UNFIT

A Novel

By Lara Cleveland Torgesen

Published and distributed by
Possibilities Publishing
PO Box 10671
Burke, VA 22009
www.possibilitiespublishingcompany.com

ISBN-13: 978-0615874494
ISBN-10: 0615874495

This is a work of fiction.

Prologue

May 9, 2012 — Today, on my 60th birthday, I feel
compelled to sit down and write something about my life,
although I scarcely know where to begin. I suppose that I have
known for some time that I would eventually tell my story, but I
have been putting it off … dreading it. My fingers click slowly
and half-heartedly along the keyboard. They, like the rest of me,
are not eager to open old wounds and relive painful
experiences. *Leave it alone*, part of me pleads, *some things are
better left unwritten and unsaid*. To be frank, I am terrified of
my past. But, as the years advance, I have become more
terrified of the idea that I will someday be gone and my story
buried along with me, undocumented. And then it will be as if it
had never happened.

It's strange that I should sit here and worry what you,
the reader, will think of me. We do not know each other. It
shouldn't matter to me what you think of me, yet it does. I
would prefer that you see me the way my friends, neighbors,
co-workers, and acquaintances see me: a typical aging, middle-
class white woman who lives with her husband in a nice house
in the suburbs of Raleigh, North Carolina. We are an ordinary
couple. You probably know dozens of other couples just like us.
There is nothing remarkable about our lives. Our neighbors
would tell you that we keep busy. They see us daily heading to
and from work. We exchange pleasantries with them on our
evening walks around the neighborhood. They'd tell you that we
spend our weekends working on house and yard-maintenance
projects and participating in community volunteer work. They
might know that we welcome frequent visits from our grown
children. They will often see me spending hours tending to my
vegetable garden in the backyard.

Occasionally, they will see me sitting alone on our front porch with my iced tea, lost in memories. It is during those times, particularly, that I can hear the voices of ghosts from my past. Some of the voices are pleasant and comforting: the sound of children laughing and playing in the North Carolina sun, the voices of teenage girls singing to the background of an acoustic guitar, the voices of elderly people sharing their own stories from what is now a very distant past. Unpleasant ghostly voices also sometimes break through and make themselves heard: mournful wails and sobs of regret, voices of accusation and endless criticism, voices of violent rage. The worst voice of all is the one that comes from deep within. It knows my deepest fears and insecurities and never fails to strike me where it hurts the most. It tells me that I'm a fake and a fraud. It shrieks at me, *"You do not deserve what you have!"*

I leave the porch to go inside and splash water on my face. And, when I look in the bathroom mirror, I can almost see that invisible word, "Unfit," scrawled across my forehead. What a cruel and spiteful word it is. Who decides that someone else is unfit for anything? What are the criteria used to determine who is unfit? The word is primarily used to dehumanize, subjugate, humiliate, and shame.

In my case, it was used as justification to commit a brutal act of violence on my body, without my consent, and strip away my God-given rights as a human being. I've spent a lifetime trying to scrub that word away, yet it always seems to find a way to reappear.

There are others like me who have also been stamped with that word, but our numbers dwindle with every year. Someday, there will be no more of us left to tell our stories. Many of the survivors are unable or unwilling to tell theirs. Shame operates as a powerful silencer. But it is time for me to break my silence.

My name is Chrissy, and I was one of those deemed "unfit to reproduce."

1

"There it is. You were born right under that rock, right there. Hard to believe it's still there after 10 years." Daddy pointed to the smooth, gray rock partially buried in the ground. I walked over and bent down to stroke the surface.

"How'd I get under there, I wonder?" I asked, beginning to dig the rock from the ground with my bare fingers.

"Beats me," Daddy said. "I was just walking on by one day, minding my own business, when suddenly I heard sort of a muffled baby cry. I searched around and did some digging. Sure enough, there you were, right underneath."

"I'll bet I was glad to get that rock off me."

"I 'spect so. It was as big as you and about as heavy too. I figured, why waste a perfectly good baby? So I threw you in the back of my pick-up and took you on home to Momma."

"I'm sure glad you did that."

"Here, let me help you with that." He helped me finish digging up the rock. We brushed off all the dirt, and I held it in my arms like it was my own baby now.

"Do you think I could keep it?" I asked.

"Well, why not? It's yours, if it's anybody's," Daddy answered.

We brought the rock home and washed it off. Daddy bought me some rock paints so that I could decorate it. I sat at the kitchen table and painted little flowers and rainbows on it and, in careful lettering, wrote, "Christine Rollings, Born May 9, 1952." Of course, the name Christine sounded so foreign to me, like some fancy rich girl from England. I was definitely more of a Chrissy, from Hilldale, North Carolina. But on formal things like this, you had to use your official name, not just what everybody called you.

"What's that you're doing?" Momma asked, wrapping an arm around my shoulders and kissing my head from behind.

"Don't mess me up. I'm painting the rock that Daddy found me under. He said I could decorate it and keep it."

"Oh, Chrissy," Momma laughed. "You know your Daddy's just pulling your chain about that. You weren't born under a rock! You were born right here in our house, in my bed, just like Trisha a few weeks ago. Just like all your brothers and sisters."

I remembered most of their births because I helped deliver them, at least the younger ones. With Baby Trisha, I even got to cut the umbilical cord and help wash her off. The midwife said I was a natural. Maybe I'd be a midwife someday because I knew exactly what to do. I was only 10 years old, but, as the oldest of six, I already knew how to do stuff some adults don't even know how to do. I could feed babies, change their diapers, give them baths, get them dressed, keep them entertained, stop them from crying, rock them to sleep. I even handled the gross stuff, like cleaning up their spit-ups and vomit and poop. Babies may be cute, but they sure do make plenty of disgusting messes! When I smelled a poop, Momma didn't even have to ask me. I'd set to work changing the diaper, rinsing it out in the toilet, squeezing it as dry as I could, and then placing it in the diaper pail for the next wash.

I helped Momma with dinner and dishes, cleaning, and laundry. I could even hang the clothes to dry on the line outside, but I needed a footstool or chair to reach the line.

Momma said she didn't know what she'd do without me. Brad was only two years younger than me, but he didn't do anything to help. He just caused trouble. He'd get mad that I'd boss him around like he was one of the little kids, but I'd tell him, "If you're gonna act like a little kid, I'm gonna treat you like one." At six, Jenny was next in line. She was pretty good about minding me and behaving herself, unlike Brad. (In my mind, I called him *Brad the Brat*). Jenny was definitely the pretty one in our family, and she was a natural artist too. She had dark hair, blue eyes, and a pretty smile. Everyone commented on how pretty she was. No one ever commented on my looks, since I was just sort of average and plain — forgettable — with light

4

brown hair, brown eyes, and a few scattered freckles across my nose.

Brad was good looking, and he knew it too. Lots of girls had a crush on him until they got to know his personality. Like I said, he was a brat, especially to girls. Then there were the three little kids of our family: Ronnie was three and so adorable you could squeeze him all day; Darlene was two, with pretty blonde curls; and Trisha was our little baby, a cutie right from the start. She's what I imagined Snow White looked like as a baby. She had a lot of dark hair and rosy cheeks and lips. She'd probably be pretty, like Jenny, when she got older. I don't know how I got stuck with all the plain looks in our family, but I was probably the smartest one, so maybe I didn't need the good looks as much as they did. No one gets everything.

We sure had our hands full — me, Daddy, and Momma. Daddy could do almost anything, and he worked real hard for us. He could fix things, he could paint, and he could build whatever you wanted. Sometimes, he had a lot of work, and we had a lot of money; other times, there was just no work, so we couldn't buy much. His Momma had died when he was in high school. He dropped out after that and went through a little "rebellious" phase before Momma set him straight. People didn't think they'd last, but they did. His daddy, my Grandpa, had died two years ago, and I still cried when I thought about it. Daddy had one younger brother who had moved out West. We didn't ever see him.

We never saw any of Momma's family either, since they had disowned her. She came from a really strict Southern Baptist family from Charleston, South Carolina. Her daddy was a minister. They weren't too happy with her when she dropped out of high school and started seeing Daddy. Then, when she got pregnant, that was it. They kicked her out and told her never to come back. They didn't even know Momma and Daddy had left South Carolina. I guess they didn't care. I asked Momma why they did that. I mean, she *did* marry Daddy and everything play an instrument, with enough time and dedication. Sure, there was the initial expense of buying an instrument, but from then on you had hours and hours of free entertainment. You didn't have to keep replacing the instrument. And I was positive I'd never get bored of playing it.

I especially wanted to learn to play the guitar because it sounded so good when played right. I imagined myself toting my own guitar wherever I went — to parties, campouts, get-togethers — and people would just call out, "Hey Chrissy, play such and such!" And I'd launch right into that particular song, and everyone who wanted to sing could join right in. In my mind, a person who could play the guitar would be welcome just about everywhere. And I wanted to be that person.

One day, when we were walking around downtown Hilldale, we spotted a music store. I peered into the window, looking at the shiny new guitar sitting right there, just waiting for an owner. "I sure would love to have something like that," I said out loud to no one in particular.

Momma looked through the window for a few moments. "Did you see the price tag on that thing? Does that look like something we could afford?" she asked.

"No." I thought for a minute and then brightened. "Hey, maybe I could ask Santa Claus to bring me a guitar for Christmas!" It was October, and I'd been pretty good that year. Surely I wouldn't mess things up before Christmas.

Momma paused for a moment and then said, "The thing about Santa Claus, honey, is that he brings you the type of things that are appropriate for your particular household and place in life. So, say for a rich kid, Santa wouldn't bring something that looked used or cheap or second-hand. That would be out of place for that kid! And, for a poor kid, he wouldn't bring some fancy, expensive toy. That would be out of place for a poor kid's home, too. The general rule of thumb is that you don't ask Santa for something that your own parents might not be able to afford. Does that make sense?"

I nodded my head. But really, it made no sense to me at all. I thought it should be just the opposite, in fact. Why should Santa be so concerned about giving nice toys to rich kids? They already had everything they wanted! And what they didn't have, they could just ask their parents for and probably get it. Santa should be spending his time worrying about poor kids and what they wanted. If he didn't get it for them, just who would? The Easter Bunny? I knew for a fact that there were a lot of poor kids in my town who were really good all year, and, for Christmas, Santa just got them some rinky-dink used toy or a pair of socks or even nothing at all.

Even worse, I heard that, for kids whose parents weren't Christians or who didn't celebrate Christmas, Santa just flew right on by their houses without a second thought. It didn't matter if these kids had been as good as gold all year long. He just flew right on by, like it was somehow those kids' fault that their parents chose the wrong religion! You know, I'd never say this out loud, but I thought Santa Claus was a bit of a butthole.

That year, I dutifully followed Momma's rule of thumb when I wrote my letter to Santa. I didn't include any of my complaints about the way his operation worked. I knew we kids typically got three or four things for Christmas that usually included something to wear that we needed, something to play with, and some sort of little treat. So I asked for a new pair of school shoes that didn't squish my toes, some colored pencils, a Nancy Drew book that I hadn't read yet, and a chocolate bar.

On Christmas day, that was exactly what I got, and I was happy with it. My brothers and sisters mostly got the little things they had asked for too. Ronnie wanted a squirt gun and Darlene wanted a little stuffed dog. Jenny got more art supplies. We had a great day playing with all our new stuff, and we shared bites of our treats with each other. Momma had bought a small ham for Christmas dinner and it tasted so good! Afterward, we gathered around our little tree and sang every Christmas carol that we knew. I couldn't help but think of how great it would sound with guitar music in the background, but I understood why I didn't get a guitar.

That night, when everyone started getting ready for bed, Momma pulled me aside and asked me to stay up for a bit with her. She had already put the baby down and we'd already cleaned up from dinner, so I wasn't sure what she needed from me. She'd even waited for Daddy to head off to bed.

"I can't wait a second longer for this," she whispered. She headed off to the coat closet and pulled something off the top shelf. It was a guitar with a big red bow on the handle.

I couldn't believe it. "Is that for me?" I asked. "Did Santa leave it?" I reached out and stroked the guitar strings. It was so beautiful, I couldn't believe it was mine.

"No," Momma said. "This gift is from me to you. I thought you deserved something extra-special for all the help that you give me. I just don't know what I'd do without you, Chrissy, and I wanted to show you how grateful I am."

I examined the guitar while she explained, "I was taking the bus to a cleaning job one day when we passed by a yard sale. I saw this guitar just sitting there. It looked brand new, and my heart started pounding so fast! I got off at the next stop and just ran over there. When they told me how much it was, I decided it was too expensive, so I started walking away. About a block later, I turned back around. I just had to get it. That's all there was to it! I bargained them down a bit, but it was still probably more than I should have spent. I couldn't let you open it in front of your brothers and sisters today because it's so out of proportion with what they got. We'll have to come up with some story about how you got this so that we don't have sore feelings around here. Whenever you see and play this guitar, I hope you'll remember that your Momma loves you more than anything in the world."

"Thank you, Momma," I said. "It's the best gift in the world." And it was. I could hardly get to sleep that night. I was itching to get started, but I couldn't wake everyone up. I just took it to bed with me and slept with it right by my side with the bow still attached. When I think back on my childhood memories of Christmas, that is my very favorite. Santa might not come through for poor kids at Christmas, but that year, Momma did instead.

The guitar and the Chrissy rock were probably the two most prized possessions that I took with me into my adulthood. They were always somewhere near my bedside, wherever I lived. They somehow took on a symbolic meaning for me: tangible evidence that my parents had once loved and cared for me. And no one could ever take that away from me.

2

It's strange how what can turn out to be the very best or worst days of our lives can start as normally as any other day. You really have no warning that your life is about to be turned upside-down. That's how it was for me, at least. It started out as a normal Friday in mid-October, the very next fall. I was 11 and in my last year of school at White Oak Elementary. We lived about a mile away. I walked with Brad and Jenny to and from school. Momma was home with the three little ones, and Daddy had a pretty good job in construction right then. There was a good chance he'd be laid off in the winter, he'd heard, but right then we were doing just fine.

There were a few different reasons I loved Fridays. We went to the school library every Friday, and I got to check out up to four books that I could take home. I always checked out four books, even if I didn't think I could read all four over the weekend. If I didn't get to a book, I'd check it out again the next Friday. I also got to buy my lunch on Fridays. (I brought lunch from home the other days.) People complain about cafeteria food, but I actually thought it was pretty good. Plus, they had chocolate milk on Fridays, so that was the best day to buy. And the third thing I loved about Fridays was that there would be no homework for the whole weekend!

That Friday was pretty normal. I bought my lunch, had my chocolate milk, checked out my four books. When the bell rang, I found Brad and Jenny outside their classrooms and made sure they had all their stuff before we started walking home. Jenny chattered non-stop about her friends at school, and Brad was kicking a rock all the way home, which was driving me crazy. "If that rock hits me in the leg, it's mine," I informed him.

"The hell it is," he mumbled.

"Brad! Watch your language!"

We had to cross two fairly busy streets on the way home, so I always made sure I held Jenny's hand when we crossed. Brad was still kicking his rock a little ways ahead. "Brad!" I called out. "We look both ways when crossing the street!"

"Go screw yourself."

"That's it. I'm telling."

"I don't care."

"Well, you should care, because you're grounded!" I didn't actually have the power to ground Brad or spank him, although I often still threatened him with both.

We walked faster so that we could catch up with him. "Chrissy, I always look both ways when I cross the street. And I never say hell or screw," Jenny said.

"That's because you're a good girl who knows how to behave herself, *unlike some people we know*," I stated extra loudly for Brad's benefit.

"And I never say damn, or shit, or...."

"Okay, okay," I interrupted. "Let's practice not saying those words by not saying them. Let's play the quiet game for the rest of the way home, starting right now." Jenny immediately pretended to zip her mouth closed and kept walking.

"I'm not playing that game," Brad said. We frantically pointed at Brad, meaning *"Ha Ha. You lose!"* He always lost the quiet game. He tried to claim that I sometimes lost too, but that's not true, because if I had something to say, I would always first say, "pause game," and then say what I had to say. But Brad would try to make a big show of frantically pointing at me anyway, as if the game hadn't been paused!

When we got home, I didn't even have time to tell on Brad because Momma needed to catch the bus for a cleaning job that afternoon. She would be gone only a couple of hours, but she needed me to watch the kids and maybe start some dinner. Brad and Jenny immediately went over to their friends' houses to play. I might have protested, but frankly it was easier having them out of my hair.

After everyone left, I woke Trisha from her nap, changed her diaper, and gave her a little snack. Darlene and Ronnie asked me if I would play a game with them. "Not today, okay? I want to start reading my book. How about you two draw me a picture at the kitchen table," I suggested, pulling out some paper and crayons for them. "And if they're really good, I'll hang them up on the wall beside my bed." They set down to work and Trisha played with her toys on the floor. I read for about an hour and then started making some spaghetti for dinner.

Momma and Daddy both came home around 6:00. "Thanks, honey, I'll take it from here." Momma started stirring the spaghetti.

Daddy came over and wrapped his arms around her waist from behind. "You're looking so good, I might just stay home tonight instead."

"Oh, I forgot, it's boys' night out tonight," Momma said. "Sit down, I'll get you a plate." I'd forgotten it was boys' night out too, and I was a little disappointed because I was hoping we could go to the drive-in movie that night.

"Nah, I don't have time. I'll just make a quick sandwich and head out."

"Daddy, that's not a very nutritious dinner. You need something more than that," I said.

"Don't worry about me, pumpkin," he said. He slapped some peanut butter on a couple of slices of bread and took a swig of orange juice from the container in the fridge.

"Germs! Use a cup!" Jenny exclaimed. She'd just come home from her friend's house. Brad was supposed to be home by 6:00 too, but of course he never watched the clock. He was always late but never got in trouble for it.

Daddy scouted around for his wallet and keys and headed out the front door with his sandwich, letting the screen door slam shut behind him.

I ran to the door and opened it, "Don't drink too much, okay Daddy?" He started his pick-up and began backing out, steering with one hand and taking a bite out of his sandwich with the other. I cupped my hands around my mouth and hollered, "Keep both hands on the wheel!"

"Go inside now, you little busybody," he said with a laugh. "I'll be home soon."

"Love you!"

"Love you more!"

I went back in and helped Momma set the table for dinner.

After dinner, I went to my room and played the guitar for a while. I was getting pretty good. I was trying to make up my own song, which turned out to be a lot harder than just learning how to play a tune I already knew. When my fingers got tired, I went out to the living room where everyone was gathered around the TV, watching a show. Momma was holding Trisha in her rocking chair. She still took a bottle at night to help her get to sleep, and she still slept in Momma's and Daddy's room, because she cried sometimes at night. Since it was Friday night, we could stay up a little later, but Momma finally shoo'ed us off to bed around 10. I got in bed with my flashlight and pulled the covers over my head so I could read my book.

I don't remember when I finally drifted off, but I do remember being woken with a start. There were voices in our living room, and I heard Momma cry out. I jumped up and ran out of the bedroom. Brad came running out of his room to see what was the matter. There were two police officers standing in the front doorway. There'd been an accident. Daddy's pick-up had plowed right into a tree at full speed, and he'd been thrown from the vehicle. An ambulance had come for him, but he'd died on the way to the hospital. I could feel the blood rush from every part of my body and couldn't breathe. I sank to the floor, unable to register what they were saying.

Momma was screaming and crying. Brad and I started crying too, and then we could hear the other kids waking up.

work out, because she could be home with the little ones during the day while the older kids were at school. And then I could handle things during her 6 p.m. to 2 a.m. shift. She would be working Tuesday through Saturday nights, starting the next week. This weekend, she said, she would buy a car with the insurance money from Daddy's wrecked pick-up. The bus didn't run those late hours, she explained, and we'd need to have some sort of family vehicle anyway. I gave her a big hug because I was so proud of her.

Life started slowly moving forward again, but it was different, sluggish and sad. We soon realized that Daddy had not only been the main breadwinner of the family, but it also seemed he'd been the source of all our happiness, fun, and laughter. We'd never again go to the drive-in, or have family game night, or do any of the family traditions we'd managed to develop over the years. In fact, I think Daddy was the glue that had always held us tightly bound to each other. So when the winds of life eventually came to beat on our family, there was just nothing left to hold us together, to keep us from blowing away.

December came far too soon after Daddy's death. We didn't get a tree or pull out any of our old decorations. We didn't even acknowledge that it was the Christmas season. There was no money to buy presents and no time to do any celebrating together. Momma was always working, and she was too tired when she *was* home. I didn't even want to try to make Christmas a special day for us anyway. Everything we would have attempted would have just made us miss Daddy more, and any effort to have a good time would have gone down in pathetic flames. So we just pretended Christmas was any other day of the year, a day we just had to get through and survive, if nothing else.

Momma was off work early on Christmas Eve since the bar was closing early that night. We all just sat at the table and silently gobbled down our dinner. Then all the kids went off to do their own thing or watch TV in the living room. After everyone had gone to bed, I sat out in the living room with my guitar in my lap. I strummed a few notes and tried to play a few of the Christmas carols I knew.

Was it only last year that Momma gave me this guitar for Christmas? It seemed like a lifetime ago, a different family, a different Momma and a different Chrissy. I wished that I could have frozen myself in time back then. I picked up my guitar by the neck and walked over to the entrance of Momma's room. She was lying face-up on top of the bed, just staring at the ceiling like she did so often now. She was always exhausted and almost never smiled anymore. I think she was hoping this was all some sort of nightmare that she would eventually wake up from.

She didn't see me standing there, but I finally spoke: "There is no Santa Claus, is there?" It was more a statement than a question.

"No. There isn't." She didn't turn her head to look at me.

"I didn't think so."

I carried my guitar to my room and climbed into bed.

4

    School started again after winter break, and we settled into our new routine. Our standard of living was quickly degrading. Food dwindled from the cupboards, and we began buying cheaper food and less of it. I could no longer buy lunches at school on Fridays. I brought my lunch every day, and there wasn't much to it. Most often we didn't have breakfast anymore. By the time 10:00 rolled around, my stomach would start growling and gurgling something awful. I would try to cough or make some noise during the really loud rumbles so that other people wouldn't hear.

    Sometimes, when I just couldn't help myself, I would gobble down my lunch right then. But then the growls would reappear around 2:00 since I hadn't eaten lunch at the normal time. I tried to work it so that I would eat a few bites of my lunch right around 10:00 and save the rest of it for lunchtime so that I could try to avoid the afternoon hunger rumbles. But, no matter how I worked it, it seemed I was always hungry. My ribs stuck out and you could even see the bones in my chest and back. It didn't bother me as much to see my own bones as when I started seeing bones sticking out of Ronnie, Darlene, and even little Trisha. They'd be laughing and playing in the bathtub like they didn't even notice all the bones sticking out of their little naked bodies. They'd grown used to not having enough to eat. It hurt me to see that. I'd end up adding to their dinners from my portion because I just couldn't bear for them to go hungry.

    Momma had bought a used Volkswagen Bug to get to and from work and to use for her errands. It had once been a pretty light blue color, but now a lot of the paint had been scratched or dinged, and there was a big crack in the windshield. It was small, but we could all fit if two of us held little kids in our laps. I'd sit in the passenger seat with Trisha in my lap, but I had to remember to lean slightly forward because the seat was broken. If you put any weight on the seat-back, it would fall straight backward into the rear seat. I usually remembered to lean forward, but a couple of times I forgot and the seat would immediately give way and fall into the laps of the people in back. I'd say, "Sorry, I forgot!" But there'd be a bunch of screaming and hollering, flailing arms, and kicking legs for a few moments until we'd get the seat back up.

Daddy probably could have fixed that seat, but without him around we just learned to live with it broken. It was the same way around our house. Things that Daddy normally would have been able to fix just stayed broken. Cracks and leaks started showing up; paint would chip and peel off the walls. We even got a big hole in the second wooden step leading to the front door. We just learned to step around it.

Not that I had ever dressed like a movie star or anything before, but when Daddy was alive I had a few nice outfits and a pair of shoes that fit. When I'd outgrown them, Momma and Daddy would make sure they were replaced. But now we wore things well past the point when they fit. And if the clothes were torn or stained, or if our shoes got holes in them, we just had to keep on wearing them like that. We didn't have anything else to wear, and we couldn't afford to replace them. If something looked really bad on you, all you could do was secretly hope it would completely disintegrate in the wash. That was the only way you'd get out of having to wear it. Either that, or it would go to the next sibling down the line. Brad wore things until they were way too small, and then poor little Ronnie would inherit clothes that were way too big for him. And you can imagine how much Jenny loved getting my stained, ugly, worn-out things. Darlene would get Jenny's old things, but she didn't much care about clothes yet, since she wasn't in school. Trisha mostly ran around in just a diaper unless we left the house to go somewhere.

Sometimes I'd look around me and feel like we were trapped on a ship that was slowly sinking. Even though we were flailing and kicking and grabbing at whatever we could to stay afloat, we were just delaying the inevitable. It felt like we were just buying time before we would eventually go under and never come back up.

That spring, Momma applied for welfare services, and we qualified. It was wonderful to have more money coming in, though we spent it as fast as we received it. It seemed there was always some crisis that popped up: the car would break down or someone needed to see a doctor, and the welfare check would immediately go for that. We weren't getting ahead, but at least now we weren't sinking quite as quickly.

The bad thing about being on welfare is that everybody hates you for taking it, even if you're a little kid and it's not really your fault that your family needs it. They know just by looking at you that you're on it. One day, we were wandering around the grocery store while Momma did some shopping. An older lady and a man with her were watching us, and I heard the lady say, "We just keep seeing more and more of these lazy women on the government dole with all their children, expecting hard-working taxpayers to support their lifestyle. It's just disgusting!"

The man agreed. "And they keep having more and more children just to get a fatter check. There should be a limit to how many kids these people should be allowed to have. If they're going to take my money, then I should have a say in what they do."

They looked right at me while they were talking, like they wanted me to hear it. I felt really bad because I didn't want to take their hard-earned money away from them. I wanted to tell them that Momma worked hard too. She wasn't lazy at all, but for some reason, it just wasn't enough. We needed help.

I told myself that someday I would pay it all back by getting a good job and working really hard and paying my taxes. I wouldn't make the welfare recipients feel bad for taking some of my tax money. I wouldn't treat them like I thought they were lazy good-for-nothings. And, especially, I wouldn't make their children feel like they should never have been born. I don't even know how people knew we were on welfare. It wasn't like we

24

went around bragging about it. Even their kids knew, and they hated us for it too.

And if I thought things were bad in elementary school, it was 100 times worse in junior high. At White Oak Elementary, there really weren't any rich kids. They were all just basically different levels of poor. But when I started school at East Junior High that fall, I couldn't believe how good some kids had it. Looking back now, I realize they were probably just everyday middle-class kids, but in my mind back then, I thought they were filthy rich. Their parents were educated and had really good jobs, like bank tellers, school teachers, and police officers. The kids wore nice, matching clothes that looked like they were bought from a department store. The girls would have bows and things in their hair that coordinated with their outfits. Sometimes I wouldn't see them wear the exact same outfit for weeks! I couldn't go more than a few days without wearing the exact same outfit.

They'd talk about things like the vacations they'd taken during the summer. Sometimes, they even left North Carolina on their vacations. These kids would go to the movies with their friends, or to restaurants or ice cream parlors on the weekends. Some of them even had an allowance. They'd carry their wallets and purses around with them at school. I could see ones, fives, sometimes even tens when they opened their wallets. I couldn't believe their parents just let them wander around with that kind of money, spending it however they liked.

I learned quickly in junior high that there are very specific groups that kids belonged to, and you don't try to mix up the groups, join a group where you don't belong, or try to be friends with someone from a different group. I learned that lesson with Jan. I had a few different classes with Jan, including English, which was my favorite subject. It was Jan's favorite subject too, and we found out that we liked almost all the exact same books. She would tell me I should read such-and-such, and I would immediately check it out from the library and read it. I would give her my book suggestions too, and she always loved them as much as I did. We both had crushes on the same characters from the books too! We laughed when we admitted that. She thought it was really neat that I had a guitar and had taught myself to play every song that I knew. She said maybe sometime I could come over for a sleepover at her house and bring my guitar. I would have loved that, but it never happened.

I usually sat by myself at lunch, and I could see Jan a few tables over sitting with the rich, popular girls. She was one of them, only with a better personality. One time she waved at me and said, "Hi, Chrissy!" as I was walking by her group at lunch. Then her friends gave her dirty looks, and I overheard one of them whisper loudly, "Jan! She's white trash!" Jan was kind of stuck in her category just like I was stuck in my welfare-kid category, and there was nothing either of us could do about it. Sometimes, I'd see her glancing over at me during lunch. I was usually reading a book. I think maybe she would have enjoyed sitting by me more than with those girls. From what I could hear of their conversations, they were pretty dumb and boring. I was glad I didn't have to waste a whole hour of my day listening to their drivel about boys and clothes. I felt sorry for Jan, and I think she felt just as sorry for me too.

I did eventually make a friend who was in my same category when Marla moved to Hilldale. Her family moved into a house that was about a half-mile away from our house. We could even walk over to each other's houses on the weekends. Marla was thin and pretty, with light brown hair and green eyes. She looked sort of like a prettier version of me. I thought Marla was lucky because she didn't have all the same responsibilities at home that I had. But then, when I learned more details about her life, I decided I preferred mine instead. She lived with her mom and step-dad and a little sister who was a year older than my sister Jenny.

Marla's step-dad was always between jobs. He'd find a job, only to get fired a few weeks later for showing up to work drunk. He drank all the time, and sometimes he hit Marla's mom. What he did to Marla and her sister was even worse, though. Now I understood why Marla always wanted to be at my house instead of her own. When Marla told me what a grown man's body looked like without clothes, I was just disgusted. She said they're awful and smelly, covered in moles and hair, with big guts that just poke right out. And when she described what they looked like you-know-where, I thought I would lose my lunch. It was no longer little and cute, like my little brother Ronnie's ding-a-ling. She said it looked like a big, ugly, disgusting pink pencil covered in hair. I sure never wanted to see one of those myself!

Marla, who had turned 13, was already developing, unlike me. I was just as flat-chested as the 12-year-old boys in our grade. But she didn't like how fast her figure was changing because it made her step-dad notice her even more. He didn't pay as much attention to her little sister, but he just couldn't keep his hands off Marla. When she tried to tell her momma about it, her momma just blamed it on her and told her she shouldn't encourage him. That's why Marla didn't want to be at her own house. Momma let me have her over for sleepovers on most Friday nights and sometimes even Saturday nights. Momma always had to work those nights anyway. As long as I still took care of things at home, she didn't mind if I had Marla over. And Marla especially liked to sleep over on weekends, because her step-dad was always drunk then.

Marla was a really good singer. She'd sing while I played the guitar. We did all the songs we knew and even started writing and playing our own songs. It was great to have a friend at school, finally, and someone who would eat lunch with me. On the days when she didn't show up at school, I felt really lonely and depressed. I was always so glad to see her again.

The nights that Marla slept over, she'd help me with all my chores: feeding the kids, cleaning up after dinner, handling their arguments, giving them baths, and putting them to bed. Then we'd stay up late and watch TV or talk in the living room. On warm nights, we'd take blankets and pillows out on the front porch and sleep out there. We could even play our music well into the night if we were outside. I think Brad had a little crush on Marla, because he did everything she said and treated her much better than he treated me. When he tried to hang out with us, though, we'd tell him to get out of our space and mind his own business.

Marla and I started having big ideas about becoming a world-famous musical duo. We looked like we could possibly be sisters, so we thought we'd form a "sister act" and travel the world playing at sold-out shows. We began coming up with songs for our first album. I wrote most of the lyrics, since I was good at that, and Marla would come up with a good way to sing them. I'd sort of just follow along with my guitar, figuring out how to play in the background with her voice. Occasionally, I would sing along with the chorus. Marla told me about this place called Las Vegas, where lots of entertainers live. They wear fancy costumes and perform their shows every night of the week. We thought that would be a perfect place for us to go someday to get started on our musical career. The more we talked about it, the more hopeful Marla would get because she really wanted to leave her house and North Carolina forever.

One night, she told me she'd really been thinking about running away to Las Vegas. Things were getting even worse at her home with her step-dad, and she said she couldn't take it much longer. But she was afraid of running off all by herself, and she tried to convince me to go with her. She said we'd just start living our dream earlier than we'd planned. I told her I couldn't leave Momma and the kids. They needed me, and somebody had to take care of things around here.

Marla said, "I got news for you, Chrissy. Your momma is using you for the free help. Just think of how much she'd have to pay someone else to do everything that you do around here. And she gets it all from you for free! There's laws against children working in this country. If you wasn't her daughter, she'd go to jail, just like my step-dad would go to jail for what he does to me. Parents get a free pass, for some reason, but that don't mean what they do is right."

28

"My momma doesn't have anybody else to help her!" I snapped. "Don't compare her to your step-dad. They're not even in the same category!" I was a little steamed that Marla would say those things about my momma.

"Okay, fine," she answered. "But one of these days, you're gonna see what I'm talking about. You'll wanna do something and your momma won't let you because she needs you to work for her. You're gonna realize that you're just a babysitter and a house servant to her."

"Let's work on our album. I don't want to talk about this anymore," I said.

But, it turned out, Marla was partially right. That spring, our school was planning a sock hop for a Friday night at the end of April. I really wanted to go. A boy that I had a little crush on at school had asked if I would be going to the dance. I told him I wasn't sure, and then he said he hoped to see me there! Maybe that meant he'd ask me to dance.

I asked Momma if I could go to the sock hop, but she said, "Chrissy, you know Friday nights are especially busy at the bar. I can't have the night off."

"I know, but why can't Brad handle things for the night? He's eleven now. I was already doing everything by the time I was his age!"

"Brad doesn't cook or clean up. I can't put him in charge. What if Trisha messed her pants or one of the kids threw up? Do you think Brad could handle that?"

"I could teach him what to do in every situation. It's just one night. Please! Everyone is going. Marla's going. I know Brad could handle it for one night."

"Chrissy, no. I just don't feel comfortable leaving Brad in charge of four kids. He's not responsible enough. I know it seems unfair. You did do all that stuff at his age. But it's different for boys. They don't do the same things that girls do. That's just how things are."

"Well, how things are *stinks*!" I replied. I ran to my room and flopped down on my bunk. My crush might look around for me at the sock hop, ready to ask me to dance. But I'd be home wiping snot noses and doing the dishes, like every Friday night. Maybe Marla was right. Maybe I was just a built-in babysitter and servant here.

Later, when I told Marla about it and I said she'd been right all along, she grew almost giddy with excitement. "So, are we gonna do this or what? There's a better life just waiting for us, Chrissy. I just know it, and I'm ready for it to start."

I told her we should probably wait until the school year was over, so we could at least complete the 7th grade and I would have turned 13 by then. But, yes, I would run away with her to start our dream life in Las Vegas.

5

We became very secretive over the next few weeks as we made our plans. We finished writing all the songs for our album and practiced them endlessly. Our plan was to leave in mid-June, the first Friday after school was out for the summer. We had about four dollars saved between us, which wouldn't get us very far. But our plan was to hitchhike across the country, earning money along the way with our performances for food. Hopefully some nice people would let us stay the night at their house, or we could just sleep on park benches and in picnic shelters. Since it was summer, the nights stayed pretty warm. We studied a map of the United States for how to get to Las Vegas. It was in Nevada and pretty far away, so it might take a few days, or maybe even a few weeks, depending on how much we could walk and how many people would be willing to give us a ride.

I was eager to start our adventure and our new life together in such an exciting place. I was sad to have to leave Momma and my brothers and sisters like this. But I would send them money once I started making a lot of it, and our lives would all be better off that way. Maybe once I became famous, I could buy Momma a nice house and she could quit her job and finally be happy again. It really was the best thing for everyone. They'd see that in time.

On the Friday that we were supposed to leave, I emptied out my schoolbag and began to pack for our journey. I'd have a pair of pants, a pair of shorts, four pairs of underwear, my jacket, and all four of the shirts that I owned. I packed my toothbrush, a small comb, my money, and some dried fruit. I contemplated leaving my Chrissy rock, since it would just add more weight and I already had my guitar to carry everywhere. But, in the end, I managed to stuff it into the schoolbag. It reminded me of Daddy, so I just couldn't leave it behind. I also packed a little hat and made a sign that read, "Donations

Accepted," so people could put money in the hat during our performances.

Finally, the hardest part: while Momma was busy working on laundry, I wrote a note to leave behind. "Dear Momma, I'm sorry about leaving like this, but I felt like I had no choice. I'm with Marla, and I'll be safe. Don't worry about us and don't try to find us. I'll send you money as soon as I can. And someday I'll be back to visit. I love all of you and I'll think of you every day. Love, Chrissy." I hid the note and my packed schoolbag in the closet and waited for Momma to leave for work for the night.

By 5:45, Momma was heading off to work and calling out that I was in charge. "Wait, Momma!" I ran into the living room. "What am I supposed to make for dinner tonight?"

Momma looked worn and haggard, with dark circles under her eyes and her mouth turned down in a permanent frown. She looked like she'd aged 10 years since Daddy died. "I don't know," she said wearily. "Just see if you can find something."

"Have you been shopping?"

"No. I have to wait till payday. Just see what you can work up from what's in the cupboards, all right? Love you. I'll see you tomorrow."

"Okay, Momma."

I felt so guilty. But what could I do? I had to think of myself this time.

I scavenged through the cupboards after she left and opened a big can of baked beans, started popping some popcorn, and set the table. When it was ready, I called the kids to dinner. Everyone ran to the table, except Brad, who stayed in front of the TV in the living room. "In a minute, I'm in the middle of a show," he said.

I sighed, hating to leave these kids in his incompetent hands, but he'd just have to learn what to do to take care of them.

32

"Chrissy, can I put a layer of popcorn over my beans to make them crunchy?" Jenny asked.

"Sure, why not?" Sometimes you had to get creative. Jenny happily built her layered concoction for dinner, with Darlene, Ronnie, and Trisha watching and following suit with their own bowls of baked beans and popcorn.

I glanced out the window and saw Marla motioning frantically at me from outside, "Come on!" she mouthed. It was five minutes past the time when we had agreed to meet. I held up my hand, "Five more minutes!" She rolled her eyes and sighed, crossing her arms and tapping her foot.

"Brad, I need to leave for a bit, so you're going to be in charge for a while, okay?"

He didn't turn his head from the television.

"Brad?"

"Fine."

"What did I just say?"

"That I'm in charge until you're back."

"Yes, that means cleaning up after dinner. Make sure the little ones brush their teeth and use the toilet before bed. And you'll need to wipe Darlene and Trisha if they make a poop. Brad!"

"I know."

"Or there will be a huge mess … Brad!"

"Fine."

"I mean it. This is very important."

"Why are you leaving for so long?"

"It's not your business. I just am."

"Then go! I'm missing my show."

I went to the closet in my room. My heart was beating rapidly. Was I actually going to go through with this? I placed the note for Momma on my bed, grabbed my guitar, and hoisted my schoolbag over my shoulder. Then I headed to the front door.

"Bye-bye, Chrissy!" came a chorus of little voices at the table. Ronnie frantically waved at me and blew kisses. I thought for a moment my heart might break, and I had to fight the urge to go over and wipe off the bit of sauce smeared across his little chin. When would I see them again?

I blew them a kiss, "Love you! Be good." My voice cracked and I quickly opened the door and headed outside, where Marla was impatiently waiting.

"We have to get a move on before dark!" she hissed at me.

We went off down the road, nervously giggling. This was all so scary, sad, and exciting at the same time. We reached one of Hilldale's busy roads by sunset and held out our thumbs at the cars while we continued to walk. After about 20 minutes, a truck pulled over and a man called out, "Where are you two heading?"

"West!" we answered.

"Hop in. I can take you about a couple of hours west to where I live in Shelton."

"Thank you!" We climbed into the truck's cab, with me by the window and Marla sitting in the middle.

We drove for a while. Marla made small talk with the man, while I drifted off to sleep beside her. When I woke up later, it was getting dark and they were still talking. I noticed he had a hand on Marla's leg, which made me a little uneasy. I was glad Marla knew how to talk to old guys like that, because I sure wouldn't know what to say to them. And I sure as hell didn't want their dirty, grubby, calloused hands on my leg!

"Do you girls have a place to stay tonight?" he asked.

"No," Marla answered. "Can we crash on your couch or floor maybe for tonight and then we'll head out tomorrow morning?"

"Sure. That shouldn't be a problem. I'll even make you some breakfast before you go."

"Thanks a lot!"

When we got to the man's house, it was about 10:00 at night. His house was small and cluttered. He had a dog in the backyard, but it looked like he had no family. We went inside and he let us have a snack at the kitchen table while he pulled out some blankets and pillows for the living room floor. "One of you can take the couch if you'd like, or you can sleep on the floor."

"Thank you, sir."

"So," he said from the living room. "Do I get any kind of payment for my generosity to you girls tonight?"

"We ain't got no money," Marla answered.

"That wasn't what I was after."

My heart was pounding a mile a minute when I looked over at Marla. She sighed and said to me, "Let me handle this. I know what I'm doing. But you're eventually gonna have to pull your own weight, Chrissy."

She went into the bedroom with him. I shakily lay down with the blankets on the couch for a while. Then I got up again and pulled my Chrissy rock out of my bag and slept with it next to me. If he came out for me in the middle of the night, I'd smash his head in with it.

When I awoke the next morning, Marla was already at the kitchen table, and the man was making scrambled eggs and toast for us at the stove. I eyed Marla and walked over to sit at the table. She looked all right, so he hadn't done anything too bad to her. We gobbled down the eggs and toast. We were so hungry, we even had second helpings.

The man offered to let us stay a second night if we wanted. I didn't like the way he was eyeing me. "No thank you, sir. Marla and I need to hit the road early this morning." He looked disappointed, but I just wanted to get out of there.

We brushed our teeth, gathered our belongings, and headed out the door, thanking the man again for the ride and food.

Marla and I walked down the road in silence for a while, and then I asked, "What did you have to do with him last night?"

"The same stuff I had to do with my step-dad. At least he wasn't drunk, and at least I got something for it this time. You get used to it and just pretend like it ain't happening. We needed the help, Chrissy. I did it for both of us, so don't give me them looks! You should be thanking me."

"Marla, I thought we were going to make money by playing our music. That's what you told me!" Now she was suddenly changing the rules of how things would be.

"I know, and we will, don't worry. But we gotta get our foot in the door, Chrissy. You don't start at the top. You work your way up. Ask any famous person. They'll tell you they had to do some things that wasn't so pleasant to get to where they are now."

"Well, we should at least try to get by without doing that stuff."

"Okay. We'll try."

We continued walking and stuck out our thumbs. This time, I was relieved when a woman pulled over. She said she could take us to a town close to the Tennessee border, so we hopped in and rode for a while. She didn't offer to let us stay at her house or give us food though. We walked to a nearby park instead. The sun was starting to set, so we just decided to stay the night in the park. But it wasn't as peaceful as I imagined sleeping under the stars would be. Bugs kept biting us. When I wasn't worried about the bugs, I was worried about being attacked in our sleep by some homeless or crazy person wandering around. It was a restless night, and we both hardly slept at all.

The next day, we decided this park might be a good place to make some money by performing. It was a big park, and there were lots of people there. I pulled out our hat and sign and we spent the whole day performing songs from our album along with other songs that we knew. By the end of the day, we'd made a total of $2.25. I couldn't believe that was all we'd made after working so hard in the hot sun all day. That was barely enough to buy what we needed. We took the money to a convenience store and bought some bread and plastic knives and peanut butter. We were starving since we hadn't eaten since that morning. We ended up eating through half that loaf in sandwiches and decided to save the other half for the next day.

I really didn't want to spend another night outside, so we tried to figure out something else. There was a little family that had been at the park for a while letting their three little kids play. They'd put a couple of quarters in our hat that day, so we hoped they might be willing to help us. Marla and I made up a story about how we were sisters who had just lost our parents, and now we were on our way to Colorado to go live with our grandparents. They were too poor to come and get us, so we had to hitchhike our way there and make money by performing our music. It was a pretty good story and worth a shot at least. We walked over and told them our story.

I wasn't sure whether they believed us, but they felt sorry for us enough to tell us we could stay at their house for one night. Their little kids were cute and they reminded me of my brothers and sisters. I taught them some riddles that I knew, and then Marla and I played some board games with them. The parents decided we were okay, and they liked how we entertained their kids. They fed us breakfast the next day and said we could stay another night if we'd like. We said we might be back after trying to make some money that day.

We thought maybe we'd just picked a bad spot to perform the day before. This time, we went to the center of town, where people were shopping, and we performed all day. But we made even less money than the day before. Discouraged, we walked back to the nice family's house and stayed another night with them.

We were learning that there were nice people in this world who just did good things and expected nothing in return. But there were also people who were not so nice and would take advantage of you if they had the chance. The hard part was, you couldn't tell just by looking at a person which kind of person they actually were. I felt so safe and secure at that family's house, I just wanted them to ask us to live there forever. We could be their nannies and help take care of their house and kids. But when I mentioned this to Marla, she just said, "You'd give up on our dream just like that, huh, Chrissy? To do what you was already doing in your old house, except in a nicer house with less kids? I'm disappointed in you."

Marla had more drive than I did, and she was right. We needed to move on and give our dreams a chance to come true.

6

We hit the road again and hitchhiked our way through Eastern Tennessee. We spent one night just sleeping out in a field next to the road. We finally made it to Nashville, the biggest city I'd ever seen. We thought maybe we could spend a couple of days there and make some money before continuing our journey. We walked through part of the city for most of the morning, looking for a place where we could set up and play our music. It was so hot and humid. We were tired, sweaty, and hungry and didn't really feel like working. But finally we found a pretty good park where we could play, and there was a convenience store next to it. We counted the money we had left. It wasn't much, but we figured we could at least stop in the store to split a Coke before we started working. I bought the Coke while Marla looked around the store.

When we were outside, I opened the Coke and took a long sip before handing it to Marla. She reached into her shirt and pulled out two candy bars. "Marla, how did you get those? You stole them, didn't you?" She knew I didn't want to resort to stealing.

"I just took these two bars, one for each of us. They can spare it. I coulda took a lot more. We gotta have something to eat, Chrissie! We can't play all day on empty stomachs. I'll eat them both myself if you ain't taking one," she threatened.

I watched as she opened her bar and started eating. My stomach was growling something fierce. "Fine. Give it to me. But no more stealing! We can only buy food with money we've earned."

The candy and Coke helped, but we really could have used a full meal. After we'd played for about an hour, and got nothing for it but a few people clapping, Marla took a break to use the park's restroom. When she came out, I saw her talking to a middle-aged man for a minute. Then she quickly ran back over and told me she'd be gone for about a half-hour. "Marla, wait! What am I supposed to do?" I asked.

"Just play for a spell by yourself. I'll be back in a jiffy."

She climbed into the man's van and took off. I sat there sweating and playing some solos on the guitar, but I kept stopping to look for the van. What if she didn't come back? What would I do? But, after a half-hour, the van pulled up and Marla hopped out. She came running over with a big smile on her face. "We're done working for the day. I just made fifteen dollars! Let's go get a real meal at a restaurant and then see a movie at a nice, cool, air-conditioned theater!"

"What? Oh my gosh, that's more than we'd make in a whole day of performing!" I knew what Marla had done, and I wanted to scold her for it. But I was also so tired, hot, hungry, and thirsty, her suggestion was just too good to pass up. We had a nice restaurant meal, and then went to a movie and bought more treats, drinks, and popcorn. For once, I think I felt like a real teenager, doing what the rich kids at my school could probably do every weekend. It was a great afternoon for both of us.

Once we left the theater, we found ourselves again with no money, no food, and no place to stay. We walked along the streets of Nashville for a while. Then Marla started talking about how I needed to pull my own weight. "I can't do everything for you all the time, Chrissy. It's your turn. We ain't famous enough yet to make a living with our music. That'll come in time. For now, we're gonna have to just give the men what they want. We'll only do it when we absolutely got to, like when we run outta money or when we need a place to stay. And we'll try to always stick together. I shouldn't a run off in that van like that, but I could tell he was a pretty safe guy. I knew he'd bring me back. I wouldn't let you do something like that though."

I knew Marla was right, but I was so scared about the whole thing. "You told me that sex is awful and that it hurts really bad. I just don't want to do it, Marla!"

"It only hurts bad in the very beginning. But you get used to it. Really, all you gotta do is take your clothes off and lay there. They do all the work. And in no time it's over and you get paid. Good money! Not just little coins dropped in a hat after hours and hours of hard work, but in bills — ones, fives, tens! For just a few minutes of laying there doing nothing. It's the only way we're gonna get by, Chrissy. Face it."

I thought about it for a few minutes. "Okay, but I always want to have you somewhere nearby, Marla. If I scream for you, I want you to hear me and get help."

"I promise," she agreed.

Just then, a truck with a middle-aged man in it slowly passed by. The man stuck his head out the window. "You girls looking for something?"

"Yeah!" Marla called out. "A place to stay the night; maybe some food and cash. You got them things?"

"Sure! What are you offering?"

"Whatever you want."

"Hop in."

Marla and I ran over to the passenger side and climbed in. We drove to the man's house. His place was a little nicer than the other man's house, but not quite as nice as the family's house where we'd stayed two nights. There was a small piano in the living room. I went over and stroked the piano keys. There was a picture on top of the piano. When I looked closer, I could see the man was in it, and he was standing next to a woman and a small boy. "My wife and kid are out of town for a little while," he explained. "Gotta have a little fun while the boss is away, right?" he joked, with a big grin on his face. I didn't smile back. I just turned and looked at some of his other photos. He had a family! I couldn't believe someone with a wife and kid would do something like this.

Marla was giving me strange looks and motioning to me. I'm sure she was trying to indicate that I should at least be a teeny bit friendly. "Is it all right if I watch your TV while you two are off together? Maybe get a snack from the kitchen?" she asked the man.

"That'd be fine," he answered. Then, motioning to me, he pointed down the hallway to his bedroom. I slowly followed him back like I was heading off to the electric chair. I did not want to do this. But I had to just get through it, like Marla said.

The man took a swig from a bottle before starting to undress. Marla was exactly right about what grown men's bodies looked like without clothes. They were horrifying. I lay there gritting my teeth with my head turned away, trying not to breathe in his bad breath while the bed squeaked away beneath us. It only took a few minutes, but it felt like a lot longer because it hurt so bad.

Afterwards, I quickly got up and put my clothes on and practically ran into the hallway bathroom. I could see the flashing images from the TV in the living room, where Marla was. I closed the door and locked it and tried to assess the damage that had been done to me. I was sore and bleeding, but not terribly bad. I ran the faucet and started cleaning up. With the faucet turned on full blast, I could cry freely now. What would Daddy think if he could see me now? He'd be so sad! And he'd punch that pervert's lights out and then let his poor wife know what kind of man she'd married. Daddy shouldn't have left us! I wouldn't be in this situation right now if he hadn't. He hadn't listened to me when I told him not to drink too much! Why hadn't he listened? I stayed in the bathroom crying with the faucet running for a long time.

Later, when I came out and sat next to Marla, she asked me how it went and I said I didn't want to talk about it. She rubbed my back for a minute and then said, "It gets easier." We both watched TV in silence as the setting sun lowered for the night.

The man let us fix something to eat for dinner, and we slept on the floor of his living room with the TV still on. The next day, we were able to bathe at his house and wash our clothes, which by now were pretty filthy with dirt and sweat. Marla took a turn with him in the bedroom, and he said we could stay one more night and then we'd have to leave because his wife and kid were coming home. When we left, he gave us twenty dollars to split.

We decided to spend a couple more days in Nashville. It was such a big city, with so many things to see and do. We didn't know when we'd be back, so we wanted to see as much of it as we could. We still played our music when we could, but Marla was right. No one wanted to pay to listen to our music. But if it was sex we were offering, it seemed there was a never-ending line of middle-aged perverts just waiting to give us their money. We'd only resort to that when we ran out of money, and we took turns on who had to do it next. It did get easier, like Marla said. It stopped hurting as much, and I just tried to pretend I was somewhere else until it was over. I reasoned to myself that it was like scraping out a poopy diaper. It's not like you *enjoyed* it or jumped up and down at the thought of having to do it again. It was just one of those nasty necessities of life that you knew you had to do. So you just held your breath and got it done, because you knew things would only get worse if you didn't.

After we'd seen as much of Nashville as we wanted, we hitchhiked west again and made it to Memphis. That was another big city, and we spent several days there as well. Sometimes we were able to stay at people's houses, and that was nice because we could often bathe there and get our things washed. Other times, we just slept on park benches or in picnic shelters or under bridges. We met a lot of other runaways and homeless kids like us, especially in the bigger cities. Most of the time, they were pretty nice. Some of them were addicted to alcohol or drugs, and it was sad to see how dependent they were on them. Marla and I had some opportunities to try that kind of stuff, and Marla would experiment, but I didn't because I still had a grudge against alcohol since I blamed it for Daddy's death. Plus it smelled like all the dirty, disgusting perverts I had to be with. We tried to stay together, but if we got split up, one of us would wait at a nearby park or rest-stop until the other one came back with the money. And we always shared our earnings 50/50, even though Marla typically made more money than I did.

After we left Memphis, we continued heading west and crossed the border into Arkansas. I couldn't believe we were now two states away from North Carolina. In some ways, it seemed like we were a world away. I remember watching the little kids playing in the park and suddenly I pictured my little brothers and sisters: Ronnie running around laughing and playing in old, stained shirts that were two sizes too big, the baked bean sauce on his chin as he happily waved goodbye to me from the kitchen table; Ronnie and Darlene working diligently on their drawings at the table; Jenny chattering non-stop about her friends at school or working on her latest art project; the sweaty curls on the back of Trisha's neck when she woke up from her nap. I even missed Brad a little. And Momma. I thought of the night she had given me my guitar, how excited she'd been to see my face when she handed it to me. I looked down at my guitar and lightly strummed the strings. I wondered what they were doing now, if they missed me as much as I missed them. I'd been gone for three weeks. It felt like three years.

We'd made it all the way to Little Rock, another pretty big city, and that was good because we'd run out of money again and needed to find some perverts. One thing we'd learned is that big cities are full of perverts. All you have to do is pick a busy road and start walking down and watching the cars, and pretty soon someone slows down to talk to you. If he's old, dirty, alone, and smells like alcohol, there's a pretty good chance he wants you for sex.

But I was feeling pretty relieved as we walked along looking for perverts, because I'd taken the last guy, and he hadn't been as old and awful as the others. So it was Marla's turn to make some money. This time, though, when the old pervert slowed down and leaned his head out the window, he barely looked at Marla. "I'll take the younger one for ten dollars," he barked at us. "I live right here in this apartment building," he nodded to the large, dilapidated building to our right.

I gave Marla a panicked look. It wasn't my turn! And there was something really creepy about the way he looked at me. I didn't like him. She called out to him, "We usually stay together. Can I come along to just hang out in your living room?"

"No, I'll just take the little girl," he answered. I wanted to run away. At least the other men pretended like they thought we were grown women, or close enough to be legal age. This guy obviously didn't even care who knew that he liked little girls more than big ones. He was a pervert *and* a sicko.

"It's okay, Chrissy," Marla nudged me forward. "I'll be right over in this park on our left waiting for you. And I'll come and find you if you ain't back in an hour."

I slowly walked to where he was parking his old Ford in the apartment's parking lot and followed him up two flights of cracked concrete stairs to his apartment. I could see Marla off across the street in the distance, heading past the trees to the covered picnic area.

When we got inside, I just stood there for a minute, looking around. His place was smelly and filthy. There were dirty dishes everywhere and garbage just thrown on the floor. "Well, what are you waiting for? Let's get started," he said.

We were still standing in his living room. "Is there a bed?" I asked.

"No. It's too dirty back there in the bedroom. There ain't no room. Let's just go right here. Get on your knees." He started unzipping his pants. When I realized what he wanted me to do, I froze with panic. There was no way I was doing that! I knew I would gag and throw up all over the place.

"Sorry, sir, I've made a mistake," I said. "I have to go now."

"Hold on there, little girl" he grabbed my arm. "I'm paying you good money for a service. Now I expect to receive that service!"

"Well, keep it!" I yelled, trying to wrench my arm out of his hand. "I don't want your money, and *I don't want you*!"

Suddenly he grabbed me by the hair and tried to force my head down to his crotch. I could feel my hair being pulled from my scalp. Screaming, I thrashed and wriggled. "I'll bite it right off!" I threatened. He pulled my head back up and slapped me across the face as hard as he could. Then he clamped his hands around my throat and started choking me. I couldn't scream anymore with his hands like a vise around my neck. His face was angry and red. He was trying to kill me! I clawed at his hands around my neck, trying to loosen them. The horrible feeling of being unable to get air overwhelmed me. What was it Daddy had said about if I ever got caught in a bad situation? *Go for the vulnerable spots — the eyes, the crotch — whatever you can get to, and use all the force you got!*

I reached up and jabbed my thumb into his eye with all the strength I had. He howled and let go of my neck. I wasted no time running out of his apartment and down the flights of stairs. I ran coughing and sputtering past little crowds of people outside the apartment building, across the street through the traffic, and into the park through the trees. I could see Marla off in the distance, sitting on top of one of the picnic tables in the picnic shelter, next to our school bags and my guitar. She was absent-mindedly scratching at the mosquito bites on her legs.

I slowed down to a walk until I caught up to her. When she caught sight of me, I rubbed at my reddened neck and burst out crying. "What is it? What happened?" she cried with alarm.

I told her through sobs and tears what the man had done. She shook her head in disgust and said, "I'm sorry, Chrissy! You done the right thing. He shouldn't a done that to you." She paused, then added, "But you know, in the future, you're probably gonna have to do that for the perverts. It's what they like."

"No! Never!" I said, wiping my tears. "I won't!"

She sighed, "Well, just rest for a bit and calm down and we'll figure out where to go from here. We probably shouldn't stick around here in case he comes back looking for us."

I sat down on one of the benches and rested my head on the table. The sun was beginning to set and we still had no money, no food, and no place to stay the night.

"Marla," I said. "I can't do this anymore. I wanna go home! I don't think we're ever gonna make it to Las Vegas. We're never gonna be a famous musical duo. That was all just a dumb fantasy! I know my life at home is boring and maybe unfair, but I wanna go back to it!"

"Chrissy, you know I can't go back there!" she shouted. "I won't!"

"I know," I said softly. I paused, then added, "I'll miss you."

We both stayed there in silence for a minute, contemplating what this meant. Marla scratched some more at the bites on her leg and then squinted off into the sunset, shading her eyes with her hand. Her lips were chapped and cracked and there were shadows under her eyes from lack of sleep. "Chrissy, I ... " she paused. Then she looked at me sadly, "Chrissy, I ain't got no place to go." For as long as I live, I'll never forget the hopeless and desperate look on her face right then.

"I'm sorry," I said. I truly was sorry for Marla, sorry that this life on the street was preferable to her than the one waiting for her at home, sorry that grown-ups took advantage of her wherever she went but no one cared about her enough to save her, sorry that I didn't have any solutions for her.

But, unlike Marla, I *did* have a place to go, and I was going there. I gave Marla a hug and took my school bag and my guitar and left her, still sitting at that picnic shelter on a hot July evening in Arkansas. I never saw or heard from Marla again. The fantasy part of me imagined that all Marla's hopes and dreams of becoming famous came true. But the reality part of me knew that Marla became another statistic, another child swallowed up by the street like thousands of children just like her.

Carrying my belongings, I walked along the streets of Little Rock back to where we had passed a local police station about two miles earlier. I took a deep breath and walked through the front door. "My name is Christine Rollings. I'm 13 years old. I ran away from Hilldale, North Carolina. And I wanna go home."

7

When I arrived at the police station in Hilldale a day later, Momma was waiting for me. She told me later that she had planned to slap me across the face and then read me the riot act for what I'd done. But, when she saw me, all she could do was run toward me shrieking, "Chrissy, Chrissy!" She caught me in a big hug and held me tight, and I hugged her back and tried not to cry. "Chrissy, I was so scared! So scared for what might happen to you out there!"

"I know. I'm sorry, Momma," I said.

"Don't ever do that again! Ever!"

"I won't. I promise! I just wanna go home. Please, can we go home?"

First we had to answer some questions for the police. They needed to fill out some paperwork. They asked me where Marla was, and I said we'd split up and I didn't know where she might be now. They asked why we'd run off, where we went, and what we did. I was as brief and nondescript as I could be, while giving them just enough information to fill out their stupid forms so we could get out of there.

The policeman turned to Momma. "Mrs. Rollings, you need to have better control over your daughter," the officer said. "This incident will go on her juvenile record."

"Yes, sir. Thank you, sir," she said. It was weird to see Momma talking with the policeman. She seemed like a little kid being chastised, just nodding her head and agreeing without even standing up for herself. I guess that's what comes from being raised in a strict, authoritarian household like the one she'd had.

We kept our arms around each other all the way out to the car, our wonderful clunker of a car with its broken passenger seat! I'd never complain about it again. When we got to the house, I jumped out of the car and ran inside. I was tackled from all sides by the kids. "Chrissy! Chrissy! You came back! We're so glad you're back!"

"Brad was a terrible babysitter," complained Jenny. "He just sat around watching TV and told us to shut up all the time!"

"Oh, shut up," Brad said, bopping Jenny in the head with his palm. But even he seemed happy to have me back. He patted me on the shoulder and said, "It's good to have you back, Chrissy." That was the most physical contact I'd ever had from him besides punches!

"It's good to be back. Oh, I missed you all so much!" Ronnie had a hold of my arm and was kissing it all the way from the shoulder down to the wrist.

We cooked up just about everything we had in the cupboards and had a big feast that night. As old and rickety and broken-down as our house was, at least I had a roof over my head again, food to eat, and people who loved me there. That night, I unpacked my school bag and set my guitar down at the foot of my bunk-bed. I placed the Chrissy rock back on the desk, where it belonged. I climbed into bed, and soon little Darlene and Trisha crawled in with me on either side. A few weeks earlier, I might have hollered at them to get back in their own beds. But that night, we fell asleep with our arms around each other, and I felt almost as happy and content as I felt before Daddy died.

Life quickly went back to normal. I was back to babysitting and doing chores when Momma went to work. But now I felt less resentful about it, since I knew first-hand what kind of world it was outside. Momma never asked me what had happened during those three weeks that I was gone. All she knew was what I had told the police officer. I don't think she really wanted to know the details. And, frankly, I didn't want to tell her. I just wanted to bury and forget the bad stuff.

School started again in the fall, and I picked up where I'd left off with my studies. It was lonely now without Marla. I was back to eating my meager lunches by myself while reading a book. There were a few people who were my acquaintances,

50

and some that I considered friends, but not the kind of friends that you confide in or do things outside of school with, like the friend Marla had been. I guess I would never be that type of outgoing, fun person who made friends everywhere she went. That just wasn't my style. But I held out hope that I might find another good friend.

Rumors started floating around school about what Marla and I had done that summer. Some of them were true and some of them weren't. I could sometimes overhear people talking or whispering about me, and they gave me funny looks. I tried not to let it get to me. God would be the judge of us, not them, I told myself.

Mid-October was always a hard time of the year for me, because it would bring back memories of Daddy's death. We didn't completely ignore the holidays like we did that first year, but we didn't make a big deal out of them either. We'd make a nicer meal and eat it together, and maybe make each other some homemade gifts. We really didn't have the money to buy store-bought gifts for each other.

That year at Christmas, though, someone knocked on our door and ran away. When we opened the door, there was a big box filled with fruit, treats, and little gifts for each person, with some of the things we really needed, like clothes and shoes. There was a toy for each of the younger kids and a board game for us older kids. That ended up being a nice holiday for all of us. We enjoyed opening all the gifts, eating the fruit and treats, and playing all day with the new board game. I played the guitar and we sang some Christmas carols. When I went to bed that night, I thought about Marla again and wondered how her Christmas had gone. Was she still out on the street? How far west had she made it? I didn't know. But I hoped she wasn't all alone that Christmas, and I wished she could have spent that day with us.

I worked hard at school and made all A's that year. In my free time, I read and played my guitar. Winter turned to spring and the days warmed up again. Sometimes, if the nights were warm enough, Momma and I would go sit out on the porch swing after the kids went to bed and just look at the stars and talk. Momma would tell me stories about when she was little and about when she and Daddy fell in love and got married. Sometimes she would smile and laugh as she talked about things they would do together, all the funny things he would say to tease her. It sounded like Daddy, all right! It was good to see her smile and laugh again. Then she would just grow quiet and stare off into the sky again. One time she told me, "He was the only man I ever loved." I placed my hand on top of hers and we just sat there, rocking in silence, lost in memories. The bad part about loving someone so much is that it tears such a big hole in your heart when they're gone. You can move on and continue with your life, but you'll never be completely whole again.

Since we were a welfare family, we had periodic visits from a social worker to check on how we were doing. For the first little while, our social worker was a man named Mr. Sterling. He seemed sort of absent-minded and not really that concerned about things with us. I think he often skipped his visits, or maybe he just stopped by when I was at school. We just didn't see him a whole lot. I didn't really appreciate him until he was gone, and we got a new social worker that spring.

Miss Pickard drove around in a shiny white car that looked like it might even be new. Her blonde hair was teased up so high that it touched the roof of her car. She wore solid blue eye shadow from the lid all the way up to her eyebrows. It was such a distraction when you looked at her. You would try to look her straight in the eye, but then your eyes would automatically start drifting up until you forced them back down. You would try to pay attention to what she was saying, but then you'd start thinking, *damn, that's a lot of blue,* and completely lose track of the conversation. I told Momma after she left one day that I predicted Miss Pickard would one day go blind from an overdose of blue eye shadow. We both started giggling. Then Momma said, "Now, be nice."

Miss Pickard carried a briefcase everywhere and clacked around in really high heels. She always seemed a bit put out when she stepped out of her car onto the gravel and dirt roads surrounding our house, like she was tee'd off that the roads and our driveway hadn't been paved since the last time she visited. I didn't like her right from the start, and it wasn't just because of her blue lids, teased-up hair, and high heels. Mainly it was because of the way she treated us for the way we lived, like we were little rodents running around by her feet, multiplying before her very eyes. She'd look at our rundown house and torn, stained, ill-fitting clothes and ask questions with a tight, false smile, then write things down on her chart. She never sat down or touched anything of ours, like she was afraid that she might catch a very bad case of poverty. The way she talked to Momma and the way Momma talked back reminded me of the exchange at the police station after I'd run away. Even though I think Miss Pickard was younger than Momma, she talked to her like she was the one in charge. She was the educated career lady and Momma was the dumb, stupid hillbilly who couldn't stop breeding. I tried to avoid her whenever she came by.

On the Friday after school was out that year, I decided to take the kids to the nearby swimming hole for the afternoon. It was a hot June day and the water felt nice. After I'd splashed around for a while, I climbed out and sat on a rock to watch the kids and to dry off. I thought about how it was one year ago that day that Marla and I had set off on our journey west. I remembered how excited we were when we first hit the road, off on our big adventure. And some of the time it *had* been exciting, like when we'd walk through the big cities at night enjoying the lights and sounds around us, that day we'd spent in Nashville going to a restaurant and movie, the nice family that had let us stay with them. But then there were the awful times, the perverts, the fear of having no protection, no place to stay, no food. I tried to put those awful parts out of my mind. I hoped Marla was doing okay and that she was safe. After I was all dry and starting to get hot again, I told the kids that it was time to go back home. They fussed about it for a bit, but I promised we'd come back soon.

When we walked back to the house, I saw the white car and the teased-up blonde hair off in the distance. Blue Lids was standing with her briefcase in one hand and her chart in the other, facing Momma, who was sitting on the porch swing. They turned when they saw us. "Oh, there you are," Blue Lids called out to us. Momma had the strangest look on her face when our eyes met. "Crystal, Crystal, I have some great news for you," Blue Lids announced once we got to the porch stairway.

"Who's Crystal?" Jenny asked.

Blue Lids glanced down at her chart. "Christine," she corrected herself.

"Wrong again. Her name is Chrissy," Jenny said.

"Okay, why don't all you little kids run along and play, all right? The big people have some talking to do, so run along now. Shoo!" She waved them away with her chart. The kids did as they were told, and I stood there at the porch steps, wondering what this was all about.

"Christine," Blue Lids started in. "I have some very good news for you! I was just talking to your mother about it, and I think you're going to be very interested in this. The state of North Carolina has a wonderful program to help out people like you. You can qualify for a very simple operation, paid for by the state and completely free to you, and after it's over you won't have to worry about having any more babies!" she gushed.

"But … I don't have any babies."

"Yes, well, you don't have to worry about having them in the future! It's called eugenic sterilization, and North Carolina is one of the few states that offers this completely free service to people like you."

"Oh … no thanks." I headed up the steps, skipping the broken step, and started for the door.

"Christine!" Blue Lids raised her voice slightly. "You haven't finished hearing me out about the program. Don't turn it down until you know all the details!"

"So finish." I stood there with my arms crossed over my chest.

"There's a special board of people in Raleigh called the Eugenics Board ..."

"What's eugenics?"

"Well, it's sort of a way of shaping the kind of society you want, what kind of people you want to have in it. Children deserve to have the right kind of parents, who can care for them properly. Certain people just shouldn't be parents. More often than not, those children turn out to be just like their parents. So the Eugenics Board authorizes the sterilization of certain people, like insane or retarded people."

"I'm not any of those things."

"Or people who are feeble-minded."

"What's that?"

"Well, it can mean a number of different things, for example, people who have a low IQ, or, say, girls who are rebellious or promiscuous, just people who shouldn't be having babies, because those babies just end up being a burden on society and to those mommas who shouldn't have had them." She smiled tightly.

"Well, I'm not any of those things either, unless 'feeble-minded' is just code for poor."

"You ran away a year ago for three weeks, isn't that correct?" Blue Lids glanced at her chart and then back at me. "You were found two states away. That sounds a little rebellious to me. And let me ask something else, are you still a virgin?"

"That's none of your business!"

"I think that answers my question right there," she said smugly.

"Well, I don't really care what you or some board thinks of me! Maybe I happen to think *you* should be sterilized, because the last thing this world needs is more blue-lidded, chart-holding busybodies, clickety-clacking around town with their noses in the air telling everybody what to do!"

Her voice rose slightly, "Well, I have already petitioned the Eugenics Board for your sterilization, and it was approved. This is a sterilization order with your name on it, Christine!"

"I don't care! I won't do it," I said.

"I don't think you've comprehended anything I've just explained, Christine."

"Yes, I do comprehend it. You think I'm some sort of dummy, or a whore, or both, and so you think I should be neutered like some barnyard animal, so you sent off a form to some jackasses in Raleigh who have never met me, and they said it was all right. But you don't know anything about me; you don't even know my name. And you don't have any authority over me!" I yelled.

Blue Lids' voice became shrill, "Well, then, let me put this in terms you'll be able to understand. If you don't comply with this state order, we're going to take this nice little government check away from your mother! Do you understand me? The free ride is over. How do you think you'll get along without that check? Your brothers and sisters will starve, Christine, and it will be your fault! When you hear them crying about their rumbly tummies and begging for something to eat, you'll know that you have only yourself to blame for their suffering. How is that going to feel?"

I was taken aback by this news. Threatening me with my siblings was the one way to get through to me. How did Blue Lids know that I couldn't stand the thought of their suffering? I'd do anything for them.

Seeing the stricken look on my face, Miss Pickard softened her tone a bit. "Now be reasonable, Christine. This really is in your best interest. You'll see that over time." Her voice lowered. "Do you really want to end up like your momma? In your young 30's, no husband, flat broke, lousy job, no education, no skills, and children up to your eyeballs? That's no kind of life." She spoke as if Momma couldn't hear her from four feet away.

"I had a husband," Momma spoke up. "He died."

"Now that I think about it, I really should have sent off a petition for you too, Mrs. Rollings," Blue Lids said, turning to Momma. "You're still of child-bearing age. I could still do that if you'd like. It'd be no trouble at all. It's such a valuable program. I try to make sure all the women and girls of child-bearing age in my caseload have access to eugenic sterilizations."

"I guess now we know what 'feeble-minded' really means, Momma," I remarked sarcastically. "It means you're a female and in Miss Pickard's caseload."

"Miss Pickard," Momma said, "my husband has been dead almost three years now. I won't be having more children."

"But you work nights in a bar, isn't that correct?" Blue Lids asked pointedly.

"What's that supposed to mean?"

"Well, I'm just saying you're probably exposed to a lot of different types of men. Some women just have trouble controlling themselves. I just think it's better to be safe than sorry," she said.

"I'm quite safe, thank you. Unless you think I'm gonna be giving birth to Jesus himself anytime soon," Momma added.

"Very well then. You can always change your mind. And I'll thank you to leave our Lord out of this."

"Seems to me you're the one playing God," Momma said, "deciding who can and can't have babies."

Emboldened that Momma was finally speaking up for us, I said, "You tell her, Momma. Tell her what she can do with her government check!"

Momma stared at the ground in front of her. "Chrissy," she stammered. "I really need that check, honey. We're barely getting by as it is, just barely getting by." Her voice started to crack. "The thought of losing it … well, we just wouldn't make it anymore. We'd go under for sure."

"Momma?" What was she trying to say?

"Your momma has already signed her consent on your sterilization order," Blue Lids stated. "You'll have the procedure before the summer is out." She babbled on with more details and about how thrilled I'd be about it, but I wasn't listening anymore. I felt like I'd just been punched in the gut and had the wind knocked out of me. Momma had already signed the consent before I was even confronted with the idea? It was *my* body, *my* life, and they could just permanently alter it without even discussing it with me first? How was this even possible?

So, this was how it would go down, I thought. People who don't even know me have the power to give me a label and then surgically alter me, taking away my God-given rights, and there was nothing I could do about it. I couldn't run away. I already knew how that ended. And the one person who *did* know me, the biggest traitor of all, was standing right in front of me, still unable to look me in the eyes as I stared her down.

"And you'll be all healed up by the time school starts this fall. Just think, you'll be starting high school in another year without a care in the world! When all your friends are getting pregnant and dropping out of school, you'll be free as a bird, able to do whatever you want. Won't that be nice?" Blue Lids flashed me her false smile.

I spent years puzzling over why Momma would sign that form. Did she really think I was any of those things Blue Lids described? Did she really think I would have been an incompetent parent? She trusted me to raise her own kids. Did she actually think I was unintelligent, rebellious, or promiscuous? Did she suspect I would run away again?

For years I tried to figure out how my own mother could have betrayed me so completely. In the end, though, I think it all came down to a matter of simple math.

She had to sacrifice one child to save five.

8

Momma and I didn't talk much that summer. I avoided being alone with her whenever possible, and we didn't talk about what had transpired with Blue Lids or the upcoming surgery in August. I knew now what my place was in that family, so I did my work, nothing more. None of my siblings knew I would be having a surgery before summer's end, and we didn't feel the need to tell them about it

On the day of the surgery, Momma drove me to the hospital. I was given a hospital gown and a place to change. I met with Dr. Blake right before the surgery. He breezed into the operating room, reading his chart, introduced himself to me, and asked if I knew what this procedure was.

"Yes, and I don't want it," I answered, bursting into tears. He was my last hope of not having to go through with it. "Please, Doctor, I really don't want to be sterilized."

"Now, Christine," he patted my hand, "there's really no need to get so emotional about this. This is a simple procedure, and I perform it all the time. No one has ever died from it. You'll be a little sore for a few weeks, and you'll have to be careful with your incision. Keep it clean and be protective of it until it's fully healed. Do you think that's something you could do?"

He talked to me like I was some sort of idiot! "That's not why I'm crying. I don't want the procedure because it's wrong! What if I want to have children someday? That should be *my* decision, not yours."

"Well, I'm very sorry, but this is the law. And it's a good one too, I might add. There are too many girls like you running around getting pregnant and expecting taxpayers to foot the bill for their babies. I'm a taxpayer too, and I'm tired of paying for all these little bastards running around. I'm glad my state is actually doing something about this problem. If more states would do this, maybe we could actually whittle down some of these welfare rolls."

"But I won't get pregnant or take any taxpayer money!" I cried. "What if I promise not to have any babies until I'm married someday?"

"Well, maybe you should have thought about that before you did whatever landed you here in the first place. I'm afraid my hands are tied, young lady. This is a state order. I have to comply."

"No, you don't!" I said desperately. "You could not do it, and just say you did. I wouldn't tell, I promise! Please, Doctor, you don't have to do this!"

"And collect money for a procedure I didn't perform? Lie to the government? Lie to the taxpayers? That might be something your kind of people think is okay, do whatever, say whatever to keep the money flowing in. But that's not how I do business. Are we clear?"

He called in some nurses who prepared me for the surgery, while he left the room for a minute. I was still sniffling and wiping my tears when he came back. I tried to stay conscious as long as I could, staring him down until the last minute. I wanted him to remember the tear-streaked look on my face as the nurse pulled the anesthesia mask over it. I hope it haunted his dreams for as long as he lived.

I don't remember being woken after the surgery. Someone helped me put my clothes back on and wheeled me over to where Momma's car waited for me out front. They helped me into the car and we drove home. Momma helped me into my bed and told my sisters to stay out of the room, saying that I wasn't feeling well and needed to sleep. I slept for several hours, drifting in and out of consciousness and having very strange dreams. Finally, I opened my eyes and stayed awake for a while, staring out of my bedroom window. It had been a dry, hot summer, and almost everything was brown and dead outside. It looked like I felt on the inside — brown, dead, lifeless. There wasn't even the slightest of breezes to make things look alive.

Soon I heard a soft knock on the door. Momma opened the door and entered with a little tray with a bowl of soup and a glass of water on it. "I brought you something to eat. They said you should eat something bland and drink liquids."

"I'm not hungry," I said flatly, still staring out the window.

Momma stood there for a moment. "You should at least try to have a sip of water, I think. That will help flush the anesthesia out of your system."

"I'm not thirsty either."

She still stood there, holding the tray. "The doctor sent you home with some medication for pain. I'd be happy to get it for you if you want. Is that what you want? Or I could bring you one of your books to read. Do you want a book?"

"What I want is to be left alone."

Momma set the tray down on top of the desk, sliding my Chrissy rock off to one side. "Just let me know if you need anything, if you start having pain or anything." She walked to the door and turned around. "I hope you're feeling better soon." She began to close the door.

"I'll never forgive you," I said.

The door clicked shut softly. I stayed there, still staring out the window for a while. Then I turned my head to look at where the tray was sitting on my desk, next to my rock. I could see the lettering and all the rainbows and flowers I'd painted on it back then, back when life was full of roses and rainbows, back when I still had Daddy. He never would have allowed this to happen, never in a million years.

I imagined sitting back in that surgical room in my hospital gown begging the doctor not to operate. Suddenly, Daddy burst through the front door of the hospital lobby and bellowed out, "Where the hell is my daughter?" Security officers tried to subdue him, but he punched them all out cold on the floor. Other people rushed to try to stop him, but he punched them out too. Daddy would never hit a woman, so I imagined they just fainted to the floor in fear. He stormed his way through the hallways, checking each room and punching out the people who tried to stop him.

Finally, he burst through the door of my room just as they were about to put the anesthesia mask over my face. He ripped it out of their hands and threw it against the wall. He punched the doctor out cold, and the nurses fainted to the floor. Miss Pickard hadn't actually been at the hospital, but I put her in my fantasy anyway. I think Daddy would have made an exception to his no-punching-women rule in her case. She held her briefcase in one hand and her chart in the other and gave Daddy one of her tight, false smiles. "Mr. Rollings, this is breaking the law. I have an order here from the state for the sterilization of your daughter."

"Oh, yeah?" Daddy yelled. "Well, I have here an order from the state to give you two *permanent* blue lids!" And with that, he punched her right in the nose. Her briefcase burst open, and all her charts and papers — describing who's a dummy and who's a whore and who needs to be sterilized — scattered so far and wide that she'd never be able to get them sorted out ever again. Then he stepped over her unconscious body and picked me up from the operating table. I wrapped my arms around his neck and buried my head in his chest while he carried me right out of that hospital, stepping over all the unconscious bodies in his path.

That's how it would have gone down if he'd still been alive. Oh, how I wished that glorious rescue story had been the way things really happened! But that was just a fantasy. And this was the real world. In the real world, you discover pretty quickly that you are *completely* on your own. And, in your darkest hour, no one is ever going to burst through that door to save you.

I slowly sat up from my bunk-bed and gingerly lifted the covers, swung my legs over, and carefully stood up, holding a protective hand over my swollen abdomen and the angry red incision underneath my thin nightgown. I slowly walked over to the desk where the tray and my rock sat. I was beginning to feel pain now, but I'd rather perish from sheer agony than have to call out to Momma asking for the pain medication she'd offered. I wouldn't give her the satisfaction of doing something to help me! I opened one of the drawers beneath the desk and pulled out my old rock paints and paintbrush and began to stroke smooth, careful lettering onto the rock's surface. When I was finished, I put the paints and brush away and carefully made my way back into bed and turned to stare at the brown, dead scenery out my window.

"Christine Kollings, Born May 9, 1952.

Died August 13, 1966."

9

A few weeks after the surgery, the new school year began. I was in my last year at East Junior High, and Brad was just beginning his first year there. If I'd been a quiet, reserved student before, I was almost a recluse now. I sat in the very back of every class and talked to no one. I didn't have any friends, join any clubs, or participate in any activities outside of school. I'm not sure that any of my classmates from back then would even recognize my name or face. I was simply part of the background scenery there.

I kept myself occupied with schoolwork. In my free time, I always had my nose in a book or my guitar in my lap. Those were my two escapes from what I considered a lonely and miserable existence. I still handled babysitting and dinner on the nights Momma worked. But even my relationship with my siblings had changed. I did what I had to do for them and nothing more. I didn't play imaginative games with them anymore; or talk and laugh with them; or hug and kiss them like I used to do. In some ways, I felt like the surgery had removed more than just my ability to reproduce. It had taken away part of something that had made me human, some of my heart and maybe even a little bit of my soul. My relationship with Momma became non-existent. We'd never again sit out on the porch swing late at night talking about the past and laughing. Those days were long gone, and they'd never come back. A few times, when I'd been sitting out there by myself, Momma came out and sat next to me, hoping to start a conversation perhaps. But I always just stood up and went back inside. Finally, she stopped trying. She often just sat out there in solitude.

It seemed to me that all my classmates had everything that I didn't have: fun, happy families, loving parents, friends, enough money and food, the confidence to speak up in class and participate in school life. I discovered there was really only one area in which I could almost always outdo them — grades.

Since I was always sitting in the back, I could typically see the grades that most of them received as various papers, quizzes, assignments, and tests were handed back. Nothing ruined my day more than seeing a grade that was higher than mine. If I had a 98 percent and "good job" written on a paper, but I saw that someone else had a 100 percent and "fantastic!" scrawled across the top, I considered it a failure of epic proportions. I wasn't even happy with a tie. If that happened, I'd work extra hard so that, next time, my score would be higher. And since I just blended into the woodwork at school, no one had any idea how fiercely I was competing against them for the better grade. Oh, how I wished I could be pitted against Blue Lids in an IQ test! I'd blow her out of the water, and then send *her* off to be gutted on the operating table, for some justice.

My teachers really didn't know my face, but they began to recognize my name as the girl who never said a word but made excellent grades. But if they were hoping the Rollings were going to produce a long line of quiet but smart students, they were in for an unpleasant surprise with Brad. His method of one-upping his classmates was by picking fights, stealing from them, and talking back to teachers and administrators when they tried to discipline him. From the 7th grade on, Brad was in and out of the principal's office and was twice that year suspended from school for two-week periods. Momma really didn't know how to handle him. She would place him on restrictions, but he would just ignore them. Yelling at him had no effect, and he was too old and too big to spank anymore. Maybe having Daddy around would have helped Brad, or maybe not. I wasn't sure. Whatever it was Brad needed, he just couldn't get it from our family or from the school system. He never did anything to help around the house. Half the time, we didn't even know where he was anyway. Looking back, I think that Brad felt as lonely and as disengaged from society as I did. He just had a different way of showing it.

I started my sophomore year at Green Level High School, a large school with about 700 students. I found it even easier to fade into the background and live the kind of anonymous life that I preferred. Every once in a while, I'd hear rumors about some girl in our grade who had gotten pregnant. I thought of Blue Lids promising me that I'd be "free as a bird" in high school, whatever that meant. If she could see me now, maybe she'd realize that she'd had me butchered for nothing. All that precious taxpayer money gone to waste! I'd never been asked on a date, nor did I even speak to the boys at my school.

With Trisha starting elementary school, Momma was able to change her hours at the bar & grill from the night shift to the day shift, working from 10 a.m. to 6 p.m. Monday through Friday. This freed me from having to make dinner and babysit most nights of the week. That was good, because it allowed me to spend more time on my studies. I found that, with more students at the high school, I had more competition for getting the best grades than ever before. I still managed to beat most of the people who sat nearby, at least from what I could see of the papers and tests that were handed back. I almost always had all A's, with sometimes an A- or the occasional B+. The lower grades typically resulted from classes in which participation in the class discussion was part of the grade. I never contributed to a discussion. I couldn't stand the thought of speaking aloud and having a bunch of faces turn around to look at me. So I had to just accept the lower grades and hope there might be some written extra credit opportunities to raise my final grades.

Even though Momma had better hours, she still always seemed just as tired and depressed as before. The tips weren't as good during the weekday shift. It seemed that the cost of everything kept going up while the money she was bringing in kept going down, the story of our lives. My relationship with her continued to be strained. Sometimes I wanted to try to talk to her, but my pride or the bitterness I carried around like the angry scar on my abdomen always prevented me from doing it. I said what needed to be said to her and nothing more.

Brad was another source of constant discontent in our house. There were continual calls from school administrators

66

and conferences with them. Momma tried to do everything they suggested, but nothing worked with him. The next year, when he was in the 9th grade, he committed his first major offense by setting the school on fire and was sent off on the first of many stints in a juvenile detention center. It's terrible to admit, but we were all a bit relieved when he was in juvie. At least then we knew where he was and that he couldn't get into more trouble there. Plus, it was one less person to feed, and Brad always ate more than his fair share when he was at home. Sometimes when he would be home, I'd secretly hope that he'd be sent back to the detention center. I don't think Momma hoped he would be sent back. She hoped he would just improve and be able to stay home, but I think even she was a bit relieved when he'd be sent off again.

Jenny was growing into the beautiful young teenager that I'd always thought she would be. She was friendly and outgoing. People were drawn to her in spite of her clothes and shoes, which were a dead giveaway that she lived in poverty. She was so gifted in her artwork. She wanted Momma to let her join the art club, but it was too expensive. Then she wanted Momma to get her a camera because she wanted to study photography. Momma couldn't get her that either. I thought about the time so many years ago when Momma bought me my guitar. I know she would have loved to do the same for Jenny with a camera, but not if it meant someone else would have to go hungry because of it. So Jenny went without her camera.

Jenny was constantly invited to her friends' houses, and she loved to be away from home and participate in their family activities. She went to sleepovers nearly every weekend and was depressed if she ever had to stay home and just be with us. She hated the way we lived, hated never having enough money for anything. If Momma ever took Jenny to any school activities or her friends' houses, she had to drop Jenny off a couple of blocks away because Jenny didn't want them to see Momma's old clunker sputtering up to the curbside. At her friends' houses, Jenny could eat whatever she wanted and not have to go without. They'd take her to the movies and parties. She never invited a single friend over to our house. I think Jenny wished that she could belong to one of her friends' families, any other family but ours.

The three youngest kids just seemed to carry on happily with life, despite the misery and dysfunction in our family. They had one another for friendship and looked out for each other. They were fairly oblivious to the unhappiness and problems going on with the older kids or with Momma. In some ways, I think they were lucky that they didn't really remember what life was like when Daddy was alive. They didn't remember going to the drive-in movies or talking and laughing together. They didn't remember celebrating holidays and having fun. They thought this was just the way family life was: a bunch of random, miserable people thrown together in an old, rickety house struggling just to get through each day. If that's what you've always known, then you think it's just normal. I felt bad for them because *I* knew what they were missing, even if they didn't. And I was sad for them, because they deserved a better life than the one they had.

My "friends" were the characters in the books I was reading and my teachers at school. I guess they were sort of one-sided friendships, because the characters were fictional, and I never really talked to my teachers. Of course, I had a few teachers who didn't really like what they did for a living and barely put any effort into it. But the teachers that I considered to be my "friends" were the ones who really loved their jobs. They liked the students and they were excited about expanding the students' knowledge on their particular subject. I especially liked the teachers who would crack jokes during class and make the whole class laugh. I got such a kick out of them, because they were really very funny. Some of them could have been comedians, I thought. They were the kind of teachers that made you look forward to coming to class because you would learn something new and be entertained at the same time. I liked the teachers who would share stories about their own lives too.

I'd think about their lives even when I wasn't at school. I'd chuckle to myself when I thought about Mr. Chandler, how, in college, he took up someone on a dare to streak across the football field with nothing but a paper bag over his head! He never got caught for that either! I felt awful for Mrs. Tanner when her cat was hit by a car right in front of her house. She had a hard time teaching class that day, and I almost wanted to go up and give her a hug after class, if I hadn't been so shy. I wondered when Mr. Sandhall's wife would have her baby. Would it be a boy or a girl? It was their first, so they were pretty excited about it. None of these teachers even had a clue how much I enjoyed coming to their classes each day. They had no idea that they were such a lifeline to the outside world for me.

When my senior year rolled around, I started to dread the end of my school career. I would be the first person to graduate from high school in my family, but I had no idea what I should do after that. The thought of not having school as my lifeline, my connection to the world, was terrifying. I didn't want to travel into this new, uncharted territory. Senior year is typically an expensive one, but I didn't engage in any of the activities that cost money. I didn't have a senior picture taken, go on the class trip, participate in activities, or attend the homecoming or prom events.

The one thing I felt I should probably do before graduation was get my driver's license. Even though I hated driving Momma's old VW — nothing worked in that car except the engine — I was 17 years old, almost 18, and probably needed a form of identification. So, in the early spring of that year, I swallowed my pride and asked Momma for the money to get my driver's license. She said it was probably a good idea and gave me the money without even hesitating. She drove me to the DMV where I took the test and passed on the first try. I was so happy when I had that little card in my hand. Most people hate their driver's license picture, but I thought mine was actually pretty good. It was issued by the state, but there was nothing on there that gave away anything about my being poor, or feeble-minded or sterilized. Looking at the card, you would think I was just a normal, everyday teenager with a happy life and a great future ahead of her. Just carrying that card around made me feel somehow validated as a normal person. I still rode the bus every day, which, for seniors, is a major disgrace. Most seniors by then either had their own cars, or borrowed a car from their parents, or they at least had a friend with access to a car who could take them to and from school. But, few people even knew who I was or what grade I was in, so it didn't really matter that I still rode the bus.

One day that spring, I walked home from the bus stop after school and saw Jenny crouched down by some pretty wildflowers near our house. She had something in her hands. When I drew closer, I could see that she had a camera, a nice one!

"Who in the world let you borrow that thing?" I asked with pleasant surprise.

She was focused on adjusting the lens and didn't look up. "It's mine," she answered. "Brad bought it for me."

That news wiped the smile off my face. "Is that right?" I immediately headed toward the house to find him. He hadn't been on the bus, so he'd either gotten a ride or had skipped classes that afternoon. Stealing something like that would land him back in juvie for sure. I couldn't believe Jenny would just accept stolen property like that! Did he steal it from a person or from a store? I wasn't sure which would put him in more trouble. Or maybe he stole the money and then bought it for Jenny or did something even worse to get the money. I'd had a sneaking suspicion for some time that Brad was using, and possibly selling, drugs.

I swung open the door to his room without knocking first. He was lying on top of his bed reading a magazine. "Did you steal that camera?" I asked accusingly.

"Nope." He didn't look up from his magazine. "Bought it with my own money."

"From what? You don't have a job!"

"How do you know?"

"Okay, what's your job?"

He thought for a minute. "Mowing lawns."

"Whose lawn? Please name names. I plan to go over there and ask them."

"I can't remember. Would you get out of my room?"

"Are you selling drugs?"

"Get out!" he yelled.

"Then you stole the camera. It's one or the other, I know it," I stated accusingly.

"Chrissy, leave him alone!" Jenny yelled from behind me. "He didn't steal it. He bought it with his own money. It's the nicest thing anyone's ever done for me and I don't wanna give it back!"

"Well, we'll just see what Momma has to say about this when she gets home," I said.

"She already knows!" Jenny cried. "Brad gave her some money too to fix her car last week."

"Oh, this just keeps getting better and better!" I yelled. I went to our room and slammed the door behind me and worked on homework until Momma came home and called us to dinner.

We all sat in silence at dinner. But once the TV was turned on and Momma headed off to her room to fold the clothes on her bed, I went over and stood in the doorway. "Isn't it a miracle?" I asked. "Brad can pull money out of his ass now," I stated sarcastically.

Momma didn't look up from folding socks. She just quietly said, "He helped me out when I was in a pinch, and I appreciated that."

"You aren't a tad bit curious where he might be getting all this money from? He got a nice, new-looking camera for Jenny. He paid to get your car fixed. Oh, my gosh, he probably paid for my driver's license too! The one thing that makes me feel legitimate. Now that's tainted too!"

Momma continued folding clothes and didn't respond.

"Do you even care that your son will likely be sent back to juvie, and then eventually to prison? Does it even bother you that he might spend the majority of adulthood behind bars?"

"Of course it bothers me!" Momma put down her folding and faced me. "But what am I supposed to do? I can't monitor his every move! It's out of my hands. I can't control him!"

"I guess it really doesn't matter. You got your car fixed. That's the important thing."

"What do you want me to do, Chrissy?"

"I want you to be a mother!" I shouted. "Mothers look out for their children. Mothers protect them as best they can. They think of their future! They don't throw them under the bus when it's convenient. Mothers teach their children right from wrong. You are a terrible mother!"

"Stop yelling at my Momma!" Trisha ran into the room and glared at me. "She's a good Momma!" She went over and hugged Momma, shooting another dirty look at me. "You're so mean!" she said. Momma patted Trisha's head and wiped away one of her own tears.

I just stood there, looking at the two of them for a moment. "You should have been the one sterilized," I blurted out at Momma and headed to my room.

10

As the end of the school year drew near, the seniors were busy making plans for the future. They ordered their caps and gowns for the graduation ceremony. They bought class rings and ordered announcements to send out in the mail. Since I would be graduating with honors, I was offered the chance to purchase an honors sash to go with the cap and gown. I didn't order anything. They all cost too much money. These ceremonies were a stupid waste of time, I told myself. I didn't want to go anyway. They could just mail me my diploma.

One of my favorite teachers, Mr. Chandler, who taught history, called my name out in class and asked if I would stay after for a bit to talk to him. I was petrified! Why in the world would he want to talk to me? What had I done? Granted, I considered him one of my best friends, but I certainly didn't ever expect that we'd have to talk face to face! After the bell rang and everyone headed out the door, I could feel my temperature rise and my heart thumped loudly in my chest. Did he think I'd cheated on something? Was I in trouble?

He smiled at me. "It's Christine, right? You're Christine Rollings?"

"My friends call me Chrissy," I replied timidly.

"Chrissy," Mr. Chandler glanced down at his grades log, "you don't say much in class, but your grades in my class are excellent. The lowest grade was one A- on a quiz. All your tests have been A's and your papers were A+ level! Congratulations!"

"Thank you, sir," I said quietly.

"I checked on your other classes, and you're doing just as well in every subject. You'll graduate in the top 10 percent of your class. The reason that I called you in was that I wanted to ask you about your future plans. Have you decided what you're going to do? Surely someone as smart as you has a bright future in store."

I shook my head, staring at the floor in front of me. "I … haven't really thought about it much. I don't know what I'll do."

"Have you thought about going to college?" he asked. "With your grades, you could get in almost anywhere you applied, possibly even with an academic scholarship. Have you applied anywhere? Is that something you'd like to pursue?"

"Yes. I mean no …. I haven't really applied anywhere." It cost money to apply to college. And I knew it was out of the question for me. It was a miracle that I was even graduating from high school, with my family background. College was a pipe dream. "But thank you for talking to me about it. I'll … really think about it."

"You should really think about it," he said. "Let me know if there's anything I can do to help you. And good luck, Chrissy," he said with a big smile.

"Thank you, sir," I shyly smiled back at him. I wanted to tell him that I'd been accepted to Harvard on scholarship, that I'd be heading to Boston at the end of the summer, anything to make his smile even broader, his recognition of me even grander.

I walked out of the room on such a high as I went off to eat my lunch but quickly deflated again as I sat alone eating my peanut butter sandwich. As smart as he was, he just didn't get it. Girls like me didn't go to college. Even if I had a scholarship, it would still cost money. I didn't even have the money to do the regular high school things, much less move on to a school that wasn't publically funded. College is a luxury, a time-out from life to better oneself. When you're poor, you don't have that luxury, and there are no time-outs, no vacations from the daily struggle to live. When you're kicking and kicking with all your might just to keep your nostrils above water, you know you can't stop kicking, even for a few moments. Because if you do, you know that you'll go under and never come back up again. People wonder why poor people just can't seem to get a leg up. But how do you explain that sometimes you need a leg up just to *get* a leg up? I avoided Mr. Chandler as much as I could after that, afraid he'd ask me for an update on my progress. And I had nothing to say.

May rolled around and I turned 18. I was officially an adult now. In some ways, it seemed that I had been thrown into adulthood long before my time. In other ways, it seemed that I'd been stuck forever in childhood, desperately clinging to a time when I used to be happy. I'd never really experienced the rites of passage of the teen years: parties, hanging out with friends, football games, dances, school clubs. I lived the contradictory life of being both the wise adult too old and mature for my peers and the little girl too young and inexperienced for them, always watching from the sidelines and waiting for the chance to join the life around me.

My little siblings were so happy when school ended for the summer. Ronnie, Darlene, and Trisha decided to have a little slumber party out on the porch that Friday night since it was a warm evening and they wanted to celebrate the start of summer. Jenny went to a sleepover at one of her friend's houses. I was glad to have the room to myself. That way I could play my guitar for as long as I wanted. Graduation was the next day and I was trying not to think about it. I played until my fingers hurt and then brushed my teeth, pulled on my pajamas, and sat on top of my bed with a pillow behind my back so I could read for a while before I was too sleepy.

Around 11:00, I heard a soft knock on the door before it quietly opened. Momma was standing there with a letter in her hand. "Chrissy, are you busy?"

"I'm reading," I answered.

"Oh," she said. "I just wanted to come in here and tell you how proud I am of you graduating from high school and all. You're the first person in our family to do that. I always wanted to get my diploma. I knew you could do it though."

"Thanks," I said, still not looking up from my book.

"Graduating with honors," she went on. "That's what this letter here says. I'm so impressed with you. And I want you to know I'll be there at the ceremony tomorrow. I can't wait to see you go up there and get your diploma."

"Well, have fun with that," I said flatly. "I won't be going myself."

"You won't?" Her smile faded.

"It's just pageantry. Monkeys handing out awards to other monkeys for imagined achievements. I find it absurd," I said, turning a page of my book.

"Oh," she said. She just stood there awkwardly. I wished she would just leave so that I could get back to my book. It was a little late to decide suddenly to go to graduation. She'd never mentioned it before.

"Chrissy?" she asked.

I sighed loudly. "What?"

"Have you thought about what you're planning to do after this?" Not her too! I thought I'd already dealt with this from Mr. Chandler.

"I don't know," I shrugged. "Probably just the usual formula: get a job and work until I die."

"I've been thinking about it. I think you should go to college. You have what it takes to go there. You're so smart. I think you should really try."

I sighed again and set my book down. "What it takes to go to college are brains, money, and clout," I said listing them out with my fingers. "I have one of those things. Are you going to provide the other two? Oh, I know! Let's have Brad rob a bank to put me through school. That would be just perfect!" I picked up my book again and tried to find my place.

"There's that junior college, Pemberton, right here in Hilldale. There's talk it's gonna turn into a four-year state school. It would be a start, at least. You could live at home, take the bus or my car when you need it. I'll bet you could even get some sort of scholarship to help with tuition. And I could start taking on some night shifts like I used to do. The tips are better. And I could get another day job. Maybe clean some houses. I think between the two of us, we could probably figure out how to get you through. I'd really like to do this for you. I really would."

I scoffed, "Well, I think I know better than to put my fate in your hands. It's best not to get my hopes up about things I know I can never have, like a college education ... or children."

The words hung in the air for a few moments. Then Momma started in again, "I know you've never forgiven me for … what happened. And, really, I don't blame you. I've thought about that time so much. You don't know how much I regret it. You were right. Mommas should protect their children, and I should have protected you!" Her voice cracked into a sob, "I'm sorry! I should never have let them touch you. I saw what you wrote on that rock, and it breaks my heart. I'm sorry!"

I felt my throat beginning to tighten, the anger and bitterness bubbling up from below. I would not let myself cry in front of her. I swallowed the lump in my throat and just stared at the blurry letters in front of me. "Well, what's done is done. There's nothing that we can do about it now."

"I hope you can … find a way to forgive me someday. Maybe we could find a way to be a family again … somehow… Maybe…"

I interrupted her, "Oh Momma! Stop kidding yourself. This family died a long time ago. We buried it along with Daddy. We're just a bunch of random people rooming and boarding together, biding our time until the day we can finally leave this rat hole!" My outburst surprised even me.

She was taken aback, a stricken look on her face. But I had the knife in now and I was going to drive it home. "And, make no mistake, Momma, the very first opportunity I have to leave this dump, to get out of this town, this state, I am taking it! I will leave all of this far, far behind me. And I'm never coming back. Ever!"

Momma was backing her way out of the room. "I hope you change your mind," she said softly and then clicked the door shut.

Don't hold your breath, I thought. I tried to get back into my book, but now I was too riled up to concentrate on it. I closed the book and switched off the lamp and climbed under the covers. After some time, I finally drifted off to sleep.

A couple of hours later, I woke up in the middle of the night to the sound of rhythmic creaking. Momma was back in her rocking chair, no doubt, drowning her sorrows in booze. Lately she'd taken to hiding bottles of liquor around the house, as if I didn't know exactly where they were. She'd sit out on the porch swing or in her rocking chair drinking and crying. Half the time her children went to school or to bed on empty stomachs, yet she still somehow found the money to buy her liquor — another thing to resent about her.

The sound of the creaking chair took me back in time so many years ago to the night after Daddy's funeral. I thought of the scared, ashen white look on Momma's face while she held a sleeping Trisha in her arms and rocked. "What am I gonna do, Chrissy? What am I gonna do?" Life hadn't turned out exactly as she'd hoped. *Well, join the club*, I thought bitterly. I thought I heard what sounded like a stifled sob coming from the living room.

Suddenly, I felt it: the slightest prick, a subtle twinge of emotion for her, sorrow for the way her life had turned out. I should go to her, I thought. I should wrap my arms around her and tell her I'm sorry for the mean things I said. I didn't mean them. Maybe I couldn't forget the past or completely forgive, but I could try to find a way to move on. We could try to be a family again. It was worth a try at least. Tell her that I wouldn't leave. Truthfully, I had nowhere to go.

But I chose to stay in bed and let the moment pass. I regret that decision so much. I cry about that horrible decision to leave Momma alone with her guilt and sorrow, loneliness, and regret. I could have saved Momma that night, just like she could have saved me once. Instead, we'd both stood by helplessly while the other one drowned.

I groggily woke to the morning sun streaming through the window. Graduation day. I threw the pillow over my head and tried to go back to sleep. A little while later, I was aware of someone standing over my bed. I heard Trisha's voice, "Chrissy. Chrissy."

"Go away," I muttered from under the pillow.

"Chrissy, Momma's not waking up."

"Then leave her alone. She's hung over. She doesn't have to work today, so just leave her in bed. And leave me in bed."

"But she's not in her bed. She's on the floor next to her rocking chair."

An eye popped open as I remembered the exchange from the night before. Suddenly, I threw my blankets off and jumped out of bed, running into the living room. "Momma! Momma! No, no, no, no, no, no! Momma! No! No!" Somehow I managed to push my way through my other siblings to where Momma was lying on the floor. I lifted her head into my lap and frantically patted her cheek. "Momma!" My voice shook from fear. "I'm sorry! I didn't mean it! Momma!" I glanced around surveying the empty bottles of liquor, an empty bottle of sleeping pills. "No! No!" I screamed, checking for a pulse. I couldn't feel anything.

"Brad! Brad!" I screamed out toward his bedroom. He came out of his room, looking sleepy and disheveled. "Call an ambulance, Brad! Momma OD'd! *There's no pulse!*" He saw the panic on my face and quickly headed for the telephone.

I held Momma's torso in my lap and rocked her back and forth, sobbing. "No, Momma! How could you? I'm sorry! I'm so sorry! I didn't mean it. No! Please!" I thought I could will her back to life just by begging and screaming and pleading.

Watching my futile efforts to revive her, the kids began to scream and cry in fear. "Momma's dead! Oh no! She's dead!" I didn't know how to comfort them, so I just added my screams and cries to theirs.

Sometimes in my nightmares I can still hear the horrifying chorus of our screams blending with the background noise of the approaching ambulance siren.

"Come back, Momma!" we cried.

But it was too late. She was already gone.

11

Momma was buried next to Daddy on a breezy June day. Somehow it comforted me to see their graves together. Maybe he was taking care of her now. Maybe she could finally be happy again. I prayed that God wouldn't send her straight to hell for what she did. She'd been so tired and depressed for so long. She wasn't in her right mind when it happened. Maybe God would understand. She'd been punished enough in life. Did she really have to be punished for all eternity too? I couldn't think about that. I also couldn't think about our exchange from the night before, my impulse to get out of bed and comfort her, my role in her death. Thinking about it would just make me feel overcome with grief, and I couldn't take it.

Except for me, all of the children in our family became wards of the state. There was really no one else who could take them. I couldn't care for them. I wasn't even sure I could take care of myself. They would be put into foster care and possibly, at least maybe the younger ones, adopted. I helped them pack their things. I searched the house for family pictures, mementoes, and keepsakes that would remind them of our family. I wanted each of them to have something of us to take with them. Goodness knows, there weren't many good times worth remembering, but I wanted them to have something at least. I tried to divide the pictures evenly, keeping some for myself. For the girls, I divided Momma's few pieces of jewelry and knick-knacks of hers that they might like. All of my siblings' belongings on earth could be packed in just a few boxes.

Brad was stoic and withdrawn on the day we said goodbye to him. I think he partially blamed me for Momma's death. When I tried to hug him, he barely went through the motions, mumbled a goodbye with his head down, and then left with the social services lady. Jenny was a different story. She cried and clung to me. "Try to remember the good stuff, okay,

Jenny? You have to be strong. Everything is going to be all right, okay? I love you. I will always be your sister."

When the car came for the three youngest, I could barely hold it together, but I didn't want to cry in front of them. They were scared enough as it was. "I don't want another family. I like this one," protested Ronnie, with tears streaming down his face.

"You will be just fine, I promise. Would I ever lie to you?" He shook his head and wiped the tears with his fists.

"Will some of us get to stay together?" Darlene asked. "I don't want to be alone."

"I don't know. I hope so. But wherever you end up, I know they will take good care of you. I know you will all be happy."

"What if my new family doesn't like me?" Trisha asked. Her wide eyes spoke volumes of fear and sorrow that an eight-year-old child should never know.

"How could that happen? That's not possible! They will love you as much as I do. I know that."

I gathered the three of them in my arms for a long, tearful hug. "When you miss me or Momma or anyone else in our family, just close your eyes and we'll be right there smiling at you. Whenever the rain falls, that means that I'm thinking about you. When you feel the sun on your back, that's me giving you a hug. And when the wind blows in your hair, that's me telling you that I love you."

I hoped they would remember the good parts of me — the loving, kind Chrissy that I could be, not the sullen, bitter, and mean Chrissy that I had been more often in recent years.

I comforted myself by telling myself that this was really the best thing for them. Maybe Brad would end up with people that could finally get through to him, who would succeed where we'd failed him. Maybe a life in the prison system did not have to be his future. Maybe Jenny would end up in the kind of family she'd always wanted, who would be able to support and encourage all of her talents and interests. Maybe she'd make lots of new friends in her new home and be able to invite them over for sleepovers and parties. She'd go on shopping trips and vacations. She'd join school clubs and attend special events. She'd be asked to homecoming and the prom. She'd go on to have a great life and become a famous artist or photographer.

I hoped and prayed that the three youngest kids could be kept together. They were so close in age and such good friends. Maybe they would end up in a family that would take them to drive-in movies and play games, talk, and laugh together. They would have nice, new clothes that fit them and never go hungry. In time, maybe they'd forget that awful morning of crying and screaming over Momma's body. Maybe over time, that memory and all the other dark, unpleasant memories would fade. They would seem like things that happened in someone else's distant, other family, not theirs. *Please, God, just give them a chance*, I prayed ... and still pray for them to this day.

I never saw them again.

The first night all alone in the house was the worst for me. I had kept myself so busy with the funeral and then packing and sorting that I didn't have time to be alone with all of my grief and regret. But now that I was alone, I could hardly bear the pain. My usual escapes — reading, playing the guitar — didn't work. I walked through the empty house and stood in each room, looking around. There was really nothing left of value in this house. The house itself was a hazard. It should be condemned. It should be bulldozed to the ground, I thought ... with me still inside. Then I burst into sobs. No one was there, so I could be as loud as I wanted. I cried and screamed and cried some more until there were no more tears left. I walked through the house and gathered all of the bottles of Momma's alcohol that remained, and in Brad's room I found some more. My original plan was to take them outside and drain every bottle into the ground, just rid this house of this awful liquid that had ushered both of my parents to their deaths.

When I was outside, though, I just sat on the porch swing and watched the sun set. I stayed there until it was dark, listening to the chorus of bugs beginning to sing. I began to drain each bottle, but, instead of pouring into the ground, I poured it down my throat. It burned my throat and tasted awful, but I didn't care. So what if it killed me, I thought, so what? I thought about Momma and Daddy — the lives that they'd led. How strange. They'd brought us all into their world and then taken themselves out. And what were we supposed to do now? When the last bottle was drained, I lay back on the porch swing and rocked back and forth, staring up at the night sky. Alcohol was supposed to make you feel better, and eventually it started doing the trick. I felt warm and tingly. I felt as if I could float up and touch the stars overhead. "Free as a bird!" I called out and began to laugh. If only Miss Pickard could see me now. "I'll be damned, Blue Lids was right about something! I'm free as a bird now!" I laughed and laughed until I started crying again. I had never been drunk before. It was such a strange feeling. I quieted down and just silently watched the stars overhead blur in and out of focus and sway from side to side. To the left, to the right. To the left, to the right. And then, finally, I passed out, still swinging on that porch.

Whatever comfort people manage to glean from getting drunk, it does not compensate for the price you have to pay the next day. When I awoke to the sunrise the next morning, I was still on the porch swing. I could hardly lift my head, it felt so heavy. But I had to get out of the light. It hurt my eyes too much. I lifted myself off the swing and stumbled over all the empty bottles, sending them rolling across the porch and down the steps. I struggled to get in past the broken screen and front door and staggered through the house to the bathroom. I vomited into the toilet and retched up as much as I could of what was left in my stomach. I sat there for a few minutes hanging onto the toilet, too weak to hold myself up without support. I wasn't sure I would have the strength, but I hoisted myself up and slowly made it to my room. I closed the curtains to block out all the light and spent the entire day sleeping in bed.

I stayed in that bed for the next few days. I was just like Momma had been after Daddy's death, unable to function. But, unlike Momma, I didn't have anyone to bring me meals or try to take care of me. It was just as well. My plan was to stay in bed and starve to death. Months from now, someone might come by to check inside this abandoned house and find my rotting corpse, still lying on the lower half of a bunk-bed set. I don't know why I kept choosing that bed, since I could sleep anywhere I wanted now. But I couldn't stand the thought of stepping foot in Momma's room. I'd entered it only to gather stuff that was worth keeping and then I'd shut the door to that room, never to enter it again.

Despite my plan to starve to death in my bed, hunger eventually got the better of me, and I found my way into the kitchen. I dug through the cupboards and fridge, eating what was left there. Finally, when there was no food left to eat, I decided I needed to leave the house. I dreaded having to go outside again, having to face people and interact with them. I reluctantly took Momma's car keys off the nail on the kitchen wall and looked for my driver's license and cash that I'd found and set aside. Fortunately, I happened to glance in the mirror before leaving the house. I looked ghastly. My hair hung in greasy strings down the side of my face. My cheeks were hollowed and gaunt looking. There were dark shadows under my eyes and bones jutting out of my chest. I needed a shower in the worst way. I couldn't leave the house looking like this. I put the keys and money down and went into the bathroom. I stood under the hot shower water until it turned cold, which, in our house, was less than five minutes. I washed my hair and face, brushed my teeth, and put on an old but clean outfit. I combed out all the tangles from my hair. Looking in the mirror once more, I didn't look that much better, but at least I was presentable now. I put the money and license in my pocket, grabbed the keys, and left the house for the first time in I don't know how many days.

I had to remind myself how to drive Momma's car. It jumped and stalled a few times, but I finally got it going. I wasn't sure where to go. We never really went to restaurants. I just wanted to go someplace where I could be anonymous. I drove around old downtown Hilldale for a while until I spotted a hole-in-the-wall type of diner. It seemed as good a place as any, so I found a place to park and went inside. A plump, balding middle-aged man greeted me as I entered and sat me down at a small table in the corner. Perfect. He handed me a menu and smiled at me. "Why such a long face on this beautiful day?" he chirped. I tried to half-smile at him. "Surely things can't be that bad," he said.

I sort of laughed and said, "Well, trust me. They can."

"Well, if our food can't put you in a better mood, then nothing can. What can I get for you?"

"I just want some sort of sandwich. Anything. Whatever is good here will be fine with me."

"I'll be right back then." He took my menu and headed back to the kitchen.

I looked around the diner. There were only a couple of other people there and they were lost in conversation, so they didn't even notice me. That was good. It looked like the middle-aged man was the only one waiting tables that day. It must have been a weekday. I wasn't even sure what day it was. The diner was nicer on the inside than it looked from the outside. It was small, but cozy and clean. There were red-checkered curtains on the windows and a small television on one end of the diner that was showing a news program. The tables all had a little fake flower in a vase in the center.

In a few minutes, the man came back with a large turkey sandwich and a glass of water. The sandwich was piled high with turkey and fixings. The bread was thick and soft. It tasted homemade. I tried to eat it slowly and savor every bite. It was the best sandwich I'd ever eaten. And I was so hungry it was gone in a matter of minutes. I drank all the water, and the man was right there to refill it the moment I set it back down. "How did you like that sandwich?" he asked.

"It was truly the best sandwich I've ever had. Maybe even the best meal I've ever had. I ate it way too quickly," I said with a small laugh. "I guess I was just really hungry." I was surprised that I could be so open and talkative with him after days of solitude and silence. Something about him set me at ease.

"Well, I told you our food would help you feel better!"

"Yes. You were right. I do feel better than I did walking in here."

The man left for a few minutes and I sat there watching the television and waiting for the check. The next thing I knew, he'd put another sandwich right in front of me and a little mug of coffee. "Oh, sir, that's very kind of you, but really, I can't pay for two sandwiches."

"It's on the house," he said. "Don't worry about it."

The sandwich looked so good that I wasn't going to argue with him about it. "Wow! Thank you so much. That's really very kind."

I gobbled down that sandwich almost as fast as the first and drank the coffee. Five minutes later, the man set a slice of cheesecake in front of me. "Oh, sir, really, you have to stop. That's so generous of you, but I can't take it. Really, I don't want to get you into trouble."

"Why would I get into trouble?" he asked. "I'm Mike." I looked at him, confused. "Mike's Diner?" He pointed to the sign. "I'm Mike."

"Oh!" I laughed, finally getting it. "Well, then okay. Thank you, Mike. I promise not to tell Mike about this if you don't either."

He laughed, "Yeah, you don't want to cross that guy! And what's your name?"

"It's Chrissy."

"Enjoy your cheesecake, Chrissy."

I ate the cheesecake slowly, savoring every bite. I'd never even had cheesecake before, and it was the best thing ever. When Mike asked me how I liked it, I told him it was so good it made me want to cry. When I was finished with the cheesecake, Mike brought the check. It had just the one turkey sandwich on it. I studied the ticket for a moment and then glanced around the room again. I didn't know where else I could go, and I dreaded having to go back home to that empty, dreary house to just lie there and rot. "Mike?" I asked timidly.

"Yes, Chrissy?" He came back over.

"Would you mind much if I just ... sat here and stayed for a while? I mean, I can leave if it gets busy and you need the table. I just ..." I tried to keep from crying in front of him, "really like being here. And I don't want to go."

"Well, sure you can!" Mike seemed flattered that I liked his diner so much. "You can stay as long as you like. Watch some TV. I have a deck of cards and some magazines and books in the back if you'd like them."

"Books?" I perked up.

"Sure. We have a big stack of paperbacks."

He took me to a place in the back of the diner, near the kitchen, and I sorted through the books that he had. "I haven't read this one," I said, pulling it out of the pile.

"Well, you'd better get busy then."

I headed back to my seat and spent the next two hours reading. I'd glance up every once in a while to check out the people coming and going from the diner. They all seemed to know Mike, and he knew all their names and things about their lives. Mike would periodically come over and refill my water or coffee mug. It was such a pleasant afternoon. Being away from the misery of that house and getting absorbed in a book was just what I needed to distract myself from all the sadness and grief that had nearly drowned me. This place felt like being at your grandmother's house, not that I even knew what that felt like. But it's what I imagined it might be like. I finished the book and closed it, sighing. The sun was beginning to set, and I really did need to leave and go back home.

I paid Mike for the sandwich and tried to leave what I thought was a generous tip, although I had no idea what a generous tip should be and I couldn't really afford it. "Are you sure there's nothing else I can help you with, Chrissy? Would you like to use the phone? Or take one of the books home? I know you'd bring it back."

"No, thank you," I said. "But I did notice you have a 'Help Wanted' sign in the window."

"Have you ever waited tables?"

"No, but I've waited on people my whole life, and I'm a fast learner. I just graduated from high school with honors. I could show you my report cards," I offered.

"That won't be necessary," he said. "When can you start?"

"Whenever you want me to. Today. Right now!" I suggested.

"Can you be here at 6:30 in the morning for the breakfast rush?"

"Yes!" I practically gushed. I could come here every day and spend all day and get paid for it! Mike brought me to the back room again and looked for a uniform that might fit me. He gave me two of them. The uniform was a white button-up dress with a collar and it had a checker-patterned apron that matched the curtains, plus a little white hat with checkers on it. The "Mike's Diner" logo was on the top left. Most people might not be too excited about wearing a uniform to work, but truthfully I hadn't had anything nice and new to wear for a long time. The uniform was now the nicest outfit that I owned. I couldn't wait to put it on.

"We'll need to get you a name tag also, but you can start tomorrow without one."

"Yes, sir!"

"Call me Mike."

"Yes, sir. I mean Mike. I'll see you tomorrow at 6:30." I resisted the urge to hug him. People are hired all the time, I told myself. It's no big deal. Just play it cool. I carried my uniforms out to the car and climbed inside.

Somehow it was easier going back to that old house, knowing now that I would just be using it for sleep. I'd be waking up early every day to head to my job.

So I didn't have a family anymore, and I didn't have school, and I didn't really have any dreams for the future. But I *did* have a job. And, for now, that was enough.

12

I was at Mike's Diner bright and early the next morning in my new uniform. Mike taught me the ins and outs of working at a diner, and I quickly learned everything. He said he was never concerned with expanding or becoming a chain. He wanted it to stay a small, cozy little hole-in-the-wall restaurant that had the best-tasting food, a place where people knew your name and treated you like family. So food and customer service were his top two priorities. He had three other waitresses, but one was eight months pregnant and wouldn't be back for a while. A second one had a child that was often sick. That's why Mike was often short-handed and needed to wait tables himself. My regular salary was pretty meager, but with tips I'd probably be pulling in about the same amount of money that Momma had.

Mike introduced me to several of the regulars. I memorized their names and faces so I'd know them when they came in again. This really wasn't the kind of job where I could just blend in the background and never speak to people. The thought terrified me at first. But then, I started thinking that none of these people knew me anyway. They had no idea that I was such a quiet, reserved, sometimes unfriendly person. I could be anybody that I wanted to be. Jenny's personality would be perfect for this job, since she was always smiling and friendly. She'd strike up conversations with perfect strangers and make them feel comfortable. It was why she had so many friends who invited her places. So I tried to take on Jenny's personality. I would ask myself, what would Jenny do or say in this situation? And then I'd try to do just that.

That strategy worked pretty well for me. I found that people responded well to a nice big smile and friendly chit-chat. I also started memorizing their exact orders without having to write them down, and I made sure that any special instructions had been followed exactly before I brought their food to them.

When their drinks were down to about one-quarter full, I would quickly refill them, so they never had to reach for a cup or glass to find it empty. My goal was to anticipate what they wanted and get it for them before they had to ask. People really appreciated just a little bit of extra attention and care and they typically left me generous tips in return. After a while, I found that I enjoyed playing the part of Jenny. Sometimes I actually felt as happy and cheerful as I pretended to be. At night I would return to my dark, dreary, broken-down, lonely home and regress to the sad, hopeless, grieving, quiet Chrissy. Everything about that house made me feel miserable and alone. I hated being there. Knowing that I would eventually put my uniform back on and head over to Mike's Diner is what kept me going those lonely nights.

After a few weeks of working, I came home one evening to find that the lights wouldn't flip on, and the electricity wasn't working. And when I tried the faucets, no water came out. It dawned on me that I had never even thought to check the mailbox since Momma's funeral. I went out to find it stuffed full of notices and bills. I brought them inside and sat on the floor with a flashlight trying to make sense of them all. Water, electricity, garbage, phone — nothing had been paid — warnings, a notice of foreclosure on the house. Why hadn't I thought of any of this? Momma had handled more things than I'd thought.

I spread all the bills around me and sat there, not knowing what I should do. I couldn't pay any of them. It was just as well, I thought. I couldn't stay here any longer.

I went around the house, gathering what I could and packing it into the car: the black-and-white television; some pots, pans, dishes and utensils; the pictures and keepsakes that I had saved for myself; my books, clothes, and guitar; my Chrissy rock and some of Jenny's drawings. I found a drawer stuffed with little homemade cards and love notes that I had saved from my siblings over the years.

"Hapy berthdey Krisy I luv yu frum Ronnie R."

"Chrissy, you're the best sister in the whole wide world. I love you, I love you, I love you. You're the best. XOXOXO Love, Jenny. P.S. I love you!" She'd drawn a picture of the two of us smiling and holding hands, surrounded by hearts and flowers.

There was a card with nothing but scribbles and "Darlene" scrawled at the bottom. Another one had just a little handprint with, "This one is from Trisha and she wants me to write Happy Birthday and that she loves you. By the way, this is written by your sister Jenny (Me again!) XOXOXO."

I put all the cards and notes in a little box in the backseat. I took a few blankets, pillows, and towels and my toiletries and personal items. That was it. There was nothing left of value in that house that I could take. After the car was all packed, I spent my last night sleeping in my bunk-bed. Daddy had built that bunk-bed shortly after Jenny was born, and I couldn't even remember the days before I slept there.

I woke up early the next morning and slipped into my uniform, combed my hair in the mirror, and applied the small amount of lipstick that I usually wore to work. Since I couldn't brush my teeth without water, I rinsed and gargled with some mouthwash. I grabbed the keys and took one more look around me. I don't know why I bothered to lock the door, but I did. At least it would provide some level of protection for the things that Daddy had built that I couldn't take with me: the beds, the kitchen table and chairs, the living room furniture, Momma's rocking chair.

As I drove down our dirt road in my packed-up car, I watched the house fade into the distance through the rear-view mirror. I watched it until it was completely out of sight.

In all the years I lived in Hilldale after that, I never went back to that home to see what had become of it. I avoided coming within even a few miles of that section of town. My past was something I wanted to bury in a deep, dark corner in the back of my mind and never think of again. Despite all my attempts to erase it, though, it would still periodically bubble up to haunt my thoughts and dreams: the sadness, anger, guilt, and remorse threatening to overcome me before I would wrestle it back to its corner again. I was afraid to come back to find the dilapidated home of my childhood looming before me. Maybe part of me was even more afraid that I might return one day to find it gone.

13

I was now living out of my car. I knew it wasn't a permanent solution, but it would have to do until I could figure out something else. Luckily, the diner had a pretty nice bathroom with a large sink. I figured I could at least wash my hair, brush my teeth, and sponge bathe using that sink. I could probably even wash my uniform in it when it was dirty and hang it in the car to dry. For once, that broken passenger seat worked to my advantage! With my blankets and pillow, it made a perfect bed since it fell down so flat. I kept the passenger side of the back seat clear so I could sleep, and everything else was stuffed into the trunk and on the driver's side of the back seat.

It was too embarrassing to let anyone at work know about my situation. They assumed I lived at home, and I told them no different. You couldn't tell how full of stuff my car was until you were right up against the glass. I would leave work at night and drive my car off to a nearby parking lot, where I would wait for everyone else to leave work, and then I would drive back and sleep right in the parking lot of Mike's Diner. I'd make sure to wake up early enough to drive my car away before people arrived in the morning. Then I'd pull in shortly after the first one or two employees arrived to start the day. The days that I had off work were more of a hassle for me. I preferred not to have days off. There was just no point to it. But I found I could do some of my food shopping then. I bought only things that didn't need to be refrigerated or cooked, mainly fruit, vegetables, bread, and crackers. For the rest of my free time, I usually went to the library and spent the day there reading books and checking out more to read in my car and on my breaks at work.

Things worked out even better when Mike gave me a key to the diner. That way, if I needed to use the bathroom during the hours it was closed, I could still get in and use it. And I certainly was not lacking for good cooked food either. I could have anything I wanted either at a discount or free at the diner, and it really *was* the best food in town. Not that I'd ever been to another restaurant to compare, but the food was so good I just assumed it had to be the best.

For living out of my car, I was actually doing quite well, and I congratulated myself for figuring out how to overcome each obstacle that arose. After a couple of weeks, though, the novelty of figuring out how to do things began to wear off. It really was crowded, cramped, and uncomfortable in there, and it was a pain to always have to leave and then come back to the parking lot as if I had some real place to go.

Early one morning, as I still snoozed in the reclined passenger seat, I heard a tap on the window. "Chrissy, is that you in there? What are you doing here so early?" I scrambled up out of the seat with a start. It was not yet 5 a.m.! It was still dark outside. What was Mike doing here so early?

"Oh, uh …" I nervously laughed and rolled down the window. "I, uh … Hi there. Actually, I was … What are *you* doing here so early?"

"I couldn't sleep, so I figured I'd get an early start on the breakfast items. And you?"

Mike was surveying all the items that had been crammed into my car. There was enough street light to see that I had quite the load stuffed in there: my food, my television, boxes and bags, my uniform hanging to dry in the back seat. There was really no way out of this. I had to come clean. "Actually," I laughed nervously again, "I'm kind of living out of my car. It's just temporary, until I can find something better."

Mike looked concerned. I thought I also saw a look of pity in his eyes, which was humiliating to me. "Chrissy, I really wish I would have known this earlier. I know a lot of people in this town. I could have helped you out. In fact, my wife and I have some friends that were recently looking for a quiet college student to rent a room in their basement. They're a really nice family. I could contact them to see if they're still looking. Even though you're not a college student, I could put in a good word for you."

It hadn't occurred to me to ask somebody for help. I'd been so concerned with trying to keep it all a secret that I hadn't stopped to consider that someone might have some useful ideas for me. "That would be really nice, thanks. I hadn't thought of that." I told myself not to get my hopes up. They'd probably already found someone.

"I'll give them a call later on today. And if that doesn't work out, we'll think of something else. You could even come to stay at our house. Both of our kids are off at college now. You could use one of their rooms if needed. I just hate the thought of you living like this." There was that look of pity again.

I really did not want to live at my boss's house or take one of his kids' rooms. How would they feel to know some homeless person had moved into their room, their personal space, and was viewing their belongings and sleeping in their bed? We went inside the diner and I got myself ready in the bathroom, feeling nervous but hopeful that I might not have to spend too many more nights in my car.

Sure enough, after the breakfast rush was over, Mike was calling his friends and talking to them. I wanted to listen to his end of the conversation, but I didn't want to appear so nosy. Once he was off the phone, he came over to me and said, "Good news! They haven't found someone yet. Their names are Judy and Ben Staker, and they live just a few miles away from here with their three children. It's a modest home, but it's in a nice area and I think you'll like it."

Mike put the other employees in charge for a little while after the lunch rush so that he could take me over to see the room and meet the family. They seemed nice. Their oldest child was in junior high, and the other two were in elementary school. It was a four-bedroom, brick home with a pretty green lawn and a lush tree out front. Mrs. Staker showed us the top level first, where the family would be. I could have one shelf in their refrigerator and one shelf in the freezer. I could use their kitchen anytime except during the family's dinner hour, from 6 to 7 at night. There was an entrance directly to the basement from the backyard, so I could come and go as I wanted without having to walk through their living room or disturb the family. We went down the concrete steps from the backyard to the basement. The basement was dark, with concrete floors and seemed a little chilly. She pointed to a door and said that would be my room. I opened the door, thinking it would look exactly like the rest of the basement.

To my surprise, I found a cute little room that had been carpeted. There was a twin bed with a pastel patchwork quilt on it in the corner and matching curtains on the two windows that let in a surprising amount of light for being on the basement level. A wooden desk and matching dresser completed the other side of the room. Next to the bed was a nightstand with a lamp on it, casting a rosy glow that made me immediately want to curl up in the bed with a good book. I thought the room was breath-taking. Across the room was another door with a bathroom that I could use. My own bathroom! Mike and Mrs. Staker were starting to look a little worried since I hadn't said anything. I was trying to hold back the tears that were threatening to come bursting out. Was it possible that this could be my room? That I would have this amazing place to wake up in every day and come home to every night?

Mrs. Staker was apologizing for the size of the bathroom. "I know it's small, but it has everything you need." Small? It was the same size bathroom as the one I'd shared with six other people! "The room is kind of plain. We could do more to decorate it, but you can see it has potential."

I couldn't hold back the tears any longer. "It's wonderful," I sobbed. "It's really, really beautiful." I continued to brush off tears and nod my head as we discussed the terms for my arrangement. It would be $65 a month for the room, plus another $15 for my share of the utilities. I could use their washer and dryer on Wednesdays. I could use the phone when needed. They just asked that I not be on the phone constantly or have people calling the house regularly. I almost laughed at the very notion of that. Who in the world would I be talking to on the phone? They continued to cast worried glances at me while I tried to contain my emotions, unsure of whether I was shedding tears of happiness or despair about my new arrangement.

I signed a lease agreement and, by that night, I had moved all of my things into my new room. My uniforms and a few other items of clothing hung in the closet. I unpacked all the boxes and bags and found a place for everything in the dresser, the desk, the closet shelf, or bathroom. I set my wind-up alarm clock on the dresser next to my Chrissy rock. I plugged in the black-and-white TV and set it on top of the dresser across from my bed. The guitar stood next to my bed. Once I finished unpacking, I just sat in my pajamas on top of the bed, surveying my lamp-lit room. No reading or playing music tonight. It was comforting just to be in my beautiful lamp-lit room and hear the sound of people moving up above me. I wasn't alone anymore. I just wanted to sit and breathe a sigh of relief. I finally had a home.

The next morning, I sat at my desk and worked out a budget based on my regular salary plus what I thought I could probably get in tips. I was making about the same amount of money as Momma had made at the bar. But, without all those extra people to support, it would go much further for me. If I lived frugally, I could put some money aside into savings every month. It felt so good to know I might have some savings in case of an emergency. We'd never had any money in savings, so every minor crisis or unexpected expense felt like a major disaster. I wasn't sure how much longer I could continue to drive Momma's car. It had been on its last legs for a long time now. I hoped it could last a few more months while I tried to build my savings. Eventually, I'd need to replace it.

Life fell into a steady, livable routine. Even though I had nice living conditions now, I still preferred to be at work as much as possible, not just because I needed the money but because I preferred not to be alone with my thoughts. At work I was the happy, smiling, cheerful waitress. I played the Jenny persona so well I sometimes wondered whether it could be my true self. Maybe the quiet, reserved persona was something I had just taken on out of necessity, as a way to protect myself. On my days off, I still regularly went to the library or ran errands. I kept my room and bathroom spotlessly clean, paid my rent to the Stakers faithfully on the first of the month, and was as quiet as a mouse in their home. I usually didn't even play my guitar unless I knew that no one was home. Or if I did play it, I would strum very lightly to make sure it couldn't be detected from above. I didn't ever go upstairs during the family's dinner hour. In fact, I tried not to go upstairs at all while they were home. I just didn't want to be an intruder in their house. I kept very few things in their refrigerator and freezer. On Wednesdays, I tried to be as quick and efficient as I could with my laundry, taking it back downstairs to fold as soon as it was dry. It was wonderful to have a dryer. I'd always hung clothes on a line to dry and I was accustomed to the stiff fabrics from line-dried clothes that had to be worn for a while before they would soften.

Fall came, and I was glad to leave that horrid summer behind me. It was all in the past now, and I tried not to think about it. We decorated the diner for all the holidays, and I enjoyed being part of that. We hung up cute little ghosts, witches, and skeleton cut-outs for Halloween and offered a wonderful pumpkin cheesecake for dessert that month. I must have had a slice of it every day. My hollow cheeks had filled out, and the bones in my chest and back disappeared. I was still thin but not emaciated anymore. Mike decided it might be nice to keep the diner open this year at Thanksgiving for people who didn't want to cook at home, so I immediately volunteered to work that day. He would pay double-time and I imagined the tips would be really good.

We planned a wonderful Thanksgiving menu. Mike's wife and their two adult children, home from college for the holiday, also spent most of the day at the diner. Several of our regular customers decided to come, and we had a wonderful, festive time.

I was hoping Mike would have the diner open for Christmas day as well, but no such luck. He decided we would close early on Christmas Eve and remain closed through the day after Christmas. The Stakers invited me to spend Christmas with them upstairs. Mike also invited me to come to their house, where his kids would be home on winter break. I turned them both down, making up a story about how I was going to spend Christmas with my grandparents in South Carolina. It was a dumb thing to say, but I just couldn't help but feel that they were asking me out of a sense of obligation. Perhaps they just felt sorry for me, since I was alone, but they'd really prefer to be with just their own families that day.

I realized I'd gotten myself into a real pickle with that lie. I lived with the Stakers. How would they not know I was hiding out in my bedroom and not in South Carolina at all on Christmas Day? I realized I was going to have to leave the house for a couple of days just to save face. I dutifully packed my car and gave everyone my best holiday wishes before leaving. Then I drove across town to a park where I'd have to spend a couple of days living out of my car again. I cursed myself for being such a dummy while I shivered beneath blankets in the broken passenger seat of my car. I could be in my nice, warm bed right now, I thought. I wondered what would happen if I were somehow able to track down my grandparents in South Carolina and show up at their door on Christmas Day. Would they be thrilled to see me? Would they take me in and tell me how much they regretted kicking out their daughter so many years ago?

I toyed with the thought for a while and then decided against it. Who was I kidding? What kind of people abandon their own children forever for some perceived transgression? How would they react to news that Momma had taken her own life and that her children were now scattered in foster homes all over North Carolina? They'd probably tell me that I should have never been born and that Momma was doomed to eternal damnation for what she did. Then I'd probably punch them in the face and be thrown in jail for assault on the elderly. No, it was better just to huddle in my car shivering all night than to try to find them. They didn't want to know me, and I sure as hell didn't want to know them either.

The next morning, after I was warm enough to come out from under my blankets, I made myself breakfast out of cheese and crackers and a little chocolate bar for dessert. I had always asked for a little treat on Christmas back in the days when I still believed in Santa Claus. Little kids started showing up at the park with their families, armed with their new toys, skateboards and roller skates, new tricycles and bikes. I got out of the car and sat on one of the swings. It was one of those nice warm winter days that you sometimes get in North Carolina. You can have snow and freezing temperatures one day and the next day go outside in 70-degree weather wearing shorts and a T-shirt. You just never knew what kind of day you'd get on Christmas in the South.

I always tried to push thoughts of my siblings immediately out of my head when they came, but today I just allowed my thoughts to turn to them and let the sadness wash over me. It was my first Christmas without them. I wondered what they were all doing right this moment. I hoped they were all having a joyous celebration with their new families. Maybe Trisha and Darlene were at another park somewhere testing out their new skates. Maybe Ronnie was somewhere nearby riding his new bicycle. Maybe Jenny had found some brand new clothes, some makeup, and some art supplies waiting for her under a beautifully decorated tree. I just hoped they were happy, and safe and well. After the families had all left the park, the temperature quickly dropped and I headed back to my car to spend one more night shivering under the blankets. The next day, I finished off the last of the food I had packed, waited for a few more hours, and then finally drove back to the Stakers' home, breathing a sigh of relief finally to be back in my bedroom again. When people asked how my Christmas in South Carolina had been, I said it had been wonderful. When they asked how my grandparents were doing, I said they were doing well and that they'd loved having me home with them for Christmas that year.

14

It was a relief to have the holidays over so I could get back to my normal life. I found that I was happiest when I had a daily routine. I didn't like surprises, and I didn't like to stray from my daily to-do list. That spring, my car finally conked out for good. The cost to repair it was more than the car was worth. I sold it to a junkyard for scrap metal, and Mike took me to a local used-car dealership and helped me find a good deal on a one-year-old white Toyota Corolla. Driving around in it was so incredibly smooth! I was in the lap of luxury. All the knobs and controls worked perfectly. It even had a working car radio! I could listen to music on my way to work. With my savings, I was able to make a pretty good down payment and Mike co-signed a loan for the rest of the money. He knew I'd be faithful about making the payments. I also purchased automobile insurance. My budget would be a little tighter now, but I knew I could handle it. Oh, the joy I felt driving around in my new car! I felt more like an adult than I ever had before.

As the one-year anniversary of Momma's death approached, I became increasingly agitated and depressed. When the day arrived in June, I was unable to get out of bed at all. I called in sick to work for the first time, closed the curtains, and lay there in the dark, crying, sleeping, and staring sadly into the room for the entire day. But the next day, I was able to pull myself together again and go back to work. My regular customers and co-workers at the diner had missed me, they said. I told them I was all right, that I'd just had a touch of the flu and was fine now.

The next year seemed to go a little easier for me. I no longer had to go through all the "firsts" of everything without my family. I still thought of them, but the pain wasn't as raw, and I didn't allow myself time to dwell on them for long. When the fall holidays rolled around, I quickly set up all the decorations at the diner again, knowing exactly where everything went. And when the Stakers and Mike invited me to spend Christmas with them, I accepted both invitations. I spent Christmas morning with the Stakers, watching their kids open presents and enjoying a nice Christmas breakfast with them. Later on, I showed up at Mike's house and ate Christmas dinner with his family. I was learning that there were many different types of families, and that sometimes you just had to form one of your own choosing. They never asked about my phantom grandparents in South Carolina whom I never called once from the Stakers' telephone or "visited" for the holidays again.

Two significant things happened to me in the late winter and early spring of the new year: I met Stan, and I was offered a new job. Shortly after the holidays, a dark-haired young man with a ruddy complexion and bulky build repeatedly came and sat in my section of the diner. I was always friendly, but for some reason I couldn't remember his name. Then one day, out of the blue, he said, "I keep visiting your work to try to talk to you, Chrissy, since you never talk to me at *my* work."

I knew he looked familiar, but I just couldn't place him. "Oh I'm sorry! Do you work at the library?" That was the only place I could think of where I frequently went and didn't take much notice of the people around me.

"No. Yuck, I hate books!" he said. "I work at the gas station. You've often worn your uniform when you come to fill up. That's how I knew your name and where you worked."

"Oh," I said. "Well, that's nice. And what's your name?" I asked just to be polite.

"It's Stan."

"Well, Stan, I will be sure to say hi the next time I fill up. Now what can I get for you today?"

He placed his order and we made small talk each time I returned to refill his drink or find out if he needed anything. I really didn't have a desire to get to know him any better than that. I mean, who in the world hates books? I couldn't imagine that.

But when I asked him at the end if there was anything else I could get for him, he said, "You could set me up on a date with the prettiest girl in this joint."

I looked at him blankly. Then I realized he was trying to ask me out on a date. I tried to think of a reason to say no. But truthfully, I was free and available every single evening that I wasn't working. So I agreed to the date.

My co-workers were more excited about it than I was. "He's cute, Chrissy! I love those cowboy types!"

"He's a cowboy?"

"Well, he was wearing cowboy boots. He just looked like a cowboy to me."

I wasn't sure what my "type" was, but I was pretty sure it *wasn't* a cowboy who hates to read. But beggars can't be choosers, I reminded myself. And it was nice to actually have a plan for the weekend.

I had Saturday evening off, so we went out to dinner and a movie. Stan mainly talked about himself at dinner, which was good for me. I didn't particularly want to talk about myself. There was nothing to say. He knew what he needed to know about me — that my name was Chrissy, that I lived alone, and I worked at a diner.

He told me that I was lucky not to have a family, because he had a huge one and it was a real "pain in the butt," as he put it. His mother had been married three times and had children from each marriage. He had seven siblings in all, and none of them were very close. He said that his mother was a disgrace to womanhood. "Women should be faithful to one man." I could only assume that Stan also held men to the same standard.

But I was pleased to learn that Stan did more than just work at the gas station. He was also taking classes part-time at Pemberton State College, which had just transitioned from being a junior college to a four-year state school. I'd heard the campus had been completely renovated, and I would have liked to visit it, but the whole idea just brought back too many sad thoughts about Momma's suggestion for me the last night she was alive. I had to just push that whole thing out of my mind.

Stan was studying business and hoped to someday own his own. He wasn't sure what type of business. He'd figure that out later. Another thing that impressed me about him was that he worked in the youth ministry at his church. He attended the Methodist church faithfully every week and led nearly every youth group activity they had. I should give him a break, I thought. He probably just didn't have time to read with working full-time, going to school, and leading the church youth group.

As we sat in the theater, I felt that familiar excitement that I used to have before the old drive-in movies began. I turned to Stan and smiled. "This is so much fun," I said. "Thank you for inviting me." Partway through the movie, Stan grabbed my hand and held it. I was 19 years old and finally experiencing my first real date, complete with hand-holding. Well, better late than never, I thought.

Stan didn't try to kiss me after our date that night, and I don't think I would have kissed him back because he had mentioned something earlier about how he could never respect a woman who kissed on the first date. All evening, I worried about what I should do if he tried to kiss me. Obviously, I couldn't kiss back after his remark. Should I slap him across the face and act really offended? Or just shy away giggling, saying, "I don't do that on the first date?" Gosh, this whole thing was so confusing. I really should have read up on dating etiquette before doing this. Luckily, he didn't try anything, so I didn't have to risk the possible demerits.

Stan and I started going out on dates frequently after that, and eventually he did kiss me at the door of the Staker home before I went in for the night. I think I did the right thing. It was a brief kiss. It was on the lips, but I didn't open my mouth. We'd had several dates, so I hoped he still respected me afterwards.

I loved dating Stan, but it wasn't because I really thought Stan was all that great. Actually, he kind of got on my nerves. He had an opinion about everything, and if you didn't agree, then you learned pretty quickly to just keep your mouth shut, because he would not leave you alone until he was sure he'd convinced you otherwise.

So it wasn't Stan that I was growing to love, it was the *idea* of Stan and the *idea* of dating someone I loved. I liked how people looked at us when we walked around holding hands. What a cute couple, they thought. I loved the idea that someone thought I was pretty enough and important enough to take out on dates. As much as I claimed to like just being by myself and reading or playing the guitar, I was also a person who had been starved of human interaction and affection for years. Dating made me feel as if I were a part of the real world, not some loner who could just fall through a crack on the sidewalk tomorrow and never be missed. So I continued to date Stan and just put up with the little annoying things. Surely every couple dealt with occasional relationship annoyances.

In early spring, my life would take another turn with an offer from Miss Cummings. She was a frequent customer at the diner and knew Mike very well. She was a single, middle-aged woman with an exuberant, sometimes boisterous, personality, but I liked her. Miss Cummings was the administrator of a nursing home a few miles away called Sunset Care Center. Sometimes, when the diner wasn't busy, I'd just go over and sit with her to visit. One day, she asked me, "Would you ever be interested in coming in for an interview? We are just desperate for good nurses' aides. I've often thought of you. You'd be so perfect for the job. You're dedicated and friendly. You're a hard worker, but you know how to laugh and have fun. It's just what we need at that place."

The center sounded interesting, and I told her I would possibly consider coming by just for a visit. I wouldn't say this to her, but I wasn't sure I wanted a formal interview. I really couldn't leave Mike and the diner. They were family to me. As if reading my thoughts, she hollered out, "Mike! I'm stealing her from you!" I was mortified that she would say that.

As soon as she left, I hurried over to Mike and said, "I don't know why she would say that. I haven't even considered leaving. Just to be polite, I told her I might visit the nursing home sometime. I wouldn't leave the diner."

Mike was busy drying off some glasses with a towel. "Chrissy, I wouldn't mind if you interviewed there. I always knew I couldn't keep you forever." He winked at me.

"So it's okay with you if I interview with them?"

"Yes! I'd be upset with you if you didn't at least pay them a visit. If it's not a good fit for you, you'll know, and you'll come right back here. But you can't spend your time wondering if it might have been the right thing for you."

So I made arrangements with Miss Cummings to visit Sunset Care Center on my next day off. The care center was large. It consisted of three single-story brick buildings that were labeled A, B, and C. The grounds were beautiful and green with lots of grass, trees, shrubs, and flowers. There was a little paved walking path where you could wheel people in wheelchairs and give them some fresh air. Miss Cummings walked me all around the Sunset campus and described what I would be doing there.

"I'm not going to lie to you, Chrissy. Some of it is very difficult work. You'll be bathing people, carrying them in and out of their bath, helping to dress them if needed, helping them use the toilet, wiping them if needed, changing adult diapers for those who use them, changing sheets, cleaning up vomit and various other messes. You may need to help feed some of them. You'll be doing what the nurses ask of you. But it can also be very rewarding work. You'll find that most of our residents are very warm, affectionate people. Seeing you will be the highlight of their day. You'll go on the various outings and excursions with those who are mobile, take them for walks, help them get some exercise, organize activities and events at the center. This job can be as much or as little fun as you make it. You won't be making that much more money than you do at the diner, but you'll have more regular hours plus benefits: vacation, holiday, sick pay, health insurance, dental. So, it's up to you whether you think it's the right position for you."

The less pleasant stuff really didn't bother me that much. I'd bathed, fed, and cleaned up after people since I could remember. Granted, it would be more difficult with an adult, but I wasn't intimidated by that. And the benefits sounded good. I just didn't know whether I could leave the diner since I thought of it as a second home and family to me. Looking around, it was a nice facility, but I just wasn't sure if this place could become my home, if these people could become my family.

I asked Miss Cummings if we could go back to the recreation room where I might have a chance to observe and visit with some of the residents. The recreation room was large. There was a lot of floor space, where I imagined I could hold some sort of exercise/stretching class for the residents. There was also a big bingo table and smaller tables for card and board games. There was a large color television and some couches and chairs set up on one side of the room. Several people were sitting at the tables to chat and some were on the couches watching TV. There was a woman with a walker doing slow laps around the room and a man in a wheelchair cracking jokes at the bingo table. I noticed he was missing a leg.

Another man sat all alone at one of the tables playing a game of checkers with an imaginary opponent. I walked up to him and exclaimed, "I love checkers! Would you mind if I played the reds?" He was delighted when I sat across from him and kept glancing up at me while we played to make sure I was still having a good time. He even made a bad move on purpose so that I could jump a couple of his checkers, but I called him on it. "You did that on purpose now, just to make me feel good." I moved his checker back. "If I win, I want it to be fair and square." I did end up losing the game, but I assured him that I had fun and introduced myself to him. He told me his name was George and that he was 87 years old. That meant he'd been born before the turn of the century, before the advent of cars, airplanes, telephones, and televisions. He'd witnessed two world wars! It was amazing to think of what he'd seen in his lifetime.

Miss Cummings had gone over to visit with the residents at the bingo table while we played. I walked with her back to her office in Building A. "Well, you've won Mr. George over, I can tell you that!" she laughed. "Really, Chrissy, that's exactly what he needed. He's the nicest, friendliest man in the world. Do you know that he has a welcome mat at his door and empty chairs scattered all over his room and that he has children, grandchildren, and great-grandchildren scattered all over the place who never come to visit but once or twice a year at most? What he'd give to have just one of them take time out of their busy lives to come and play a game of checkers with him! Or read a chapter of a book to him."

"I already know the perfect book that I could read to him," I volunteered.

"It just breaks my heart for some of them, Chrissy. It's like they worked so hard and spent a lifetime contributing to their society and their families. And then the moment they become somewhat of an inconvenience, they're shipped off here. They become the throw-aways."

There was something about hearing that word *throw-away*. That's when I knew I would be taking the job at Sunset Care Center. No one would be thrown away under my watch, I resolved. Mike's Diner wanted me, but Sunset Care Center needed me. And I was the kind of person who needed to be needed. I filled out the necessary paperwork and told Miss Cummings that I couldn't start until Mike had found someone to replace me. She was so happy that I'd accepted that she agreed to anything I wanted.

It was evening when I made it over to the diner. The dinner rush was over and Mike was in the back room moving boxes around and restocking the pantry. I just stood there and watched him for a moment before I found the courage to speak.

"How do you even begin to know how to thank someone who has done so much for you? How do you let them know how much they mean to you?"

He paused, but didn't turn around. "You accepted the job."

"Yes."

"That's good. I told you that you would know if it's right for you."

I still couldn't help but feel like a bit of a traitor. My heart felt so heavy. "You plucked me out of the garbage. You gave me something to eat, you gave me a job, you found me a place to live, you took me into your family and made me feel part of it." I started to cry and Mike came over and hugged me. "You co-signed the loan for my car," I squeaked out. "I mean, how do you ever repay something like that?"

Mike replied, "You don't repay it. You turn around and you pluck the next person out of the garbage. There's never a shortage of people who need help, Chrissy. So you find them. And you give them the benefit of the doubt. You give them the tools to succeed and then trust that they will succeed."

I nodded my head. "I will," I said.

"Now look what you did. I'm starting to cry myself," Mike reached for a box of tissues and handed one to me and took one for himself. "You'll come back to visit, right?"

"Not only that, I'm going to be back here in the fall with a bus full of elderly people for pumpkin cheesecake!"

"We'll be ready for you."

We decided that I should begin the following Monday at the care center. I would work through the weekend at the diner and Mike would pick up the slack waiting tables until he had someone to replace me.

I couldn't wait to tell Stan about my new job. He didn't seem all that impressed. "Man, I can't think of a worse job than that! Changing diapers on old people and giving them baths? I can't believe you're actually excited about that, Chrissy."

"Well, I'll be doing a lot more than that. I get to plan activities and fun events for them, kind of like what you do with the youth group!"

"It's not at all like what I do. But I guess waiting tables isn't that great a job either. You're moving from digging holes to scooping poop. Not much difference."

I wanted to point out that pumping gas wasn't that much higher on the list of dignified jobs, but I knew that wouldn't go over very well with Stan. He didn't like to admit that's what he did. When people asked, he usually just told them that he was a college student and a "counselor for young people."

Oh well. I wasn't going to let Stan dampen my mood. I had a new job, and it was exciting to me. On my last night at the diner, I turned in one of my uniforms, washed and pressed, and told Mike that I would wash and press the one I had on and give it back to him sometime the next week.

"Keep it," Mike said. "Leave it hanging in your closet as a reminder that you can always come back if things don't work out." And that's just what I did. After I finished my shift and cleaned up that night, I boxed up a small slice of cheesecake to bring home with me and walked out the door. I turned around and looked at the sign to Mike's Diner, remembering the day I had driven around aimlessly looking for some hole-in-the-wall place to eat. I walked to the side of the building where the parking lot was and stood there for a few minutes, recalling the nights I spent there wrapped in blankets in the passenger seat of Momma's Volkswagen Bug. I unlocked my Corolla and slowly slid into the driver's seat, started the car, and for the second time in my life, I watched as my home faded into the distance through the rear-view mirror.

15

On Monday morning, I woke up bright and early and headed off to Sunset Care Center to start my new job. Miss Cummings greeted me, smiling, and had me fill out some additional paperwork in her office before she walked me to Building C, where I would be stationed. Each building had three to five nurses' aides who cared for the residents in that building. We would rarely do things with the residents from the other buildings because it was difficult to move some of them from building to building. We'd have monthly staff meetings all together. I was glad to be in Building C because that had the largest recreation room of the three residential buildings.

Miss Cummings introduced me to the head nurse of Building C who would be my boss. Her name was Nadine, a tall, pretty black woman with an athletic build. She looked to be in her mid-20's. She sat down to talk with me about her expectations of me. "I don't really care about titles. I don't care about who's over who. That just breeds drama and resentment in my view. We're all equals here: the residents, the staff, and the administrators. We all treat each other with respect. That's the main rule here. Respect is something that is earned. I'll agree to try to earn your respect if you agree to try to earn mine. We're a team, and we work together to do things."

I liked Nadine's attitude immediately and was eager to get started on earning her respect. "Now, as for the residents," she continued, "we especially treat them with respect. Sometimes you're going to see them in unpleasant circumstances. No one enjoys having to clean up someone else's vomit or waste or have to feed them or give them a bath. But, just remember, however humiliating or unpleasant you may find it, it is 100 times worse for them. Imagine how upsetting or discouraging it is to have to rely on someone else to do the things that you've handled by yourself, in private, your entire life. Sometimes they get a little upset about that. Sometimes they can be nasty and resentful. Just remember that all these people are someone else's mothers, grandmothers, fathers, brothers, sisters, and friends. Someday you may be in the position of having to rely on someone else for your basic needs too. And how do you want to be treated then? Just try to be patient and understanding, and treat them how you would want to be treated someday if you're ever in that situation."

I nodded my head in agreement. That was a good way to think of it. Nadine told me that I would be "shadowing" one of the other aides, a girl named Charlene, for the first week to get a feel for the various duties I would need to perform. Charlene seemed nice, and the morning went by quickly as I shadowed her. There was a lot to do, and some of it was very hard work — lifting people in and out of bathtubs and beds, helping them with toilet needs, bringing their meals and feeding them by hand if necessary. The philosophy at Sunset was to give the residents as much autonomy as possible — and that could vary on a day-to-day basis. Charlene said there were some days when residents had so much energy and strength, they could do everything for themselves and you wondered why they even needed to be here. And then the next day, that same person might not even have enough strength to lift a spoon to their own mouth. So you played it by ear and developed a feel for who needed extra help on that particular day.

Before I knew it, it was already lunchtime, so I went to C's breakroom and sat there alone, reading a book while slowly chewing my peanut butter sandwich. Nadine came in to grab something from the fridge. When she saw me she said, "Stop that! You're depressing me. Who would sit in a dark, windowless breakroom reading a book on such a nice day? Come on outside on the lawn to eat with me and Tyrone."

I figured she was probably right. I'd spent plenty of hours holed up alone reading books while life went on around me. Maybe it was time for me to venture from my comfort zone a little.

115

I walked outside with her, and she'd been right. It was a beautiful, cloudless spring day. We walked toward a tall, nice-looking black man already sitting under a shade tree eating lunch on the lawn. He smiled and waved at us. I thought maybe he worked at Sunset also, but it turned out he was Nadine's boyfriend. He worked as a teacher and coach at West Junior High, just a mile away from Sunset, so he would often come over to eat lunch with her. They didn't seem to mind having me there with them. Ty reminded me of the teachers that I had really enjoyed while in school. He was outgoing and funny and won me over immediately.

Nadine and Ty had been going out together since they met in high school, and they were obviously still very much in love. They rented a little house together not far away from the care center. I wondered why they weren't married, but I didn't want to pry. It really wasn't my business. We all chatted and ate and laughed until Ty needed to go. He gave Nadine a quick good-bye kiss and told me that it was nice to meet me. Nadine and I walked back to Building C and I found Charlene to get back to the rounds that day.

Nadine had been right. There was very much a team atmosphere there. It felt as if we were busy beehive workers, buzzing around moving from one task to the next but not in a hurried or stressed way. Nadine and the other nurses did treat the aides with respect. They would ask you to do something, like change someone's diaper, if it was needed. But if you were busy doing something else, and there was no other aide around, they'd just do it themselves. They wouldn't just leave it for you to get to later. There seemed to be no sense of anyone being "above" a certain task. People just saw what needed to be done and they did it. I wasn't sure if that was the way it was in all three buildings, but at least that's the way it was in C.

The day was over before I knew it, and I said goodbye to Nadine, Charlene, and some of the other staff and residents that I'd met. I was looking forward to getting to know everyone in my building and in the other buildings. I was pretty sure I was going to like my job.

I saw Stan that evening. He didn't even ask how my first day had gone. I think he'd forgotten it was my first day there. He complained all evening about his own job. He had a hard time getting along with his boss. So I decided not to say anything about how I liked mine. Stan would take it the wrong way. He had to compare himself with everyone, so getting along with my boss would be a slap in the face about his relationship with his. Then he complained about school and how stressful it was, and he was also planning a major event with the youth group. He was just so busy and stressed out all the time, he said.

"Well, since your church work is on a volunteer basis, maybe you could scale some of that back," I suggested, "at least for now. That way you could concentrate on work and school."

"No! Working with the kids at church and spending time with you are the only two things I actually *enjoy* about my life," he said.

For some reason, hearing that he enjoyed spending time with me came as a pleasant surprise. He spent so much time lecturing or criticizing me that I sometimes questioned whether he actually even liked me as person. Maybe I was some sort of church project for him, I wondered.

Near the end of March, Stan invited me to the Spring Fling at his church. I was excited to go — my first dance! And I actually had a real date to take me. I'd decided to spend my next day off shopping for something to wear.

But Stan beat me to it when he told me he'd bought me something to wear to the dance. "Oh?" I asked, trying not to sound disappointed.

He handed me a shopping bag and I looked inside. There was a pale pink spring sweater with a matching skirt and some sort of hair bow thing, also pale pink. "I think women look best in soft, feminine colors, like pink," he said. "You'd look really good in that. And I also like it when you wear your hair pulled back instead of down. It just looks more pulled together. I like women with their hair pulled back in ribbons or bows. It looks very feminine."

I guess Stan was just used to seeing me with my hair pulled back, since I'd had to wear it that way at the diner. But I actually preferred to wear my hair down most of the time when I wasn't working.

I didn't have a huge wardrobe, either, but when I did buy clothes, I was always drawn to bold, bright, rich colors: reds, blacks, deep greens, royal blues. My whole life I'd had to wear faded, worn, washed-out looking clothes. Now that I actually had a chance to pick out my own clothes, I opted for things that looked fresh and new. I didn't own a single thing in pastel colors … until now. On my list of favorite colors, pastel pink came only slightly ahead of dirty, dingy, yellow-tinged white.

"Thanks, Stan. That was really thoughtful of you. It's … really pretty." I kissed him on the cheek. I shouldn't be ungrateful, I told myself. Just because we didn't share the same taste in colors or clothes or hairstyle preferences didn't mean I couldn't try to wear something to please him once in a while.

So the night of the dance, I put on the pink outfit. The sweater was scratchy and uncomfortable. I'd worn curlers all day under a scarf. Now when I took them out, my hair fell into soft curls down my back. I pulled it into a ponytail and did my best to secure the pink contraption around it. It was the biggest bow I'd ever seen, almost larger than my head, I thought miserably as I struggled with the metal clasp. Now for the makeup. I typically didn't wear makeup, but Stan said that men liked women with a little bit, just not so much that it made them look like a whore, he cautioned me. I applied a small amount of lipstick and blush and then a little bit of mascara. That looked pretty good. Then I made the mistake of trying to draw on a little bit of eyeliner. The line immediately smudged. When I tried to fix it, I ended up smearing the mascara so that I looked like a football player. I washed off my whole face in frustration and started over again, this time leaving out the eyeliner. This would just have to do, I thought, giving myself a final once over in the mirror. I could hear Stan at the Stakers' front door.

I managed to have a good time that evening, despite the scratchy sweater and bow in my hair. Stan said I looked beautiful, which was nice except for the nagging fear that I'd have to go to all the trouble with my appearance every time I saw him. The people at his church were very friendly. Many of them came up and introduced themselves to me. I noticed that most of the girls were dressed in pastel sweaters and skirts, with their hair pulled back in ribbons and bows, just like me. They were all white girls, and they all wore just a touch of makeup to bring out their best features. It almost felt as if we'd all been stamped out of white cookie dough with the same cookie cutter. We were all slight variations of the exact same person.

*****

"It's just plain weird if you ask me," Nadine remarked when I told her about it at lunch the following Monday. I'd tried several times to go back to eating by myself in the breakroom, but Nadine would have none of it. She'd drag me outside to eat with her and Tyrone, saying that I needed to get some color so that the residents could tell me apart from the wall. "You wouldn't ever see me running around town in a pink tutu just 'cuz some man thought it looked good!"

"What if I said pretty please?" Ty teased, nudging her with his foot.

"*Especially* not then!" she shot back.

"C'mon Nadine," he countered. "You'd look so adorable, like a giant, walking stick of cotton candy!"

"You two aren't making me feel much better," I said, biting into an apple.

"We're sorry, Chrissy," said Ty. "The important thing is that you had a good time."

"I did have a good time. They want me to start going to church there with Stan, which I'd like to do. But I guess that means I have to pull on the pink contraption every week."

"Why in the world would you have to do that?" asked Nadine. "You wore it once for a special occasion. You did your time in it. Now you can go back to your own style."

"Well, it's not that simple. Now that Stan's basically outlined what he finds attractive, it'll look somehow defiant if I go back to my own style. I mean, maybe when it's just the two of us on a date, I can wear what I want, but if I'm in *his* territory, like church, I need to look the way he wants me to look."

Nadine just gave me an exasperated look. "There are so many things wrong with that statement, I don't even know where to begin. Since when is church *Stan's* territory? I thought it was God's territory. And if he doesn't like the way you normally look, then he should find someone else to date. Tyrone knows that when it comes to commenting on my appearance, he has two choices: he can either tell me how wonderful I look, or he can keep his damn mouth closed about it!"

Ty nodded in agreement, "It's true," he said. "I shudder to think of what might happen if I ever strayed from either of those two options."

"Well," I sighed. "You're probably right. I've actually been thinking it might be time to break up with Stan. As nice as it is to have someone to go out with every weekend, we probably just aren't a very good match."

"Now you're finally starting to make some sense," said Nadine. "So, when are you going to lower the ax?"

"Well, he invited me to one of his youth group activities for Wednesday night."

"Don't go to it. Just break up with him over the phone."

"Nadine! I wouldn't be that rude. Maybe I'll go to the activity and then ask him if we can have a talk afterwards. I'll try to be nice about it."

16

That Wednesday, I gave in and wore the pink sweater and bow, but replaced the skirt with a pair of slacks. Stan still gave me an approving glance when he picked me up. We drove to the church. That night's activity was going to be a short lesson followed by a game of volleyball and refreshments. The youth group was so friendly. The kids seemed excited to have "Stan's girlfriend" there. They told me what a great guy he was, how he was always there to listen to them and to give them advice. Listening to Stan give his lesson, I almost felt that I was seeing a completely different person from the one I'd come to know. He was outgoing, funny, motivating. He really did seem in his element with the youth group. He read various quotes from the Bible and then talked about how the kids could apply that message to their lives. I even felt a little motivated myself to improve my life.

I'd had my break-up speech all prepared, but now I didn't really want to give it. Maybe there was more to Stan than I had previously thought. Sure, he could be a little rough around the edges at times, but he was a good person at heart. Maybe he just needed a good woman to help smooth out those rough edges. Momma had said that Daddy went through a "rebellious" phase, and I knew she'd helped straighten him out. I couldn't imagine Daddy ever saying some of the insensitive things to Momma that Stan said to me. But who knows? Even Daddy might have had his difficult moments.

By the time we'd finished a fun game of volleyball and eaten our refreshments, I had completely thrown out my prepared break-up speech. Instead, Stan and I had a good make-out in his car before I snuck in to the Staker home through the back entrance so that they wouldn't see my disheveled hair falling out its pink bow and smeared lipstick.

* * * * *

"Boo! Hiss! Boo!" yelled Nadine at lunch the next day when I told her about it.

"Did you just 'boo' at Chrissy?" Ty asked, incredulously.

"Yes, I did boo her for having no backbone whatsoever! So what if he had a good night? Even serial killers have their good moments! You could have just ended things on a good note with him, Chrissy. You still should have broken up with him."

"Nadine, you should have seen him with those kids. He was really wonderful. I think I've misjudged him. He's a great guy, a really great catch for someone like me."

I avoided Nadine's accusing glances for the rest of lunch and was relieved when Ty changed the subject to talk about something that had happened at the junior high that day. She'd never even met Stan. All she knew was what I'd told her about him, so perhaps I just needed to emphasize the good things and de-emphasize the bad.

I did start attending church with Stan, and I enjoyed playing the role of "Stan's girlfriend." We were the dynamic, young church couple that everyone wanted to be around. I enjoyed the popularity. I barely paid any attention to the things that were said in church. I just liked sitting there with Stan holding my hand, checking out the outfits and hairstyles of the other girls and women at church, and going over my schedule for the upcoming week in my head. It was like being part of a social club.

Easter was coming soon, and I helped Stan and the youth group color Easter Eggs so that we could hide them for the little kids on the Saturday before Easter Sunday. The hunt was followed by a nice picnic lunch. It was a beautiful day, and I was starting to feel that it was my church now too. I was getting to know some of the names and faces there. I liked being around Stan when he was with the people from church because he became that person that I admired whenever he was around them. I just wished he thought of me as one of them, because he seemed to change back into his moody, critical self whenever we were back alone again. No matter how hard I tried to play the loving, supportive female role, no matter how hard I tried to pattern myself after the other church women, Stan seemed to know that it was all an act.

Stan had invited me to his family's house for Easter dinner. He lived at home, and I'd been to his house once or twice before. It was always uncomfortable there because he had so many siblings, and none of them got along very well. I didn't even know which ones were Stan's full or half-siblings. I just knew his mom had been married three times, so I guessed about a third of them were full siblings and two-thirds were half-siblings. There were eight in total, a mixture of teenagers and young adults, and some of them had also brought friends or significant others to the dinner. There wasn't enough room for everyone to sit at the table at once, so some people took plates and went into the living room or outside. Stan and I sat in the living room. I ate silently listening to Stan get into an increasingly heated debate with one of his sisters. All of a sudden, he jumped up, grabbed my hand and said we were leaving.

We walked outside in a huff for about a half-mile before Stan started calming down. He said, "I just can't stand living there anymore with those idiots. We should get married. It would be so much better if it was just the two of us. Would you marry me, Chrissy?"

I'd just been thinking I wanted to go back to get another roll. His question took me by surprise. Was this a proposal? What was I supposed to say? "We've only been dating a couple of months, Stan. Don't you think this is a little premature?"

"If two people love each other, there's really no reason to wait around. It just breeds temptation. Don't you want to start a real life? You can't rent somebody's room forever."

I couldn't really think of a reason to refuse. Besides, I didn't want him to get mad at me. It really was probably the best offer I was going to get. "I guess so," I said.

We returned to the house and walked in as if nothing had happened before. Stan had a bad temper, but then he'd just get over it and pretend like nothing had happened. I, on the other hand, seldom had outbursts. I'd just get sullen and moody, holding grudges and nursing the seeds of resentment for years before lashing out. Stan announced that we were getting married — probably in June, which was just two months away. People came up and congratulated me and welcomed me to the family, so I put on a big smile and thanked them while scouting out that basket of rolls. When I finally made my way over to them, they were all gone.

*****

"Have you lost your fool head?" Nadine exclaimed. "That is the craziest thing I've ever heard!"

"Nadine, come on now. This is Chrissy's life. She's an adult and she makes her own decisions. Follow your own advice: if you can't say something nice, keep your mouth shut," said Ty when we sat eating lunch the next day. I'd been dreading telling them both, but it had to come out.

Nadine was ticked and hardly spoke to me at all that day unless it was work related. But she and Ty must have talked that evening, because she was much nicer to me the next day and told me she would support me however she could.

For the next couple of months, every spare moment of my life was consumed with wedding preparations. We couldn't afford a big, fancy wedding, but we were planning on 50 to 60 guests. Stan was able to book the church for a June 24 wedding. The people at church were wonderful with offering to donate their time and services. Someone offered to do our cake, and another person would handle the flowers. Still another offered to be our wedding photographer. Mike decided to close the diner to the public that afternoon so that everyone could come over for lunch on him. There were just enough tables and chairs to fit everyone as long as extra people didn't show up.

Stan and I needed to find an apartment, get our marriage license, and buy wedding bands. I needed to find a dress. I was so grateful when Nadine offered to take me shopping, because I had no clue where to begin. Looking at the price tags on the dresses at the first store, I refused to try on any of them. We ended up going to a second-hand shop, where I found a really pretty white wedding dress with a veil. Nadine helped me try it on. It was about two sizes too big for me. I slumped and started to take it off.

"Now hold on. Don't get so discouraged," Nadine said. "I have a sewing machine at home and I'm a pretty good seamstress. I can take this in and make it look like it was made for you. You'll need to come over to my house for a couple of fittings."

I turned around and hugged her. "You're the best!"

"Mmmm. Especially considering how much I despise the groom. I'm doing this for *you*. Let's see, we've got about a month now. Why do you have to get married so soon? You should have a longer engagement so everything's not so rushed!"

"Well, Stan doesn't believe in having sex before marriage, so he's kind of in a hurry to get married."

"Is he now?" she said with distaste.

I thought it was admirable that Stan wanted to wait. He assumed I was still a virgin, since he knew I'd never had a boyfriend before. For all intents and purposes, I practically *was* a virgin, I told myself. After all, those men had just used me for sex back then. I was so young and didn't know what I was doing. And I didn't enjoy it, so it didn't really count. Stan hadn't actually asked if I was a virgin, so I hadn't lied.

That was just one of the many deceptive narratives that I harbored during this time. Stan also knew nothing about my past. He didn't know I'd been sterilized. My scar had faded to a thin, white line, and if he ever asked about it, I'd just tell him I'd had my appendix taken out. I wasn't exactly sure where a scar would be from having your appendix out, but I was pretty sure that if *I* didn't know, Stan wouldn't either. I vacillated among three different narratives for dealing with my sterility. My favorite, yet probably least likely, narrative was that I imagined Dr. Blake had taken pity on me at the last minute and not cut and tied off that second fallopian tube during my surgery. Then, once I was married, pregnancy would turn out to be a pleasant surprise. I'd never have to tell Stan. It would almost be as if the surgery had never happened.

In the second narrative, I begged and pleaded silently with God to heal me from my sterility. I mean, if God could heal the blind and the sick and raise people from the dead, then surely He knew how to fix a couple of broken fallopian tubes. And He had cured barren women in the Bible if they were faithful enough. If he could do that for women in biblical times, then he could do it for me in modern times.

In the third, and probably most likely, narrative, I imagined that Stan and I "tried" to have children naturally for a long time, and then finally accepted the fact that one of us probably had some type of fertility issue. We would be sad over it initially, but then we would adopt some children or take in foster children. It's what lots of infertile couples ended up doing. Why should we be any different?

In none of my narratives did I ever admit to Stan the truth about my past. Somehow, I sensed he wouldn't take it very well. During one of his cruel moments, he'd use it to tear me apart. It's why I continued to hide from the truth of my past. It was the one tool that could be wielded to break me forever. I ran my finger along my thin, barely detectable scar. Why tear this thing back open when it had healed so nicely?

At the beginning of June, Nadine and Ty invited Stan and me to their house on a Saturday night for dinner. I was excited to get them together. I loved Nadine and Ty so much and I hoped that we could hang out as couples together. They'd see that Stan really was a great person. And Stan would see why I liked them so much. He had grown somewhat weary of listening to me talk about them. "Nadine says this. Nadine says that. Do you ever think for yourself, Chrissy?"

The first thing Stan said when we drove up to their house was that it was "small," even though it was larger than the size of the two-bedroom apartment that we had just picked. Nadine and Ty met us at the door and welcomed us inside. They'd made a really nice chicken dinner with salad and rolls. We'd brought something for dessert. We made small talk at the dinner table for a little while when suddenly Stan asked, "So how long have you two been living here?"

"Let's see," Ty said, looking at Nadine. "It's probably been, what, three years that we've been renting this place?"

"Yeah, that's about right. 'Cuz, yeah, we found it right around the time we both got our jobs. We wanted some place that was fairly close to work."

"So," Stan continued, "when are you two finally going to get married? That's a long time to be living in sin."

"Excuse me?" Nadine asked.

"I said that's a long time to be living in sin. You really should be married by now. I don't see any reason why you should choose to live this way."

Nadine looked like she was about to explode. I could feel the blood rush to my head and beads of sweat begin to form on the back of my neck. What was Stan thinking? I just wanted to lunge across the table and cover his mouth with my bare hands.

Fortunately, Tyrone stepped in to defuse the tension. He just chuckled and said, "Oh, we'll eventually get married. I don't think there's any question about that. Definitely, before we have kids, we'll get married. We're just not the kind of people who are in a big hurry. It'll be easier for us to take on the expense of a wedding once all our student loans and such are paid off."

"Well, Chrissy and I have managed to plan a wedding that we can afford and still keep the Lord's commandments. What kind of marriage do you think you're going to end up having with such a shaky beginning? If you really wanted to be married by now, you would have found a way to do it."

Nadine finally spoke up, "Well, Stan, if you want to do things in a rushed, haphazard way, that's up to you. You get married your way, and we'll get married our way."

"It really isn't *my* way though. It's keeping the commandments of God. I'm not trying to push my own agenda onto other people. However, I *will* speak up for God's, even when it's not the popular thing to do. All it takes is making that decision and then moving forward with it. Ty, when are you going to ask her?"

Ty glanced at Nadine and laughed, "Well, I suppose I'll ask her whenever she tells me to ask her." He and Nadine both erupted in laughter and I joined in nervously. My laughter sounded a little too high and shrill to be genuine. I was actually on the verge of tears. I was silently willing Stan to keep his mouth closed, but having no luck.

"As the head of the household, Ty, you should really take the initiative to make sure it happens. Then Nadine can either accept or refuse your proposal."

"He's the head of the what-hold?" Nadine asked. "This is the first I've heard of that. Ty, did you get a new job and not tell me about it?"

Ty just shrugged and laughed, "Nobody ever tells me anything. I'm not sure what I am around here. Nadine's not really into titles."

"*Especially* when it comes to my own household," Nadine added pointedly at Stan. "There's no need for titles. I believe in working as a team at work and at home. Everybody does their share. Everybody is equal."

"Well, that all sounds well and good, but I think it's difficult to put into practice. Someone has to be in charge and God has laid out the order for us. It says very plainly in the Bible that God is the head of the man, and man is the head of the woman."

"Why can't God just be the head of the man and the woman? Take out the middle man, so to speak?" Nadine argued.

"I don't question what God has already laid out for us," Stan stated.

"That's probably because it works out so dandily for you. If *you* were the one at the bottom of the totem pole, you would probably question its structure. All I know is *I've* already got a head. It's sitting square on my shoulders, where it's always been." She and Ty both erupted into laughter again.

The rest of the evening's conversation was equally painful, with Stan and Nadine showing barely concealed disdain for each other's worldview, Tyrone's attempts to smooth out the ruffled feathers, and my nervous, shrill laughter and red face in the background.

At one point, we were talking about how Nadine had done part of her nurse's training in the labor and delivery ward. Nadine remarked, "I decided on that very first day, if I ever have a baby, I'm going to be numbed from the neck down from the moment I get to the hospital. No way am I going through that without the meds."

Stan flatly remarked, "I just don't believe in that. It's wrong."

"Well, good," countered Nadine. "When you have a baby, don't get numbed. Hopefully you'll allow Chrissy the opportunity to make that decision for herself."

Oh, if only they knew how pointless this conversation was! But I kept my mouth closed.

"Chrissy will go without medication when she delivers our children. As part of Eve's punishment for breaking God's commandment, He commanded that she would bear children in pain. That punishment still applies to the daughters of Eve."

"Oh really? We're taking the Bible that literally now? Then please excuse me and Tyrone while we go run to put our shackles and chains back on!"

There was an uncomfortable, awkward silence. Ty couldn't think of a remark to defuse the tension this time, and I was hoping this was all just a very bad dream.

Stan answered, "I think we can all agree that certain things found in the Bible, such as slavery and polygamy, are wrong today. God condoned them at a certain time for reasons known only to Him. It's not our place to question Him. But there are certain truths found in the Bible that are timeless, and if we ignore them, we will suffer the consequences."

"Well, pardon me if I don't happen to think the subjugation of women is a 'timeless truth.' There is one part of the Bible that I do think is a timeless truth, the part about treating other people the way you want to be treated. Personally, I think if we all just took that one piece to heart, we could probably just toss out the rest of the Bible and be just fine. Let's face it, a lot of it is just mumbo-jumbo about nothing."

Stan seethed the entire way back to the Stakers' house. "I just despise those sassy, negro-lady types. They have an opinion on everything, and watch out if you don't agree with them. You'll never hear the end of it. That Tyrone guy is all right, but he needs a backbone. He needs to be the man in that relationship. It's painful to see a grown man led around by the nose like he is."

"He's madly in love with her and she with him," I said. "I think there's a lot to admire about their relationship. It's not perfect, but whose is really? They've been together since high school."

"That's another thing," Stan said. "Your unwillingness to stand up for righteousness is a bit concerning, Chrissy. It says something to me about your morals or lack thereof. I guess I can let it slide since she is your boss, so maybe you feel like it isn't your place. However, *I* will not be silent when it comes to standing up for the truth."

We pulled up to the house and sat there in silence. I hated it when he made me feel like I wasn't a moral, decent person. "I'm sorry," I said quietly. "I shouldn't have brought you together. You both have strong personalities, and I love you both, so I was hoping you'd like each other."

"Just remember that your true loyalty rests with your husband. Everyone else is secondary. And I sincerely hope that her sassiness and disrespectful attitude doesn't rub off on you, Chrissy. If it does, I'll have to insist that you not associate with her beyond work, not even to eat lunch with her."

He didn't kiss me goodnight or walk me to the door. I exited the car by myself, and Stan sped off while I slowly walked to the back entrance of the Stakers' house.

On Monday morning, I was dreading having to face Nadine. She was writing something down on a chart when I found her. "Nadine, I am so sorry about this weekend. You were so kind to invite us into your home, and he was so insulting."

"Mm-mmm," Nadine looked up from her chart. "Chrissy, you are welcome in our home anytime. But do not ever bring that scripture-quoting snake into my home again. I know you've chosen him, and that's your decision. I will say this one time and then I will never say it again: There's still time to break off the engagement."

"Nadine," I said in exasperation, "I think Stan was just feeling a little jealous that night. He's very stressed out! He has a lot of responsibilities. You have a nice home and I think he was a little jealous of that. Plus, I talk about you all the time, so he's jealous of that too. That's the way he deals with jealousy. He has to find some way to be better than other people. I think that's why he came up with the whole 'I'm more righteous than you' thing. It's just his way of dealing with stuff like that."

Nadine was back to writing on her chart, but she still had that skeptical look on her face. She thought I was just making excuses for him. "Nadine, I just really wish you could see him the way he is with his youth group. I mean, those kids just love him, and he's so funny and outgoing. You'd just really love him. He said something so funny the other day to them. What was it?

... I can't think of it right now, but it was hilarious, believe me. You would have laughed so hard."

She let out another skeptical, "Mm-mmm," and looked up from her chart. "Snakes sometimes have their nice days too," she said pointedly. "I still wouldn't be friends with one." And with that, she walked out of the room to finish her rounds. I sighed. Nadine had a certain tone in the way she talked. Even if she knew absolutely nothing about a subject, you would swear she was the world's leading expert on it. What did she know about snakes having nice days! Yet she said it so convincingly, I had to wonder myself whether it might be true.

The last few weeks before the wedding were so busy and flurried. We'd made a deposit on a small, two-bedroom apartment, but we still needed to furnish it. We poked through yard-sales and second-hand stores for some good deals. The people at work held a surprise wedding shower for me and had taken up a collection. Instead of buying me gifts, they just pooled their money and gave me one large check. I was so grateful. It was exactly what we needed. When people had asked what I wanted, I'd just said, "Anything is fine," even though I really wanted to say we needed the money. It feels too weird to ask people for money instead of gifts, so you just hope that they decide on their own to opt for cash. Even though things were so stressful and busy, I was excited about starting our new life together. It would be so wonderful to have a place of our own. As much as I liked living with the Stakers, it would be nice to have my own kitchen, my own living room, and not have to feel always like someone's house guest. Stan was equally looking forward to moving out of his mother's house.

A few weeks before the wedding, I went back over to Nadine and Ty's house for my dress fitting. "Girl, you need to put some meat on these bones," Nadine sighed as she pinned in every seam in my dress by a couple of inches.

"I know. I think I've lost some weight since leaving Mike's Diner. Food just doesn't taste as good when I make it myself. Plus there's been the stress of learning my job at the care center and the stress of being engaged to Stan."

"It wouldn't be as stressful if you weren't rushing all of this so much, and if he wasn't such an asshole."

"Nadine, please. That's my future husband you're talking about."

She sighed again. "Let's get your arms in these sleeves. You're going to roast to death wearing a long-sleeved dress for a June wedding."

"I like the long sleeves. It looks elegant. I don't care if I'm roasting."

Nadine held out one of my arms with a look of distaste. "If chickens had arms, this is what they'd look like," she remarked.

"Well, then, it's good I'm wearing a long-sleeved dress."

The day of the wedding was approaching too quickly. There was still so much left that we needed to do. Every morning, I would jump out of bed when my alarm clock rang and keep moving non-stop until I fell into bed at night in sheer exhaustion. I didn't even have spare hours to read or play my guitar. Things would calm down after the wedding, I told myself. Then Stan and I would stop snapping at each other all the time. Sometimes I thought he was purposely trying to get on my nerves. But I told myself I just needed to be patient and understanding. He was dealing with work and school and church work and preparing for the wedding. He was even busier than I was.

Two weeks before the wedding, I was hurrying through my day at work. I was making a note on one of the resident's charts and caught sight of the date. It hit me like a ton of bricks and I nearly passed out. It was the anniversary of Momma's death. I'd been so caught up in my own little whirlwind that I hadn't even thought of it until now. Last year, I couldn't even get out of bed on the one-year anniversary. This year, it had completely escaped my mind until now. How could I forget Momma in only two years? How had that awful day not been seared into my memory, coloring every day since then? How could I have thought so little of the family that had been torn from me?

I tried to put on a good face to finish out my day, but I could already feel the horrible pounding headache beginning behind my eyes and spreading throughout my brain. I just had to make it until quitting time, I told myself. Then I would rush home, close the curtains, turn out the lights, and lie in bed crying and grieving for the rest of the night. Finally, I clocked out and practically ran out the door without saying good-bye to anyone. My head was pounding and hurting so much, I wondered if I would be able to make the drive home.

Stan was waiting outside in the parking lot for me. Oh no! I'd completely forgotten that we were supposed to go over and taste the samples of different cakes from the woman who was doing our wedding cake. Well, Stan would just have to handle this one. I needed to get home.

"Are you ready?" he asked.

"Stan, I feel terrible right now. My head is pounding and I think I'm going to be sick. I'm really not up for tasting cakes tonight. I need to go home."

"What? You can't do this to me, Chrissy. She prepared those samples specifically for us today. We *have* to go over there. There's no other time to do it. Just suck it up and put on a happy face. You obviously made it through work. One more hour won't kill you."

"Stan, one more hour *will* kill me. You'll have to just handle this one yourself. Just pick the one that tastes the best and we'll go with that. I don't care. Cake is cake."

"I can't do it by myself!" he yelled. "This is a woman's job. You have to come!"

"You know what, Stan? Not every job in the world has a gender attached to it. Sometimes when something needs to be done, you just do it without figuring out whose 'role' it is. I don't care what flavor you pick. Or do eeny-meeny-miney-mo. I really don't give a shit."

"That kind of language is very unbecoming on a woman."

"It's also very unbecoming on a man, but that doesn't seem to stop them!" I fumbled with my keys and started unlocking my car door.

Stan reached out and grabbed my upper arm tightly. "You're not getting in that car!"

"Yes I am! Let go of my arm! You're hurting me! Let go of my arm!"

He gripped it tighter and tighter, "Or what? What will you do? Huh?"

"Ow! You're hurting me! I'll scream!"

"No one can hear you. What will you do if I don't let go? Huh?" My arm felt like it was in a vise.

"I'll call off the wedding!" I yelled.

Suddenly he grabbed the other arm and shook me like a rag doll against the car. I could almost feel my brain rattling against my skull. I screamed and howled, "Let go! Let go of me!"

Finally he let go and shoved me against the car. "Then go! Get the hell out of here!" he yelled.

"It's over, Stan!" I screamed. "I'm done with you!" I yelled as I unlocked the door.

I started the car and screeched out of the parking lot. I cried all the way home, alternating between thoughts of the horror that had just happened and the horror of what happened two years ago this day. I made it back home and stumbled into my bed. I lay there in the dark for hours crying. My head still hurt and my upper arms felt sore and tender where he'd gripped them so hard.

So the wedding wouldn't happen. It was almost a relief. I dreaded the thought of all the people we'd have to tell and the arrangements we'd have to cancel. We'd need to give back all the money and gifts we'd already received. But it was better to cancel now while I still had the chance. Nadine would be proud of me, I thought.

When I was too tired to cry anymore, I just lay there in the dark. I could hear the phone ringing off in the distance, and a few moments later Mrs. Staker knocked on my door. "Chrissy? Honey, it's Stan on the phone. He needs to talk to you."

"Mrs. Staker, I'm very ill right now, and Stan knows that. Would you tell him I can't come to the phone? Please?" I tried to steady my voice.

Mrs. Staker relayed the news and then hung up. The phone rang again 15 minutes later and then 10 minutes after that. Finally, there was another knock on my door. "Chrissy? He really insists on speaking with you."

I threw off the bed covers and went to open the door to my room. Mrs. Staker seemed taken aback by my appearance. My hair was disheveled, my eyes were red and bloodshot and my face was puffy from all the crying. "Mrs. Staker, I'm sorry about all this. But I really can't talk to him right now. The wedding is off. Would you just please hang up and then take the phone off the hook? Please! I am so sorry."

Mrs. Staker went back upstairs and murmured something into the phone. I didn't hear it ring again, so she must have taken it off the hook as I'd asked. I put on my pajamas, washed my face, brushed my teeth, and went to bed.

The next morning, there was a knock on my door again. I heard Mrs. Staker's voice, "Chrissy, are you awake? Chrissy?"

"What is it?" Surely he hadn't called this early in the morning.

"Stan is here. He wants to come in."

I didn't want to put Mrs. Staker in more of an awkward position. "Fine then."

The door opened and I tried to smile cheerily at Mrs. Staker. "Thank you, Mrs. Staker," I said. As soon as she went back up the stairs, I threw the covers back over my head. I didn't even want to look at Stan. "Can't you take a hint? I want you out of here right now."

Stan sighed and I heard him pull out the chair to my desk and sit down. "Chrissy, I can't tell you how sorry I am for how I behaved last night. I've just been so busy and stressed with work, and school and the wedding. I figured the cake-tasting was the one thing you could handle. And then when you said you wouldn't do it, I just sort of snapped. And I'm sorry about that. Can you forgive me?"

I didn't answer. He was silent for a few moments, probably glancing around my bedroom. This was the first time he'd seen it. I thought about my Chrissy rock right in front of him on the desk. I held my breath for a few moments wondering if he'd ask me about it. But if he saw it, he must have dismissed it as some sort of child's artwork. Then he spoke again, "I picked the lemon sample."

So he had gone over there after all on his own. Somehow that knowledge softened me. I spoke from under the covers. "That's a good choice. Everybody likes lemon."

"Does that mean you'll still marry me?"

I contemplated this for a few moments. Then I said, "Don't ever touch me in anger again. Ever."

"I won't. I promise."

I could almost hear Nadine telling me to stand my ground: *Don't give in.* But right then I just needed to be held. I slipped out from the bed and cuddled up to him in the chair. I was glad Nadine couldn't see me. We held each other and then made out for a while. And, for the next few days, our relationship was never better.

I opted not to tell Nadine about the incident since it was water under the bridge now. She probably wouldn't have handled it well. The only thing that reminded me of it was the soreness in my arms when I would lift the residents throughout my workday. Two horrific-looking bruises had formed on my upper arms where he had grabbed and shaken me. Both bruises were swirled with shades of blue, pink, and purple. There was maybe even a tinge of yellow and green in there. And you could see the marks from individual fingers. There was no mistaking I'd been grabbed roughly by human hands. Luckily, my dress had long sleeves. The elegant white sleeves would perfectly conceal the dark bruises I had underneath.

Two days before the wedding, I went over to Nadine's for a final fitting. She'd been working hard on the dress and was really pleased with how it had turned out. It wasn't until she was in the room to help me change that I realized she might catch sight of the bruises. She stood there holding out the dress. I pulled off my pants but kept my shirt on. I took the dress from her and started to pull on the lower half.

"I might just leave this shirt on underneath. It's cold in here," I said.

"What? Don't be ridiculous. It won't fit right with a bulky shirt underneath. It's a summer day in the South, Chrissy. Even a person who's just skin and bones like you shouldn't be cold. Take it off."

I began to lift up the lower half of the shirt. Nadine was still watching me. I pointed to the wall behind her. "Okay, but look that way."

"Oh, so now you're shy," she sighed and turned her head away while I quickly yanked off the shirt and pulled the sleeves up until they covered the bruises. "It's not like you have anything worth seeing," she continued. "Have I ever told you that you have the body of a 12-year-old boy?"

"Several times. There. Now you can look." She turned me around and helped me with the zipper in back.

She brought me over to the full-length mirror and stood behind me. We both began to smile. The dress was a perfect fit and it transformed me into a princess. She brought the veil over and secured it over my head. "Nadine, it's wonderful. It really does look like it was made just for me. Thank you!"

Nadine just smiled back at me in the mirror. "For a 12-year-old boy, you clean up real nice," she said.

Two days later we gathered at the Methodist Church and had a wonderful wedding with about 50 people in attendance, just as we'd planned. There was Stan's family and some of his church friends. My family was there too: Mike and his wife, the

Stakers, Nadine and Tyrone, and a couple of others from work and church who had become my friends. The pictures could attest we were the perfect happy newlyweds.

17

After the wedding, we moved into our new apartment and began to settle into a new routine of living together and adjusting to one another's habits. We didn't see each other that much more than when we were dating because we were both on the go so much. I was hoping that life would calm down and be less stressful, especially for Stan, now that we didn't have the wedding to plan. But it seemed that he was just as stressed as ever. I wasn't pleased to learn that Stan had been taking all remedial courses at the college. He needed to get up to speed in both reading and math before he could take the general education classes at Pemberton. I tried to help tutor him in both, but we'd both end up getting frustrated. I just didn't understand how he couldn't grasp the simplest of concepts. Then he would sense my frustration and get angry with me. The only good thing about our frequent arguments was the make-up sex afterwards. At those times, he would be so passionate and loving. It was his way of telling me he was sorry. They were the only times that I felt really valued and loved as his wife.

One Saturday afternoon, we sat at the kitchen table eating lunch while I tried to explain a fraction problem to him. "So, you take two apples and slice them into eight sections each. Then you eat five of the sections. How many apples do you have left?"

He sighed and ate a spoonful of soup, "How should I know? It's all in pieces now! There are no apples left."

"Yes, there are! Say it in fractions."

"Well, why'd you slice up two apples if you were only going to eat a few slices from one?"

"The *point* is that I'm trying to get you to visualize how this mathematical problem on paper might work in real life. Honestly, Stan, this is really not that hard."

"Well, it is when you're working full-time *and* going to school *and* leading a youth group *and* when you're married to a nagging bitch who thinks she knows everything!" And with that, he threw the books, papers, and pencils off the table and dumped a bowl of chicken noodle soup over my head. Then he stormed off.

"Real mature, Stan!" I called after him furiously. I headed over to the sink to pick the noodles out of my hair and rinse it out. Then I cleaned up the mess at the kitchen table. He truly acted like a little bratty kid sometimes. And somehow he could twist every situation so that it ended up being my fault. It was going to take him forever to get through school. With going part-time and not even beginning the general education requirements yet, it would be years before he had his business degree. How I would have loved to have been the one going to college in his place! But the man was supposed to be the main breadwinner of the household. It didn't matter if the woman would do better in school and had better income-earning potential. You followed the cookie-cutter plan and never strayed from or questioned its logic.

Within weeks of our wedding, Stan had already forgotten the promise he'd made me about never touching me in anger. One day, I had our wedding pictures laid out on the kitchen table figuring which way to arrange them in our wedding album. Stan began looking through and studying the pictures. He noted with glee that there were many more guests who were there "for him" than "for me." He started adding them up, listing everyone from church as a guest for him. Then he proudly told me that he'd had twice as many guests compared to the number for me.

I continued placing pictures in the book and just casually shrugged my shoulders. "I really don't care about small-minded stuff like that," I said nonchalantly.

Suddenly, Stan reached out and backhanded me across the face with so much force that it nearly knocked me out of my chair. I screamed and stood up holding the side of my face. "Why'd you do that?" I screamed at him. "You promised, Stan!

We haven't even been married a month, and you've already broken your promise!"

"Well, then that makes *two* of us!" he barked back. "You promised to honor, respect, and obey me, and instead you undermine and insult me every chance you get! You think I'm a stupid idiot!"

"When have I ever called you stupid or an idiot?" I cried, still holding my face.

"I can see it in your eyes! You are my *wife* and it's time you showed a little respect!"

I ran out of the apartment, still holding the side of my face, which stung and felt red hot. I ran for a while before slowing down to a walk while I cried. He had promised not to touch me in anger again. This time, I had nothing to use as leverage against him. I couldn't tell him I wouldn't marry him. I had already done it. I couldn't tell anyone about it. Nadine had warned me, and I just wouldn't listen. After walking for about an hour, I turned around and started walking back. We'd just have to work this out. All married couples have their problems. We'd just have to learn to work them out together. Somehow I needed to show him more patience, understanding, and respect. And he needed to learn how to control his quick temper.

When I came home, Stan apologized and we sat down and discussed strategies for how to solve our problems maturely. Then we sat cuddling during our television programs that night while I held an ice pack to the side of my face.

Sure enough, another bruise formed, but this one would be more difficult to conceal. I went to the store and bought some foundation that matched my skin, as well as some concealer and powder. A woman at the make-up counter showed me how to use it. I told her I'd been playing softball with my church group when I was hit with the ball in the side of my face by accident.

When I showed up at work with my made-up face, Nadine gave me a strange look. "Why all the make-up?" she asked. "You look like a clown. In this heat, that stuff's gonna melt right off of your face."

"Stan likes women to wear a little make-up to accent their best features."

"Oh, well, if Stan likes it, then by all means, pile it on. Use a spatula."

I sighed and started my rounds. Nadine was right. The make-up began to sweat off. I kept running into the bathroom to reapply the concealer and then pat it down with powder. Hopefully this bruise would fade faster than the ones on my arms had.

I'd really grown to like my job at Sunset. Nadine rarely had to ask me to do anything. I was busy from the moment I arrived until quitting time. Often, I'd still handle things even after I'd clocked out for the day. I just hated leaving when there were still things left undone. Nadine would sometimes have to order me to go home.

The residents loved to chat with me, but I felt too guilty to engage in much conversation while I was being paid to work. I'd often ask them to hold onto a thought, then, once I'd clocked out, I would go back to their room and finish the conversation on my own time. They especially liked to share stories from their past. History had always been one of my favorite subjects in school, and talking to the residents was almost better than reading history books. Many of them had lived through the events that I liked to read about. They could tell me in person exactly what it was like. I'd spent so much of my time in solitude, I'd almost forgotten how nice it was just to sit and visit with someone. Honestly, the residents and I were a perfect match. They needed someone to listen to them, and I was hungry for information and human interaction. I enjoyed visiting with them far more than visiting with Stan.

One day, as I was helping to dress and feed Miss Anna, she commented on what a hard worker I was. Then her train of thought began to drift and suddenly she was telling me about remembering the sign at the entrance, "*Arbeit macht frei —*

work shall make you free." And she started talking about the barking dogs, the hounds from hell, she called them. I froze as I realized what she talking about ... Auschwitz! She'd been there! She'd lived to talk about it.

I knelt down beside her and held her hands. "You were there!" I exclaimed breathlessly. Her eyes widened and she nodded her head slowly. "Will you tell me about it? I'll come right back here after my shift today."

I thought about it for the rest of the day as I went about my duties and then immediately went to Miss Anna's room after I clocked out. She talked well into the evening about what had happened there. She'd lost her entire family and so many of her friends. She'd seen people beaten and starved to death. She'd seen the smoke stacks and heard rumors of massive death chambers. Even then, she couldn't believe it was real. She lived to walk out of the gates of Auschwitz in 1945, but she told me that, in her nightmares, she is always back there. When I went home from work that night, I sat and ate by myself and went to bed before Stan came home from a church activity. I dreamed of the smoking chimney stacks and the barking hounds of Auschwitz.

Besides always treating one another with respect, there were two other main rules at Sunset that I would find a little more difficult to follow. Nadine insisted that we never cry over someone's death and that we didn't have favorites. So far, the only residents that had passed away in Building C were people that I didn't know very well. Even then, it was difficult for me to look at their empty beds or pass their rooms once they had died. I knew that, one of these days, one of the residents that I had grown to love would pass on. We were supposed to "celebrate" the life that they'd had and be grateful that they had moved on and were no longer in pain or suffering. I told myself when the time came, I would do my best to put on a happy face and just get through the day. Then I would go home and bawl my eyes out.

As far as the rule about not having favorites, I decided to change that to not *playing* favorites. I could treat them all equally, but I definitely had my favorites and my not-so-favorite patients. Some of the residents were grumpy or downright nasty. I tried just to be patient with them, remembering that many of them were here against their will and resented the loss of their autonomy. Some of them had grown children who could have taken care of them so that they didn't have to be in a nursing home. But, even remembering this, it was sometimes hard to take care of a person who does nothing but bark at you and criticize everything you do. I already had one of those at home to deal with. Fortunately, that type of person was a rarity at Sunset.

There were also a couple of residents who just did annoying or bothersome things, like Mr. Oscar. He considered himself a real "ladies' man," which meant he never left any of the women he considered attractive in peace. He was constantly flirting with the female residents and staff. He liked to carry around little toys and figurines, and he would come up from behind and set it on your shoulder—as if the figurine were peering down your shirt into your cleavage. He had done that to me several times, although, admittedly, there was nothing down there worth seeing. He asked me nearly every day if I was still married, and I always answered, "Yes, Mr. Oscar, I'm still very much married."

Many of the female residents complained about Mr. Oscar. "Would you keep that pervert away from me?" one asked. "He had a mirror on his shoe that he was using to try to look up my skirt!" If we were ever in a group activity and I saw Mr. Oscar harassing someone, I would quickly go over and try to distract him, drawing him away from the poor woman. I heard someone chastise him one day, "This is a nursing home, not a singles bar! Sell your goods somewhere else. This woman isn't buying." I had to chuckle to myself sometimes. In some ways, the nursing home was not that different from being in high school.

The only female that Mr. Oscar didn't flirt with was Nadine, even though she was probably the prettiest woman at Sunset. He said black women weren't his type. "Well, this is one instance where I say hallelujah for racism," Nadine remarked when she found out that was why he left her alone. I was grateful when Nadine offered to help him with his bath. Needless to say, he made me very uncomfortable when I had to be the one helping him. Sometimes, when he found out it would be Nadine, he'd decide to bathe himself, which was just fine with all of us.

I also definitely had my favorites at Sunset, the people like Miss Anna, who talked to me and shared their histories, the people who treated me like family. One such person was Miss Candace. She came to Sunset that summer, shortly after my wedding. Miss Candace was born in 1890 and was now 82. She'd been living on her own in her house for the past 10 years, ever since her husband died. She'd hoped to stay in her home until she died. There had been a nurse coming to her home once a day to check on her and bring her meals. But, after a fall in which she'd spent five hours on the floor before the nurse came, she'd finally decided it was time to go to a care center. When I'd heard her story, I just assumed she'd initially be like most residents when they first came to Sunset after being independent for so long, slightly bitter and resentful about ending up in a nursing home.

Miss Candace was different though. She was always bright-eyed with a huge smile on her face from the day she entered Sunset. You'd have thought she'd just transferred to a five-star resort hotel with the way she raved about how nice the facility and grounds were. "It's just breathtaking!" she exclaimed, when I wheeled her around the grounds for the first time. "Can we do this every day?"

When she ate our regular old cafeteria food, she'd act like every meal was the best one yet. "I must get the recipe for this cobbler. It's the best I've ever had!" Even though I knew she was living in a dream world, it was impossible to feel sullen and moody around Miss Candace. Some mornings, I'd come into work after a fight with Stan feeling so miserable about the world. Then, the moment I'd see Miss Candace, my mood would lighten, and I'd start to feel better again. I'd always be ready to go home and patch things up with him again after a day with Miss Candace.

When I'd help her use the toilet, or give her a bath, or help her get dressed, she'd say, "Oh, this must be so awful for you. It's so embarrassing!"

"I don't mind a bit," I'd tell her. "This just comes with the job. We get through it quickly and then we can move on to the fun stuff."

Miss Candace had joined the Mormon Church shortly after her husband had died, 10 years ago. Every Sunday, people would come and pick her up to attend church. Or, if she was too weak to sit through all the meetings, a couple of the men from her church would come and administer the bread and water sacrament. Stan told me Mormonism was a cult, but I had a hard time imagining any of the Mormons who came to visit Miss Candace were cult members. They seemed pretty normal to me.

Stan and I were still regulars every Sunday at our own church, and he still met with the youth group at least once a week, sometimes more. In early August, they'd planned a campout on a Friday night, and Stan asked if I might be able to come and play my guitar for the kids around the campfire. Would I! From the moment I first began dreaming of learning to play the guitar, I'd imagined myself with a group of people around a campfire, roasting marshmallows and singing every song we knew. I was so excited for the event I brushed up on my guitar skills weeks ahead of time. We packed the car on that Thursday night, so that on Friday after work we could immediately head to the campsite.

That Friday, I rushed through the day and watched the clock, which seemed to be moving extra slowly. Finally, when it was quitting time, I clocked out, but then I heard some sort of commotion coming from the recreation room. One of the residents had fallen and broken a hip. I went over and ended up staying until the ambulance arrived to take the resident to the hospital. I was a little shaken by the whole event, not to mention that I was about 15 minutes behind schedule.

I rushed home. There really was no time to change clothes or fix my hair and make-up the way Stan liked. No matter, I thought. It's just a campout. Who's going to be dressed up for a campout? I had on Levi's and a red button-down shirt. I quickly glanced in the mirror, ran my fingers through my loose hair and put on some lipstick.

Stan came through the front door, as I was heading to get my guitar from the bedroom. He was just as rushed as I was. He frowned when he saw my Levi's, red shirt, and hair that was down. It wasn't a look he liked on me. "You look like a harlot," he said.

"Well good! It's precisely the look I was going for!" I stormed out the door, carrying my guitar. "I am not going to a campout dressed as a toddler!" I yelled at Stan. Some people who were walking by turned around to look at us as we got into the car.

"Shh! Keep it down! You don't have to make a scene in front of everyone!" he hissed as we climbed into Stan's car and slammed the doors closed. We drove in silence all the way to the campground. Then we put on our big smiles to greet the youth group when we saw them.

We all set up our tents and then built a big fire to gather around and roast our hot dogs and marshmallows while we sang songs. I pulled out my guitar and was fortunately able to play most of the songs that the kids requested. We talked, laughed, and sang until well into the night. The kids taught me some of their own camp songs and we even made up a few crazy songs of our own. I was having such a good time, I had completely forgotten about the earlier unpleasant exchange with Stan. I tried to catch his eye and smile at him a few times, but he was always busy talking or doing something else.

"Chrissy, can you come to more of our activities? It's so fun having someone here to play the guitar. You and Stan are such a cool couple," one of the kids remarked. Some of the other kids agreed.

"Well, thank you! That's a nice thing to say. I'll talk to Stan about it. I could probably work some youth group activities into my schedule." Watching the fire, talking, laughing, and singing with this group was everything I'd always hoped it would be. I was having such a good time. Finally, I caught Stan's eye and smiled at him while I sang and played. I gave him a wink to let him know I wasn't mad at him anymore.

He didn't smile back. He was sitting in the background and not the center of attention, where he liked to be when he was with this group. Suddenly, I had the distinct feeling that I was stealing his limelight, and he didn't like it one bit.

Later on, it was time for everyone to go to their tents and sleep. The girls were in separate tents across from the boys. Stan and I needed to periodically check in on them to make sure they stayed separate. After everything had quieted down for a while, I made my first check in the girls' tents and came back to the tent I shared with Stan. "All's clear on the fornication front," I joked, as I sifted through my overnight bag for my toothbrush.

"It's not a laughing matter, Chrissy," Stan said as he climbed into his sleeping bag. "This job needs to be taken seriously. It's not all laughter and goofy song performances. We're the grown-ups here. You're acting like one of the teenagers."

"Sorry," I said, and paused for a minute. "Hey, just because they can't get close doesn't mean *we* can't. Should we zip our sleeping bags together?" I teased.

"No," he said, zipping up his own bag and turning his back to me. "We have to set an example for the kids."

"Even though they can't even see us?" He didn't answer.

I sighed and climbed into my own bag and fell asleep for a few hours before Stan woke me for another tent check.

The next morning, we cooked a hot breakfast and sat around by the campfire for a little longer before we finally packed our things and took down the tents. The kids once again asked if I could participate in more of the youth activities. I promised them that I would try.

On the drive home, Stan was still quiet and sullen. I told him that I was sorry for yelling at him the night before. He kept driving and didn't respond. Then I said, "I had a really good time at the campout. I can see why you enjoy being with the youth group so much. They're great kids."

Stan still didn't respond, so I tried again. "I'd like to help out more if I could, with the activities and stuff and whatever you might need me to do."

"We really don't need more help," Stan said. "Having too many leaders just confuses the kids. But, I'll let you know if there's anything else you can do."

I continued to see the youth group teens at Sunday services, but Stan never asked me to help out with one of their activities again.

18

Near the end of August, Stan started the fall semester at Pemberton. This was his first semester of taking actual college courses. He registered for a basic earth science class and a composition class. They were both difficult for him, especially the composition class. He needed to turn in a weekly reflection paper on articles that his professor distributed. Since I was a fast typist, Stan asked me if I would type his hand-written papers for him on our typewriter.

I sat down that first weekend with his hand-written paper and typed the first line, then stopped. His spelling and grammar were so bad, I could hardly make out what he was trying to convey. Half of his sentences weren't even complete sentences. I read through the whole thing. It was a terrible paper. It made absolutely no sense.

"Stan? Could you please come here for a minute? I'm having trouble understanding what you've written here."

He came and peered over my shoulder. "Just type out what I've written. You can correct anything that's misspelled."

"But ... there are a lot of grammar problems too. I don't even understand what you're trying to say in some of these sentences. It makes no sense."

"Just type what's there."

"Will you just explain to me in your own words what your thoughts were on this article? And maybe then I can help reword some of these sentences to better convey the message."

"I've already written down my thoughts. It's on the paper. Just type it."

"I cannot type a paper that makes absolutely no sense to me! Would you please just sit down, summarize the article that you read, and give me your thoughts on it?"

"Here's the damn article!" Stan slapped it down in front of me. "If you're so smart, just read it and type out your own thoughts on it. I don't have time for this!" He stormed out the door to go to work.

I read through the article, and then typed out a three-page essay on my reflections of the article. I tried to incorporate some of the things from Stan's hand-written paper that made sense into the essay. When I finished, I stapled the pages together and read through it again. I wasn't sure if it was college-level work, but it was much better than what he'd been prepared to turn in.

When Stan came home from work, I handed him the paper and asked him what he thought. I told him that I'd started with his ideas and then just elaborated a bit and corrected some of the grammar and spelling. He scanned through it, smiling, and kissed me on the cheek. "Thanks, Babe." He put his name at the top and saved it to turn in the next class period.

A week later, when the paper came back, he came home excitedly and showed me the score. There was a solid "A" at the top, with a note from the professor that read, "Well thought-out arguments. Very well written." I smiled and took the essay from him. I couldn't help but be filled with that familiar pride, that sense of accomplishment that I'd had when I was back at Green Level High School. This meant I could do college-level work and succeed!

Stan began to have me write all of his weekly papers. He didn't bother to attempt a hand-written version anymore. Initially, he'd at least read the article and tell me what he thought about it. Then I'd read the article and type out the paper, trying to incorporate some of what he'd said. After a while, he didn't even bother to read the article. He'd just hand it over to me and let me figure out what to say about it. I quite enjoyed the work. I was learning a lot, and it felt good to be "back in school" again, even if it was through someone else. One time, we got an A- and a suggestion for improvement from the professor. That just made me work harder on the next paper. The next time, Stan came home with an A+ and "Fantastic!" written at the top. We were both ecstatic about that.

Shortly after the A+ paper, Stan and I attended a picnic for the young married couples at church. We were hoping to get to know some more couples our age. It would be nice to have some people to hang out with occasionally. I'd pretty much given up hope that we could be "couple friends" with Nadine and Ty. Stan made it clear that they were my work friends and that we wouldn't be doing anything with them outside of work.

While at the picnic, I sat with some of the other women to chit-chat. I could overhear Stan talking at a nearby table. I'll be damned if he wasn't bragging about the A+ paper he'd just received, and how he'd never scored anything less than an A- in his English class! Not that I expected him to give me any credit for the good grades in that class, but he should at least have the decency to keep his mouth shut about it.

"That's terrific, Stan. How do you get such good grades on top of working full-time and your volunteer work?" I heard one of them ask.

"Oh, Stan has a little help here and there," I interrupted with a little wink.

Stan shot me a warning glance before laughing off my comment, "Yeah, Chrissy does a little bit of editing with some of my grammar and spelling."

"Well, that's good," someone commented. "It's always nice to get a second eye on your work."

They moved onto another topic and I went back to the conversation with the women. After the picnic, we drove home in silence. I tried to make small talk with Stan, but he seemed to be in one of his moods. When we got out of the car, we gathered some of the leftovers from the picnic and made our way up the steps to our apartment. I was ahead of Stan, carrying a large Tupperware bowl full of chips.

"I had a good time today," I said. "There were more newlywed couples than I thought. I liked Alice and Pete. I'll have to get that potato salad recipe from her. It was so good."

I opened the door to our apartment. Just as I stepped through the entrance, I was hit with the powerful force of a boot in my back. It sent me sprawling to the ground, and I lost my grip on the bowl of chips, sending the chips flying in every direction.

I turned around on the floor in surprise and shock to see what had hit me. Stan loomed up above me and slammed the front door closed behind him. "You conniving little bitch!" he yelled. "You just couldn't wait for the first opportunity to tell somebody about those papers. You just can't stand for me to get a little credit for what I do! I bust my ass every day without a single thank you. You talk back to me, disrespect me, and undermine me at every opportunity! You're turning into that sassy Negro bitch that you work with, and I won't have it, Chrissy! Not under my roof!"

"I just said I helped!" I cried out in my defense. "No one thought it was peculiar. They said it was a good idea!"

"You should have kept your damn mouth shut! Don't cross me, Chrissy! Don't you dare try anything like that again! Now clean up this mess! You pick up every last speck of a chip on this floor. There will be hell to pay if I find one crumb!"

He stomped off to the bedroom. I crawled around on the carpet with the chip bowl. My vision blurred with tears, but I made sure I picked up every last crumb.

Later, Stan came up and hugged me from behind, apologizing for his behavior. He was grateful for my help, he said. He was just feeling a bit overwhelmed with his classes, plus work, plus the youth group. He'd never lose his temper with me again. He'd never touch me in anger again. It was beginning to sound like the refrain of a very terrible song. I lay awake that night with Stan's arm across me in bed. I felt the same horrible sinking feeling that I'd had as a kid in a welfare family, that no matter what I did, no matter how hard I tried, it was no use. I would eventually go under.

That fall, things with Stan continued to go downhill. After his apologies for losing his temper, he would be good for a while and treat me well. Then, the old irritations would begin again, the snapping back and forth, the moodiness. Finally, there

154

would be an eruption followed again by lots of apologies and remorse. The rough grabbing and shoving and pushing eventually gave way to slaps and pinches and hair-pulling. And then he was outright punching, kicking, and choking me into submission.

I became very adept with foundations, concealers, and powders. I would dab, blot, and blend away all the signs of my abuse. Long-sleeved turtlenecks shirts were my best friends. Luckily, the weather was getting cooler so it was more comfortable to stay covered up. We remained the happy, young newlywed couple at church that everybody loved. We'd often argue the whole way to church and then put on our fake plaster smiles and sit through the services, Stan's arm around me protectively. No one from church would ever guess, or probably even believe, the kinds of brutality he was capable of behind closed doors. Who, Stan? He's the nicest, friendliest guy in the world. He wouldn't hurt a flea! Once we'd get back in the car to go home, we'd pick up where we'd left off with our argument or just sit in silence.

Despite my skilled cover-up tactics, I felt as if Nadine had bionic eyes and could see right through my layers of make-up and clothes to the bruises and welts beneath. One day, as we sat at lunch, she stared at me skeptically while Ty and I chatted. Suddenly, she broke in, "Chrissy, do you have anything you'd like to talk to us about?"

"Nope," I replied, biting into my sandwich.

"Well, if you ever do, you know that Ty and I would like to help you."

"Thank you, but I don't need help with anything."

"You know you're not fooling anybody with all that make-up."

I ignored her and turned back to Ty to ask him about his classes at school. There was really nothing they could do to help. I knew now that I'd made a big mistake marrying Stan. But I'd made my choices and I'd taken my vows. I took them seriously. Lots of married couples had their problems. They just had to learn how to work through them together. There was no way Nadine would be able to understand anyway. She had a relationship that was based on equality, love, and mutual respect. The only thing she would be able to do was lecture me, and I already had enough lectures at home.

As promised, I organized a fall trip to Mike's diner with all the residents who were mobile enough to go. Mike had prepared plenty of pumpkin cheesecake and had closed the diner to the public for that afternoon so that there would be enough room for the seniors. He had even booked a little group of baton twirlers to perform for the residents. The residents were thrilled with the whole thing.

The diner was all decorated for the fall, and I began to wax nostalgic as I looked around me. Sometimes I just longed to go back to the simpler life of living with the Stakers, coming to work at the diner every day, and spending my spare time at the library or playing my guitar. It's too bad that I'd ever accepted that first date with Stan. Mike gave me several concerned glances as I buzzed around with my plastered-on smile and caked-on make-up. At one point, he pulled me aside and asked, "Chrissy, are you all right? Are you happy?"

My smile faltered for a split second before I regained it and answered, "Yes. I'm extremely happy. You know, marriage has its ups and downs, but I have no major complaints." I nodded my head. "I'm quite happy."

I knew that people like Mike and Nadine cared for me and wanted to help. But I just couldn't come clean on what was happening behind closed doors in my married life. It was too embarrassing. What kind of person gets married in the summer and is ready to call it quits by the fall? I would not be that person.

So, no, I really couldn't talk to anyone about, or even admit to myself, what was happening. And then one day, I found I had a comrade in the most unlikely person imaginable. I was helping to bathe Miss Candace in her bathroom and pulled up the sleeves of my turtleneck to keep them from getting wet.

156

Suddenly, Miss Candace ran her withered hands down my arms, with a concerned look on her face, "I know these marks," she said. "I know them well. Not you, Chrissy. Oh no! You're much too nice of a person to have this happen to you." Her silvery blue eyes seemed to be looking right through me to my very soul.

I froze for a moment, then regained my composure. "Oh!" I laughed. "These marks. I'm just so clumsy. I'm always hurting myself! Here, let's get you dried off and in some clean clothes."

I helped her over to the bed and began getting her dressed. Miss Candace wore the strangest looking under-garments I'd ever seen. They looked like white long-johns from the 1800's, and they had some stitched-in markings on them. I thought they were for religious purposes, but I didn't ask about them. It really wasn't any of my business. Anyway, she was so frail and thin, she could probably benefit from that extra layer of clothing, I figured.

She grabbed my arm and spoke again. "It's terrible, isn't it? It's so terrible when the person who's sworn to love and protect you becomes your greatest tormenter. So heart-breaking and terrible!" Her silver-blue eyes welled up with tears as she watched me.

I hastily finished dressing her, making up some excuse about being late for a staff meeting and practically ran out of the room. I was shaken by her words for the rest of the day. Here I'd been presuming she'd never known a day of sadness in her life. She always seemed so happy. We really know so little about the people around us. We see them every day and make our own assumptions about their lives based on the few minutes of chit-chat that we have with them. Yet we rarely even scratch the surface of knowing who they really are.

By the end of the day, I decided I needed to know more. After clocking out, I went and tapped on the door to her room. She called out a cheery, "Come in!"

I walked in and pulled a chair over to her bed. "I'm so sorry for rushing out the way I did today. I was just very taken aback by what you said to me. No one knows what's really going on with my life. Nadine suspects something but, I don't know, I can't talk to her about it."

"It's a difficult thing to discuss. It's difficult even to admit to yourself what's happening. They blame it on you so much that, after a while, you begin to blame yourself for it too. You begin to believe you deserve every blow and more." She smiled sadly at me.

"Tell me your story. I have some time right now. Stan's at an activity tonight."

She sighed and stared off out the window for a few moments. "It was a different age, a different time for women back then. In 1915, I was 25 years old and still unmarried, practically an old maid by the standards back then. To be a spinster was considered a fate almost worse than death. Women were nothing without a man back then. They couldn't vote. They didn't even count as a person, really. There were few career options available to women. You could perhaps become a teacher, or a nurse, or a librarian. That was about it. But I always wanted to be married, to be a wife and a mother. That was my dream.

"So when I was introduced by a family friend to my husband, I was thrilled. He was 10 years my senior, but that was okay with me. I liked the idea of a mature fellow. He'd been a bachelor for a long time, and he should have stayed one. We had a very short courtship and engagement. It didn't take long after being married for me to realize that I'd made a terrible mistake. He was a gruff, abrasive man, even when he was sober. And when he was drunk, he was vicious and brutal. I can't tell you how many times I was beaten to within an inch of my life, too many times to count.

"I was so hopeful and eager for Prohibition to pass. I thought it would be the answer to all my problems. If I could just get the liquor out of his hands, life would be so different, so much better. And it *was* initially. He was sober for a good three months, and it was the best three months of our marriage. That's when our son was conceived. But then he just found a way to get alcohol through the black market. And it was low-grade, terrible stuff that made him even more violent and vicious. I knew then that things would never change. People never talked about violence in the home. What happened in a man's home was a man's business. The law stayed out of it. People stayed out of it. A woman was the property of her husband. You can do whatever you like with your own property It's no one else's affair—that was the thinking of the day.

"After a few years, he didn't even live in the house with me anymore, which was just fine by me. He slept in a cot out in his workshop that he'd built in the backyard. He was a hard worker, I'll give him that. He was a skilled craftsman and machinist. He provided a roof over our heads and food on the table. His drinking didn't seem to affect his work, although he often drank while he worked. He was a perfectionist. Anything that he built was pristine, with attention paid to every detail.

"We were married for almost 50 years. The last five years he was bedridden and ill, with diabetes, cancer, and dementia. I took care of him every day. I hated every bone in his body. I breathed a sigh of relief when he finally gasped out his last breath. He couldn't hurt me anymore. To this day, I still hate the bones rotting in his grave."

Hearing those words from such a sweet, loving, happy woman was such a shock to me. "Why did you stay with him all those years? Why didn't you leave him?"

She smiled sadly again, "Women didn't have the option to leave back then. Where would we go? Your place was with your husband. He was your dictator. Some women were blessed with kind, benevolent dictators who treated them so well. Other women, like me, had not-so-kind dictators. In either case, you'd made your choice and you had to live with it. And, once children entered the picture, you couldn't even entertain thoughts of leaving. What would become of them? You had to think of more than just yourself.

"Oh, but things are so different for women now, Chrissy. They have rights. They have so many more opportunities. There's never been a better time to be a woman than right here, right now in 1972! You don't have to stay in a bad relationship. You don't have to have a ruined, battered life. You can leave! Oh, please leave him, Chrissy. You're a smart girl! You have a job. You don't have children yet. Oh, please leave now while there's still time."

I shook my head, "It isn't as easy as you think. And Stan's not as bad as that. He doesn't really drink much at all, and he's never drunk. And he does really love me. He's always sorry afterwards and treats me well for a few days. Did you see? He sent me flowers today at work with a card saying he loved me. I'm not ready to give up on my marriage. I just got married in June. Some couples need time to adjust to each other. We need to try harder and be more patient with each other. I'm just as guilty. I can be nasty and sarcastic at times."

"I've never seen you that way."

"That's because you bring out the good person in me. I have other sides as well."

She shook her head. "It doesn't matter. There is never a good excuse for a man to beat his spouse. They don't change, Chrissy. Oh, they can be sorry. They can make promises, but the next fight only proves that they haven't changed a bit. In fact, they only get worse over time. When they see what they can get away with, they keep pushing the line further and further. You have to have the courage to say it ends here. You have to be braver than I was."

I looked at my watch. "I should probably go. It feels good to finally talk to somebody about this. But please don't tell anyone about me. I don't want them poking their noses in my business. My marriage is different from yours. I'm going to find a way to make it work."

I could feel her piercing eyes on my back as I headed out her door. I went to the front office to pick up my bouquet of flowers from Stan. I tried to keep Miss Candace's words from echoing through my mind as I drove home.

*****

I had a good review on my work performance at Sunset and received a small raise. It wasn't much, but I was now making more than Stan did at the gas station. He was happy that we had a little more money coming in, especially now with the holidays upon us. But it was also a bit of a blow to his pride to have me making more money than he did. He frequently reminded me that there was no real opportunity for advancement at the nursing home. I'd advanced as far as I could in my position. I would never be more than I was right now, whereas he would eventually have a college degree and unlimited opportunities for advancement.

I continued to write weekly papers for Stan's English class. He was doing well and getting an A in that class, but he struggled with his earth science class. I tried to help tutor him, but then he'd just get frustrated and take it out on me. I couldn't take his tests for him in that class. He struggled to maintain a C average. He also despised his job at the gas station. The only thing he really liked doing was working with the youth group. I had stopped suggesting he cut back in that area because he'd get so angry with me for even suggesting it. But when he complained about all of his responsibilities and time constraints and made excuses about why he didn't have time to study, I couldn't help but see that the simple answer was to let go of his volunteer work or at least cut back significantly.

We'd be spending the holidays with Stan's family, which wasn't thrilling to me. It was always so tense and awkward being around his family. I never could keep track of who wasn't speaking to whom at the moment. But, at least if Stan was focused on griping about his own family, he would lay off me for a while. We made Christmas wreaths and fruit baskets for his mom and his siblings.

One nice thing about having two full-time incomes and no children was that we lived pretty comfortably now. We were frugal and rarely went out to dinner or the movies together. Our main entertainment was going to church activities, which were free, or just watching TV at home. I'd often look around our cute little furnished apartment and think about how I would have viewed this place and our lifestyle when I was a poor welfare child living in a shack on a dirt road. I would have thought we were filthy rich! We had plenty of food to eat. We had two working cars, a small but nicely decorated little apartment, a color TV in our living room, and my old black-and-white TV in our bedroom. I had a small but decent wardrobe, with maybe a few too many turtlenecks and pink items for my taste. All in all, we lived like royalty! Sometimes I'd go into my closet and pull down my Chrissy rock from the top shelf and think about that girl that I used to be. What would she think of the person I was now? How would she view my life? If Stan ever saw the rock, he never mentioned it or asked me about it. He just assumed it was some child's artwork creation. I doubt he ever bothered to read it. It wouldn't make any sense to him anyway. He knew so little about my past.

Stan was in a better mood over winter break since he didn't have to worry about school, and we had a fairly pleasant Christmas and New Year's, all things considered. In January though, when spring semester began, Stan's mood quickly soured. He was taking two more classes, and there was very little writing this time, so I couldn't help him much. After two weeks, he was ready to drop out of school altogether. He just wasn't cut out for this, he told me. We argued one morning about it while we were getting ready in the bathroom. I had just showered and was wrapped in a towel, detangling my hair with a brush. Stan's plan was to resign from school that day so that we could get some of the tuition money back. He'd decided he wanted to become a motivational speaker for young people.

"Stan," I argued, "how do you even establish a career like that? What kind of training do you need? It's not like 'youth motivational speaker' is advertised as a job in the want ads. I think you need to form a plan for how to do this. In the meantime, I think it is very unwise to drop out of school. You need to have a back-up plan in case the motivational speaker thing doesn't work out."

"I should have known you'd have nothing but negative things to say about this. You're never supportive of anything I want to do. You don't support any of my dreams."

"I don't mean to be negative, but I'm trying to think about this practically. What are you going to motivate young people to do? Will it be religion-based? Not every teenager out there is a Methodist or even a Christian. It's fine to do that on a volunteer basis at your local church, but no one is going to pay you to go out and do it as a profession. Are you going to persuade them to avoid drugs? What do you know about that life? You can only speculate. Are you going to persuade them to stay in school? That's a bit ironic, wouldn't you say?"

Suddenly Stan reached out and pulled the brush out of my hand and began hitting me with it. "Ow! Stop it!" I cried. "That hurts!"

I started to run out of the bathroom, but he grabbed onto me by my towel and yanked me down to the hallway floor. While I was face down on the carpet, he pounced onto my back and bit me hard right on the back. I screamed and turned around trying to fight him off. My towel was off, and before I knew what was happening, he had yanked down the top of his pants and raped me right there on the floor. I screamed and cried for him to get off me the whole time. When it was over, I sat up and put the towel back around me. I cried and told him I should have him arrested for rape. He buckled his pants and casually said, "I'm your husband. It's my right. There's no such thing as rape when it's your spouse."

I slowly began to finish getting ready. His teeth had broken through the skin on my back and it really hurt. I dabbed at it with some salve and gingerly pulled my shirt on over the top. Stan came over and kissed me on the cheek as if nothing had happened. "I'm sorry if I was a little rough on you," he said. "Things will get a lot better after I've dropped out. You'll see. I think it's the pressure of school that makes me do stuff like that to you. I know it will get better after today." With that, he strode out the front door to go to work.

All day long at work, I could hardly force a smile. I felt so depressed, so degraded after what had happened that morning. The bite on my back throbbed continuously. When I went for a bathroom break, I lifted my shirt and turned around to check on it in the mirror. The individual teeth marks were visible, and swirls of colors were beginning to form around them — yellow, green, and blue. It would darken and look horrible for several days, I was sure. I just couldn't live like this anymore. Something had to change.

I sat quietly through lunch with Nadine and Ty, barely paying attention to anything they said. I took a few bites of my sandwich and then wrapped up the rest of it to save for later.

"Somebody's awfully quiet today," commented Ty in my direction.

"It's just been a bad morning."

"Anything you want to talk about?" Nadine asked.

I hesitated, then shook my head. What could they do about it? Nothing. I could feel the bite stinging through my shirt. Nadine still waited for me to say something.

Finally, I spoke. "If I show you two something will you promise to remain calm? Just don't go flying off the handle about it?"

Nadine promised and Ty nodded in agreement. I stood and turned around and slowly lifted my shirt just high enough to show the mark on my back where I'd been bitten.

Nadine gasped in horror. "What *in the hell* is that on your back?"

"It's a bite." I lowered my shirt and turned back around.

"A bite? A bite! From what, may I ask? What wild, vicious animal pounced on you in the woods and bit into your flesh like that? What rabid dog attacked you? Tell me so I can call the pound to come and get it."

"You know very well that it wasn't an animal that bit me."

"Because that's what wild animals do, Chrissy. They bite! *People* do not bite."

"One of them does," I said grimly, searching through my lunchbag for anything that looked edible to me right now. I couldn't tell them about the rape. It was just too private and humiliating. The bite was bad enough.

A look of pure anger flashed across Ty's face. He slammed his fist into his palm. "I'd like to have just five minutes alone with that little weasel. Just five minutes alone to cure him for good!"

"Somehow I doubt that more violence is going to help my situation," I said.

"Maybe not," responded Nadine, "but it would sure do us a world of good to see that snake get what's coming to him. I knew he was hurting you! Ty and I both suspected that's what was happening and you just wouldn't admit it. I'm glad you finally came clean. Now the question is what are you going to *do* about this? You can't stay in that apartment any longer. Why don't you move out and come to live with me and Ty for a while? We've already talked about it. We have a spare bedroom and you could stay there for as long as you needed. Divorce that bastard before it's too late!"

"Nadine, I am *not* getting a divorce. Do you think I want to be a 20-year-old divorced woman? I can't stand the thought of that! I haven't even been married a year. Yes, I made a mistake, all right? I admit that. I shouldn't have married Stan. You were right. I was wrong. Are you happy now?"

"No. I am not happy at all. I am worried about my friend. I just want you to know that you have someone to turn to, a place to go where you'll be safe. Just say the word, Chrissy, and we'll help you out of this mess."

"The *word* is that I am staying married. Yes, I recognize that we have our problems. Lots of couples have problems. They have to learn to work them out. I think we need to get some marital counseling with one of the church leaders. I'm going to insist to Stan that we need joint counseling. He'll be really nice to me over the next few days since the incident just happened this morning. I'll be able to get whatever I want, and I'll tell him I want counseling."

"Oh, counseling from church, yes, that's perfect," said Nadine sarcastically. "Someone who is unlicensed, untrained, and ill-equipped to handle this kind of serious problem is going to tell you to work harder, be more patient, and stay together no matter what! Then they'll read you some mumbo-jumbo thing from the Bible that makes no sense and send you along your merry way. If you ask me, that kind of thing is a big waste of everyone's time."

"It's inspired advice," I stubbornly countered.

"Inspired by what, who knows? Maybe it's inspired by the baloney sandwich they ate for lunch that day. One thing I do know, it is *not* inspired by God. Any God who would have a woman stay with a man who beats her is a fictional God. 'I distrust those who know so well what God wants them to do because I notice that it always coincides with their own desires.' Susan B. Anthony said that. You just remember that quote when people start to talk with such surety about what God wants."

I wasn't sure I'd done the right thing by telling Nadine and Tyrone about Stan and me, but it felt better just knowing I had some people in my corner in addition to Miss Candace. If I ended up dead, at least they'd know. They'd make sure justice was done. It was a crazy, morbid thought, but it somehow made me feel a little better.

We did start attending marital counseling sessions at the church. We were discreet, because we didn't want anyone from church to know there was anything more behind our happy Sunday smiles and warm chit-chat with fellow members.

From the moment we sat down with the counselor, Stan would start talking and wouldn't finish until we'd get up to leave. I barely said a word. Stan's narrative of what was happening was so convincing, even I was almost sucked in by it. He would begin to cry as he talked about his mother's multiple marriages and the different men she'd brought into their home, some of whom had mistreated Stan, his siblings, and his mother. Then Stan would talk about all the pressures and stress that he had to deal with, and how I ended up causing more stress by constantly putting him down and making him feel like less than a man. Yes, he'd slapped me "once or twice," he admitted, and he knew that was wrong. He'd repented of those sins and promised to treat me with love and respect, but I needed to do the same.

The counselor asked me if I was willing to do the same. All I could do was nod my head and say yes. At the beginning of every session, I would have a little speech prepared in which I tried to explain how things really were. But, by the end of Stan's explanation, I was just as convinced as the counselor that the problem really wasn't Stan. It was everyone around Stan, and, most especially, it was me. I really needed to work harder at being a better wife. And if I could do that, then our marriage would greatly improve. Then the counselor would open up the Bible and we'd each take turns reading verses from an entire section. I tried to pay attention to the words on the page in front of me. I tried to ignore the echoes of Nadine's voice quoting Susan B. Anthony in my head. Damn, it was uncanny how Nadine was always so spot-on.

After a few sessions with the counselor, Stan and I agreed that we probably didn't need to go anymore. Our marriage had been saved, and Stan now had some really good ideas for a future youth group lesson on marriage and family relationships.

19

My participation in church really began to dwindle that spring. The novelty of being the young, fresh, popular married couple had worn off. I was tired of playing the happy, submissive little "wifey." It just wasn't me, and I was sick of pretending that it was.

Besides having to fake a happy marriage, there were a couple of things about church itself that gnawed at me. The times when I did pay attention to what was being said at church, which, admittedly weren't very often, they always seemed to be talking about some variation of the same tired theme: the "righteous vs. the wicked." There were the righteous folks (us) versus the wicked folks (not us), and we righteous folks seemed to be more than a little preoccupied with the actions and inevitable fate of the wicked folks. And it seemed like the circle of wicked folks was quite broad and sweeping. It not only included people who were obviously wicked, like murderers and child rapists, but it also seemed to include just average, everyday people who didn't believe in the same things as us. It didn't seem right that good people of other religions would be included with the wicked group just because they held different religious beliefs. What if that was what they'd been taught since they were little kids? What if they thought *they* were the ones who had the truth and *we* were the ones going to hell? Maybe they were in church right now discussing *our* wickedness. That seemed so odd.

And the wicked group also included the people who just plain weren't religious. Maybe they were people like Momma, who just didn't go to church or believe in it much, but that didn't mean they didn't try hard to be good people. I remembered one time when Marla and I were talking about God, and she said she wasn't even sure if God was real because she'd prayed a lot for Him to help her out of her situation with her step-father and He never did. She had to be the one to get herself out of there. I told Marla that maybe God was just busy with other things at the moment, because He had a big to-do list with the whole world's problems. Just because He didn't answer her prayers didn't mean He didn't exist, I told her. Marla just said, "Well, I figure whether He's real or not, it don't matter. Either way, you're pretty much on your own." Marla would also have been counted as one of the wicked people by our church's standards, and maybe she did make some bad decisions. But I still didn't think she deserved to go to hell with the truly wicked people. Even my brother Brad wasn't wicked in my view. He definitely had his faults, lots and lots of them, and I'd be the first person who could name them all. But deep down inside, I knew he still had a good heart. Why would he have helped Momma with expenses or bought Jenny that camera if there weren't some little specks of goodness inside him?

I'd be thinking about all these things while we sat in church discussing the righteous vs. the wicked, and it just didn't sit right with me. But the problem with questioning one thing about your church is that it leads to questioning more and more. And after a while, you find that you hardly believe any of it anymore. Even the songs we sang, which had always been my favorite part of church before, began to irritate me once I started really paying attention to the words. It would be some beautiful song about love and faith and Jesus set to a beautiful melody. But then I'd find some one-liner in one of the verses about how the wicked would get what's coming to them in the end. And, to me, it would just ruin the whole song.

So I started volunteering to work the Sunday shift, since it gave me a good excuse not to go to church. After a while, I told Stan that I had to work, even on Sundays that I had off. He wondered why I had to work so many Sundays now, and I told him that we were short-handed since one of the aides had recently quit.

I would go to the nursing home and spend my Sunday mornings and afternoons there just visiting with the residents. I'd take them for walks around the grounds or play games with them in the recreation room. Sometimes I would take Miss Candace to her Mormon church services. Stan would have been horrified, since he maintained that it was a cult, but the services there weren't really that different from regular Christian services as far as I could tell. They prayed, talked at the podium, and sang songs. They did have their own version of that same "righteous versus the wicked" theme that I found so irritating, but for some reason I could take it better sitting next to Miss Candace than sitting next to Stan. I didn't feel the weight of her judgment upon me — the "are you getting this, Chrissy?" vibe that I got from sitting next to Stan in church.

My favorite time to visit the Mormons was always the first Sunday of the month. On the first Sunday, they didn't have any speakers planned. People would just get up out of the audience and walk up to the microphone and say whatever they felt like saying. They'd just get up there and shoot the breeze about what was happening in their lives, and then they'd close by saying how much they knew the church was true, and that the Book of Mormon was true, and that their Mormon prophet was a true prophet. I thought that was so fascinating. There's no way I could ever get up in front of a crowd like that and just start talking about my life without something prepared beforehand. Just like when I was in school, I was the type of person who sat in the back and never said a word. I did notice there were other people like me at the church. Some never got up, and I noticed over time that it was often the same people getting up to talk month after month. They must have been the brave ones who didn't mind sharing things about their lives. I told Miss Candace that I would help her if she ever wanted to get up there, but she was more of a sit-in-the-back-and-listen kind of person, just like me.

Sundays also gave me a chance to get to know my patients on a more personal level. And I was glad I had that chance, because, just as Nadine had warned, I eventually began losing some of the people I'd grown to care about there. It was very difficult, but I learned to save my tears for when I was in private. When someone in Building C passed away, we would hold a special "celebration of life" memorial. We would invite their family members to come and share pictures, mementoes, and special things about their loved one's life with us. If they had enough pictures, I would create a slide show that we could play during the memorial. I'd bring my guitar and play some of the deceased's favorite songs while the pictures flashed by on the wall screen. It was a moving tribute to life that the residents grew to love, and we felt as if we couldn't say good-bye to any of our friends until we'd had our memorial.

I actually grew to love the days that I'd spend at the nursing home when I wasn't being paid. Then I could just visit and spend quality time with the residents without feeling guilty about it. I'd bring books to read to them, my guitar to play for them, or simply play a board game or card games with them. Sometimes they just wanted me to sit and listen to them. I considered it such a privilege to get to know these people in their final days before they passed away. I'd heard a saying once that people's lives were like the leaves of a tree. They are their brightest, most colorful and brilliant right before the very end of their lives. And that's how I saw the residents of Sunset. I was privileged just to be able know them in the brilliant autumns of their lives.

It's odd how work and home had managed to trade places in my mind. Work was my safe haven, my escape place, the place where I felt I had family and people who loved and accepted me no matter what. Home was the real workplace for me, the place I dreaded, the place where I felt overworked and under-appreciated, the place where I had a nitpicking boss who was just waiting for the chance to pounce on me about something. Is it any wonder that, on my days off, I chose to go back to work?

One beautiful spring Sunday afternoon, I decided to wheel Miss Candace around the grounds so she could see all the trees that were blossoming and get some fresh air. We stopped under a shade tree to take in the view.

"Tell me about your son," I said.

"Oh," she smiled. "He was the one bright spot, the great joy of my life. How I loved my Danny! He was a gift from God," she said, "right when I had lost all hope."

"I'm sure you were a great mom," I said. "I'm actually surprised you didn't have more children."

"Oh, I desperately wanted more," Miss Candace said. "And there would have been more too. But my Mr. Awful never let up on me. Ever. Even when I was pregnant. I had five pregnancies in all. And only one child made it out of the womb alive."

"Oh," I said, "I'm so sorry. That must have been awful." At least I already knew I'd never get pregnant. It would be so terrible to get your hopes up so many times and have them dashed all over again.

"The first three miscarriages happened in the first trimester. I would head straight to bed after a beating and pray that my unborn child had survived it. But then the terrible cramping would begin. And I'd go to the bathroom and horrible clots of blood would come out of me. He couldn't even let me have this, I would think. He couldn't allow me to have someone to love, who would love me back.

"The fourth one was by far the worst. I'd made it to the second trimester. I was five months along. I was starting to be hopeful that this one might make it. But, no, after a terrible beating the same cramping started. The pain was horrendous this time. I thought I might die. The others had just been clots of blood. But this one was a tiny baby, a little girl. Can you believe that?" Her silver blue eyes welled up. "I could have had a daughter, maybe somebody like you. I would have liked that very much."

I smiled and grabbed her hand. "I'm sorry," I said. "I'm so sorry you went through that."

She nodded and swallowed hard. "I cleaned her off, wrapped her up and put her in a little hatbox. Later, I dug a hole in the field beside our house and buried her there. I placed a

172

large gray rock over it so that I would have a place to go and visit from time to time."

I sat on one of the benches next to Miss Candace's wheelchair. Now I understood why she harbored such deep hatred for her dead husband and why she could never forgive him. Truthfully, I wouldn't be able to forgive something like that either. I'd still hate the bones in his grave just as she did.

"You want to hear something really strange?" I asked her. "My daddy used to tell me that I'd been born under a rock just like the one you described. It was in a field too, I think. He took me there one day and showed it to me. He said he was just walking by one day and heard a baby crying under the rock. He picked it up and found me right there. I still have that rock. I believed that story for years." I laughed. It had been so long since I'd mentioned anyone from my past. But for some reason, it seemed safe to tell this story to Miss Candace.

Miss Candace smiled and squeezed my hand. "Well, isn't that something …" she remarked. "Isn't that something …"

"And so, after the baby girl, then you became pregnant with Danny?"

"Yes. I was 30 years old and had all but given up hope. Then, like I told you, when Prohibition passed, there was a brief period of sobriety. And I think that helped me get through that first trimester. But then Mr. Awful started up again and it was worse than ever. I knew I would lose the baby, but my Danny, he was a fighter. He won every battle he ever fought except that last one to cancer. Even in the womb, he was a fighter. I'd go through a beating and head to bed just crying and praying that this child survived. He'd be real quiet and still for a while. There'd be no movement, and I was so terrified that the cramping would start. But then I'd start to feel those little kicks again. He made it through! Every single time, he made it through. And then one day, he was in my arms. God had finally answered my prayer, and there was no way I was going to let any harm come to this child."

"How were you able to protect your son?"

"Well, when he was a baby, Mr. Awful left him alone. Actually, he hardly ever acknowledged the baby's existence. He wasn't in the house when Danny cried, which was a good thing. Mr. Awful stayed in the workshop most of the time by then. But then, as Danny grew into a toddler, he became more mobile and started climbing and getting into things. One time, Mr. Awful yelled at him and picked him up and threw him across the room onto the couch. That scared him, and it scared me too. With all the courage I could muster, I stood up to him and told him never to touch my child. Ever. I said, 'If you want to hit something, hit me. If you want to kick something, kick me. But don't you ever touch my child again or I promise that we will vanish from your life! You'll never see or hear from us again.' He looked into my eyes and he knew I meant every word."

"You took the brunt of the beatings so that Danny wouldn't have to," I said quietly.

"Well, of course I did!" Miss Candace's eyes shone brightly. "That's what a parent does. You don't bring a child into this world and then let the wolves get it."

I felt that old bitter knife twist deep inside me. No one had been there to stop the wolves when they'd come for me.

I brought Miss Candace back to her room in Building C and tucked her in bed.

"Are you comfortable?"

"Yes."

"Get some sleep now. I'll be back tomorrow." I grabbed my things and started for the door.

"Chrissy?"

"Yes?"

"Learn from me. It doesn't have to be that way. There's still a chance for you. There's still hope."

I clicked the door closed and walked out to my car. As I drove home in the dusk, I thought about Miss Candace's life.

It's strange to think of the things that were going on while you were at various stages of life. It's even stranger how events that happen before you were even born can have such an effect on your life today. I wondered if I would grow to hate Stan the way Miss Candace had hated her husband. They'd been married 47 years, more than twice my current age. Stan and I were just approaching our one-year anniversary, and it already felt as if we'd been together a miserable eternity. How had Miss Candace lasted that long? How had she managed to stay sane through all of that? Her bright eyes and smiling, happy face were real, not like the plastered fakeness that I managed to muster day in and day out. She had hope, real hope, and she was convinced that there was hope for me too.

20

Spring gave way to summer. I managed to get through the anniversary of Momma's death for another year with the same happy smiles and fakeness that were second nature to me now. When I was alone, I would turn back into the quiet, sullen, brooding person, thinking dark, bitter thoughts about Stan and my life with him. Just as he blamed all of his troubles on me, I began to link every negative thing in my life back to him. Just the sound of his boots walking across the linoleum floor was annoying to me, as was the way he chewed his food with a grinding sound in the back of his mouth and a jaw that clicked and popped occasionally. It made me lose my appetite. Of course, I'd never say anything about those annoying things to him. Any negativity expressed would only rain back down on me a thousand-fold, so it wasn't worth it.

We spent our one-year anniversary at a local bar. I sat at the bar all evening nursing a club soda while Stan played pool and the pinball machine and had a few beers. "Such romance," I said to myself bitterly. At one point, a fairly nice looking man about my age came up and asked if he could buy me a drink.

"Oh, uh, I'm married," I said, "to that guy," pointing with my thumb over in Stan's general direction.

"Don't look so excited about it," the man said teasingly.

"Yeah, well, it's our one-year anniversary," I offered for no particular reason.

The man shook his head and grabbed his drink. "And that," he said, "is precisely why I'll never get married."

I just shrugged my shoulders and took another sip while he walked away. I glanced back over at Stan. It was good that he hadn't seen someone trying to hit on me. He'd probably just end up blaming it all on me. Perhaps I was sipping my club soda too seductively. He'd come up with some reason why it was my fault, and I'd pay for it.

That summer, we embarked on a number of home-decorating projects. We put together two bookcases and a coffee table for the living room and bought some additional furniture for the living room, not without plenty of quarrelling, but we were pleased with the results. Stan figured that now, since we didn't have to pay for tuition anymore, we could afford some things like this.

He hadn't made any headway on his career path to become a "motivational speaker." I had plenty of sarcastic comments that I would never actually voice about *that* particular idea. It seemed the motivational speaker needed some motivation to get motivated about training to become a motivational speaker! I'd laugh about it if it weren't so pathetic.

One Saturday we were on our way out of a discount furniture store, walking to our car in the parking lot when Stan suddenly cried out, "Man, I wish I had a brick to put through this stupid lady's windshield."

"Why? What'd she do? Did she take the parking space you wanted?"

"No, dummy," he replied. "It's her bumper sticker."

I read it as Stan put some things in the trunk. "Pass the Equal Rights Amendment for Women."

I climbed into the passenger seat while Stan finished what he was doing. Then he walked over and climbed into the driver's side.

"Yeah, equal rights for women. That would be such a big bummer," I noted sarcastically as he started the engine.

"Chrissy, women already have equality. These stupid feminists want a lot more than that. Men and women are equals, but they have very different roles and functions in our society. Women's libbers are always trying to say that there's no difference, that men and women are exactly the same. Do you know how dangerous that would be for our society if we just pretended that everyone is the same?"

"It sounds like they are asking for equal rights, equal treatment under the law. That's not saying that there's absolutely no difference between men and women."

"Don't get sucked in by their arguments, Chrissy! You have no idea how dangerous that kind of thinking is. Women already have equal treatment. I mean, look at how good women have it nowadays! They're put on a pedestal all the time! Haven't you ever heard the saying, 'Behind every great man is a good woman?' Men would be absolutely nothing without the good women that support them and help them achieve their dreams. There would be absolutely no greatness in this world without good, supportive women. But that's not enough for these feminists."

Stan angrily steered through traffic. "They hate all men, Chrissy. And yet they want to turn themselves into men. They won't be happy until they've completely switched the God-ordained roles of men and women. They want to turn all men into effeminate little wimps, and they want women to become the dominant sex and rule the world. That's the ultimate aim of the equal rights amendment, Chrissy, to completely switch the places of men and women."

"Well, now *I'm* a little confused. On the one hand, you're telling me that men and women already *are* completely equal. But then you say feminists want to switch places and become the dominant sex. That implies that you currently believe there *is* a dominant sex, the male sex. If they were truly equal, then switching places would make them still equal."

"That's not what I'm saying at all! All I said ... You've completely twisted my words around. You're too dense to understand something like this. These feminists are popping up everywhere and their plan is to completely destroy society as we know it. Look, there's another one." He pointed to the bumper sticker on the car in front of us. "See how crass and rude they are? They're not women at all."

The sticker read, "We are the women for the ERA. Screw us and we multiply!"

178

I had to suppress the urge to smile. Clever!

We were stopped at a stoplight, and as soon as it turned green, Stan leaned on his horn. "Move it, you dumb bitch!" he yelled. "Out of the way!" He illegally sped around her, yelling out the window, "Learn how to drive!" I ducked down into the seat so she wouldn't see me as we sped past.

I knew better than to criticize Stan's driving, especially when he was in a mood like this. But I did say, "I'm just pointing out that it seems illogical to me to say that two people are already completely equal, but if they switch places, one will ultimately dominate the other one."

"Well, they're equal in value to God. But there's a definite order to things, which God has laid out for us. If you try to mess up that order, things turn to complete chaos and nobody knows what their role is anymore. It's explained a lot better in church. If you ever *went* to church, you'd already know this."

"I *do* go to church sometimes. Just not with you. I've been taking Miss Candace to her church sometimes on Sundays."

"With the Mormons?! Good grief, Chrissy! I've warned you about them. They're not Christians! It's not even a religion. It's a cult!"

"It is not a cult! The people there are very normal and very nice. It's just a church, like any other church out there. They sing, they talk, they pray, and they get together for activities. How is that different from any other church we've known?"

"Their beliefs are completely different, Chrissy! Okay, so maybe a regular church service at one of their meeting houses seems normal. But they perform secret rituals in their temples, they wear underwear that they believe is magical, they have their own scriptures, they do everything their prophet leader tells them to do. They don't even believe in the same God we do."

"If they're not hurting anybody, what does it matter what they believe? How does it harm you personally if someone wears different underwear than you? I know Miss Candace believes in the Bible too. She has other scriptures also, but so what? Maybe Mormons just like extra reading! And she has a picture of Jesus on her wall right next to her bed!"

"It's a different Jesus."

"Well, how many of them are there?" I asked in exasperation. "Honestly, Christians can't even agree on who's actually a Christian. How can we ever expect the religions of the world to ever see eye-to-eye on anything? Why can't we just live and let live if it's not hurting anyone?"

"Because we are warned against false religions and false teachings!"

"Maybe they think *yours* is the false religion!"

"Well, they're wrong! The very thought that they'd think that about another religion is just further proof that they believe in a *false* religion. If you don't watch your guard, they'll try to rope you in and get you to believe all the same crazy stuff."

"They have never tried that. They know I'm just a caregiver for Miss Candace."

"Well, it's coming. Mark my words. They can't wait to unleash those missionaries on you and try to force you to read their scriptures and wear their magical underwear. Let one of their minions bring her to church. That's not part of your job."

"Okay, Stan, we're not getting anywhere with this conversation. You'll never be able to step outside your own lens to see the world differently. So let's pretend we didn't have this conversation."

"Chrissy, I forbid you to attend church with those Mormons again."

"Fine." I found it easier to just verbally agree to Stan's mandates, whether or not I actually obeyed them.

"Remember, *I'm* the expert on religion, not you. You stick to your areas of expertise, wiping butts and playing the banjo." He laughed at his clever joke. "And I'll stick to my areas of expertise."

Pumping gas and being an asshole, I thought to myself. I stared out the passenger window while Stan continued to steer through traffic. I'd learned not to voice most of my thoughts around him. But it saddened me to realize that I'd regressed back to the sullen, bitter, sarcastic Chrissy that I'd become around Momma and my siblings after my sterilization. Stan just seemed to bring out that person in me. The people at work probably wouldn't even recognize me at home with Stan. I was so different with him from the person that I was at work. And it was a good thing Stan wasn't a mind reader. Let's just say he'd have to quit his job so that he could stay home and beat me full-time if he knew all the disrespectful thoughts I had about him.

Now that we'd been married for over a year, Stan began to voice open concern over the fact that I hadn't yet become pregnant. Most couples who weren't using birth control were pregnant within a year, he said. He wondered what we weren't doing right. After reading a magazine article and talking to some people at church about optimizing fertility, he began to chart my menstrual cycle on the calendar. We needed to have sex every other day between days 10 and 19 of my cycle. This mandate, like so many others of Stan's, was met with my usual lack of enthusiasm. Now, the one area of our life that had been somewhat decent would be turned into something forced and mechanical. It also felt like such an invasion of my privacy that he needed to know the exact day I started my period so he could go chart it out on the calendar, marking with little foil sticker stars the days we needed to have sex. It was as if I were a prized horse he was trying to breed, rather than his wife.

And, yes, I felt guilt too as he charted and planned, knowing that this was all futile. Somehow I knew I couldn't come clean about my sterilization, ever. It was better if he just realized, over time, that I was infertile. And then maybe we could decide to adopt or take in foster children. But telling the truth would rain devastating consequences on my head. I knew that without a doubt. And so I put up with the week and a half of quick, methodical, purposeful sex every month and the invasion of my privacy, the feeling that my own body did not fully belong to me. And I breathed a sigh of relief when that week and a half was over, because then I wouldn't have to do it again until next month. Since sex was now a chore, we couldn't imagine engaging in it outside of that ten-day window.

While the autumn brought with it the excitement of upcoming holidays, it also brought with it the cold and flu season, which at a nursing home can be devastating. We had more deaths during cold and flu season than during the late spring and summer, so we were more vigilant about washing hands and trying to keep sick residents isolated from the healthy ones. If you were sick, you were not to come into work, no matter how short-handed we were. I hadn't taken any sick days so far, and I rarely was sick, so the policy didn't affect me as much as some of the other staff.

But my luck ran out that fall when I caught one of the worst flu viruses I'd ever had. I woke up in the middle of a Sunday night to the horrible gurgling in my stomach. I tried to go back to sleep, thinking it was just something I'd eaten that day that hadn't settled well. Very soon, I began feeling hot, cold and clammy all at the same time. The wave of nausea came quickly, and I barely made it out of bed and into the bathroom to vomit into the toilet. I felt a little better after that. But then it would begin to build again until I was running back to the toilet. The fourth time happened right after my alarm went off. After cleaning myself up again, I made my way to the phone and called into work, saying I wouldn't be in today due to illness.

Stan was just waking up as I climbed back into bed. "What? You're not going to work today?"

"I'm sick. I was up all night throwing up. I just called work."

Stan grumbled to himself and got out of bed. I could hear him stomping around the apartment and slamming things around. *What is the matter with that moron now?* I knew that

182

he had a busy schedule for today. He had to work all day and then was in charge of a youth group activity later that evening. He'd hoped to be home in time to catch the football game on TV that night. He was acting as though my illness somehow threw a wrench in his plans, and I wasn't sure how that worked out in his mind. He'd have his things to do regardless of whether or not I was sick.

As he grumbled and threw on his clothes, I asked if he was okay. He ignored me for a few moments and then commented, "It would sure be nice to have the day off too, but *I* don't have that luxury!"

"I would much rather be at work today too, Stan. Believe me, this is no picnic."

"You look fine to me. You just want the day off."

"Did you not hear me getting up all night to vomit in the bathroom?"

"No."

"Well, I was. If you're here for a while longer, I'm sure I'll vomit again to prove it."

"Well, I have places to be today! Unlike you, I have to show up at my job."

I felt too ill to argue with him. He finished getting ready and slammed some things around in the kitchen. "I have to make my own lunch too?!" he shouted. Usually I packed our lunches the night before, but last night I figured I'd just do it in the morning before we left. It was one day. He could buy his lunch if necessary. "Enjoy your day off!" he shouted at me from the living room and then slammed the door.

"Yeah, go to hell, creep. I hope you catch my germs." I spent all morning and most of the afternoon in bed, occasionally getting up to run to the bathroom again. Eventually there was nothing left in my system to throw up. I would just lean over the toilet and dry heave when the nausea overtook me.

By late afternoon, I felt well enough to move my pillow and blankets into the living room so I could at least lie on the couch and watch TV for a while. My stomach was starting to settle down enough that I thought I might be able to keep something down. I went into the kitchen and made myself a slice of dry toast and poured a small glass of apple juice. I brought them back to the couch and slowly ate. The food did seem to help settle my stomach. I sat back down on the couch and fell asleep until I heard Stan's boots coming up the stairway to our apartment.

He rushed through the door and headed back to our bedroom to change and get ready for the activity. "How many soap operas did you watch today?" he asked sarcastically.

"Zero. I was sick all day. And I have no interest in soap operas. How was work?"

"Terrible. I don't know how much of that place I can take any longer. I'm overworked and under-appreciated there. I'm just about ready to quit that job. I've been thinking about going back to school."

"But you hated school too."

"That's because I was in the wrong field, Chrissy. I don't want to go into business anymore. Maybe if I majored in something like communications or public relations, I would enjoy it much more."

I decided not to point out to him that all he'd taken were a couple of general education classes, which he'd have to take regardless of his choice of a major. I sighed and repositioned my pillows and blankets. Stan didn't like working for other people. He wanted to be his own boss in a high-level position where he could feel important, but he wasn't willing to put in the time and effort to get there.

He came back out of the room. "I have to go. You didn't even get dressed today?" he asked in annoyance.

"Why would I?"

"You look like crap."

"Thank you."

He grabbed his keys and left in a huff. I'd have to remember never to have the audacity to get sick again. I heard his car speeding off and then stood to switch off the TV. There was nothing that I wanted to watch anyway. I went back to my place on the couch, wrapped up in blankets, worrying about what would happen if Stan quit his job. It would devastate us financially. We needed that second full-time income. And I'd already seen how well he handled being in school. He just wasn't cut out for college-level work. He'd drop out again and be more frustrated with his life than ever. And I'd bear the brunt of that frustration. Stan was really a child in a grown man's body. He was impulsive and immature. He couldn't control his emotions. He wasn't even a nice, sweet child at that. He was more of the schoolyard bully type of child.

After dozing off again, I woke up and felt hungry again. I went back into the kitchen to make another slice of toast and pour another cup of juice. I hoped I would feel better by the next morning. I couldn't stand the thought of another day in bed. I didn't know how some of the seniors who were bedridden handled it. The days went by so slowly when I had nothing to do but stare at the wall and listen to clock tick. I would much rather be busy. The day just flew by so quickly when I was busy.

Stan came back at about 8:30. He was upset because it hadn't gone well. The kids were restless. They didn't pay attention to the lesson, and some of them made jokes the whole time. Usually Stan was in a better mood after being with the youth group, but tonight he was in an especially foul mood. I listened while he complained about his entire day. He didn't even ask how I was feeling. Not that it mattered. I didn't want to remind him that I was sick, because for some reason my illness was just another annoyance to his day.

I got up to put my plate and cup in the kitchen sink. I would wash them tomorrow. For now, I just wanted to brush my teeth and go to bed for the night.

"Where's my dinner?" Stan asked as he switched on the TV and plopped down on a chair to watch football for the rest of the evening.

"What?"

"I said, where's my dinner? I'm starved. I haven't eaten since lunch and I've had a terrible day!"

"I haven't even been able to *think* about food all day without getting nauseous. Dry toast is the only thing I've been able to keep down."

"Well, if you can make toast for yourself, you can make dinner for me."

I stood in the entrance to the living room from the kitchen, looking at him incredulously. Did he really expect a piping hot meal to be waiting for him when he got home? I hadn't asked him to do anything for me, and I was the one who was sick. "Make it yourself," I said. I grabbed my pillow and blanket from the couch and headed to the bedroom.

Suddenly, I felt my hair being pulled from behind. Stan dragged me by my hair back to the kitchen while I screamed in protest and threw me down on the kitchen floor. "I said make my dinner!" he bellowed.

"No! I won't!" I yelled back and picked myself up off the floor. He immediately shoved me back down.

I began to cry and stood up again. "I'm calling the police if you won't leave me alone!" I yelled.

I headed toward the phone, but Stan grabbed the receiver and held it high above me. "Not if you can't reach the phone," he said. I tried to grab it out of his hand and he hit me across the face with it. "Just make me dinner! Why can't you do just one thing I ask of you?"

"Because I said no!" I held my face where he'd hit it with the receiver and headed from the kitchen into the living room.

Stan tackled me from behind and I was down on the ground again. He turned me around and began to pummel my face with his fists. His legs pinned my arms down so I couldn't defend myself. "Stop it!" I cried. "Stop! Please! Okay, I'll make you dinner." He got off of me and I stood up, feeling so weak and faint. But the hatred I felt for him burned red hot. "I'll make you dinner," I said. "But you have to promise not to watch me make it. And you have to promise to eat the whole thing!" Oh, I'd make him dinner all right, a dinner he'd never forget.

I started for the kitchen when Stan tackled me down on the living room floor again. "You are such a lousy bitch!" he yelled. "You're a terrible wife, the worst wife in the world!" He pummeled me with more punches. This time, my arms were free, so I tried to ward off his blows, but they kept coming faster. "You're supposed to make our home a place of refuge from the world, where a man can come home after a bad day and be taken care of. You do none of those things! You've been sitting around on your lazy ass all day doing nothing. I asked one thing from you, and you just won't do it! You'd much rather spend your time with old people, and Mormons, and Negroes, doing things for them rather than doing things for your own husband!"

Stan was sitting on my stomach as he yelled and pounded me. Seeing his angry red face above me, tasting the blood in my mouth, and feeling his weight on my weak stomach was too much. The toast and apple juice that I'd managed to get down came gurgling back up my throat. I began to vomit. Stan jumped up in disgust. It missed him, barely. I turned my face to the side and continued vomiting into the carpet.

He strode angrily into the kitchen and I could hear him opening the knife drawer. This is it, I thought. This is how I'm going to die. I would be stabbed to death while lying in a pool of my own vomit on my living room floor. Fine, let him kill me, I thought. I didn't have the strength to get up and run away or to fight. I'd just lie here while he stabbed me to death. I hoped for a quick end, if nothing else. A knife. How fitting! Stan knew I was terrified of knives. He seemed to be rummaging around in there for quite some time. What was he doing? Finding the perfect weapon for slicing and dicing me to pieces? What a sadist he was!

After a few more minutes, he strode back into the living room, but, instead of wielding a knife, he carried a plate with a sandwich and a side of chips and a can of soda. He turned up the volume on the television and sat down on the couch, propping up his boots on the coffee table while he watched the game and ate his food. I stayed on the floor for a few more minutes. Was it over? Was he finished with me? During the commercial break, he glanced over at me still lying on the floor and said between bites, "Clean that mess up before I lose my appetite."

I slowly lifted my head from the puddle of vomit and picked myself up from the floor. I walked into the kitchen to fill a bucket with water and disinfectant. I grabbed a sponge and some old rags and brought everything back to the living room. I crouched over the mess and cleaned for the next several minutes. Stan glanced over again during the next commercial break while he picked off the crumbs from his plate. "See? You could have avoided all of this just by making me a sandwich."

Looking back on that moment in time is still painful to me, so many years later. I can still taste the blood, smell the vomit and disinfectant, feel the wet strands of hair clinging to my swollen, red, clammy face as I weakly scrubbed away at the carpet beneath me. I can still hear the background noise of the football game, the endless chatter of commentators, the roaring cheers of fans in the stadium.

21

The next morning when I awoke, my nausea was gone, but my face and upper torso looked horrific. Two black eyes had formed, and my entire face was mottled and bruised. I applied layer after layer of make-up and cover-up. That muted most of the discoloration, but my face looked puffy and shiny. I could just blame it on the illness from the day before, I decided. I slipped on a turtleneck to hide the bruises on my neck, chest, and arms. I left my hair down to provide more coverage. I was sore and stiff and would need to take it a bit slower today, but I'd probably have to do that anyway after how sick I'd been.

Stan was apologetic when he saw me after waking up. He again told me about how terrible his day had gone and that he was sorry for taking it out on me. He didn't bring up quitting his job and going back to school, so I was thankful at least for that. I was careful to pack his lunch for him, and he gave me a solid embrace when I handed it to him. I kept my arms down by my sides. I wasn't ready to hug him back yet. He told me how much he loved me and headed off to work. My guess was I'd be getting some sort of flower bouquet delivery from Stan at work today.

"You look terrible! Go back home if you're still sick," Nadine said as soon as she saw me.

"Oh, I feel much better today. I think this is just, you know, the after-effects of being sick."

"After-effects?"

"Yes."

"Like after-shocks from an earthquake?"

I cleared my throat. "Yes. Something like that."

Nadine peered at me closely over her patient chart. She wasn't fooled a bit.

One of the new nurse's aides came over gushing, "Chrissy! You're so lucky. You're always getting flowers from your husband. You just got a delivery from him this morning. That must be because you were sick yesterday."

"Thanks, Olivia. I'll pick it up later."

Nadine was still peering at me over her chart. "Mmm-hmm," she said and started off on her rounds. I was pretty sure I'd be getting another "say the word" lecture from her and Tyrone at lunch that day.

When I went in to help feed Miss Candace her lunch, she was happy to see me again. "Chrissy! You're back! I was so worried about you yesterday."

"It was just a little flu bug, nothing to worry about. Let's see. It's soup today, surprise, surprise. Do you ever get tired of soup?"

"No! It's very tasty soup."

"Well, I'm glad you like it. *I* would get tired of it. How are those hands today?"

"A bit shaky. I don't think I can hold the spoon very well. Are you sure you're okay? You look a little different."

"Oh, I'm fine. Okay, here comes a bite," I said. "Is that too hot? Too cold?"

"Just right." She was still looking closely at my face while I dipped her spoon back into the soup. Suddenly, she placed her withered hand on top of mine. "Leave him," she said fiercely. Her silver blue eyes seemed to plead with me.

My smile faltered and I couldn't stop the tears from welling up. "I can't."

"Yes, you can!"

"No, Miss Candace," I said. "I know you think things are so much easier for women now. And maybe they are in many ways. But I still am trapped in this relationship. I can't just walk out. This is the life that I chose."

How could I explain to her so that she would understand? We'd both been trapped in birdcages during our marriages. Hers had been a cage of concrete. There was no escape from it. Mine was more a cage of thin wires, but it was still a cage. There was no single wire alone that could have held me in my cage, no single thing I could point to and say, "That's the reason I have to stay." It was the combination of all of them together: not wanting to give up on my young marriage, not wanting to be a divorced woman at 21, fear of being alone, fear of what Stan might do to me if I left him, reluctance to lower my standard of living without that second income, reluctance to give up my apartment and go back to renting a room in someone else's house again, a sense of loyalty and obligation to Stan in spite of his abusiveness, a sense that a barren, defective person like me didn't deserve anything better than Stan. Each of these things acted as a wire keeping me trapped in my cage.

I helped Miss Candace finish her lunch and then avoided her, as well as Nadine and Ty, for the rest of the day. I didn't want any more inquiries, advice, or lectures about my home situation. Besides, there was always a sense of relief after a particularly violent episode with Stan. He always seemed genuinely sorry and dedicated to the idea of improving things between us. It meant he would be really nice to me for the next few days. The sex would be tender and passionate instead of methodical and purposeful. It was at those times I thought perhaps that I really loved him, in spite of his faults. I craved those days, even though I had to go through hell first before getting them.

I was glad when I was finally able to clock out, pick up my flowers, and go home for the day.

Sure enough, Stan was on his best behavior. He was in Motivational Speaker Stan mode, full of ideas for how to improve our relationship. He told me I could have "anything I wanted," within reason. I decided not to make him promise never to hurt me again. It had never worked before. There was no reason to hope for anything different this time. It was better to ask for something more specific, something I could real- istically get. I thought about it for a while and then told him what I really wanted.

"I don't want to spend the holidays with your family this year. I want to be with the people I care about, the people who care about me. I want to spend Thanksgiving at Mike's Diner and Christmas at Sunset Care Center this year. If you want to join me, that's fine. I don't really care either way. You can make up whatever excuse you want to tell your family about my absence. Tell them I had to work or something because we're short-handed."

Stan's jaw tensed the way it did when he got angry with me, but he agreed to my request. He said he would join me for Thanksgiving at Mike's Diner and then he would go to his family's house alone on Christmas Day and make up an excuse for me. That would work out perfectly. They could tolerate Stan at Mike's Diner. It was where we'd met. I had a feeling he would not be very welcome at Sunset. Rumors had been going around among the staff and residents about what was happening to me at home. Nadine and Miss Candace hadn't given away my secret, but enough of the outward signs of my abuse had been apparent to the others. That, coupled with the phone calls to check on me and flower deliveries from Stan, was enough for people there to figure out on their own what was happening.

Mr. Carl had offered to teach me hand-to-hand combat moves that he'd learned during his military service. "Chrissy, let me show you how to kill a man using your bare hands. You could drive his nose through his brain like this." He showed me in slow motion how to do it.

"Thank you, Mr. Carl," I said. "But I really don't think I have any need to kill someone with my bare hands."

Miss Stacey introduced me to her son, who was a divorce lawyer. "He's the best in town," she assured me.

"Well, that's wonderful," I said.

"Would you like his card?" she asked.

She looked so hopeful I agreed to take his business card. "All right. I guess one never knows when a divorce lawyer might come in handy."

I appreciated their concern, although it wasn't the kind of attention I enjoyed. I pretended not to notice the sideways glances and looks of pity thrown in my direction while I was at work.

True to Stan's agreement with me, we had Thanksgiving at Mike's Diner. It had been a while since I'd last seen Mike. Once again, being back in the diner made me feel nostalgic for a simpler time in my life, when I could just focus on my job and spend my days off at the library or relaxing in my room at the Stakers' home. I never had to worry about my safety. I didn't have to cook, clean, and do laundry for someone who had nothing but criticism for me.

Mike looked over at me with concern several times, but this time he didn't ask me whether or not I was happy. Being happy was sort of irrelevant, anyway, when I really thought about it. I mean, is anyone ever really that happy? There's always something that's ready to tear down your happiness, whether it's emotionally, mentally, or physically. And as soon as you finally have one thing conquered, there's something else standing in line to take its place. Mike could tell there was something different about me. Perhaps it was some sort of innocence lost. Looking back on that forlorn and desperate 18-year-old girl that he knew back then, it's hard to imagine that there was any innocence left to lose, but I suppose there was a little bit. When Mike asked us about the various things going on in our married life, Stan would step in and talk for us both. I sat there and picked at the turkey and stuffing on my plate. I would have been more like my old self if Stan hadn't been there, speaking for the two of us.

Luckily I had Christmas without him to anticipate. I couldn't wait to get started on my preparations for Christmas at the nursing home. It can be a depressing time of year for the elderly, especially when they've lost so many of their friends and family members. But I was determined that this year would be different. It would be one of their best yet, a holiday to remember. I set to work baking cookies and brownies and making nut clusters. Our freezer was so packed with baked items that there was no room for our regular frozen food. I ignored Stan's complaints about it. "You'll live," was my reply.

I found some cute holiday tins at a discount store and bought enough for all the residents in my building. They would each have a tin filled with goodies plus a handmade ornament. I bought enough supplies at a local craft shop to make little wreaths for each resident. I brushed up on all the Christmas carols that I knew on my guitar and even learned some new ones. I wanted to be able to play any song that was requested. I decorated the hallways and common areas of our building. Luckily, there was a budget for holiday events, so I didn't have to spend my own money on that. I asked several of the residents to share their favorite Christmas memories. Miss Anna would share some Hanukkah traditions and memories with us. I wanted it to be an inclusive event, not something just for those who celebrated Christmas. I arranged to have lots of holiday goodies and snacks at the event. Several people had invited friends and family members to join us, so I arranged for more folding chairs and tables to be brought into the recreation room.

And, despite our rule about not having favorites, I couldn't help myself when I found an old black-and-white portrait of Miss Candace's son Danny dressed in his military uniform. The picture was just tucked between the pages of one of her old books on a shelf in her room. I didn't think she'd notice if it went missing for a few days. She was rarely mobile without assistance anymore, and I didn't think she'd touched those books since she'd first moved in. I took the picture to a frame shop, where I had it matted and framed in a beautiful gold ornate frame. I couldn't wait to see her reaction when she opened it. I would wait until the festivities were over so that the other residents wouldn't see. She could just tell them later that she'd had the picture brought from her home.

Stan complained about all the time I was spending on the nursing home event. If I put this much time and effort into our own home and marriage, he said, we wouldn't have all the problems we had. Out of a sense of guilt, I pulled out a box of

Christmas decorations from the storage closet and haphazardly spread them around our living room. We had a small fake tree that I quickly set up. I threw some colored balls and tinsel on it and topped it with a big aluminum star.

The star reminded me all our futile "baby-making" foil star sticker dates on the calendar. There was still no pregnancy — surprise, surprise. I wondered when Stan would finally declare us infertile, so we could stop this useless exercise. I was tired of having to report my monthly bodily functions to him. I would have been content to dwindle our lovemaking down to once a month, or even once a year, maybe even never again. Sometimes I was tempted not to tell him when I'd started my period. Maybe we could just skip a month or two of the foil stars. But then I decided against it. He'd get his hopes up that I was pregnant. It was better to just get it done and out of the way.

Christmas Day finally arrived and I stuffed the trunk and back seat of my car full of tins, wreath ornaments, sheets of Christmas music, and my guitar. Stan's car was stacked with the gifts that we'd purchased for his family, mainly boxes of candy because we couldn't remember what everyone liked. We'd forgotten to get gifts for each other, but he said my main gift was getting to spend Christmas at the nursing home. That was fine with me. It was the only thing I wanted. We wished each other a Merry Christmas and gave each other a quick peck before we took off in our separate cars. Stan wasn't looking forward to an entire day with his family. I didn't blame him. I pictured his house with people losing their temper all day and various members storming out of the house for one reason or another. I'd much rather be going where I was going.

Our holiday event went off without a hitch. Several of the seniors in Building C had invited friends and family members to come. We gathered in the recreation room, which looked especially festive with all of the decorations I had put up. We even had a big decorated tree. We had a large table filled with goodies and another for drinks.

Several of the residents shared their Christmas memories with us, memories all the way back from their childhood days, as well as Christmas memories from when they were adults and had children of their own. I sat and listened. I didn't share any of my Christmas memories, but I knew which one I'd share if I did. I glanced over at my guitar standing in the corner of the room and pictured it as it had been with the giant red bow. Suddenly my heart ached with sadness. I missed Momma and Daddy and my siblings so much. To prevent myself from being consumed with grief, I jumped up and started gathering all of my tins with the goodies and the wreaths. It was always better to distract myself from my grief.

The seniors loved everything. They were surprised that I had gone to so much effort for them. I pulled out my guitar and sat down on a stool. I played every Christmas song they requested. We had a wonderful time, and I was once again successful at burying the memories and sadness that had tried to plague me again. The cafeteria had made a delicious turkey dinner for the residents, which we were allowed to eat in the recreation room surrounded by the Christmas lights and decorations. We stayed up talking and reminiscing until I noticed a few people beginning to nod off. I hated to call it quits. It had been such a lovely day, and I had no interest in returning home either to a dark, empty apartment or Stan's complaints about how the day had been for him. Neither option was very appealing to me at the moment.

I helped to return the residents to their rooms and to bed. Since Miss Candace didn't have anyone visiting her that day, I wheeled her to her room myself. Once we were inside, I turned and shut her door. "I've been looking forward to this all day," I said. "I couldn't give it to you in front of the other residents, but I have a little gift for you." I pulled out the wrapped box and handed it to her.

"Oh no," Miss Candace said. "I didn't know we were exchanging presents. I didn't have a chance to get anything for you!"

"Don't be silly," I said. "I know you're not able to shop. And truthfully, this is more exciting to me than getting a gift. I can't wait for you to open it."

She reluctantly took the gift and unwrapped it. "Oh my," she said, pulling the framed picture from the box. "It's beautiful! How thoughtful of you. It's my boy exactly as I remember him." She touched the side of his face. "Wasn't he handsome?" she asked.

"Yes, he was. He was just as you described him. Now he can watch over you every day." I'd brought a small hammer and some nails. There was no one on the other side of her room, so I could hang it up that night without waking anyone. The residents were allowed one picture hanging in their room, and Miss Candace already had her Jesus picture up there. She reminded me of that, but I just shrugged my shoulders and kept hammering. "I seem to be breaking a lot of rules lately. I'm not obeying the one-picture rule. If Danny were still alive, he'd tell us it's a stupid rule.'"

Miss Candace laughed. "That's exactly what he'd say." She watched as I hung up the framed picture. "It looks wonderful. Thank you! Now I can just glance up there every time I start missing him. He waits patiently for me to join him someday. Just a little while longer, son," she called out. "It won't be long before I'll be there with you."

"Don't say that," I said. "I don't like to hear it."

"Oh, honey, I'm not afraid of death. Death has already been conquered. Now that I know so much about the afterlife, I can hardly wait to get there. I'm ready whenever God wants to call me home."

I tucked her bedding around her and added another blanket from her drawer. "May I ask you a personal question, Miss Candace?"

"Go right ahead."

"Do you believe your underwear is magical?"

She looked surprised at first and then began to laugh. "Well, no, I don't think it has magical powers. I suppose it does look a little strange to someone who hasn't seen them before. It's just something that I wear daily to help remind me of some of the promises that I made to God when I was in the temple, promises of how I'm going to live my life. So I do believe it is sacred, but not magical. Do you think there's a difference?"

"Yes," I answered. "I just wondered. I'd heard rumors. I'm sorry for prying."

"Don't be. I'm glad you asked. If I actually did have magical underwear, you'd know. I'd show up at your door with a bat the next time your Mr. Awful laid a hand on you."

I couldn't help but laugh imagining that. "I'd like to see that. You wouldn't even have to take a swing. Stan would fall over dead of heart attack at the sight of you. And the last thing he'd hear before he left this life would be me asking about how I might get myself a pair of magical underwear!"

We both giggled like a couple of teenage girls. Then I sighed, "Well, speaking of Mr. Awful, I should probably go home to him now. The nice thing about having him with his family all day is that he'll have plenty of things to complain about without having to focus on *my* shortcomings. People who get on Stan's nerves are never in short supply, I've noticed. Merry Christmas!" I bent over and gave her a little hug.

"It's been a merry one indeed. And thank you again for the framed picture. I just love it. I think of him every day. I carry him around in my heart always."

22

Stan and I stayed home on New Year's Eve and watched Dick Clark announce the ball drop in Times Square. We had decided that this year, 1974, would be the year to really work on improving our marriage. Stan had worked up a poster that he was pretty excited about. It pictured a giant triangle, with a picture of a man on one side and a woman on the other side. At the base of the triangle was a picture of Jesus.

Stan explained that when men and women rely solely on each other in a relationship, it just doesn't work. They fail because there is no solid structure to support them. But when a man and a woman include Jesus in their relationship, it forms a solid triangle that is structurally sound and can withstand all the obstacles facing that relationship, he said.

I sat there while he explained the whole poster to me, nodding my head and acting as if it were the most profound thing I'd ever heard in my life. I didn't really get how that whole concept translated to real life, but if it made sense to Stan, if it made him a nicer person just by imagining being in a giant triangle with Jesus and me, then I was all for it. Jesus could come right on in and join our marriage as far as I was concerned. He could pull up a chair and make Himself at home if it meant my husband would no longer hurt me whenever the urge hit.

So we hung the triangle poster in our bedroom as a reminder, and we toasted to our New Year's Resolution for 1974: to go an entire year without fighting. Yes, it was a lofty goal and it would be hard, but if other couples could do it, then so could we. The first couple of days of our "year of no arguments" went surprisingly well. There were a few slight annoyances, but we managed to overlook them to keep the peace. By day five though, the small annoyances had become major grievances. We had our first blow-up argument of the new year.

We concluded that we had set our goal too high and that's why we'd failed. You can't just go from almost daily bickering to an entire year of marital bliss, even with the best of intentions. We decided to start over again, this time aiming for six months of no arguments. And, if we could make it that far, then maybe we could go ahead and extend the peace through the year's end and beyond. Maybe we'd learn new habits and ways of dealing with each other that would last us the rest of our lives together. When that idea failed, we decided we should start small: three months. We could go one season of the year without a fight. And then, maybe next year, we'd aim for two seasons, then three, and finally the entire year. It could still work. We weren't ready to give up on our resolution.

A few days later, we reduced it once again, to one month. Surely we could last an entire month without a fight. We had our resolve, our determination, our triangle poster. What more could we possibly need? Sure enough, a few days later we reduced it again, to two weeks. A month is actually a pretty long time when you're dealing with someone on a day-to-day basis. Then it was 10 days, and, finally, our resolution, originally intended to last one year, had been reduced to one week. One solid week. Anyone could do that! A pack of wild dogs could go a week without fighting. Surely, with our human ability to reason and talk things out, we could outlast a pack of wild dogs in keeping the peace. (Ironically, it was my comparison of us to wild dogs that instigated the fight that ultimately brought down the one-week resolution.)

By mid-February, we had abandoned our New Year's resolution altogether. I mean, who really keeps a New Year's resolution beyond that point anyway? We'd set ourselves up for failure just by calling it a resolution. At least we'd learned some valuable things in the process. Besides, there was always next year ...

The triangle poster in our room eventually came down, but Stan had other plans for it. He'd decided to put on a Saturday afternoon workshop for the youth group that spring on marital relationships. He excitedly told me about all his plans for the workshop as we drove around running errands one Saturday morning. He wanted to focus on moral dating strategies, what to look for in a future spouse, and strategies for strengthening marital relationships. "I want to help the kids to avoid making mistakes when it comes to dating and choosing a future spouse," he added.

I could have used a workshop like that, I thought sarcastically as we drove along. Stan wanted to ask different couples from church to come and speak at the workshop. He'd ask them to focus on the different areas and what they had found to work best for them. He started listing off the couples that he was thinking of asking to speak, Jean and Thomas Francom, Karen and Charles Summers, Collette and Bill Tankersly. I nodded my head as he listed out the couples that should participate in the workshop. Those were good choices. I didn't know them that well, but they all seemed to have happy marriages and stable families. "And then of course you and I will be speakers. You'll need to make sure you don't have to work that Saturday."

I froze. Was he serious? Did he honestly think we had the type of relationship that should be propped up as a model for others to follow? We were the couple that couldn't even outlast a pack of wild dogs in maintaining the peace! Was he in the same marriage that I was? I cleared my throat and then said carefully, "I think the three couples that you listed are good choices. You should just go with them. I don't think that we should be a featured couple."

"That would look a little strange, Chrissy. I'm the leader of the youth group and I've been married almost two years. If we don't participate, they're going to wonder what's up."

"Well, make up some excuse about why I can't be there. Say I had to work. Face it, the two of us have nothing to say that would benefit those teenagers at all, unless we were the example of what *not* to be."

"What are you talking about, Chrissy? Our relationship isn't that bad. Yes, we've had our fair share of problems, but we're learning how to deal with them. It might be good for the youth group to hear about strategies that married couples use to deal with disagreements and difficulties."

"And just what strategies have we learned, Stan? Please enlighten me. From my perspective, our way of handling our disagreements and difficulties is by yelling and screaming at each other, followed by you slapping me or punching me across the room. But, hey, let's focus on the positive. I do always get flowers and a few days of kindness after you've beaten the tar out of me!"

"Stop exaggerating all the time. You love to paint yourself as the victim. I barely ever hit you. And you're going to speak at the workshop. That's an order."

"Fine then. I'll speak to the youth group about what to look for when dating someone. I'll tell them that if someone spends all their time talking about themselves, and doesn't really care about your life except as it relates to them, that's a red flag. If someone can't even get along with anyone in their own family and dreads every family get-together because they know it will be miserable, that's a red flag. If someone belittles you and tears you down constantly to make himself somehow feel better, that's a red flag. If someone can't ever be happy for your successes because they view them as their own failures, that's a red flag. I'll tell them they shouldn't just walk away from such a person. They should run."

Stan held up a warning hand to me as he used the other hand to steer through traffic. "Chrissy, this is exactly what I'm talking about when I say you never talk to me with respect. You're never supportive of anything I say or do. You make sarcastic comments and roll your eyes like you think I'm the dumbest person in the world. If you treated me with the respect I deserve, as your husband and as your head, I'd never have to lay a hand on you."

"Stan, respect is not something that you can just demand from another person and expect to receive. It's not something you will ever be able to beat into them with your fists! Respect is something that is *earned*. And, you know what? You haven't earned my respect!"

Stan suddenly reached out his arm and I cowered down in my seat to ward off the blows. But, instead of hitting me, he reached his arm past me to try to grab the handle to my door. "I want you out of my car right now! Get out! I can't stand to have you next to me another minute!"

I screamed and tried to pull his arm away from the door. "Stan! Stop it! Stop the car! You'll kill me!"

"I want you out now! Get out!"

"Stop the car!"

"Get out!"

"Stop the car! I will not jump out of a moving vehicle!"

"Out!"

"Pull over and I will get out! Stop the car! Pull over!"

Stan braked so quickly that the car screeched over to the curb. My heart pounded as I reached for the door handle. As soon as the door was ajar, he shoved me out. I toppled onto the sidewalk, twisting my ankle beneath me. He reached over, red-faced and grabbed the passenger door. "You can walk home!" he yelled. Then he slammed the door shut and sped off, leaving me still sprawled on the sidewalk.

A car that had been behind us pulled up to the curb. A woman opened the driver's door and stood up. "Oh my gosh! I just saw what happened. Are you okay?" she asked with concern.

I stood and tried to put some weight on my hurt ankle. I brushed off some of the dirt on my trousers. "Oh, I'm all right," I said. I tried to laugh it off, "Just a little couple's quarrel, that's all. He has a quick temper. I'll be fine. I'm embarrassed you had to see that."

I waited for her to climb back in her car and drive away, but she still stood there. "I could take you to the hospital if you'd like."

"Oh no, that won't be necessary. I just tweaked my ankle a bit when I landed on it. I'll ice it later. I'm sure it's fine."

"I could take you to the police station and you could file a report. I could be a witness to it. You really don't have to take that kind of abuse, you know."

"I'm really quite all right. Thank you for your concern. But, really, it's not necessary."

"Well, okay, then. If I can't convince you ..." She reluctantly got back into her car and drove away.

I tested out my ankle. I didn't think it was broken since I could put weight on it. And it wasn't swelling up. I probably just strained it. I hobbled toward the end of the street. My purse was still in the car with Stan, and I was about two miles from home. I stood there for a while wondering what I should do. Would I be able to walk the two miles on a hurt ankle? I limped down another block and then stopped again. I was starting to wish I'd accepted the lady's offer to give me a ride. My ankle really throbbed. Why was I so stubborn? Why couldn't I accept offers of help from others?

Down the road a distance, I could see a pay phone. I picked up my limping gait a little bit. Did I have money? I checked in my trouser pockets and felt some change in there. What a relief! I had enough for a phone call. But once I made it to the phone booth, I realized that I didn't really know whom to call. I didn't know Nadine's number. I could look it up in the telephone book but she probably wasn't home. Even if she had been home, I wasn't sure that I wanted to let her know what had happened. I just wasn't in the mood for another one of her "say the word" lectures. There was Mike, but I didn't really want to bother him at work. Saturdays were always busy at the diner. The only person I'd feel comfortable calling would be Miss Candace, but she couldn't come to get me.

The only other number I knew was our home number. I was pretty sure Stan wouldn't come to get me. And I wouldn't ask him anyway. After a few minutes of contemplating my options, I put the change back in my pocket. It took me about an hour and a half to limp the two miles home.

Stan was apologetic later on that evening. He held my ankle in his lap and iced it. He got takeout food for us instead of expecting me to cook. "If I would have known you'd twisted your ankle, I wouldn't have let you walk home. You should have said something."

I suppose I should have shouted something during that three-second window before he slammed the door shut and sped off. "Someone drove up right after it happened and offered to give me a ride," I mentioned to him.

"Was it a man or a woman?"

"A woman."

"You should have taken it."

"She said she could take me to the police station to file a report. She witnessed the whole thing."

"She should mind her own damn business," Stan said. "She's probably one of those busybody feminists. There's nothing they love more than accusing men of abuse."

At least this episode got me out of having to participate in the relationship workshop. Stan said he would tell the group that I'd really wanted to make it, but that I had to work that day. Then he said he had written something from me that he would read to the youth group about being a wife in a Godly marital relationship. He seemed pretty proud of it and wanted me to read it, but I declined. "I've never really enjoyed fairy tales," I told him.

It turned out I didn't have to work that Saturday when Stan had his workshop. But it was such a warm, beautiful spring day that I decided to go over to the care center anyway. All the trees seemed to have blossomed overnight. I thought it would be nice for Miss Candace to get outside and see all the blossoming trees. She was happy to see me, and I helped her into her wheelchair. As we walked around she'd exclaim, "Isn't that just lovely!" over every blossoming tree or bush we passed. We stopped at one of the benches. I sat down and admired the grounds around us.

"I loved these grounds immediately," I said. "It was one of the reasons I decided to accept my position here."

"Chrissy," Miss Candace spoke, "tell me what your dream is. Surely you don't want to be a nurse's aide for the rest of your life."

"I love my job!" I said defensively.

"Oh, I know. And we certainly love having you here. I'd be so lonely if you left. But you're such a bright, capable person. Is this really what you want to do forever?

"I don't know," I shrugged. "I don't have a lot of options really. This is a steady job with good benefits. The pay isn't that great, but at least it's consistent. And I'm a pretty frugal person. I don't need a lot of things."

"If you had unlimited resources and time, what would you want to do?"

"Well," I thought for a moment. "I used to think I was going to be a world-famous musician." We both chuckled. "That didn't work out so well for me. Gosh," I stared off into the trees in the distance, "I haven't really thought about it much. I did always love going to school. I was actually a pretty good student."

"I can believe that," Miss Candace nodded her head.

"So, I guess if I had the opportunity and means, I'd love to go to college."

"What would you study?"

"You know, I kind of had a difficult time in my youth. Some bad things happened to me. But I really felt like my teachers in school were my lifeline to the world. They taught me everything. They made me love learning. And I was so shy back then, they hardly even noticed me. They had no idea how important they were to my life. So I guess if I could be anything, I would want to be a high school teacher. It doesn't sound that

206

lofty a dream. They don't make a lot of money, but they make a difference in so many lives. I'd want to be somebody who makes a difference."

"What would you teach?" she asked.

"English," I said. "If you can instill a love of reading and good communication skills in students, that provides a solid foundation for anything else they might want to pursue. I love every subject, but English has always made it to the top of my list."

"Don't let go of that dream. There's always hope. I think that's what ultimately keeps us humans going, even during the worst of times. If we can cling to hope for something different, something better in the future, it keeps us from drowning in despair."

Suddenly, part of the words of an old poem that I'd memorized in high school flashed through my mind. "'Hope is the thing with feathers. That perches in the soul, And sings the tune without the words, And never stops at all.' Emily Dickinson wrote that. It's just part of the poem, but I always liked it."

"That's beautiful," said Miss Candace. Her silver-blue eyes shone in the sunlight. "That's exactly what hope is like. Something with feathers that rests within each of us, always ready to soar. I need to write that down so I can share it in church."

"Miss Candace, may I ask you why you decided to be a Mormon?"

"Well," she sighed. "You know that my son Danny died in his mid-30s." I nodded. "It was 1955. It broke my heart. I felt like I had nothing left to live for. I wanted to die. I contemplated lots of different ways to take my own life, but I just couldn't come up with anything that was painless and guaranteed to do the job. Mr. Awful became ill shortly after that. I figured I'd lasted this long taking care of him, I might as well see it through to the end. There was really no one else who could do it. I shouldn't have felt any responsibility for him after the way he'd treated me all of our married life, but I still felt some strange sense of obligation anyway. He had always kept a roof over our heads and food on the table. Maybe I did owe him something. So I stayed. I took care of him. He lived for several more years after Danny died."

I stood from the bench and began wheeling her along the path again. Miss Candace continued, "He began to suffer from dementia in those final years. It was difficult to take care of him. I was getting old too. I couldn't lift him. But I'd help him to the bathroom. I'd give him sponge baths. I kept him clean and fed. I thought he might not ever die. He was becoming such a burden to me."

I couldn't imagine Miss Candace having to do all the things I did now for the residents. It was very physically taxing. Some days I just felt so exhausted, and I was in my early 20's! Miss Candace was in her early 70's by the time her husband finally passed away. It must have been so difficult for her. I wheeled her back inside Building C, and we headed down the hall toward her bedroom.

"Do you want to know the nicest thing he ever said to me? It was just before he died, when his mind was nearly gone from the dementia. He looked at me in confusion one day when I walked in and he asked, 'Where's that nice lady who takes care of me?' Can you believe that? He said I was nice! I was very taken aback by that. Could it be that, somewhere in the back of his mind, he saw something good in me? But," she shook her head, "it's pathetic that an old woman like me would even cling to those words trying to find some comfort in them. It was much too little, much too late. I watched him struggle to take his last breath and I felt no sorrow for him, only relief that he was finally gone, out of my life forever.

"But in the days that followed his funeral, I sank back into the deep depression that I'd been in after Danny's death. There was really no reason for me to be around, no one needed me anymore. I had nothing. I had nobody. And I didn't want to become a burden to someone else the way Mr. Awful had been to me those final years. I began to contemplate ending it all again. This time I would be brave enough to do it, I knew that. But first I decided to sort through all of our stuff and get rid of things. I wanted to have everything in order, so that it wouldn't be left for someone else to go through. I went through all of our things and either donated them to charity or tossed them.

"As I went through all of my belongings and mementoes, I seemed to be having an ongoing conversation with God. Everything was sad to me, everything just added to my depression. My life had been a failure, I told God. None of my dreams had come true. And now my life was over and I really had nothing to show for it. I had always wanted a happy family, a good marriage, a good life, lots of children. I wanted grandchildren laughing and playing nearby. The only thing God had ever allowed me to have, my brilliant boy, was taken from me far too early. And, in some ways, I felt resentful of God. How could He have let my life be such a waste?

"And then one day, as I was going through some of my old books, I came across a quote that somehow just struck me: 'It's never too late to be what you might have been.' That's a quote by George Eliot." I nodded my head. George Eliot was the pen name for Mary Anne Evans, an English novelist in the 1800's. She'd used a male-sounding name because only men were typically published back then.

Miss Candace continued, "Anyway, that quote just stayed with me. I couldn't get it out of my mind. I felt like it was God trying to tell me something. It's never too late to be what you might have been? Was that possible? But I was an old woman, I argued in my mind. I'd lived my life. I'd failed. It *was* too late for all of my dreams to come true. I was 72 years old. That quote didn't apply to me. But for some reason, it gave me just a little bit of hope. It made 'that thing with feathers' inside my soul start to stir again. And I started re-thinking my plan to end my life. Was it possible that God still might have plans for an old woman like me?

"That was the day the Mormon missionaries showed up at my door. They taught me about God's plan for me. They told me about how I could be with my son again. Mormons believe in eternal families and eternal progression. You can continue to learn, grow, and develop in the afterlife. And the family bonds you form in this life can continue in the life beyond through ordinances that are performed in the temple. And you can be married in the afterlife. You can have more children. It just continues on and on through eternity. I'll get a second chance, Chrissy, after I die. My dreams still have a chance to come true. When the missionaries taught me all of this, I felt like it was God's way of telling me how that quote still applies to me."

"What about Mr. Awful? You won't be married to him anymore, right? Will he go to hell?" I asked.

"Well, Mormons really don't believe in hell. It's more like different kingdoms of glory. He'll be in a place far, far away from me. That's all I care about."

"I still think he should go to hell though."

"Well," she said, "he won't be my concern anymore. I'll get a new husband, and he'll be the kind of husband I always wanted."

"A 'Mr. Wonderful'?" I asked, smiling.

"Yes, that's exactly right. I'll get a Mr. Wonderful of my own." Her silver-blue eyes shined brightly with hope. "My son will join us. And we'll have lots more children besides. Chrissy, wheel me over to my bookcase. I want to show you something."

I wheeled her over and she pulled out an old photo album. She flipped through a few pages and then lifted one of the photos out from behind the plastic page cover. She handed it to me. It was an old black-and-white photo. A young woman in the photo smiled back at me. She had soft curls around her head and wore a white feminine-looking button-up blouse with a lace collar. "Who do you think that is?" Miss Candace asked me.

I studied it closely for a moment. There was no mistaking those eyes and that smile. "It's you!" I said. "Miss Candace, you were such a beautiful young woman."

"Yes, that was me," she said proudly. "I had soft, curly hair and delicate features. My teeth were naturally straight and white. People used to tell me I could be an actress. I don't mean to brag, but they did say that. The years of beatings and unkindness, they aged me quite a bit." She touched the wrinkles on the side of her face.

"I still recognized your eyes and smile though. I still knew it was you."

"Chrissy, the woman in that picture is who I still *am* on the inside. I look in the mirror now and I see an old woman looking back at me. I don't know who that woman is. This is who I am," she pointed at the woman in the picture. I handed it back to her and she studied it for a moment before shakily placing it back inside its plastic cover. "It's who I'll be again someday. In the afterlife, we won't be old, wrinkled people who have to be wheeled around in chairs. We'll look and feel like we did back in the prime of our lives. Everything will be restored just as it should be. And we'll be immortal then. We won't ever die again. That's why I joined the Mormon Church, because it had all the answers I was looking for. That was about 12 years ago, and I haven't looked back. I'm happy again because I know what's in store for me. It really isn't too late for me to be what I might have been after all. It's never too late."

She handed the photo album back so I could return it to the bookshelf. I helped her with her dinner and then tucked her into bed for the night. She had me turn on the television to one of the comedy shows she liked to watch. I gave her a quick hug and a kiss on the forehead and headed out the door, as canned laughter on low volume emanated from the television. She'd typically lie there propped up on her pillows laughing through the first 15 minutes, and she was usually asleep with her head tilted to one side by the time the show ended.

I had dinner waiting for Stan when he came home from the relationship workshop that evening. He was on a high since the day had gone really well. He said the featured couples had all done an excellent job and the kids seemed enthusiastic about everything. We ate quickly while he talked, and then I cleared the table and began doing the dishes at the kitchen sink while Stan gave me a play-by-play account of the entire workshop from the kitchen table. "I really wish you could have gone, Chrissy," he said. "This workshop would have been very beneficial for you."

I rolled my eyes as I rinsed off the suds. Of course the workshop would have benefited *me*, since I was the one who needed all the pointers. Stan never saw how any of the guidance might apply to him as well. It was always other people who needed to improve their lives, not him. I wasn't sure why it was so grating to hear Stan pontificate on the fundamentals of a Godly marital relationship to me. Hadn't I just spent the afternoon listening to Miss Candace talk about her religious beliefs? That hadn't bothered me a bit. In fact, I thought it was fascinating. And it wasn't even that I found Miss Candace's religious beliefs to be particularly believable. I mean, it was a nice storyline, but I felt like that was all it was. Who really knows what comes after this life anyway? It's all just speculation.

I think what really bugged me about listening to Stan's religious talk versus Miss Candace's was the level of hypocrisy that I saw behind his. Miss Candace and Stan both fervently believed in the fundamentals of their religions. But Miss Candace lived her life in a way that was congruent with her belief system. That was something I could respect even if I didn't believe in the same theological narrative. Stan, on the other hand, was almost the exact opposite of what he claimed to be. He could preach to those kids all day long about Christian love, charity, kindness, unselfish behavior, and Godly relationships. Yet, he was judgmental, harsh, selfish, unkind, even brutal behind closed doors. Even worse, he didn't have a clue about how hypocritical his own behavior was. In his mind, he *was* the person he claimed to be. He even lied to himself about how much he brutalized me. He had never admitted to giving me anything more than a couple of well-deserved slaps. And if a person can't even admit to himself that he has a problem, there's no way he's ever going to be able to address that problem or try to remedy it.

I finished drying the last dish while Stan wrapped up his summary of the workshop. Then he gave me copies of all the handouts that they'd given to the attendees. "I would admonish you to study these worksheets, Chrissy, and make more of an effort to be the kind of wife that a Godly marriage requires."

I took the papers from him. "Thanks, Stan, I'll do that."

He left the kitchen to go turn on the television in the living room while I quietly stuffed the papers into the garbage.

23

I turned 22 years old in May. The days continued to grow longer and warmer as summer approached. People in North Carolina try to take advantage of these long, warm days before the humidity of mid-summer rolls in to stay. Wherever you went this time of year, you could usually see people out walking or working in their yards. Kids rode their bikes everywhere and filled the playgrounds. They become anxious for school to let out for the summer.

I noticed that I was becoming increasingly tired, listless, and depressed through the end of May and into June. I wasn't exactly sure why until I glanced at the calendar at work one day and realized what it was. It was the four-year anniversary of Momma's death and my family being scattered everywhere. Had that been only four years ago? In some ways it seemed like a lifetime ago. I realized that I could hardly remember the individual faces of Momma and my siblings. I could hardly remember what their voices sounded like. In pushing the miseries of my past so far out of my conscious mind, would I eventually forget them completely, as if they'd never existed at all?

The weight of my sadness, remorse, and guilt grew heavier throughout the day. I felt as if I hardly had the strength to do all the lifting my job required. I wore my fake plastic smile and made cheery remarks all day long, but on the inside I was screaming and crying and cursing out the entire world. *Just get through this day, Chrissy,* I repeated to myself over and over. *Just get through.* Would this be the mantra for my entire life? Just barely getting through the day? I finally clocked out and practically ran to my car. I just needed to get home and be alone with my thoughts for a while.

Luckily Stan wasn't home when I got there. I dropped my bag on the floor and went over to sit on the couch, holding my knees close to my chest. I hadn't allowed myself to think of my siblings for so long. But now I just sat there and tried to remember little details about them. I tried to remember the exact shade of their hair color, the exact location of each little freckle or mole, the way each one of them laughed or talked excitedly about something they were doing at school. I just let the pain wash over me; wave after wave came crashing over me. I was tempted to pull down the little box from the top of my closet where I'd kept the pictures, letters, cards, and mementoes from our old house. It was right next to my Chrissy rock. But I decided against pulling all of that stuff down. It was enough to know they were there. I couldn't look at them.

I wondered where each of them was now. Had they pushed me out of their minds the way I'd pushed them out of mine? Brad would be 20 years old now. Was he in prison? Was he safe? Jenny would be 18, maybe just graduating from high school. What was she planning to do? Did she have more options than I'd had? Was she happy? Ronnie would be 15. I'll bet he was tall and that his voice had changed. I wondered what he looked like. Did he go by "Ron" now? Had someone adopted him? I'd always hoped the three youngest would have been adopted together in the same family. It was a lot to ask, but maybe some family out there would have been able to take on three sweet children who had lost everything. Darlene would be 14, a teenager now. What did she look like? Trisha, my little baby, would be 12. Were they happy? Did they have enough to eat? Did they have nice families? Did they have friends? I had so many questions and no clue how to get the answers. Tomorrow I would push them out of my mind again. But tonight I thought of them and missed them dearly.

I heard Stan's boots coming up the front stairs to our apartment. I tried to regain my composure as he unlocked the door. "What's the matter with you?" he asked as he strode past me to the bedroom. "You're just going to sit there staring off into space all night like an idiot?"

"No," I answered. "I'm about to make dinner. I just had a long, hard day, that's all."

"Well, it couldn't have been worse than my day," he said as he changed into a new shirt. "I nearly quit today. I don't know how much more of that job I can take."

I just sat there, still clutching my knees and staring off into the distance.

"Oh, guess what?" Stan said, "The Humphries had their baby today. It's a boy."

"That's great. That's wonderful news." I was trying to remember who exactly the Humphries were. It had been so long since I'd been to church. All those married couples having babies had started to blur into one for me. I couldn't distinguish them from each other anymore.

"I told them I would stop by the hospital to visit this evening. Why don't you come with me? Maybe it will spark some desire in you to have a baby."

"I'm too tired," I said. "Give them my best."

"Are you sure? I think it would be good for you to see the baby. Maybe you could hold it for a while. You haven't seemed all that enthusiastic about starting a family. I thought all women wanted to have babies. What's wrong with you?"

I just shrugged my shoulders. "I guess some have a greater desire than others."

Stan stopped in front of me in the living room. "What is that supposed to mean? You don't have a great desire to have a baby?"

"It's not that I don't want one. I do. I just don't place all of my hopes and dreams on being a mother. I like to think that there's more to me than just being a baby factory."

"There's no greater calling for a woman than being a mother, Chrissy. Everything else is just secondary to that. You could be a success at everything else in life, but if you're a bad mother, or not a mother at all, you'd still be a failure."

"Gee, I'd better get busy then, coaxing my womb to grow a baby. I wouldn't want my life to be a total failure. I'd hate to be a waste of precious space on this planet."

216

Stan grabbed his wallet and keys. "I'm going to go spend some time with people who are positive and enjoyable to be around. Don't sit around here feeling sorry for yourself all night. Do something useful."

He slammed the front door. I still sat on the couch clutching my knees to my chest. Four years. What had I really done with my life? Maybe Stan was right and I really *was* a failure, a feeble-minded waste of space on this planet. At that moment, I felt as if I were staring off into the great abyss that was my life, just as Momma had done so many years ago after Daddy's death. She didn't know what to do. And I didn't know either. Is this how my life would always be? Would I constantly be running from and trying to bury my past? Would I always have to distract myself from the misery of my present and lie to myself about my future? Would I always be this unhappy? At that moment I wanted to dissolve into tears, but I was too tired for the effort it would take to have a good cry.

After several minutes, I decided I'd better get up off the couch to start dinner. Stan would have a fit if he came home and still found me there doing nothing. Maybe I could tell him that I was sitting there pining away for a child. He'd be okay with that excuse if he thought I was sincere, but Stan never thought I was sincere. And truthfully, he was right. I never said anything to him anymore that wasn't laced with sarcasm or tinged with exasperation. It hadn't always been that way. At one time, I thought I loved him, or at least the idea of him. I could have been a good wife to someone who was a little bit nicer and less hypocritical than Stan. We'd been married almost two years and it felt like an eternity. Miss Candace had talked about the Mormon marriages that last forever — you stayed married after death and lived together for eternity. I couldn't imagine anything worse. At least I knew that Stan and I could finally part at death. I could be rid of him then. Being married to him forever would definitely be worse than hell.

I pulled items out of the cupboards and fridge and started dinner, still thinking my dark thoughts. I set out two plates and waited for a few minutes for Stan. Then I decided to eat my dinner while it was still warm. I could reheat Stan's later. After finishing dinner, I went back into the living room and turned on the television. The canned laughter and stupid comedy shows would distract me from my miserable thoughts. This day was almost over, and I told myself I would feel better tomorrow. During one of the commercial breaks I went and grabbed a bag of chips to snack on while I watched TV. I heard Stan's boots on the steps and then his key in the lock of the front door.

"Hi," I said. "There's dinner on the table. I can heat it up for you if it's cold."

"I grabbed a burger on my way home."

"Oh." That was all right. I'd just save the rest of it for leftovers.

Stan sat down, watching me for a minute. I kept my eyes focused on the television and crunched away on my potato chips. "Chrissy, you really should have come with me tonight. I think you really would have enjoyed seeing that baby."

I continued to stare at the TV and crunch my chips. I did not want to pursue this subject any further. Hopefully he would get the hint. "They looked so happy," Stan continued. "I watched them and I thought maybe that's what's missing from our marriage. Maybe we just need a baby."

I didn't respond.

Stan continued, "You know, I was thinking about something while I was driving home."

"Oh?" Uh, oh.

"Yeah, I was thinking, we've been married almost two years, right?"

I nodded, still watching the TV.

"In that two years' time, Luke and Stella met each other, started dating, got engaged, got married and had a baby. Can you believe that? They did all that just during the time that we've been married."

He looked at me expectantly. Finally, I said, "Well, whoop-de-do for Luke and Stella Humphries. I'm not sure how you want me to respond to that. It sounds a lot like our relationship, minus the honeymoon baby. Some people rush through these things. It works out fine for some and it's a complete disaster for others."

"I just don't understand why you don't want to have a baby."

"Stan, can we talk about something remotely interesting? Otherwise, I'd rather just sit and watch this show."

We sat in silence watching the show for a few minutes. Suddenly Stan stood up and turned off the television. He turned to me and asked, "Is there something you'd like to tell me?"

The little bird of panic fluttered within me briefly, but I regained my composure. He couldn't possibly know about me. I hadn't told a soul. And he wasn't smart enough to figure it out.

"You're using something, aren't you? You're using something to prevent a pregnancy because you don't *want* to get pregnant!"

I breathed a little sigh of relief. He didn't know. "Don't be ridiculous, Stan. I haven't used anything, ever, to prevent a pregnancy."

Stan sat back down. "Then why haven't you gotten pregnant after all this time trying?"

"I don't know. It's not an exact science. There are no guarantees of when, or even if, it will happen."

Stan sat in silence for a minute, watching me accusingly. Then he jumped up and walked right past me to the hallway and into our bedroom. I didn't like the look he had on his face. He didn't believe me. I followed him into the bedroom and found him rummaging through my dresser drawers. He tossed my personal belongings onto the floor: nightgowns, bras, panties. It felt like such an invasion of my privacy to see them scattered all over the floor like that.

"What are you doing?" I hissed. "You're messing up my things! Get out of my things!"

"Where is it, Chrissy?" he yelled. "Where is the birth control you're using? I won't stop until I find it. I know you're lying to me!"

"I'm not using anything! I promise!" I started gathering up all the things he'd tossed aside. I had all my drawers organized a certain way, and I was furious that he'd just toss everything out like that. He'd opened up more of my drawers and was rummaging and tossing while I tried to tuck my things back into the first drawer. When he saw me with my hands in the drawer, he reached over and slammed the drawer closed on my fingers. "Owww!" I screamed. On impulse, my stinging hand reached out and struck him across the face.

We were both dumbstruck by that move for a moment. My hands flew up to cover my open mouth, "I'm sorry!" I whispered.

His face reddened in anger and he lunged at me, throwing me to the floor and pounding me with his fists. I screamed and tried to protect my head with my arms. The blows seemed to be coming from every direction. "Stop, Stan! Stop!" I screamed.

Finally, he got off of me and I sat up. "You can make this easier on yourself by telling me where you keep your birth control," he said.

"I don't have any. I swear it!" My nose was bleeding profusely and I was crying. I reached for several tissues and tried to stop the bleeding.

"I don't believe you," Stan said. He headed for the bathroom and started rummaging through all the drawers and cabinets in there.

"You can search all you want," I said. "You won't find anything."

"Well, then, I'll just have to keep searching, won't I?" he answered. "Either that, or you'll come clean with me about what you're using."

I held the tissues to my nose and tilted my head back. Stan came walking back to the bedroom after a few minutes.

This time he headed for the closet. He tossed aside all my shoes on the lower shelves, rummaged through my clothes that were hanging up, and then started throwing down all the items that were stored on the top shelf. I watched in horror as my rock tumbled to the floor. He opened the box of keepsakes and mementoes that I hadn't opened since I tucked them safely in there. He dumped everything on the floor. "Why do you keep all this crap?" I stared down at the pictures from my past, the homemade cards and letters, the misspelled scrawling of little children. I shakily reached down to pick them up. Stan's boot came down on top of them. "Leave them! We're not packrats. I'm throwing all of this stuff away."

My rage swelled and I lunged for Stan, hurling my fists at him to hurt him as much as I could. "How dare you! How dare you! You have no right!"

"I have every right!"

I punched, scratched, kicked, and fought him as hard as I could. We tumbled to the floor and rolled around. I tried not to let him get on top of me, but he was too powerful. He pinned me down and then slammed his fist into me wherever he could find a place to punch: my face, chest, arms. I tried to ward off his fists, but they came faster than I could fight them off. My nose was bleeding back into my throat, and I began coughing, sputtering, crying, "Stop, Stan, please! Stop!"

"Then tell me!"

"You've gone through everything! There's nothing! Please, just stop!" I sobbed.

He pushed himself off of me and stood up, panting. "Get some tissues. You're a mess!" he said. He watched as I picked myself up and grabbed the box of tissues for my nose. My whole head pounded and my lip was split open. He continued, "Then there must be something really wrong with you then. If you're not using birth control, then there must be something wrong with your body to keep you from getting pregnant. I know it's not me, so it has to be you. You can't even do the one thing that women are good for. You're barren."

I stopped breathing for a second as I held the tissues to my nose and mouth. I couldn't believe it. In all of Stan's crazy charges and wild accusations, he'd managed to stumble right onto the truth! And just then, the whole thing struck me as being wildly, insanely funny. I began to laugh.

"What's so funny, huh?" Stan strode over and struck me across the face, but I continued to laugh right in his face. "I want to know what is so damn funny." He struck me again and I laughed again. His face had reddened. His anger was incredible. I must have looked like a raging lunatic, with my bloodied face and my insane laughing, but I just couldn't stop. He struck me a third time. "Tell me!" he shouted.

"You are!" I hissed out at him. "You are so damn funny because you're so stupid!"

"What?" He struck me again.

"I said you're *so stupid!* Stan, you are so stupid, that you've come full circle, all the way back around to actually being a little bit smart."

He stood there with his clenched fists, confused.

I held out my arms and laughed again, "You're on to me, Stan! The jig is up! You've stumbled onto my terrible secret. Now you know. I can't have children! I will *never* be a parent, not now, not ever! How do I know? Because I was sterilized as a young teenager, and I've known about it the *whole* time," I sneered, "through every gold-starred, baby-making attempt, I've known! I was sterilized by a state order. Do you want to know why? Because I was poor and promiscuous! That's right, Stan. I come from trash. I *am* trash! And the state decided that trashy girls like me shouldn't be having babies, so they had me fixed. Oh, and I ran away at 13 and worked as a teenaged prostitute too. Basically, I'm your dream wife!" I laughed again.

It took a moment for all of this to register. Then I could see the red rage build in Stan's face as he came at me. "You lied to me, you awful bitch! I never would have married you! I never would have married you if I'd known!"

"Oh, well now I'm *really* regretting not telling you!" I shouted back at him.

His hands clamped onto my upper arms and he shook me until my head rattled. Then they clamped around my neck and he began to choke me. I couldn't get air, and from the look on his face I knew he meant to kill me. I clawed at his hands around my neck and began to panic. I stomped my feet against the floor, hoping that the people down below us would come up to intervene, to save me from being strangled to death. They'd never done anything before, but maybe this time they'd sense the urgency and do something. I started seeing stars and growing weak from lack of air. But, with all the strength I had left, I kneed Stan in the groin. He grunted and doubled over enough to loosen his grip around my neck. I was able to break free and ran into the hallway.

Stan was right on my heels and caught me in the hallway. He grabbed me by the shoulders and slammed my head over and over into the wall. He was going to kill me tonight, but I would not go down without a fight.

I tasted blood in my mouth and spat it into his face. "Did you really think I would ever have a child of yours, even if I could?" I shouted. "Did you think I would bring your child into this world, to be greeted by your clenched fist?"

Stan struck me across the face and then tried to get his hands around my neck again. He was trying to choke the words off, to keep me from talking, but I would say what I had to say to him if it was the last thing I ever did. I pulled on his hands with all my might and yelled out, "Your child would hate you as much as I do! Because he'd see past that church-man veneer to what you really are on the inside: a rabid animal who should be put down!"

Stan flung me full-force into the hallway mirror. It shattered and I fell to the hallway floor, with shattered mirror pieces raining down all around me. This time I knew I would not be getting back up. "A monster," I finished. I remember the next few moments only in flashes: a boot coming at my head, my head turning and my hands flying upward, the instinct to protect my face. There was a sickening thud followed by a popping sound in my ear, then another thud. Then everything went black.

I'm not sure how long I remained passed out, but when I regained consciousness, I was still lying on the hallway floor, surrounded by broken pieces of mirror. I could hear Stan's voice, but it sounded distant and tinny. It echoed, "Chrissy, wake up. Chrissy, can you hear my voice? Chrissy?" His voice had an edge of panic to it. "Chrissy?" I felt his fingers on my carotid, checking for a pulse. "Chrissy?"

I turned my head and opened my eyes. I saw stars. My surroundings seemed to be spinning. There was a loud ringing in my ears. And there was something else too, in that dimly lit hallway. I could barely make it out. "Chrissy, can you focus?"

Yes, there was definitely something else there. I lifted my head slightly and felt something trickling out of my ear. I squinted my eyes to see better. It was the figure of a little girl standing there, maybe about three or four years old. She had long, brown hair and was looking at me with a very distraught expression on her face.

"Chrissy, what are you looking at?" Stan's voice came from off in the distance. "Chrissy?"

I knew who she was. She was my daughter — the ghost of a child who would never exist. She held out her arms to me and said one word, "Mommy." Then she vanished back into the hallway wall.

It's better for her that way, I thought, *better for her never to have existed at all*. I nodded my head and swallowed more blood. Then I rested my head back down on the spinning floor beneath me.

"Chrissy, can you hear me? Can you understand?"
Better for her.
"Chrissy?"
Better for her.

"Chrissy, can you put your arm around my neck? I'm going to carry you into bed and clean you off, all right? Everything's going to be okay."

Better for her.

I felt myself being lifted and carried away from that hallway. "You'll feel better in the morning. Don't worry about all this mess. I'll clean all this up, okay? You're going to be just fine."

Better for her.

You don't bring a child into the world and then let the wolves get it.

24

The sun shone brightly through the window the next morning when I awoke. I slowly turned to the side. Stan was already out of bed and doing something in the kitchen. I lifted the covers and slowly eased my body up. My head pounded. Everything hurt. I was still wearing the clothes I had been wearing last night, but my face had been wiped clean of blood. Everything that had been tossed around in our bedroom had been put back in place. I eased my legs over the edge of the bed and headed for the bathroom. I used the toilet and then turned on the water for the shower to let it warm up. I began to undress and glanced in the mirror. I was a mess. I had two black eyes and a split lip. My face was mottled with discoloration. There were welts across my neck and chest and all over my upper arms. My lower arms were scratched and discolored as well. Only the lower half of my body looked normal.

Stan appeared in the doorway. "How do you feel?"

"About as good as I look."

"I was a little worried about you last night. I kept checking to make sure you were still breathing. I was afraid you might have a concussion or something."

I continued undressing.

"Maybe you should take the day off today and rest."

"Can't. I have an important staff meeting today."

Stan was quiet for a moment. Then he said, "I cleaned up everything from last night. I have breakfast waiting for you in the kitchen."

"I'm not hungry."

"I also packed my own lunch."

"How thoughtful of you." I stepped into the shower and pulled the curtain closed.

Stan continued talking while I showered. "I'm sorry that I got a little rough with you last night. I overreacted. But you were in the wrong too, Chrissy. You've been very dishonest with me for a very long time. I think we can work through this though. We could look into adoption or something like that. I still think having a baby would be very beneficial for us."

He waited for some sort of response from me, but I remained silent in the shower.

"I've also been thinking about ways we can improve our relationship. I think one of the reasons we failed on our New Year's resolution is that we focused on the negative rather than the positive. We focused on *not* doing something rather than *doing* something. I think we should sit down tonight after work and come up with five active goals that we'll both agree to do in our marriage. I think the first goal should be 'always be completely honest with each other.' I think you've learned your lesson from last night about what happens when we are dishonest or deceitful with one another. Marriage should be based on complete openness and honesty."

I closed my eyes, leaned my head back, and just let the warm water wash over my body.

"Secondly, I think we should always start and end each day with a compliment for each other, such as 'That was a very nice meal you made Chrissy,' or 'You look very nice today Chrissy,' or 'Thank you, Stan, for how hard you work each day.'"

Shut up! Shut up! Why won't you just shut the hell up! I screamed on the inside.

"Anyway, we can come up with the other three positive goals tonight, but I think that's a good start."

I finished washing and rinsing my hair. He obviously wasn't going to leave, so I wrapped a towel around my hair and another around my body and stepped out of the shower. "You sure do bruise easily," he commented.

"Is that my compliment for this morning?"

"No. We haven't started that yet."

He stood there while I brushed my teeth. Then he followed me into the bedroom. He went to the closet and pulled out a pink, long-sleeved turtleneck. "You should probably wear this today," he said. I put on my bra and panties and pulled the turtleneck over my head, then slipped on some trousers. I sat down in front of the mirror and detangled my hair, then started applying my layers and layers of make-up and cover-up. Stan stood there watching anxiously, then began to visibly relax as he watched the black eyes disappear, the mottled bruising fade away. I dabbed, blotted, and blended away nearly all the signs of last night's attack. "That's looking better," he said. "You should probably wear your hair down today too."

I pawed at my ear with annoyance. "I can hardly hear out of this ear."

"Maybe you should have a doctor look at it. You could say you got hit with a softball during a game."

Was he just going to stand there and watch me the whole time? I wanted him to go. He pointed out a place on my face that could use more cover-up.

"Stan, I really don't need any of your help with this. I'm the expert at cover-ups. Remember? You stick to your area of expertise, and I'll stick to mine."

"Okay," he said.

He reached over to give me a kiss good-bye and I shrank away from him. "Don't touch. Everything hurts."

"All right. I said I was sorry. We'll talk some more tonight. You still have some explaining to do about all the lies and deceit, but I'm confident we can work it out together. I'm looking forward to developing our five-goal relationship plan."

He left the room and I heard him grab his keys. He opened the front door and called out, "You know how much I love you, right?"

"Yep."

The door clicked closed behind him. I heard his boots going down the front steps and his car starting in the parking lot. I was sure I was due for a lovely bouquet of fresh flowers today at work, together with a card telling me how much he loves me, and maybe a 10-point list of how I can be a better wife to avoid this kind of punishment in the future.

I stared into the mirror at my shiny, painted face. It was a hot June day, and I was going to show up at work looking like a clown who thought it was the middle of winter. I was so tired of this … so very, very tired. I was tired of flower bouquets and promises that things would improve. I was tired of wearing winter clothes on summer days and constantly running to the bathroom to touch up my melting make-up. I was tired of sideways glances and looks of pity from the residents and staff, tired of pleas from Miss Candace and "say the word" lectures from Nadine, tired of faking a smile and a cheery voice when I really wanted to scream and cry and pound my fists on the walls and break all the windows.

I wondered what would happen if I went into the bathroom and took every pill in the medicine cabinet. This must have been how Momma felt that last night as she rocked back and forth, back and forth, in that rocking chair. Just tired, so very, very tired and lacking the strength to go on anymore.

I thought of that little girl who had appeared in the hallway last night. Was that just a delusion? Had I imagined her? She'd seemed so real. I wondered what kind of a mother I might have been to her. Would I be the kind of mother who cowered in a corner while her husband beat her? Or, even worse, would I be the kind who stood by helplessly while he did the same thing to her child? Maybe I couldn't be brave for myself, but could I be brave for her? I stared into the mirror for a few moments.

Then I reached over and grabbed my cold cream and began to tissue off the make-up around my eyes, revealing the dark, mottled skin beneath. I sponged off all the makeup on my cheeks, forehead, nose, and chin, revealing the bruising, red, swollen skin it had been hiding. I stood and went to the closet, pulling off my turtleneck. It was much too hot a day for a shirt like that. I pulled on a tank top, revealing the bruises and scratches going down my arms, the welts on my upper arms, chest and upper back, the finger-grip marks around my neck. There. That felt much better. I pulled my hair back into a ponytail. This was much more summer-appropriate attire. I wiped off the lipstick and dabbed my split lips with Chapstick. I took a quick glance in the mirror. Perfect. Then I grabbed my purse and keys and headed off to work.

When I arrived at Sunset, I stood outside Building C for a moment. Part of me wanted to run and hide, to pull all my cover-ups back on and pretend like nothing had ever happened. *I am brave*, I told myself. *I am calm and deliberate.* I took a deep breath and walked through the front doors. The first person I saw was Miss Cummings, giving some instructions to a couple of staff members. Her eyes widened and she gasped when she saw me. The others looked at me in horror. "Chrissy! What in the world happened to you? You look like you've been hit by a truck!"

"I need to speak to Nadine," I said. "Have you seen her?"

"She's doing her rounds."

I headed down the hallway, feeling the stares and hearing the low murmurs of concern. I heard Nadine's voice coming from one of the patient's rooms. The door was slightly ajar so I knocked softly on it to interrupt. Nadine glanced up at me and immediately cried out in horror. She held her chart in one hand and the other flew up to cover her mouth. "Chrissy!" she gasped.

"Nadine, may I speak with you in private?" I asked.

She followed me out to the hallway and we walked in silence to the medicine room, went inside, and closed the door. Nadine stood in front of me. Her eyes filled with tears and she held the chart up near her face, as if to partially shield me from her view. For once in Nadine's life, she had been struck totally speechless.

"Nadine, I …" I fumbled for a moment. *I am brave. I am calm and deliberate.* "Nadine, I need to know … what word is it that you want me to say?"

She lowered her chart slowly and began to smile through her tears. "You just said it," she said softly.

Even though Nadine had urged me to leave Stan since I first started dating him, I had no idea how she had been planning for this day. She had already figured out exactly how to proceed. Miss Stacey's son, the divorce lawyer, had agreed to represent me for free. Since there was abuse involved, he could probably expedite the divorce proceedings, especially if Stan didn't contest it. I could be a divorced woman in just a few months' time and I could go back to my maiden name. I would get a restraining order against Stan so that he couldn't come near me. I would live with Nadine and Ty in their spare bedroom, and I could not go anywhere by myself for the next little while, at least until they knew I was safe.

"He can't know that I'm leaving," I said. "He'll never let me go. He thinks of me as his personal property, so he won't handle this well."

"That's why you are going to move out with no warning. He'll come home to find you gone, and the only communication he'll have with you after that will be through your lawyer. This is for real, Chrissy. If we're going to do this, it's going to be all the way. None of this 'I think Stan has really changed this time, I should give him another chance' crap. Do you understand? Are you serious about this?"

"Yes, I am."

"Good. When is the next time that Stan will be gone for a few hours on a day that you're off? I'll schedule it off too, and I'll get a little group of people together to come over to your place with boxes. You need to make up lists with everything that you want us to pack up. We'll aim to have you completely out of there in less than two hours. Is that feasible?"

I nodded my head. I told her that Stan was in charge of a youth group car wash a week from this Saturday. He'd be gone for several hours. That was the best time to do it. That would give me a few days to make up my lists of belongings to gather, meet with the lawyer to start the paperwork, and get the restraining order.

"He can keep all the stuff that we bought together except the bookshelves. They're all my books anyway. I just want the stuff that's definitely mine. I don't want to argue with him over things. I'll close our checking account and he can take half of it. He won't be able to afford the apartment anymore on his own. He'll either have to move back in with his mom or get a roommate. I don't know what he'll do."

"Well, it won't be your problem anymore."

We decided to finish our planning with Ty at lunch that day. We were already behind on rounds that morning. It felt good to have a plan and to start it into motion. None of the residents handled my appearance very well, but they were happy to know that I was going to leave Stan. Miss Stacey beamed when she told everyone that her son was going to handle my divorce, and that I was in good hands because he was the best divorce lawyer in town.

"Now for the really hard part," I said to myself as I knocked on Miss Candace's door.

"Come in!" she called out.

I opened the door softly and walked inside. When she saw me, she cried out, "Oh no, Chrissy! No! No! No!" she sobbed.

"It's okay! It's okay!" I rushed over to her bed, knelt down and grabbed her hands. "It's all right, Miss Candace, I'm going to leave him. Okay?" She began to calm down, as she looked in my eyes and saw that I was serious. "I'm going to leave him."

"Today," she said.

"Soon," I answered.

"Today."

"A week from Saturday. I'll be all right until then. He's on his very best behavior right now, so I'll be okay. He won't know a thing until I'm already gone." I told her all about our plans for moving me out the Saturday of the youth group car wash.

"Oh, I won't sleep a wink until you're out of there. I'm so nervous! What if he figures it out?"

"Come on. We're talking about Stan here."

She touched the bruises on my face. "How could he?" she said.

232

"He'll never touch me again," I promised. How many times had Stan made me that promise? But I was the one promising this time, and I kept my promises.

As predicted, a bouquet from Stan arrived that afternoon with a little note reading, "I'm sorry. I love you, Stan."

I almost put it out in the dumpster, but then I decided that these colorful, pretty flowers shouldn't have to pay for what Stan did. I took apart the bouquet and put little flowers on the dinner trays of the residents when I brought them their meals. "This is from Stan to you," I told Miss Anna as I handed her the flower.

"Well, this is from me to him," she said dryly, pointing up her middle finger. I stifled a laugh. I loved my residents.

The next few days were challenging. I had to pretend that everything was back to normal with Stan. I had to sit through his latest lecture on how we could improve our relationship and feign enthusiasm for it. I avoided any physical contact with him whatsoever. There was no way I could have sex with him now that I knew I was leaving. With all my bruising, he knew without being told that I was in no mood for any kind of physical relations with him. It was a relief to know that I'd never have to have sex with him again. With my experiences in that department, frankly I didn't care if I never had sex with anyone again. At 22 years old, I was ready to be celibate for the rest of my life.

I walked through the apartment when he wasn't home, making lists of things I wanted boxed up to take with me. How strange to think that I would go from this life as Stan's wife one night to being gone without a trace the next. As Stan talked about our future, about adopting children together, about doing things this summer and fall, about plans for next year and beyond, I just nodded my head and smiled, calmly and deliberately. I'd let him kiss me goodnight and then, as he rolled over and soon began the steady, low rumbling snore, I'd think about how much I hated and despised the man lying beside me. I wanted him to know every miserable thought I'd ever had about him. But I had to bide my time just a few more days. This lie was almost over. My disappearance without words would tell him everything.

When I awoke the final Friday morning, I had a nervous fluttering feeling inside. It was my last day here. I just needed to hold it together one more day. *I am calm. I am deliberate.* I made breakfast and packed one last lunch for Stan and kissed him as he headed off to work. He said he'd take me out to dinner on Saturday night after the youth group carwash. I smiled and said that would be nice. He noticed that my bruises were fading away nicely and I agreed. They were definitely fading.

I finished getting ready and headed off to work. Most of the people at work knew what was going to happen. A couple of co-workers who had Saturday off were planning to come and help with the move that morning. Stan would be leaving around 10 a.m., so they planned to arrive by 10:15. We hoped to be completely gone by noon. My lawyer would show up at the apartment in the late afternoon with the restraining order and divorce papers. He would tell Stan that I was gone for good, that I wanted nothing more to do with him, and that he could make this divorce as easy or as difficult as he liked but it would happen nonetheless. I smiled when I imagined the look on Stan's face, the rage he would feel with no one to punch.

Miss Candace had been a nervous wreck since the day I'd told her I was leaving. She was worried that Stan would catch onto my plans and do something terrible. I'd thought of that too. So many times during Stan's rages, he'd threatened to kill me. He'd told me once that he'd carve me up so badly that no one would be able to recognize me. But that was just to scare me. Stan beat me during fits of rage in the privacy of his own home. Later on, he was always sorry. He didn't plan things out in advance. He saw himself as a very peaceful, God-fearing man who sometimes lost his temper when provoked.

On Friday, though, Miss Candace gave me a peaceful, serene smile as we finalized details with Nadine in her room.

234

She couldn't come, of course, but she wanted to know exactly what would happen and when so that she could watch the clock and be there with us "in spirit."

"Everything is going to turn out just fine. I know that now. I have faith," she said.

"Well, I'm glad *you* do," I said. "Now, I'm the one starting to get a little nervous. I keep worrying about some little detail or important thing that I've missed. I hardly slept at all last night, and I'm sure it will be the same way tonight."

"You won't forget a thing. I know that. I've been praying non-stop. And I put your name in the prayer rolls at the temple. I have enough faith for both of us."

"Well, thank you," I said, sincerely. "I need all the prayers I can get."

"And I've been fasting too."

"What! Miss Candace, no, no no! You are in no condition to be fasting. How long have you gone without food?"

"Oh," she thought for a moment, "about 24 hours now."

"Oh, Good Lord," said Nadine. "I can't believe we didn't notice she wasn't eating. Let's get some food down this poor woman." She quickly headed down the hallway to the cafeteria.

"How long were you planning to starve yourself? I feel terrible!" I exclaimed.

"It's not starving, it's fasting."

I knelt down by her face. "Either way it's the same thing. I appreciate so much that you're trying to help. But you need to eat something right away. Okay, Miss Candace? Do it for me."

"But," she protested, "fasting makes the prayer stronger."

"God will understand. Okay, Miss Candace? He knows what's in your heart. Please eat something right now. For me." I put her face in my hands. "I need you to stick around here. You can't just waste away. You're all I have left. Okay?" My voice broke with emotion.

Miss Candace looked at me with those wide silver-blue eyes and then nodded her head slowly. "Okay," she agreed.

Now I definitely had to make sure nothing bad happened. Miss Candace would think it was because she broke her fast.

That evening, I made dinner for Stan one last time. We watched our Friday night television shows one last time. He complained about his day at work one last time. After he headed off to bed, I went to where he kept his keys and quietly slipped my spare car key off of his key ring and put it in my purse. Hopefully he wouldn't notice it was missing.

The next morning, as he got ready to go to the car wash, he asked me what my plans were for that afternoon. "Oh, I don't know. After I get ready, I'll probably run a few errands. I should be home by the time you're home," I lied. *I am calm. I am deliberate.*

Stan was still there when I got out of the shower and as I blow-dried my hair and brushed my teeth. I got dressed and put on my makeup. I watched the clock. It was almost 10. "You have to be there at 10, right?"

"Yes. I'm running a little late. I'm looking for more spare rags."

"There might be some under the kitchen sink."

I heard his boots going into the kitchen and then back into the living room.

"You don't want to be late," I reminded him.

"Since when do you care how punctual I am for a church activity?"

"I just ... don't want those kids to be waiting around for you. That's all." My heart thumped a little faster. *I am calm. I am deliberate.*

He quickly strode into the bedroom and came right at me. "I'm off." He kissed my cheek. "I'll see you later."

"Yes." I took a deep breath and held it until I heard the front door click behind him and his boots heading down the stairs.

I went to the closet and pulled out the overnight bag that I'd packed earlier in the week. Nadine had all the lists of things to box up. I didn't feel comfortable having them at our apartment in case Stan somehow found them. We always stored the overnight bags in this closet. He wouldn't think it was unusual to see it there unless he discovered that it was packed.

I looked at the clock. It was 10:10. Suddenly, I heard someone coming through the front door. It was Stan.

"Chrissy!" he called out angrily. I jumped and turned around to face him.

"What is it?" I said with alarm.

"The key to your car is missing from my key ring!"

I am calm. "That's strange. It must have fallen off."

"Keys don't just fall off."

"Or it slipped off somehow. I don't know. That's very strange. I'm sure it will turn up though."

Stan started looking around the room. He picked up the overnight bag and placed it back in the closet. My heart thumped wildly. He didn't seem to notice that it was heavier than usual or question why it was out. *I am calm.* He headed into the kitchen to look for the key there.

"Stan, you're very late," I said. "Do you really need my car for something right now?"

"No, it's just … I hate it when things go missing."

Then you're going to hate this afternoon.

"Check at the church to see if it's in the lost and found. I'll look around here for it."

He sighed. "Okay. I just worry that someone will steal your car."

"That's very unlikely. Let me worry about that."

He reluctantly headed for the door. "I'm looking forward to our night out tonight."

"Yep."

"Remember that I love you."

"Mm-hmm."

Just minutes after Stan's car pulled away, Nadine and her group pulled into the parking lot. They'd borrowed a truck from one of her friends, which Tyrone drove. I was waiting for them when they came to the top of the stairs. Nadine introduced me to her friends and I thanked them for coming. A couple of people from work also arrived to help.

Nadine was in no mood for chit-chat. "Okay. There's no time to lose. Everyone has their list and their empty boxes. Each person will be assigned one section of this apartment to handle. We're going to aim to be out of here by noon. Chrissy needs to take a look at each box before we close it and stack it in the truck. There are two men, so we'll need them to handle the heavy lifting. Mainly that will consist of Chrissy's bookcases and books."

We worked quietly for the next 90 minutes. The silence was periodically broken with questions for me. Most of my things could fit into the back of the truck. I put a couple of the more fragile boxes in the trunk of my car, and I also made sure that my guitar, box of pictures and keepsakes from home, and my Chrissy rock were in the backseat of my car.

By noon, the truck was completely packed. I gave Tyrone some money to get a couple of pizzas and some drinks. I could at least buy everyone lunch for helping me out like this. The truck with Tyrone and Nadine's friends took off to their house. I told Nadine she could go too. I wanted to walk around the apartment one last time to make sure I had everything and to say good-bye.

"Nope," Nadine said. "You're not to be alone for the next little while. That's part of the rules, remember? What if Stan came home unexpectedly and it was just you here with all your stuff gone? I'll wait out in my car in the parking lot to follow you to our place. That will give you a few minutes to walk through the apartment one last time. Remember, this place may have some good memories for you, but it has more bad memories than good ones. Don't waste your time and energy feeling sad about it."

I walked alone through the apartment. It wasn't empty. I'd left almost everything for Stan. I didn't want him to contact me to argue over something that he thought rightfully belonged to him. Of course, he thought that *I* rightfully belonged to him too, and he wouldn't react well to the way I left or the very fact that I was leaving at all. I had emptied enough stuff that he would notice something was very different from the moment he walked in. And I imagined his rage building as he stomped through the apartment calling out my name and opening drawers, cabinets, and closets looking for my things. His face would redden and his fists would clench as he found them all empty. I had no idea how he would react to my lawyer showing up with divorce papers a little while later. It's just a good thing the lawyer wasn't a woman. Stan wouldn't try to pick a fight with a man. He picked only the physical battles that he knew he could win.

If he'd known how serious I was this time, he would have sworn up and down to change, to go to marriage counseling, to agree to any and all of my requests. But, this time, I wanted only one thing: to be freed from my birdcage. I took my keys and purse and exited the front door one last time. I turned around and locked the door, then slipped the door key off of my key ring and put it under the mat. I wouldn't need it anymore.

I went down the steps to my car in the parking lot, where Nadine waited to follow me in her car. I started the engine and pulled out of the parking lot. As I drove down that familiar street, I didn't even bother to look through the rear-view mirror. Instead, I looked straight ahead and drove calmly, deliberately into my future.

25

We were a little more relaxed and less hurried once we got to Nadine and Tyrone's house and started moving me in. Someone turned on some music and we ate pizza while bringing in all the boxes and shelves. Nadine and Ty had cleared out their spare bedroom except for a small twin bed, a nightstand with a lamp and a chest of drawers. Once all the boxes were in and the shelves set up, I thanked everyone for their help and told them I could unpack everything myself. Nadine and Ty had said I could live there for free, but I insisted on paying a third of the rent and utility expenses. That would help them build their savings, since they eventually wanted to buy a house. The house that they rented had two bathrooms, so the one in the hallway would basically be my bathroom. It was a nice arrangement and close to work.

I stayed busy all afternoon unpacking the boxes, hanging up my clothes, stacking my bookshelves and deciding where everything else would go. Nadine and Ty started preparing a nice meal for our first dinner together as roommates. I hoped they didn't mind having me there or see me as a burden. I wondered what was happening with Stan back at the apartment, but I was pretty sure I could guess.

Right before dinner, the phone started ringing. We all looked at each other in fear. For some reason, I felt like a naughty child who had been caught with my hand in the cookie jar. By now, Stan knew that I had just been playing along with the reconciliation efforts for the past several days. He knew now that I had been planning to leave him all along. "Don't answer that," I said.

We let it ring about 20 times before it finally stopped. Five minutes later, it started back up again. "All right, let's just get this over with," Nadine said. She picked up the phone. "Hello." She paused for a moment. "And just what is your question?" She paused again. "I am not at liberty to say." From across the room I could hear Stan's voice picking up volume. "Please do not raise your voice to me. I'm not your wife, and I do not put up with grown men who have tantrums." She paused again. "Anything you have to say to her should be said through her attorney. She's gone, Stan. She never wants to see you or speak to you again. And if you show up here or at Sunset, we'll have your ass thrown in jail where you belong. It's over. Get used to it." She hung up.

We ate our dinner in a nervous silence. Tyrone tried to break the tension with a few comments here and there. The phone rang again. This time when Nadine picked up, I could clearly hear Stan yelling, *"Let me speak to my wife right now!"*

"It sounds like someone needs a diaper change and a nap!" She hung up the phone.

"Just take it off the hook, Nadine. He won't stop calling tonight," I said.

"What if your lawyer needs to reach you?"

"I'll call him after dinner."

She took the receiver off the hook and placed it inside a kitchen drawer. We sat in silence eating while the phone beeped its off-the-hook sound and then finally went silent.

On Sunday, we put the receiver back on the hook. It was silent all morning. "He's at church. But he's stewing," I said.

By the afternoon, it started ringing again. We ignored it for several hours. Nadine didn't want to keep it off the hook all day. Finally, that evening, she picked up again. "Would you please stop calling here? There is nothing you could say to her that will make her change her mind. I am expecting a phone call from my mother tonight and I would appreciate leaving this line open ..."

I could hear more yelling through the receiver. Nadine pulled the receiver away from her face and stared at it. "Well, if that isn't the rudest guy I've ever known! Now he's attacking *me*. He just called me the N-word."

"What!" Ty yelled so loudly that I jumped. I'd never seen him angry before. "Give me that phone!" He yanked it out of

Nadine's hand. "Listen up, you little cowardly prick. I want to know exactly where you are right now, because I'm coming for you the second I get off this phone. Are you at your apartment? You like to beat up women, do you? Well, guess what! *I* like to beat up men! And I'm about to give you what you deserve! I'm gonna tear your head right off your shoulders and shove it up your ass, you maggot! Here I come!"

He slammed the phone down and searched around for his keys.

"Get 'im, Ty!" said Nadine.

I stood up in horror, and ran to block the doorway. "No! This has to stop, right now," I pleaded. "Ty, if you go over there and something horrible happens, you'll be the one to get blamed. You know that, right? It doesn't matter what your excuse is. You're black and he's white. And this is the South. You're no help to me in jail! You'd get fired from your job. It would ruin your life. And I can't have that on my head. I need you here. Nadine needs you here. Please don't go!"

His chest still heaved in and out, but he was calming down. He looked over at Nadine. She reluctantly sighed. "She's probably right. Don't go over there. Besides, he's probably busy rinsing out the pants he just crapped."

All three of us began to chuckle. "Oh, that I could be a fly in that apartment right now to see that!" I commented. We talked and laughed for the rest of the evening. Somehow that whole incident had eased the tension. The phone stayed silent for the rest of the night. We made brownie sundaes for dessert to celebrate my freedom.

My attorney came to Sunset the next day to visit his mother and to let me know that Stan had called him and had agreed to cooperate with the divorce. We would divide what we had in our checking account evenly and then close the account. He would sell most of our furniture and give me half of the money. He would move back in with his mom. I planned to open my own account just as soon as I had my maiden name back. I used my married name only on official documents, but in my mind, I was already Chrissy Rollings again. And it was a good feeling.

We settled into a routine that summer. For several weeks, Nadine made sure we had the same work schedule so that I could ride with her to and from work. I wasn't allowed to go off on my own to the library or to go grocery shopping, or even to take a walk on my own. She was afraid that Stan would try to confront me if he could get to me when I was alone. I was added to the chore chart on Nadine and Ty's refrigerator. There were rotating assignments for all the household chores, cooking dinner, and doing the dishes. Everyone did his or her fair share.

It was strange for me to go from doing all the domestic work for two people to doing just a third of it. I suddenly had more free time on my hands. I rediscovered some of my old pastimes: reading and playing the guitar. The only thing I did less of now was watch TV. Nadine and Ty rarely had the television on. After dinner, we would often just sit around the table and talk or play board games and cards. I'd never realized how much TV Stan and I watched at home. It was a good distraction from actually having to interact with each other. So many of our conversations ended in a fight that, after a while, we just avoided any unnecessary talking.

I enjoyed living in a peaceful household with Nadine and Ty. I hoped that they didn't mind having me around all the time or grow to see me as a nuisance. Sometimes I'd watch their playful, loving back-and-forth banter and grow a little bit sad. It reminded me of the banter that Momma and Daddy would sometimes have together back when I was little, before everything fell apart. I wondered what it was about Nadine and Momma that could inspire that kind of love in a man. Whatever it was, I didn't have it. Maybe men could sense that part of me that was dead inside, the part that was unlovable. I'd never have a relationship like Nadine and Ty's, one that was based on love, equality, and mutual respect. I'd have to be content with being alone. Luckily, I wasn't the kind of person who really needed a man to love me in order to be happy. I had everything I really needed after all.

One day at work, I ran into someone I remembered from church who was visiting one of our residents. We chatted for a minute. Then she told me that she didn't believe the rumors about me at church. Apparently, Stan's story at church was that we were getting a divorce because I'd had an affair with someone at work. He'd tried to forgive me and move on, but I was unrepentant, so he eventually gave up. Poor Stan, everybody thought. That's why I never came to church, they thought. I felt too guilty over my illicit affair.

I caught Nadine in Miss Candace's room later on that day and told them Stan's story.

Miss Candace was appalled. "You have to call one of the church leaders and set the record straight. You can't let something like that go."

I shook my head. "What's the point? It doesn't matter. They can believe whatever they want about me. I have the truth on my side, and that's all I need. Stan knows it too. Maybe that will eat him up inside over time. But, most likely, it won't. He'll tell that lie long enough that he'll eventually come to believe it himself."

Nadine stood there, shaking her head in disgust. "And just who in the world, I wonder, would you possibly have an illicit affair with? Mr. Oscar?"

At that moment, the image of me having an affair with the "ladies' man of Sunset Care Center" struck us all as being absurdly funny. We simultaneously erupted into laughter. "Shhh! Somebody might hear us," I whispered with my finger to my lips and stumbled over to the door to close it, still laughing.

Miss Candace was laughing so hard that tears glistened in her eyes. I grabbed a tissue and handed it to her and then grabbed another for myself. "Oh my. Sometimes all you can do is just laugh," I commented.

Once Nadine had an audience, there was no stopping her. "Oh, I know! I know! Let's start circulating a rumor of our own. We could say that you were having an affair with Mr. Oscar because he was *waaaay* better in the sack than poor little Stan. Watch how quickly that boy would backpedal on his own damn lie!"

We howled with laughter, Miss Candace sitting in her wheelchair, slapping her thigh. I worried about what this hard laughter might do to her heart. I stood behind her and patted her back. "Take a breath now, Miss Candace."

She dabbed at her eyes with the tissue. "Oh my goodness, I'm going to repent for all this dirty talk later, but right now I'm just having too much fun." She sighed. "Oh, I wish you two girls had been around back when I had *my* Mr. Awful. I sure could have used a good laugh or two at his expense back then."

The laughter finally died down, and we all sighed, lost in thought for a moment. Then Nadine broke the silence. "Well, hell, let's go dig 'im up. I've got enough insults for that bag of bones to go on all day." We erupted into gales of laughter again. I hadn't laughed like that in a long time, and I'd forgotten how healing it could be.

By the end of the summer, Nadine and Ty felt it was safe enough for me to go places without an "escort." Stan had not tried to contact me at all since that last phone call at the house. Maybe he missed me a little. I didn't know. I sure didn't miss him at all. I knew he wouldn't try to come after me at this point. Stan's anger was brutal and abrupt, but it was always unplanned and didn't last long. He wasn't a premeditator. I guess I could be grateful for that at least. I started going to the library again and going for long walks. I even started jogging a little. It was nice to get outdoors and fill my lungs with fresh air, especially as the weather cooled down that fall.

When my divorce was final, we went out to celebrate. There was even a cake for me at work with "Congratulations on your divorce, Chrissy!" written in chocolate icing. It seemed a bit strange to treat the event as cause for celebration, but I wasn't the type of person to turn down a spontaneous party. When I came home from work that day, I sorted through my clothes and decided to give all my pink things to Goodwill. I also got rid of all of my turtlenecks, probably not the smartest thing to do at the onset of winter, but I figured it would give me a good excuse to go shopping. Nadine sat on my bed and gave her opinions on what I should keep or toss. "Get rid of all those ugly hair contraptions he liked you to wear too. We'll put all that crap in a bag and maybe mail it to his next wife."

"You think he'll get married again?"

"Of course he will. He's probably dating some young thing he met in that youth group right now. They breed those girls to want nothing more out of life than to be some man's house servant."

"I feel like I should warn her or something."

"What can you do? She probably wouldn't believe you anyway. Stan would have some explanation about how you're just a bitter ex who wants to ruin his life."

Nadine was probably right. I thought about those nice, young, trusting girls in that youth group. I hated the thought that someone else might end up in the situation I'd endured. But I didn't know what I could do to intervene. Hopefully she had people she could turn to for help, as I should have done much earlier in our marriage.

Hilldale had recently opened its first shopping mall. Nadine and I were astounded when we walked through it. You could go into store after store without ever having to step foot outside. "Oh, I could live at this place," Nadine remarked. "I never want to leave!" What used to take several trips could now be done all at one place. We especially loved the food court. It was like a little mini-mall of restaurants. Whenever Ty had a weekend game to attend, we decided that we would head to the mall. We could always come up with something that one of us needed. And, of course, the other person needed to come along to give an opinion. Once we'd find the perfect item, we had to go celebrate with a snack or drink at the food court.

It was fun for me to have a good female friend again. It reminded me of when Marla and I would hang out together, laughing and talking and enjoying each other's company. Stan hadn't allowed me do anything with Nadine beyond work. I'd never been the type of person to have lots of friends, but I realized that having even just one really good friend made all the difference for me.

Every once in a while, Nadine would share stories from her past. She didn't know much about my past and would try to ask me about my upbringing and my family. I would immediately freeze whenever she would do that. I knew I could probably trust her with some of the things that had happened in my past without her judgment, but I just wasn't ready to face those memories, to acknowledge that they'd happened. It might send me into the sort of depression from which I couldn't escape. So, instead, I'd turn the conversation back around to focus on Nadine's life. I told her there wasn't much to say except that I'd lost everyone I'd ever loved and that it was too painful to talk about. She just nodded and accepted that this was all I could share.

Only Miss Candace had even a vague clue about my past. One day during one of our conversations, I told her I'd been thinking about what she'd told me about how the Mormons don't really believe in heaven and hell. It's more like they just think people attain different levels of glory, which she called kingdoms. And she said all the kingdoms are pretty good. They're all better than life on earth, she said. Even really awful sinners get to go to a lower kingdom.

"So what happens to good people who do bad things? What about, like, someone who commits suicide?" I began to feel the lump forming in my throat. "You don't think that God judges them too harshly?"

Miss Candace hesitated for a moment, looking up at her Jesus picture. "I think," she said, "that God walks a mile in everybody's shoes before judging them. Isn't that what He always tells us to do? Why would He be any different? So, no, I

247

don't think that God judges them too harshly. When I think about how close I came at one time … to ending it all, I just remember that I was in a lot of pain. And I just wanted the pain to end. I'm glad that I didn't go through with it, because look at everything I would have missed. But I like to think that, if I had done it, the God waiting for me on the other side would be one who understood and still loved me and wouldn't condemn me. When you think about the life of Christ and how He treated other people, especially the downtrodden, wouldn't you agree?"

I nodded my head and swallowed my lump. I couldn't tell her about what had happened. And she would never ask. But I think she knew. "Miss Candace, someday when you get to that other side, not for a long time, if you see my momma … " I faltered for a moment, "tell her that I'm sorry. That I didn't mean those awful things I said. Tell her that I never stopped loving her."

"Oh, honey, she already knows," Miss Candace put her hand over mine. "But I'll tell her anyway just to be sure. I'll tell her what a fine person you turned out to be. I think she already knows that too. I'll bet she's a lot closer than you might think."

I nodded my head, swallowing the lump in my throat, and stared out the window. I hoped she was right.

Nadine and Ty had gone on their first date in high school on a Valentine's Day, so they considered February 14 their "anniversary." They'd been together for 12 years now. They'd planned a nice date for that evening, so Nadine wanted to go shopping with me for something to wear. "I never thought I'd say this, but I'm actually getting tired of the mall. Let's go somewhere else," she suggested.

We drove to a more upscale area in Hilldale where there were some nice dress shops and jewelry stores. I spotted a nail salon nearby. "Hey Nadine, let's stop at that nail salon and get our nails done. I've always wanted to do that!" We parked the car and walked toward the salon. "Maybe we could even get pedicures if they're not too expensive."

"Oh, aren't we getting fancy-pantsy today!" she exclaimed.

"Well it's your anniversary, isn't it? I think we should splurge."

When we walked into the salon, I immediately felt out of place. It was full of wealthy-looking white women. They glanced at us disdainfully. "Yes? Can I help you?" one of the workers asked.

"Um, we'd like to get our nails done today. And, how much are your pedicures?" I asked.

"Just sign your name and what you want here. Tassie, this one's yours."

Tassie gave Nadine a dirty look and reluctantly stood and sighed, heading for the supplies. "This is my second Negro this week," she muttered loud enough for us to hear. "We're going to need more sanitizer!" she yelled out.

"You know what? Never mind. This place smells like something is rotting," I said.

I stormed out the front door with Nadine right behind me. "Who do they think they are?" I yelled. "How dare they treat potential customers with such disrespect! What is the matter with them?"

"Welcome to being black in the South, Chrissy. Enjoy the ride," Nadine remarked.

"What? That's what this is about? I thought they assumed we were poor or something."

"There's nothing about us that indicates we're poor," she said. "But there's definitely something about me that indicates I'm black."

"I have a mind to go back there and put a 'Bigots Only' sign on their door!" I fumed. "And every time they take it down, I'll put another one back up."

"I've been dealing with this all my life, Chrissy. Things are actually a lot better now than they used to be around here. I remember the days when I couldn't go to school with white kids, or eat in the same restaurants, or drink from the same fountains, or even crap in the same toilets as them. I'm only five years older than you. Don't you remember those days when everything was separate between blacks and whites in Hilldale?" I did remember thinking it was a big waste to have to build two of everything when we could all just as easily use the same facilities. And it always seemed like the things reserved for black people were never quite as nice as the things built for white people.

It didn't seem very fair to me, but I just assumed the grown-ups knew what they were doing. I remembered one teacher in elementary school who scared us to death by telling us that terrible, terrible things would happen if we intermingled with black people, especially if we ended up "inter-breeding" with them and having kids that were half-black and half-white. I'd raised my hand in class and asked her specifically what terrible, terrible things would happen if we did that. She looked at me, perplexed, and said, "I just told you! They might end up mixing and having children."

"But what terrible, terrible things would happen?" I thought she meant that we'd get hit with the plague or something like an earthquake or a hurricane. Or maybe a swarm of locusts might descend upon Hilldale if we permitted race mixing.

"Chrissy, pay attention! I just told you. The races should not inter-breed."

I just didn't see how falling in love with someone of a different race and forming a family together qualified as a terrible, terrible thing. But I was already getting dirty looks from the teacher and my classmates, so I decided to just keep my mouth shut about it. Somehow biased people have it all worked out in their minds so that nonsensical things make perfect sense. And they get really mad if you question their logic or ask for supporting evidence for their claims. The fact that they said so and that they have a deep gut feeling about it should be enough to convince you of their point of view.

It was like Stan's explanation of how women were completely equal with, yet also subservient to, their male counterparts. It made perfect sense in his mind. And since he believed it was God's design for women, no amount of evidence to the contrary could convince him otherwise. If you question people like that long enough about their views, you'll usually find that it almost always boils down to what they want to believe. They'll go to any length to defend a hierarchal social system that benefits them personally.

I think Nadine's experiences growing up in the Jim Crow South were the main reason she wasn't into labels and titles at work and why she placed so much emphasis on perfect equality both at work and at home. Maybe it's even the reason why she hadn't yet married Tyrone. She knew she could trust him not to try to become dictatorial with her, but she still felt reluctance to take on a formal role that even hinted at subservience to someone else.

When the weather began to warm, I spent more time at the care center to take Miss Candace for walks. She seemed more tired lately, and she could use some fresh air. One day, as I wheeled her around the grounds of Sunset, she asked me what kind of religious upbringing I'd had. I could be brief, without touching on any areas that were painful for me.

"My mother had been raised in a very strict Southern Baptist home and was disowned," I said. "I think that kind of turned her off on the institution of religion. But we considered ourselves Christians. I mean, we believed in the Bible and everything. A few times we tried out different nearby churches. But I guess we never really found a good fit because we didn't stick with any of them for long. The longest I've ever consistently gone to church was in the early days with Stan. I can see the appeal of having a religious community to count on. Stan made it pretty clear though that it was *his* community, not mine. I was just along for the ride."

"Did you like going to church?" she asked.

"Yes, for the most part. There's a little part of organized religion that bugs me though. It seems like everybody in the same congregation has this whole 'us vs. them' mentality. Everyone thinks they're going to heaven and everyone else is going to hell. I mean, I know Mormons don't believe in hell, but they still talk an awful lot about wicked people. And they think that they're the only ones that have the truth, right?"

"Well, yes," Miss Candace thought about it for a moment. "I guess I can see how someone might see it that way. Mormons do think they have the only true church of Jesus Christ. But one thing I like about it is that everyone will get a chance to join at some point. If they don't hear about the gospel in their lifetime, then after they die, they'll get a chance to learn about it and they can convert then."

I nodded my head. "That does sound a little more fair."

"That's why I haven't really pushed the church on you too hard. I just know you'll join when you really learn about it in the afterlife," Miss Candace said. "You'd make such a good Mormon! But I'm afraid I'll explain it all wrong and mess up your chances. You only get one chance to accept it."

She looked up at me with those hopeful silver-blue eyes. I was almost tempted to tell her that I would join right then, just to make her happy. Instead, I said, "Well, I'll tell you what: when I someday get to that other side, if I see a young Miss Candace standing there smiling at me and waving her Book of Mormon, I don't even need to be taught the gospel. I will convert right then and there."

"Don't say it unless you mean it, because I'll be there."

"I do mean it." I kissed the top of her white hair as I wheeled her back to Building C. "And I'll remember just what you look like from that picture you showed me."

"And instead of wheeling me around all over the place, I'll walk right next to your side. Won't that be lovely?" she remarked.

I tucked her into bed and stayed there until she fell asleep. For some reason, I felt a sad and mournful feeling come over me. Change was in the air. I could feel it.

I'd just found out that Tyrone had applied for a coaching job at a prestigious high school in New York. Nadine and Ty both felt that there were better coaching opportunities for a man of color in the Northeast. And, with Nadine's skills, she could get a job anywhere. I felt guilty for secretly hoping he wouldn't get the job. I wanted the best for them, of course, but I didn't want them to leave. I didn't want to be all alone again. And Miss Candace wouldn't be around forever.

Try to stay positive, I told myself as I drove home. Whatever will be will be. That night I had a dream that I was standing at the edge of a lake and I could see a boat out in the middle. I heard voices coming from the boat, and they were voices I recognized. I could hear Daddy's and Momma's voices talking. I could hear my brothers and sisters laughing and playing. I could even hear Nadine, Ty, and Miss Candace all talking. But the boat began drifting away.

"Wait!" I called. "Wait for me! I'm coming!" I jumped into the lake and began to swim, but the boat kept drifting farther and farther away. They couldn't hear me. "Stop!" I called. "Wait!"

I tried to swim faster but it seemed that the water was getting thicker, as if I were swimming through sludge. I struggled and gasped trying to swim through it. When I finally reached the middle of the lake, I stopped and looked around. The boat was gone. I spun around and around calling for anyone to hear. Then I grew silent. I realized I was completely alone.

26

"I feel like you're missing something," I told the doctor when he came around to check Miss Candace. "Something's not right with her. Her eyes aren't as bright, and she doesn't have the pep that she used to have."

"Chrissy, there's nothing we can do for her," he said. "It's old age. Surely you've seen this in the other patients. They grow older and weaker. They eventually die of old age if something else doesn't get them first."

I sighed. He just wasn't listening to me. If no one else was looking out for her, it would have to be me. She never felt strong enough anymore to go to her Sunday church service, so the elders would come on Sundays and administer the bread and water to her in her bed. I began to monitor everything she ate and drank. She just needed to eat better and stay hydrated. Whenever she woke from a nap, I would typically be standing there with a glass of juice and a straw. "Drink."

She needed better circulation. I moved her arms and legs up and down for several minutes a day. I would read to her from the classics and play songs for her on my guitar. She would smile and close her eyes, trying to hum along to the tune. She needed more fresh air and sunshine. "Let's get you outside for your daily dose of nature. That's better than any pill."

"I'm too tired," she said one day.

"Nonsense. Give me your arm." I helped her into the wheelchair and took her outside. A nice conversation would help her perk up, I was sure. "Tell me some more about your son Danny," I said.

She was quiet.

"Miss Candace?"

"You talk," she said with a tired smile.

What should I talk about? It needed to be something positive. I began to tell her about working at the diner. I told her about how I'd been living in my car and really had nothing. I told her how the people at the diner became my substitute family. Mike had helped me find a place to live at the Stakers' house. I told her about how we grew to know everyone who came there regularly. We knew their names and details about their lives. We celebrated birthdays, anniversaries, and holidays together. And that's how I'd come to feel about the people at Sunset Care Center as well. They'd become my family.

"Isn't it interesting," I said, "how people can come together and form a family even when they're not related? And that's how it is now living with Nadine and Ty. I feel like we're a little family. We look out for each other. We take care of each other. And I feel like you're part of my family too, like the grandmother I never really had."

I didn't tell her that Ty was in New York right now for a job interview. I didn't want to think about the possibility of our little family breaking up. I would worry about that when the time came. I told her about how Nadine and I liked to go shopping at the mall on the days that Ty had to be at a game. I described how big it was, how it took almost an hour of walking just to go past every store. I told her about the food court and all the choices available for meals, drinks, and snacks. I wheeled Miss Candace back down the hall to her room.

"And someday real soon, I'm going to take you to that mall so you can see that I'm not kidding about how big it is. Just as soon as you're up to it, we'll go. So you need to work hard to get your strength back, okay? We'll go to any store you like. And at the end, we'll stop at the food court for a little treat, maybe a strawberry milkshake. How does that sound?" I asked as I tucked her back into bed.

"Chrissy," she said weakly, "you need to let me go."

"Nope," I shook my head stubbornly, fighting back the tears. "No, I don't."

"God needs me," she said.

"No, He doesn't," I countered. "He has billions and billions of people to choose from. I'm just asking for one. He can spare one person."

She looked at me sadly and then nodded her head. "Okay," she said. "I'll try to stay a little while longer."

"Don't just try. Do it. I know you can get better if you just try hard enough. You just have to make up your mind to want to live."

"Okay."

"So you will?"

"Yes." She nodded her head and closed her eyes. I stayed there holding her hand until she fell asleep. It was my day off, so I could go home.

I left her room wiping my eyes and passed Nadine in the hallway. "Are you all right?" she asked.

"Yes. I'll see you at home."

I spent most of the evening in my room playing the guitar. When I came out for a snack, Nadine confronted me in the kitchen.

"Chrissy, I'm worried about you. You are way too attached to Miss Candace. You spend half your time waiting on her. There are other patients that need you too."

"Most of the time I spend with her is my own time. I've never neglected any of my patients!"

"But how do you think it looks to the other patients that you spend your free time with Miss Candace? She is quite obviously your favorite. It's very important in our business to be professional and impartial."

"She doesn't have anyone else, Nadine! The others all do," I argued.

"She has the people from her church," Nadine pointed out while I rolled my eyes.

"Oh please! They come once a week for 15 minutes, and then they can't wait to get out of there!" I replied.

"Chrissy, I'm speaking not only as your boss but as your friend. I'm worried about you." Nadine took a deep breath. "She's dying, all right? You have to accept that. If she had relatives at a distance, now is the time that we'd be calling them to come and say their good-byes. I think, deep inside, you know it too, but you're in denial."

I felt an angry lump forming in my throat. "She is not dying! She's been a little under the weather lately, but she's determined to get better. You don't know everything, Nadine! You don't know her like I do. She's very strong-willed and determined. If she really wants to live, she will."

I wanted to tell Nadine to just stay out of it, to mind her own business. But, since she was my boss, it probably *was* her business. "The human body knows when it's time to go," Nadine said. "No amount of strong will and determination will ward off death in the end."

"Would you please stop saying that? You aren't always right about everything!" I couldn't recall a time when she had been wrong, but I was sure she had been at some point in her life. "What am I supposed to do, Nadine? Should I just sit back and let her wither away and die all alone in the middle of the night?"

"That's not what I said at all."

"… because I'm not going to let that happen."

"I'm just worried about you, that's all."

"Well let me worry about me. Okay?"

I left the house to go for a walk. Maybe I *was* in denial. It felt as if my dream about the boat in the lake were coming true. But what else could I do except swim after it through the sludge? And so I would continue to dote on Miss Candace, moving her limbs every day, forcing her to eat and drink, taking her outside for fresh air, reading to her and trying to engage her in conversation. I would continue to believe that she could ward off death with sheer will and determination. Because what else could I believe?

And then one morning in late April, I walked into work and Miss Cummings was standing there with a couple of nurse's aides. She looked up at me with a look of dread as I wished her a good morning. "Chrissy," she said with a sorrowful tone. "We tried to call you but no one picked up. I'm sorry to tell you that Miss Candace passed away early this morning."

"What? No! No! No! I didn't get a chance to say good-bye!"

I ran down the hallway toward her room still carrying my purse and my packed lunch. I sobbed loudly and openly, turning every head as I ran past. I was breaking every rule, but I didn't care. I pushed my way through her door. She was still lying in her bed, silent and still. Her eyes were closed. I would never see those silver-blue eyes again. I would never see that smile or hear her cheery voice again. I collapsed into a chair by her bed with my head in my hands, still crying.

Nadine came in behind me with Sally, the new nurse's aide who was shadowing me this week. "I tried to call home as soon as I found out. You must have been in the shower," Nadine said.

I ignored her and kept sobbing.

I could hear Sally speak up. "I thought we weren't supposed to cry when people died."

"She wasn't just 'people,'" I spat out. "She was special."

"But I thought …"

"Would you just leave?" I spun around angrily to face the young girl. "Get out! Just go! I don't want to hear about any crappy rules!"

"Sally," Nadine turned to her and spoke, "I think I'm going to have you shadow Shantel this week instead. Chrissy is going to take the day off today. Let's give her a little bit of space. There are some sheets and towels in the laundry room that need to be folded, okay?"

I heard Sally leave the room. I was holding Miss Candace's hand and I felt Nadine's hand on my back. "She died all alone in the middle of the night, just like my Mo… just like I feared," I said.

"She died peacefully in her sleep. And she knew she was loved. You made sure of that. Remembering that will help you to accept it, Chrissy. It's what she wanted."

258

Nadine reached out and touched Miss Candace's face, then squeezed her lifeless hand. "We'll miss you here, sweet lady." She nodded up at the pictures on the wall. "Go with them." Then she returned her hand to my back. "Take all the time that you need with her to say good-bye. You're taking the day off. We can handle things here just fine."

I heard the door click shut behind her. I stayed alone in the room with Miss Candace holding her hand. I cried until there were no more tears left. Then I just sat in silence for a while, thinking about her life and all the things she'd endured. Then I stood and bent over her to kiss her forehead one last time and drew the sheet over her head.

I walked over to the bookshelf where her photo album rested. I opened it up to the page with the black-and-white portrait of young Miss Candace. She looked to be about my age, so happy and full of life, so full of hope for what life had in store for her. I slipped the picture from underneath its plastic cover and put it with my things. No one would miss this photo. And I think she would have wanted me to have it.

Her funeral was held the following weekend at her church. The person handling the funeral program asked me if I would share a few thoughts about Miss Candace. I thought about doing it for a little while, but my old school shyness got the better of me and I declined. I couldn't bear the thought of all those faces turned in my direction as I spoke. What if I lost my composure and cried in front of them? I couldn't let that happen.

Instead I sat and stared at the floor of the chapel during her funeral. Nadine sat next to me, and a few other people from the care center were there. There were also lots of people from her church. I was surprised that we managed to fill the chapel. A few people who were close to her at church spoke about her. They talked about how eager she was to learn and how happy she was to serve in various church roles and to participate in all the church functions during the time that she still able. They spoke about how she maintained a cheery disposition even after becoming confined to a wheelchair. She always chose to see the positive side of everything and was admired by everyone who knew her.

I began to wish that I'd had the courage to speak. It wasn't that the speakers portrayed an inaccurate version of Miss Candace. It was all true. But it really took knowing about her past to appreciate how far she'd come. That was a perspective that only I could have provided because she hadn't shared those things with anyone else.

When I'd first met Miss Candace, I'd assumed that she'd had a wonderful life, that she'd never known a day of sorrow. It's easy to be happy if that's the kind of life you've led. It's much more difficult if you've faced tremendous sorrows and heartbreak the way she had.

I didn't join in singing any of the songs or listen to the prayers. In some ways I felt angry with God for always taking people away from me. Sometimes I think it would just be easier to believe in no God than one who doesn't seem to hear your cries and pleas for help. I wasn't going to ask God for help anymore, I decided. The message from Him was loud and clear: You're on your own, Chrissy.

We rode in silence in Nadine's car to the cemetery where Miss Candace's coffin would be buried. Nadine knew I needed some space, so she didn't try to force a conversation. We sat through more words, prayers, and songs at her burial plot and then lowered her coffin into the ground. I kept my eyes focused on her coffin the whole time. As people began to disperse, I told Nadine that I wanted to stay awhile longer and that I would just walk home. It was a few miles, but the walk would do me good.

After she left, a middle-aged man came up to me and smiled. "Christine Rollings?"

"Yes," I answered apprehensively. How did he know my name?

"I'm Michael Broder, Mrs. Thorngood's attorney. I was wondering if you might be able to stop by my office sometime next week to discuss some things." He handed me his business card.

I reluctantly took it. "Um, okay." Had I done something wrong? Was I being sued? "Is everything okay?" I asked.

"Oh, yes. This is just a formality. Could you come by on Wednesday afternoon, around 2 p.m.?"

"That's probably all right. I'll call if I can't get that afternoon off."

"Thank you. I'll see you Wednesday."

I slipped the business card in my purse. Hopefully this was just something harmless. I wouldn't worry about it for now, I decided. I stayed and watched while the hole in the ground was filled. Everyone left to go home. But I wanted to sit by the gravesite for a while.

Sunset Care Center just wouldn't be the same without Miss Candace. Every time I walked past her room, it made me sad. The room hadn't been filled yet, but it would be soon, and that would make me sadder still. It would be as if we'd replaced her with someone else. I had to just remind myself of what Nadine had said. She'd died peacefully. She'd died knowing she was loved, unlike Momma. Over time, I would be able to accept Miss Candace's death, I told myself.

I walked over to where the beautiful, colorful bouquets of flowers were placed on Miss Candace's gravesite. I pulled out two of the long-stemmed yellow roses and slowly made my way over to the other side of the cemetery. It took me a while to find the two small side-by-side grave markers. Both markers were covered in dirt and overgrown with grass and weeds. I got down on my hands and knees and spent the next several minutes pulling up grass, dirt, and weeds until my hands and fingernails were filthy.

When the markers were finally presentable, I sat silently on the grass between the graves of my buried parents. They were born the same year and died seven years apart and were together forever now in death. I stayed there, lost in memories, until it grew to dusk. Finally, I arose from the ground and bent to place a long-stemmed rose on each of their graves. Shades of pink and orange streaked across the sky in the distance as I walked home.

Fortunately, I had remembered how to plaster on a fake smile and feign a cheery voice, even when I felt lifeless inside. That's how I made it through the next few days at work. Keeping busy had always proved to be the best way for me to cope with loss. If I could distract myself with the tedious business of everyday life, I couldn't be swallowed by my grief.

I'd asked for Wednesday afternoon off so that I could visit Mr. Broder's office. That was another thing that I tried not to dwell on. He'd assured me that the visit was some sort of harmless formality, but the unknown was always a bit scary to me. Maybe it was because of the briefcase he carried at his side. Somehow it reminded me of the day that a briefcase-toting Blue Lids had shown up at my house all those years ago to give me the wonderful news about a fabulous program for "people like me." I knew how that story ended, which made me wary of Michael Broder, even though he'd seemed nice enough.

I had to call his office and ask his receptionist for directions to their office building. I was not familiar with that part of Hilldale. As I drove there, I tried to assure myself that everything would be fine. If I were in some sort of legal trouble, I could always call Miss Stacey's son for guidance and I'm sure he would help me. He'd been so wonderful handling all the details of my divorce and hadn't charged me a penny. Some people like to portray all lawyers as scoundrels, but that certainly hadn't been my experience with them at least.

The office building was located in a really beautiful part of town. The streets were lined with trees. All the office buildings sat on well-manicured lawns, with well-placed bushes, flowers, and rocks to add to the landscaping. I parked in the building's lot and checked the address against the business card to make sure I was in the right place. I walked through the glass front entrance doors and was greeted by Michael Broder's receptionist in the front lobby. She asked me to wait a few minutes. I sat down on a soft brown couch and took a few deep breaths to remain calm. This was no big deal. I reminded myself that he'd been Miss Candace's attorney. She would never authorize some sort of lawsuit or anything that would cause me grief.

After a few minutes, the receptionist brought me to Mr. Broder's office, a nice room with big windows and mahogany furniture. Mr. Broder stood from his desk and walked over to shake my hand.

"Thank you for meeting with me today, Miss Rollings. This won't take very long. But there is some paperwork and things for you to sign. Won't you sit down?"

"What exactly am I supposed to be signing?" I asked.

"Please have a seat."

I reluctantly sat down and waited for him to continue.

"As you probably know, Mrs. Thorngood was very organized and mentally competent right until the very end."

It seemed so odd to hear Miss Candace's last name. At her funeral, people had referred to her as "Sister Thorngood." It just didn't seem to fit her.

"Yes, I know that."

"She was very meticulous in her will and laid out exactly what she wanted to happen following her death. Her estate was not very large, but she did have some savings as well as the property that was left to her by her husband. Now the house on that property is extremely old and should probably be demolished, but it sits on a two-acre lot that is pretty valuable. We've already had a lot of interest in the property. It should sell right away."

I'd almost completely forgotten that Miss Candace had owned a home in Hilldale. It had seemed to me that her home was her room at Sunset and all the property she owned could be found in her dresser and bookshelves there.

Mr. Broder continued. "There are a few expenses and bills that still need to be paid, her care at Sunset, her property taxes, funeral expenses and attorney fees. She wanted 10 percent of all her money to go to her church." I nodded my head. Why did I need to know this minutia? "She wanted the remainder, or 90 percent of the leftover estate, to go to you."

My mouth dropped open. To me? A nurse's aide? Why in the world would she do that? Was there no one else?

"Based on our estimates of the property's value after taxes, you'll be getting a total of about $30,000." My mouth dropped open even wider. That was more money than I could even comprehend. It was about three times my yearly salary!

Mr. Broder continued, but I could hardly listen to what he was saying. I was just trying to make sense of what was happening here. I wasn't being sued! I was the main beneficiary in Miss Candace's will.

Mr. Broder continued to go over details, looking up at me distractedly from time to time. Maybe he knew I wasn't really paying attention anymore. Finally he interrupted himself, "Uh, Miss Rollings? Are you all right?"

"Oh, sorry! Yes, I'm just very surprised. I really can't quite believe this is happening!"

He continued to talk and I nodded and tried to pay attention. But my mind kept wandering off again. What in the world was she thinking? How come she hadn't said anything to me about this? Why would anyone leave that kind of money in my hands? What did she think I was going to do with it? It was as if I'd won the lottery without even knowing I was in the drawing!

There were several forms for me to sign. Mr. Broder said that he had a check to give to me that day in the amount of $5,000, and the remaining $25,000 would be given to me after the sale of the Thorngood property.

After I'd signed everything, he handed me the check for $5,000. I just stared at it in disbelief. So many zeros! And this was just a fraction of what was to come. I didn't even feel comfortable putting it in my purse. I needed to have it right next to me, where I could feel it was still there. I put it in my pocket.

"She also dictated this letter to be given to you."

He handed me the letter, and I folded it and slipped it into my pocket as well. I couldn't read it right now. I could hardly even focus on his instructions.

I don't remember even saying good-bye to the receptionist as I walked out of there. I felt like this was some sort of dream. My hands shook as I reached for the keys in my purse.

There was no place I really needed to be right now. I decided to go for a walk to get some air and try to sort out the events of the last hour. I didn't feel steady enough to handle a car at the moment, but I could walk.

I walked through the tree-lined streets for several blocks, admiring the pretty residential area where kids were riding their bikes and playing kickball in the streets.

It was too much money! To me, money came in amounts of tens and twenties — occasionally, large bills went into the hundreds. But I never even thought of money in the thousands or tens of thousands. Thirty thousand dollars! It would take me all day long just to count that high.

Surely somebody else needed it more. I could pay all my bills. I didn't have a lot, but I had enough. I was comfortable.

Maybe she had some instructions for me for what I was to do with this fortune. Maybe I was supposed to spend it a certain way. I felt in my pocket for the folded note and took it out. My pace slowed as I read the note:

Dear Chrissy,

Well, I'll bet this is a surprise! I've been so excited about this day. How I would love to see your face when you found out the news. But, unfortunately, I have to be gone before you can hear it.

I want to thank you for making the last few years of my life so sweet and special. It was such a treat for me every day to be greeted by your smiling face and cheery voice. You never seemed to mind all the drudgery of doing the things for me that I used to do for myself. You've been a wonderful caregiver as well as a friend.

You don't know how many times I've thought about your story of being found under a rock as a baby. I think of that awful day, so many years ago, when I buried my baby girl under a rock. Back then, I thought God had abandoned me and was deaf to my cries. It may sound silly, but I like to think now that maybe that little baby never really died at all. She just lay there dormant for decades and emerged years later in the form of Chrissy Rollings! So maybe you understand a little bit why I think of you as part of my family and why I feel the inheritance rightfully belongs to you. That rock is our connection.

Now, don't you worry about me or waste any time on sadness and sorrow. You know that I'm right where I want to be and I'm happy. My days were numbered when we met, but you have many, many more days ahead of you. And I think there is much happiness in store for you.

I have sensed that there are some things in your past that have scarred you and filled you with sorrow and regret. I didn't want to press you about those things, thinking that you would tell me when you were ready. We ran out of time, but I do want to tell you now that I know what it's like to live with sorrow and regret, and I know what it's like to get past it. We are shaped by the events of our past, but those events do not define us. Nor do they determine our future.

You were so strong and determined when you finally decided to leave a toxic marriage. I wish I could have had your strength a long time ago. You are much stronger than you realize. Now use that strength to confidently pursue your hopes and dreams. And always remember my favorite quote: "It's never too late to be what you might have been."

I will miss you dearly, but I know we'll meet again. And I can't wait to see what the future has in store for you.

With much love,
Miss Candace

The letter was neatly typed and Miss Candace had scrawled her shaky signature at the bottom. I read the letter a few more times and then tucked it back into my pocket alongside the check.

I had no idea where my legs were taking me, but I felt the need to just let them go where they wanted to go, taking note of the street names that I passed so that I would remember how to get back to my car eventually.

I walked along, thinking about Miss Candace's life and the strange twist and turn of events that had brought us together. Miss Candace had led a life marked by fear, pain, and sorrow. But, in her last decade, she'd decided that life was still good and worth living. She wanted me to discover that sooner than she'd discovered it.

At that moment, the world *did* seem full of hope and wonder. I could feel the warm North Carolina breezes blowing through my hair and see the sun dancing and glinting through the leaves of the tree-lined streets as I walked. The dancing lights seemed to be pointing in the direction that I should take and I trustingly followed where they beckoned. I felt the check again in my pocket, a check for $5,000 made out in my name, and the promise of more to come. I thought about the enormity of the gift I'd just been given. It wasn't just the gift of money. It was also the gift of hope. For the first time, I felt that I could see the pathway to an open, undetermined but bright future. I realized that I had just been given a leg up!

And suddenly I recognized the place where my legs had decided to take me. I found myself striding purposefully across the Pemberton State College campus and through the front doors of the administration building.

"May I help you?" asked the girl at the front desk.

"Yes, please. I'd like an application for admission."

27

I'd been right all along. Change *was* in the air. But I no longer feared change or tried to stop it. To live is to change.

Tyrone got the coaching job in New York, just as I knew he would. He and Nadine planned to move by summer's end so that he could start with the new school year. I'd be alone again, but I knew I had the confidence and means to get by on my own now.

In June, Nadine told Ty that he could ask her to marry him if he wanted. He proposed with a ring as we sat on a picnic blanket under the annual Fourth of July fireworks show at a large park in Hilldale. She, of course, accepted. As I watched them hold hands and dream of their future together under the exploding colors of light in the night sky, I thought I had never seen anything so pure. Stan had once told me that their relationship was evil because they lived together before marriage. But he'd been wrong. *Ours* was the relationship that was evil and impure, not theirs. Nadine and Ty planned to hold their wedding the following spring in New York. They hoped I would come, and I said of course I would. I wouldn't miss it.

That summer, Nadine and I reluctantly halted our frequent shopping trips to the mall. Now was the time to get rid of things rather than accumulate more. We sorted through all the household items and boxed up things for the move. We held a few weekend yard sales to get rid of the stuff we didn't need or want.

I'd been accepted for admission at Pemberton State College. I spoke with Miss Cummings about wanting to go back to school in the fall, and she agreed that I could reduce my work hours and that Sunset would work around my class schedule as needed. I wanted to keep my job and go to school concurrently if I could manage both. My plan was to start out as a part-time student. I registered for two classes. If that went well and I thought I could handle more, I would increase my course-load at school. I figured I'd waited this long to go to college. Why start rushing through now? There was no huge hurry to graduate by a specific time. And I didn't want to be overwhelmed in my first semester at school.

I found a one-bedroom apartment about midway between work and school. It was perfect for me. I didn't want to have to deal with a roommate. I worked out my budget on paper and realized that, if I lived frugally, I could basically live off of what I earned, even with my reduced pay. I would need to dip into my savings from Miss Candace only for the big expenses like tuition and books.

It was satisfying knowing that I could live alone, work and go to school, all on my own. Once I settled into my new schedule of work and school, I knew that I would stay busy and not have time to feel lonely or sorry for myself. Nadine, Ty, and I planned to move out of the rental house at the same time in August. They'd recruited some friends to help with the move. We first moved all of my stuff into my new apartment and then went back and reloaded the moving truck for their long drive to New York.

I knew that I would miss Nadine and Ty immensely. It was hard to imagine work and home life without them. I would miss our lunches out on the lawns of Sunset Care Center. I would miss having Nadine as my boss, a boss who allowed me to be my own boss. I'd miss our conversations and laughter at the dinner table. I'd miss our shopping excursions, food court treats, and card games. I'd even miss our chore chart. But most of all, I'd miss the kind of rare friend that I'd managed to find in Nadine. I'd make other friends, sure, but I knew it just wouldn't be the same.

We said our final good-byes, and I watched them pull away in their moving truck, thinking how much I'd depended on them the past few years. Honestly, I don't know how I would have gotten by without them.

Friends like Nadine are truly hard to come by — the kind of friend who tells you truth, even when you don't want to hear it; the kind of friend who is always there for you, no matter what.

After they were gone, I busied myself setting up my apartment and getting ready for my first day of school. I had registered for two general education courses: a life science class and an English composition class. Both classes met on Monday, Wednesday, and Friday. The English class was immediately after the science class. I would be working full days on Tuesdays and Thursdays and reduced hours on the remaining days and weekends. I visited the campus to buy my books and to visit the buildings in which I had classes. I timed how long it would take me to get from building to building. They were both on the side of campus that was close to the library. I loved having access to a college library! It was a spacious with plenty of sitting areas. I assumed I would be going there for most of my research and studying.

On the morning that fall semester began, I sprang from bed and got myself ready for my first day of school. I was more than a little excited. It had been five years since I'd been in a classroom and I couldn't wait to be back! My life science class was large, about 50 students. That was just to my liking. I could sit in the back and be comfortably anonymous. Most of the students looked to be fresh out of high school. I was a few years older than they were, but I didn't mind. They probably would have no idea about my age unless they somehow found out that I was a divorced woman.

I studied the course syllabus and was happy to see that grades were completely dependent upon completion and quality of homework assignments, quizzes, tests, and a research paper. I would need to get started on the research paper this weekend. I already knew I'd be up most of the night coming up with a topic.

Even though I had been more excited about registering for the English class than the science class, I wondered if I should drop the English class from the moment I walked into the room. It was much smaller, about 20 students. The seats were arranged in a large semi-circle around the room. I couldn't sit in the back and blend into the wall. Reading through the syllabus, my heart dropped further. On top of reading and written assignments, a full one-third of my grade would be dependent upon sharing in class things that I'd written and participating in class discussions! I felt a wave of panic go through me. I wasn't cut out for this. Here I was, a self-declared English major, ready to drop out after reading the course syllabus of a general education English class!

After class, I headed for the library to get started on my homework and to think. I reminded myself of the words in Miss Candace's letter. She'd told me that I was stronger than I thought I was. There was no way I could drop out after having come this far. Just because I'd never made a peep in high school didn't mean I had to be the same way in college. No one knew about me. No one knew a thing about my past. *We are shaped by the events of our past, but those events do not define us. Nor do they determine our future.*

I vowed to march back into that English class on Wednesday, sit smack dab in the middle of the room, and make some sort of brilliant comment every time the professor asked a question. It didn't end up working out quite that way though. I chickened out at the last minute and sat as far to one side of the semi-circle as I could. When the professor asked a question, several people raised their hands and started a class discussion. Every time I thought of something "brilliant" to contribute, my heart would start pounding fast and my face would turn red before I even had the courage to raise my hand. Then, by the time I worked up the courage to try and raise my hand, they would already be onto a different topic so that my comment was no longer relevant. I would try to think of something else to say and the vicious cycle continued until the class period was over.

The same thing happened on Friday, and then the entire next week. That class was so full of jabberwockies, I'd never be able to get a word in edgewise! To make matters worse, one young man sat opposite from me in the semi-circle and constantly stared at me, as if amused by my quiet torment and frustration. He stared so much that I became a little self-conscious. Did I have a milk mustache or a giant red pimple erupting on my forehead? Why couldn't he annoy somebody else with his staring problem?

Most of the time I just tried to ignore him and pretend I hadn't noticed his constant staring. But when I would throw him a stern, "stop looking at me" glance, his face would erupt into a huge smile, punctuated with a dimple on each cheek. It was infuriating! I never returned the smile, but that didn't seem to stop him. He had a small space between his two front teeth that was, admittedly, rather charming. But I wasn't about to fall for something like that. I'd had enough "charming" men to last me a lifetime, thank you very much. I suppose he might have been objectively nice looking, if you're an objective kind of person. He was tall and had sandy-blonde hair that fell into his eyes and olive skin that gave him the look of having a year-round tan.

He'd raise his hand every once in a while and make some clever comment that was directly relevant to the class discussion. Sometimes it was almost verbatim to the comment I was trying to muster the courage to make, and he stole it from me before I ever had the chance to say it. Then the professor would rave over it, as if he'd just said the most profound thing the world had ever known. I would slump back in my seat, thwarted once again, waiting for the annoying onslaught of dimples. I'd noted his name was Trevor, Trevor Townsend, not that I cared. I mean, what kind of name was that? Clever Trevor. Well, he could go be clever somewhere else. He probably assumed I was some young, fresh-out-of-high-school girl who would swoon over a couple of clever comments and a big, dimpled grin. Well, he would soon learn that smiles, stares, and clever comments had no effect on me. And I didn't swoon.

The first couple of weeks of class, we mainly read well-known essays, wrote about them, and then discussed them in class. But I'd noticed that a "personal essay" was listed on the syllabus, and I'd already started to lose sleep over what it might entail before the professor even mentioned it. Sure enough, it was just what I feared. We were to write a one-page personal essay that would give people a "snapshot" into our own lives. Some of us would be asked to read our essays aloud to the class! My heart sank as I packed my book-bag and headed to the library after class that day. I didn't share things about my life, ever, even with people I loved. How could I provide a "snapshot" of my life for perfect strangers? There was nothing to say! I couldn't, or wouldn't, share anything about my past. Could I fill an entire page about how I lived alone, played the guitar, read books, attended school, and worked at a nursing home? The entire class would be asleep before I finished reading the page!

Fortunately, that night as I lay awake in my apartment, some ideas started forming. I could slightly deflect the essay from focusing solely on me so that it provided a "snapshot" instead of my work-life. I may not have led a life that was worth sharing in an essay, but I knew plenty of people who'd led interesting, fascinating lives. It was a perfect plan. I had the whole thing written in my head by the time I finally drifted to sleep around 3 a.m. It wasn't a wonderful essay, but it would have to do.

We turned in our essays the following Friday as we were leaving class. Clever Trevor turned in his right after mine and smiled at me. "That was a tough one, huh?" he commented.

"Not really," I replied curtly and quickened my pace so that he wouldn't try to walk with me as I headed toward the library.

The next week, when our essays were handed back, mine had been given a solid "A." The professor had written "Very unique snapshot. I hope you'll be willing to share in class." I was thrilled, except for the sharing in class part. Hopefully, the professor would forget about that by the time he started asking people to read their essays. I did *not* want to read mine. I hadn't even summoned the courage to make a single comment in class.

The professor spent most of the class period talking about writing style, which was good. I watched the clock, willing it to move faster. Then he started calling on people to read their essays for the class. My heart quickened and I could feel beads of sweat collecting on the back of my neck. I didn't pay attention at all to the other essays being read aloud. I just watched the clock and hoped the jabberwockies would analyze every sentence to death until class was over.

With five minutes to spare, the professor interrupted the discussion. "I wanted to make sure we had time to hear Christine Rollings' essay. She used an interesting writing technique for her snapshot, but I think it's very effective. Christine, would you mind reading yours?"

Clever Trevor was grinning at me. The dimples were in full force today.

"Um. All right," I said. My hands shook as I held up my paper, so I set it back down on the desk and cleared my throat.

The Unexpected

Looking at Mr. George's wheelchair-bound legs, you wouldn't expect that he'd used them to run across the battlefields of two World Wars, but he did.
Looking at Miss Jenny's arthritic, withered hands, you wouldn't expect that she'd used them to raise nine children all on her own, but she did.

When you see Mr. Aaron's hearing aid, you wouldn't expect that he'd spent decades playing concert violin in the finest symphony in the state, but he did.
When you see Mr. William leaning against his cane for support, you wouldn't expect that he'd once been a track champion in the Olympic games, but he was.

Looking into Miss Anna's soft brown eyes, you wouldn't expect that she'd witnessed the barking hounds, unimaginable horrors, and the gates of hell at Auschwitz Concentration Camp, but she did.

Looking at Mr. Henry's mottled, shaking hands, you wouldn't expect that he'd saved hundreds of lives and trained the most skilled surgeons in the South, but he did.

When you see Miss Velma's smiling face, her welcome mat at the door, and the empty chairs set out in her room, you wouldn't expect that she has 15 family members within driving distance who never come to visit her, but she does.

As I spoon-fed Miss Candace and lifted her in and out of her wheelchair, I didn't expect that she'd end up being the one to take care of me, but she was.

When I first came to work at Sunset Care Center, I never expected that the sterile white hallways and the smell of antiseptic and medicine would become the sights and sounds of home to me, but they did.

I never expected that the strangers living and working there would become my closest friends and family, but they did.

I never expected to find that the mundane and the extraordinary, the plain and the beautiful, the weak and the strong, the fading old and the vibrantly young at heart, the everyday and the sublime could coexist and co-mingle in the same place at the same time, but they can.

So, if you ask me what to expect at Sunset Care Center, the best I can tell you is this:

You should expect the unexpected."

The class was silent after I finished. They must have hated it, I thought. But one girl dabbed at her eyes with a tissue and said, "I'm calling my grandma as soon as I get home today." A few people chuckled.

The professor said, "We don't have enough time for a thorough discussion, but you can see how she juxtaposes seemingly opposite things to really make each line a powerful statement in itself. I think this is a wonderful 'snapshot' into the life at a care center. She really humanizes it. Excellent job, Christine."

People nodded their heads and gathered their things as we prepared to leave class. I was just happy that I'd survived the ordeal and that it had been at the end of class so that the attention hadn't been focused on me for an unbearable length of time. My face still felt hot, but my heart was slowing down. I planned to head over to the library for some study time before I had to be at work later that day.

As we left the building, I noticed someone speeding to catch up with me. "Wow! That was an amazing essay you wrote." It was Clever Trevor.

"Oh, uh," I cleared my throat, "thank you."

"I sure hope I don't have to read my essay to the class now. It will sound pretty bland and boring after that."

"I'm sure that's not true. You've said some neat stuff in class." Neat stuff? *Chrissy! Get a hold of yourself!*

I kept on walking, but he kept pace with me. "It's Christine, right?"

"Well, most people just call me Chrissy."

"I'm Trevor, by the way."

"Oh. Okay." I pretended I hadn't known his name before.

"Where'd you learn to write like that?"

"I … um … don't really know."

"Listen, Chrissy, do you have class or anything right now?" I just looked at him blankly. "There's a coffee shop down the street. Maybe we could walk over there and get a coffee or something and just chat. Do you have time? You could give me some writing pointers."

"I don't really have any writing pointers," I said lamely. "And … I have to be at work in," I glanced at my watch, "two-and-a-half hours."

He looked at me so hopefully. The dimples appeared again. "Well, that does kill my original plan to drone on for three hours about baseball stats. But we really don't have to take that long. We can watch the clock to make sure you leave on time."

I hesitated, looking at my watch again and then glancing in the direction of the library. I really had planned to use that time to do research for my science paper, due at the end of the semester, but it would seem too much like a made-up excuse not to join him.

"Tell you what," he said. "I'll sweeten the deal by promising to try not to spill hot coffee all over your lap. I've learned the hard way it does not impress girls much."

There was something so familiar about him, I realized. It was the way he could say something funny with a completely serious face. Only the glint in his eye told you he was just trying to get a reaction out of you. It reminded me of Daddy! The way he'd described in such detail how he'd found me under a rock.

"Well, okay," I said. *Damn those dimples!*

We walked over to the coffee shop and spent the next two hours talking. It was very comfortable talking to him, but my guard was still up. I remembered thinking Stan had been a nice guy too. Men are always on their best behavior until they've won you over. Then the ugliness comes out.

But I really had no hint then of whatever ugliness was beneath those dimples. He told me that he'd grown up in Hilldale. He'd graduated from Central High School, which was the rival school to Green Level High. He had a younger brother named Jessie who still went to Central. Trevor was actually a third-year student at the University of North Carolina in Chapel Hill studying "city and regional planning." But he'd decided to come home for a little while for family reasons. He told me that his mother's breast cancer, which they thought she'd beaten a few years ago, had returned. The doctors had given her a year, at best, to live.

"I'm so sorry," I said.

"Well," he said. "I wouldn't write her off just yet. The doctors don't know her the way I do. She's pretty stubborn. But I decided I'm probably needed more at home right now than in Chapel Hill. I can get some of the general education courses that I don't really enjoy out of the way at Pemberton."

"Like English composition?" I teased.

He smiled, "Well, it's probably not my favorite subject. I told you, I'm not a very good writer. But mainly I just felt the need to be in Hilldale right now. I can always go back to UNC to finish my degree later. I don't want to have any regrets."

I nodded my head, staring at the floor. "It's terrible to live with regrets."

Trevor paused for a moment. "But enough about me, I want to hear about you. Tell me about yourself. Are you from Hilldale?"

"Yes," I said. "I graduated from Green Level High about five years ago. This is my first year in college."

I deflected the topic of conversation from me by getting him to tell me about UNC. I'd never been to Chapel Hill, but I'd heard it was a nice place and that UNC was a very good school. Trevor obviously wasn't your typical Hilldale hillbilly. He talked for a little while and then turned the conversation back to me. He wasn't satisfied with the little I'd offered about myself. I wasn't used to having to come up with things to say about myself. I'd always been able to avoid the subject by saying a few brief words and then turning the topic around. Let's face it, most people find themselves to be a fascinating conversational topic. Stan had never grown tired of talking about himself.

"I think you've already heard the most interesting things about me from my essay."

"But that wasn't really about you. It was about your place of work. It was terrific, don't get me wrong, but it doesn't tell me much about you."

"Well, let's see," I began. "I was born under a rock, or so the story goes."

"That explains a lot about you." We both chuckled. He waited for me to continue.

"So I live alone. I read and play the guitar. I don't have any family. My parents are dead. I really don't like to talk about my past. It's full of tragedy and misery. I really don't have any close friends. I did, but they moved. Or died. I don't like to party. I don't socialize much. That's pretty much it. Oh, and I had a two-year train wreck of a marriage. I don't really like to talk about that either."

"Boy, you sure know how to reel a guy in."

His observation caught me by surprise, and I started to laugh. "Yes, well, I'm quite the catch, you know. Normally, there's a line of men down the street just waiting for a chance to date me. You just happened to catch me during a little … lull."

"I have excellent timing," he said.

I was amazed at how at ease I felt talking to Trevor. He seemed genuinely interested in what I had to say and wasn't completely put off by the fact that I was a couple of years older than he was and obviously had some sort of rocky past.

"Well, I should probably take advantage of this 'lull' since it probably won't last long," he said. "Would you care to go out with me on a real date this weekend?"

"I can probably make some time," I answered.

I gave him my phone number and then he walked me back to where my car was parked in the school parking lot. I floated through the rest of my day at work with a dreamy look on my face. All the while, the sensible part of me demanded that I come back down to earth. Trevor seemed nice enough, but then again, I'd thought Stan was nice in the beginning too. Now I started wishing I still had Nadine around so that she could meet Trevor and tell me what she thought.

Even if Trevor wasn't perfect, it would still be nice to have someone to do things with occasionally, I told myself. And, he wasn't here permanently. Eventually he'd go back to Chapel Hill to finish his degree. That worked out perfectly for me. Since I knew he was leaving, I would view him as a temporary pleasant distraction, a nice little break from school and work. I wouldn't allow myself to get attached to him. Even if we did form some sort of relationship during the time he was in Hilldale, we'd eventually drift apart once he went back to Chapel Hill. We wouldn't have to have a messy break-up. We'd just realize that it wasn't going to work out.

Trevor and I went out that weekend, and then every weekend after that. In fact, we spent pretty much all of our spare time together. It still hardly seemed enough to me. I'd say good-bye to him one day and immediately begin anticipating the next time I would see him. I spent an extraordinary amount of time planning my outfits and how I would wear my hair and make-up the next time I saw Trevor, whether it was in class or on an outing together. Would Trevor like this outfit? Would Trevor think my hair looked good this way? Still, I berated myself for falling back into this trap of trying to look good for a man. Hadn't I vowed to never again so much as lift a finger or pluck a single stray eyebrow hair in the name of looking good for a man? But Trevor was different. He was smart. He was funny. He saw something worthwhile in me. And, best of all, Trevor was temporary.

28

"Mmmm, try this one, Trevor. I give it a 10." I handed him my chip dip sample at the grocery store sample table.

"I don't trust your ratings. You rate everything too high. Tens should be handed out very sparingly, if at all. But you give a 10 to nearly anything that's palatable." He tasted the dip and smacked his lips a few times. "It's an 8.2," he said matter-of-factly.

"Enough with the decimals!" I protested. "Use whole numbers!"

"I like to be precise when taste testing."

We loved stores that gave out free samples and typically went out of our way to visit the stores that offered plenty of samples. It seemed that everything was fun with Trevor, even mundane things like going to the grocery store to pick up items for dinner. We'd been dating only a few weeks and we were already past the point of going on formal "dates." We just automatically assumed that we'd be together if we both had a free evening. We'd study together, take a break to go for a walk, and then cook a meal together at my apartment.

Trevor didn't have preconceived notions about "female roles" and "male roles" the way Stan did. In fact, everything with Trevor was such a contrast to life with Stan. I remembered how much I hated running errands with Stan. We'd always get on each other's nerves. Even when we weren't outright fighting, there were still the constant put-downs from him. He never wanted me to think too highly of myself. By contrast, Trevor was always building me up. He seemed to think I was a better person than I actually was.

I kept waiting for Trevor to show some signs of nastiness or ugliness now that we'd come to know each other better. But if Trevor had flaws, they'd so far escaped my notice. I really did wish I could get a second opinion of him from someone who could be objective. Not only did I like Trevor more the more I got to know him, I liked *myself* better too when I was around him. I realized that I could joke around, laugh, and enjoy life when I was with the right person. I liked the person that being with Trevor brought out in me.

He no longer sat across from me in English class "tormenting" me with his grins. Instead, he sat next to me. And, just knowing that I had a friend right next to me somehow gave me the courage to speak up and make comments in that class. I still hadn't turned into one of the "jabberwockies," but I could hold my own. I was glad that I had registered just part-time that semester. I was busy, but I still had enough time to enjoy some free moments with Trevor. And the first time that he kissed me I actually felt weak in the knees. I'd always thought that was just an expression people used to describe what it felt like to kiss someone, but it turns out it's a real thing if you're kissing the right person.

Trevor invited me to come to his house to celebrate Halloween. I'd never been to his house or met his family, and it made me a little nervous. I remembered how uncomfortable I'd always felt around Stan's family. I secretly wished that it could be just Trevor and me without the "add-ons" of his family members. What if they didn't like me? His family was very important to him. He could probably be swayed by their opinion of me. But they were curious about this person who was taking all of Trevor's free time lately, so it was time to meet them in person.

They weren't having a party, he said. They were just planning to hand out candy to the trick-or-treaters that night. "But I have to warn you, my mom really 'gets into the spirit' of things." I wasn't really sure what that meant. Growing up, I'd never really considered Halloween to be much of a holiday. We didn't get the day off of school. We couldn't afford costumes and seldom bothered to come up with home-made ones. No trick-or-treaters came to our poverty-stricken area, which was good because we didn't have candy for them anyway. We could barely feed our own family and certainly couldn't afford to hand out candy to other people's children.

Trevor's family lived in one of the nicer neighborhoods in Hilldale. They had a large, two-story brick home with black shutters alongside the windows and a large rocking-chair porch spanning the front of the house. We arrived just as it was getting dark and the first trick-or-treaters were coming out. Trevor's mom had the entire porch decorated with what looked to be hand-crafted goblins, ghouls, ghosts, black cats, and witches. She was dressed as a witch and stood on the porch stirring a giant black cauldron with dry ice in it. A tape recorder in the background played scary-sounding music, and she cackled as the children came up to the porch for candy. Now I could see what Trevor meant by his mom really "getting into the spirit of things." She barely broke character as we were introduced, since there were still trick-or-treaters on the porch. I also met Trevor's dad and his younger brother Jessie, who was on his way out to a Halloween party with his friends.

Trevor and I went inside the house and he showed me around. It was a beautiful home that looked like it could be showcased in a decorator's magazine. What would it have been like to grow up in a place like this instead of where I'd been raised? The living room area was just as decorated for Halloween as the outside porch with all kinds of Halloween crafts.

"Boy, your family sure does like Halloween," I commented.

"Chrissy, this is just the tip of the iceberg," Trevor responded as his mom came inside and waited for more trick-or-treaters. "Our house is decorated this much for every holiday, practically year-round. In fact, there aren't enough holidays in the year for my mom. She has to make up some of her own. Let's see. There's a 'beach vacation' theme for June, a 'back to school' theme for September, a 'flower explosion' in May …"

"It's 'blossom festival' in May," Trevor's mom corrected him with a bop from her witch's broom on his head. She turned to me and explained, "Maybe it seems a little extreme, but I just enjoy all the seasons of the year and what they have to offer. I think life should be celebrated year-round. I've been accumulating this stuff for years, and I always buy it on sale. This is what I love, and the neighborhood has come to expect it now."

"Well, Mrs. Townsend, your decorations are fantastic!" I said.

"Please, call me Joyce. I'm too young to be Mrs. Townsend."

"I do a little bit of decorating myself from time to time as part of my job," I said. "I work at a nursing home. The residents just love it when I decorate our building for various things. It's nothing like the decorations here. I wouldn't even know where to find some of these crafts."

"She makes most of them," Trevor offered. "She spends about 90 percent of her time at the Hobby Barn."

"Trevor, you exaggerate!" Joyce said. Then, turning to me, she said, "They do have everything there. I like to go right after a holiday when everything is marked down and I buy my stuff for next year."

"I've never been there," I said. "I'll have to make it over there though. We could use some updated decorations at the care center."

"You'd be welcome to go through the boxes in our attic. I have everything sorted and labeled. I've been doing this for years, so we have much more than we need. You're welcome to use anything you like."

I was dying to go up there and sort through those boxes that very moment. Trevor laughed at the look on my face, "Chrissy, you look like you've just won the lottery."

"I have! I'm coming back here tomorrow to load up on Thanksgiving decorations."

284

Joyce seemed pleased that I liked the decorations as much as she did. Just then, more trick-or-treaters came to the door. Joyce put her witch's hat back on, grabbed her broom, and hurried out the door, cackling with glee. I watched as she stayed in her witch's persona, handing out candy to the children in costumes.

"What are you making in the pot?" they asked.

"Oh, it's a special brew made with frog's tongue, snake eyes, rat's tail, and cockroaches. Would you like to try some?"

"No!" The kids ran off, screaming.

Joyce laughed and continued stirring her smoky pot. I wasn't sure what I had expected at the prospect of meeting Trevor's mother, but she was nothing like I would have imagined. "Okay," I said, "I think I need to get in on some of this action."

Joyce rounded up another witch's hat and a cloak for me. Trevor put on a scary mask and we spent all evening out on the porch handing out candy and scaring children. By the end of the night, I could cackle almost as well as Joyce. "I'm starting to see the appeal of being a great cackler," I remarked to Trevor. "From now on, I will not laugh, giggle, or even chuckle. I will only cackle."

"Mom, what have you done? You've created a monster!" said Trevor.

After the trick-or-treaters went home for the night, Joyce told us we could take what we wanted from the leftover candy. Trevor and I dove for the pot of candy and bartered and traded for our favorite candies like little kids. I had never laughed so much or felt so at ease in someone else's family environment.

Trevor's dad, Hal, seemed to have a great marriage with Joyce. He joked around and teased all evening. Pretend bickering seemed to be a Townsend family trait, but you could sense the love beneath it. I'd take pretend bickering any day over the real thing. It wasn't until I'd gone home for the night that I even remembered that Joyce had a life-threatening illness. She hadn't seemed sick at all to me. I was around sickness and death all the time at my job, but I didn't sense it coming from her. Maybe Trevor was right and the doctors were wrong about her. There was no way she could be gone within a year.

The next day, I went back over to the Townsend home to see what Thanksgiving decorations I might be able to borrow for the care center. Trevor had gone to play tennis with his brother, since he wasn't really interested in going through decorations with us. Joyce led me to the attic and I was astounded by what I saw up there. There were boxes and plastic totes stacked all the way up to the ceiling of the attic. Everything was organized and labeled. It was like a public library of holiday and seasonal decorations. There were five large boxes labeled "Thanksgiving" alone. Joyce was busy taking down all of her Halloween decorations, so I picked out the things I thought could be used at the care center and filled one box with them.

I made sure Joyce saw everything I was taking before I took the box out to my car. I'd picked out a couple of stuffed scarecrows, some beaded pumpkins, a cornucopia, a set of pilgrims, and a few wreaths decorated with fall-colored leaves.

"What I think I'll do is get a few hay bales for the entrance, and I'll put the scarecrows and pumpkins on them. The wreaths will go in the hallways and the pilgrims and cornucopia will be in the rec room," I explained to her.

With every item that I took from the box to show her, she would exclaim, "Isn't that adorable!" and proceed to tell me how she'd made it or found it on clearance at the Hobby Barn.

I would ask, "Did you want to keep this? I don't want to take it if you'll use it here."

"Oh, no, no, no. You take it. You can even take more than that. I'll still have plenty of things left over."

By the end of the morning, she'd talked me into taking two of the boxes with me. I'd be able to find a place for everything, I was sure. When I brought it all to the care center, it took me a couple of hours to decorate, but the feedback was immediate. The residents loved how festive it looked in our building. I felt a little guilty now that the other buildings didn't look as good as Building C, but I wasn't about to offer to decorate all the buildings at Sunset. The other staff could handle their own buildings.

The weather grew colder and the leaves turned brilliant that fall. Trevor and I liked to take long walks to enjoy the scenery and each other's company. I felt that I'd never been happier. Still, the nagging voice inside of me reminded me that nothing ever stays happy for long. There had to be something wrong with Trevor. I just couldn't see it yet. I tried to probe him for information that would help me uncover his flaws. There was only one time I even came close to finding something.

"Are you a Methodist? Please say you're not a Methodist," I asked as we took a walk around a pond in a local park. We'd brought some leftover bread to feed the ducks.

"I'm not a Methodist," he answered. He cast a sideways glance at the relieved look on my face as I tossed bread crumbs into the water. "I must say, you're the first 'anti-Methodist' I've ever met."

"Well, I'm not really 'anti' all of them. Just one of them."

"I see. You're a micro-bigot."

"Yes, but with good reason. I should have guessed that you weren't one. You would have told me." I wrapped my arms around his neck and kissed him.

Trevor hesitated for a moment, and then haltingly offered, "Actually, uh, I'm an atheist."

"You're a whatiest?"

"It's a person who doesn't believe in God."

"I know what it is. I just can't believe you are one! How could you not believe in God?"

"How could you not believe in Santa Claus?"

"That's different!"

"Not to an atheist."

"But I've heard that atheism is like its own religion. It has its own leaders and followers. They go around making fun of

287

religious people and try to take religion away from everyone else."

"Atheism is a 'religion' like not collecting stamps is a hobby," he said. "And no one talked me into being an atheist. I just figured it out on my own over time. I just don't believe in things that have no proof. Sorry. I'm not a subscriber. That doesn't mean I go around trying to cancel everyone else's subscription. But I would appreciate it if they weren't always trying to sell me theirs."

I considered this for a moment. In a way it was a relief to me. I'd found a "flaw" in Trevor! And it was one I could accept.

We began kissing again, our favorite pastime of late.

Suddenly he pulled away. "Wait a minute. You're not Amish, are you? Please say you're not Amish."

"No, but I might join the Mormons someday."

"Oh, dear."

I told him about Miss Candace and how Mormons believe that all people will get a chance to hear their version of the gospel, either now or after they die, and they can convert then. I told him how I had promised Miss Candace that I would convert if I found her waiting for me on the other side waving her Book of Mormon.

"Well, I'll tell you what," Trevor said. "I'm pretty sure that I'm right and that there is no such thing as an afterlife. But, if I'm wrong, and I see you and Miss Candace standing there waving your scriptures at me, then, what the hell, I'll join the Mormons too."

"That would be lovely." With Trevor, even disagreements could be pleasant.

I, of course, introduced Trevor to the best food in Hilldale at Mike's Diner. He'd never heard of it, but he agreed with me that it had great food. Mike never let us pay for anything. He even gave us extra slices of pumpkin cheesecake to take home to Trevor's family. When Trevor went to use the restroom, Mike came over and said, "I don't even have to ask you if you're happy, Chrissy. I can see just by the look on your face that you are. It's about time."

I spent Thanksgiving at the Townsend home. We had a wonderful feast and then sat down to watch football. The Townsend men were content to watch football and pick at the leftovers and pie for the rest of the day. After my food had digested enough for me to be comfortable again, I looked over at Joyce and mouthed the words, "Christmas decorations."

She laughed and said, "You read my mind, Chrissy. Let's go up to the attic."

We spent the rest of the day taking down the Thanksgiving decorations and putting up the Christmas things at the Townsend home. Then we filled the entire backseat of my car and the trunk with decorations for the nursing home.

Joyce said, "Once I'm gone, the care center can just have most of my decorations. The boys won't want to put up all this stuff every month. And it'll do me good to know my things are being appreciated. I'll let you decide what things you want to take for the care center."

"Don't talk that way, Joyce." I felt the same icy fear forming that I used to feel when Miss Candace would talk so casually about her own impending death.

She sighed, "Well, I know it's hard to hear. And, as good as I feel right now, I don't really believe myself that it's actually going to happen. But, at some point, we're probably going to have to face the reality of it."

"Are you scared?"

"No. I'm not scared of death. None of us are getting out of it, you know. I've had a wonderful life and I've lived it to the fullest. I've tried to celebrate every day I've been given with the people I love. I hope they'll remember that and carry on the tradition. I do wish I had been given a little more time, though, time to see my boys get married." She smiled at me. "I would have liked the time to get to know my grandchildren. But I can imagine the kind of families that they'll have, and it makes me happy to know that they'll be happy."

I smiled sadly. Her sons *would* have great lives and happy families. How could they not? They had everything going for them. I'd already figured out by now that Trevor was well out of my league. He was my boyfriend by a strange twist of events that kept him in Hilldale for this short time. I'd have to remind myself of that someday when I had to let him go. I was lucky to have him for the time that I did. Maybe compared to the other girls in Hilldale and at Pemberton, I might have seemed like a decent catch. But, once he went back to UNC, he'd be back in his own league again. There were loads of girls there who were smart, beautiful, and well-spoken. They came from respectable families and they'd had a good upbringing. He'd find someone like that, someone who'd never been married, someone who could give him children. And he'd forget all about me. The thought made me so inexplicably sad that I had to push it out of my mind. I'd deal with that when the time came. But he was mine for now.

I'd become a regular at the Townsend home. I loved the feeling that I was part of their family. Trevor was actually the one who sometimes suggested that we spend a little more time at my apartment so we could have some privacy once in a while. That was nice too. We tried to balance the time spent between our two homes. We finished out the fall semester and had a few weeks off for winter break. Trevor got a B+ in our English class. I had a solid A, but I was a little disappointed with my A- in my life science class. That could have been an A too if I had spent a little more time studying and a little less time with Trevor. But, I figured I'd have plenty of time to raise my GPA once I was alone again and had nothing better to do than to study all the time.

Trevor came over to my apartment to help me set up my Christmas tree. I would be spending Christmas at the Townsend home, but I still wanted my apartment to look a little festive.

"Mom wants to know if you want to come over to help out with the Christmas Box for this year," he said.

"What's the Christmas Box?"

"It's something we do every year. Mom has a friend who works in social services. She comes across a lot of families in need in this area who probably wouldn't be having a Christmas without help. She gives Mom some information about the family, their address, and the kids' ages and sizes. We put together a big box of stuff for them and leave it on their doorstep."

My heart skipped a beat, remembering the box left at our front door so many years ago. Could that have been from the Townsends? It would be too much of a coincidence. I was itching to ask Trevor whether he remembered delivering a box to a widow with six children about 10 years ago. But, it would have given away too much information about me and opened a door to all the skeletons hidden in my closet, a door I preferred to keep shut.

"I'd love to help," I said.

Later, when we were at the Townsend home, Joyce wasted no time putting us all to work. "Okay, the theme for this year's Christmas box is 'snowmen,' so I have everything divided out by person and it all needs to be wrapped in this snowmen wrapping paper and labeled for that person."

"The Christmas box has to have a theme?" I asked. "Wouldn't the theme just be Christmas?"

Trevor sighed. "Chrissy, get with the program, would you? It's a holiday box put together by Joyce Townsend. Of course it has to have a theme! To use the theme of 'Christmas' would be way too obvious. That's only for people with no imagination."

Joyce ignored him. "The family has a single mom in her 30's with three kids: two girls, ages 14 and 8, and a 5-year-old boy. So there are clothes, shoes, and a jacket for each child. They all need to be wrapped. The youngest two have toys, and the older girl has books and some costume jewelry. And, can you believe this? I found this 'snowman' board game for them. Is that perfect or what?"

I spotted something in the piles. "Nancy Drew! I loved these books!" I exclaimed reading the back covers. "I'll wrap the older girl's things," I offered.

"Along with the wrapped stuff we'll have a separate box with Christmas dinner. There's a ham and some fixings. There's a basket of fruit. There are snowman stockings filled with little goodies for each of the kids. And I also made these snowman sugar cookies. Aren't these cute?" she exclaimed, pulling out a snowman-shaped tray filled with snowman cookies.

"Adorable," said Trevor. "But I'm not sure how to wrap the ham and mashed potatoes in this snowman paper."

"Oh, you're such a wiseguy!" Joyce bopped him over the head with her roll of wrapping paper. "Chrissy, you're going to love this. I made this for the mom," she pulled out a little set of three handcrafted snowmen "Christmas carolers." Joyce had made them out of cotton quilt stuffing. They wore little winter hats and held sheets of music in front of them. The rounded "O's" of their mouth indicated they were belting out a festive tune.

"Oh, my gosh! I want a set of those. I love them," I said.

"More than you love me?" asked Trevor.

"Yes!" I said, playfully grabbing a roll of wrapping paper out of his hands. "They're much cuter!" I'd become as good at "pretend bickering" as any of the Townsends.

"Oh, and Chrissy," Joyce pulled out a beautiful, downy soft handmade snowman quilt and spread it wide. "Do you think she'll like this? I made it. I figured we could just fold this up and drape it over the other items in the box. That'll help cushion the presents."

"She'll love it. She'll definitely love it." I pictured Momma wrapped in that quilt, sitting in her rocking chair on Christmas Eve, feeling immensely relieved that her children didn't have to experience a Christmas with no presents. "She definitely will."

We wrapped and labeled everything and decided to deliver it the next evening, Christmas Eve. I was now even more excited about delivering the box than I was to spend Christmas with the Townsends. Holidays were an everyday occurrence at the Townsend home, which is not to say that Christmas wouldn't still be special. It was just nice to see that, in the midst of their own happiness and prosperity, the Townsends recognized that for some families Christmas can be a very sad, even tragic time of year.

Fortunately, Hal's van was big enough to fit all five of us as well as the overstuffed box of snowman stuff and the Christmas feast. Joyce had written down the address and directions to the family's home. We drove across town singing Christmas carols, laughing, and talking along the way. I loved admiring the Christmas lights illuminating each home and feeling Trevor's hand holding mine as we drove across town. It felt like a magical evening.

We crossed the train tracks to the "poor" side of town. We noticed immediately that the homes here were smaller and less decorated. The Christmas lights became scattered and scarce, and the streets darkened as we drove further through this area. I grew quiet as I watched the old familiar streets and buildings pass by. I hadn't been back here since the day I'd packed up Momma's car and abandoned our old house. As we drew closer and closer to my old neighborhood, I felt my heart quicken and my temperature rise. I didn't want to see that old shack that haunted my dreams. I wanted to jump out of the van and start running back to the other side of the tracks. I pulled my hand out of Trevor's and pretended to fiddle with my hair so that he wouldn't feel it shaking and sweating. We passed by Marla's old broken-down house. I couldn't pull my eyes away from it as we slowly drove past. Marla …

We made another few turns and then Hal switched off the headlights and we pulled to a quiet stop along one of the dirt roads. Joyce turned around whispering, "Okay. The house is the second on the left just ahead of us with the porch light on. It's going to take all three of you to unload the stuff. Try to be quick but careful. Watch your step. Quietly load the porch while Hal and I pull forward a few houses ahead with the headlights still off. When it's all loaded, ring the doorbell and run. You'll jump inside the van and then we'll take off."

Trevor whispered, "Is there a reason why we are whispering? I'm pretty sure they can't hear us, unless they have bionic ears."

Jessie and I started to laugh.

Joyce rolled her eyes but went back to her regular voice, "Chrissy, how do you put up with this smart-ass all the time?"

"I don't know. I have a thing for obnoxious men, I guess."

"Well, that's good to know," said Trevor. "I was keeping things pretty tame before, but now I'm going to let all the obnoxious out!"

Joyce and I pretended to groan in misery. Then, Jessie, Trevor, and I gathered all the stuff. The box was so large that Trevor and Jessie had to carry it together. I hauled a separate large laundry basket that was filled with food for the Christmas feast. We quietly made our way through the dark to the front porch. It was falling apart, just as our old porch had been falling apart. "Watch your step," I whispered. "Some of this wood is splintered."

I was relieved that Trevor and Jessie made no comments about the state of the homes or bigoted assumptions about the types of people who lived in this area. They'd been coming here enough over the years to know what to expect and just wanted to do something to help.

When we had everything set up in a nice array in front of the front door, Trevor whispered, "Ready?" Jessie and I nodded our heads. Trevor rang the doorbell and we took off running toward the van a few houses ahead. Joyce had the sliding door open for us, so we hopped in and closed the door. We felt a bit like bank robbers on the run.

"Go! Go! Go!" Joyce said as Hal hit the gas. We all began to laugh from the exhilaration of it all. We'd done it!

We headed back toward the train tracks. The Townsends talked and laughed while I stared out the dark window, wishing I could see the looks on the faces of the family as they opened

294

the door and discovered what was waiting for them. I wished I could have been a fly on their wall for the entire Christmas day, watching as the children reacted to their new clothes, shoes, and toys. I imagined the look on the 14-year-old girl's face as she touched her bright, new, never-worn clothes and Nancy Drew books. Suddenly, I felt overwhelmed with emotion and began to cry, keeping my head turned toward the window so no one would see. But all my sniffling and hand-wiping of my tears gave me away.

"Chrissy, are you all right back there?" asked Joyce. All the attention was now turned toward me.

"Yes, I'm fine," I said through a sob. "I'm not sad. This was really great. It's just," I fumbled for the right words, "I was on the receiving end of something like this a long time ago. And I can tell you that it's very much needed, and very much appreciated." I nodded my head emphatically and wiped more tears.

The Townsends were all quiet now. They patiently waited for me to say something more. They were all curious about my past, but Trevor had told them I didn't talk about it. He'd tried and failed a few more times to get more information from me. I felt Trevor's hand on my back and it gave me the strength to dry my tears and smile again. As we crossed over the train tracks, I silently willed those old ghosts to stay behind where they belonged. I wanted nothing to do with them. They were not allowed into the nice part of town.

29

Some of Trevor's high school buddies had invited him to a New Year's Eve party at one of their houses and Trevor asked me if I wanted to go. I wasn't really the partying type, but it would be nice to get to know some of Trevor's friends. He hadn't spent any time with them since returning to Hilldale, so he felt somewhat obligated to go. Once again, I wished that I'd had Nadine around to help me find the right dress, but I finally found a pretty cream-colored dress at the mall that was reasonably priced. Joyce let me borrow her matching pearl earrings and necklace set to go with it.

Trevor looked so handsome in a button-down shirt and tie. He'd cut his hair shorter and it made him look more grown up. Jessie was also going to a New Year's Eve party with some of his friends. Hal and Joyce had plans at home. I was hoping we could all be together like at Christmas, which had been so much fun. But not everything had to be celebrated as a family.

At the party, Trevor introduced me to some of his friends. I could hardly hear what people were saying, the music was so loud. Some of his friends were already clearly drunk and wouldn't remember me after that night. Someone stumbled past me, spilling a drink on me and then went over and vomited into the kitchen sink. I plastered a smile onto my face and went over to grab some napkins to blot my dress. If this was Trevor's idea of a good time, I wondered why he'd chosen a serious girl like me to date.

"The Duke man is back!" I heard a female call out. A girl with long hair, tons of make-up, and half of her cleavage spilling out of her dress went running over to Trevor and threw her arms around his neck. "Are you home for the holidays? Why didn't you call me?" she whined.

"It's UNC. I'm a Tar Heel," Trevor replied.

"I get them all mixed up!" she shouted above the music. "How long are you home?"

"I've actually been here since last summer. I'm at Pemberton for a little while."

"I didn't even know! We should get together! Do you still have my number?"

I wanted to grab the garden hose from outside and spray her off of Trevor.

"Actually, I'm dating someone right now. This is Chrissy." He waved me over to his side.

With a look of distaste, the girl gave me the once-over. "Oh," she said. She reluctantly pulled her arms off of Trevor. "I need another drink!" She stumbled away.

Trevor looked at me. "Sorry about that. She's just a friend from high school."

"Oh," I said.

"So, are you having a good time?" Trevor shouted.

"What? I can't hear you!"

"I said, are you having a good time?"

"Yes!" I shouted back. "Your friends are very nice."

"What?"

"I said your friends are very nice! How about you? Are you having a good time?"

"Not really!"

It was too late for me to change my previous answer, since I'd already told him I was having a splendid time. I reached up to tug at my bad ear.

"Are you all right?" Trevor shouted.

"Yes! It's just ... I have a bad ear. The eardrum ruptured a couple of years ago and it never healed quite right. The loud music kind of irritates it."

"Let's go outside for a while to get a break from the noise!"

We grabbed our coats and hats and stepped outside on the front porch. We could still hear the rhythmic booming of the bass from outside, but it was much more tolerable out there.

"So," Trevor said, "it's almost 1976! Do you have any New Year's resolutions?"

I shook my head. "No. I don't believe in those. People rarely keep them. If you want to make changes to your life or be a better person, you should just do it starting right now, in my view."

Trevor nodded. "That's a good way to view it."

"How about you? Do you have any resolutions?"

He shrugged. "Not really," he said. "Actually, I've been kind of dreading the new year. I'd rather just stay in 1975. It's been a good year."

"It has," I agreed. I knew what Trevor meant but would never say out loud. He didn't want to see what 1976 had in store. It was the year he would probably lose his mother. It was the year I would probably lose Trevor. I admired the profile of Trevor's face against the winter sky and wished we could stay frozen in time together, frozen in 1975 with the people we loved.

I reached up and touched his face and he bent down to kiss me. After a few minutes, I said, "I wonder what Joyce and Hal are doing right now."

"Oh, I can probably guess." Trevor chuckled. "They do the same thing every year: put on music, dance around like fools, and set off fireworks in the backyard. They still haven't figured out that they're not teenagers anymore." I laughed, picturing that.

Trevor continued, "And then the very worst part comes after the clock strikes midnight. They race up and down the street in their party hats with noisemakers shouting 'Happy New Year!' and totally embarrassing themselves. Oh, and they also pig out on chocolate and cheese fondue all evening. I'm sure Mom has already pulled out her fondue pots by now."

"Fondue?" I'd always wanted to make fondue.

Trevor glanced at me. "You want to join them, don't you?"

"I want to be wherever you are."

He held onto my fingers. "Your fingers are freezing!" he remarked.

"It's all right," I said. He rubbed my hands between his to try to warm them.

"Come on. Let's go."

We happily ditched the party without even saying good-bye. I don't think anyone even noticed that we left. We drove back to the Townsend home. When we entered the front door, I saw Joyce in the dining room setting up her fondue pots.

"Chrissy would rather hang out with you nerds," Trevor announced to his parents.

"Well, Chrissy knows where all the fun is," replied his mom.

"Joyce, I've always wanted to make fondue. Show me what you do."

I followed Joyce into the kitchen while Trevor and his dad sat down in the family room to watch the New Year's Eve party in Times Square on television. Joyce and I worked on dicing various types of fruit, vegetables, and bread for dipping in the cheese and chocolate. I told her a little bit about the party and the girl who had thrown herself on Trevor.

Joyce shook her head in disgust. "I always worried about him with girls. He's so nice and never wants to hurt anyone's feelings. There are girls who sense that and just latch on."

I hoped Joyce didn't see me that way. I hesitated for a moment, then asked, "Joyce, did it bother you at all when you first learned about me, I mean that Trevor was dating an older, divorced woman?"

Joyce kept on dicing chunks of cheese. "Why would it bother me? I'm an older, divorced woman too."

"I mean because ... wait. What did you just say?"

"Did Trevor not tell you? I was married briefly before I met Hal."

"Wow! I never would have guessed that. I can't even picture you with anyone but Hal," I said.

"Well, I was young and thought I knew what I was doing. After graduation, I married my high school sweetheart. It didn't take me long to figure out I'd made a big mistake. I grew up. He didn't. We were divorced within a year."

"Did he … abuse you?"

"Oh heavens, no! Why would you think that? No, there was never any abuse. But he was a child. He couldn't keep a job, he spent money he didn't have and he lied whenever it was convenient. I realized I could never have a family with this man. And I really wanted children. So I divorced him and I was single for a few years. Then I met Hal, and I knew he was the right one for me. Personally, I think we 'older, divorced' women are wiser, more mature, and more discriminating. You're such a refreshing change from some of the other girls he's brought home in the past." Joyce winked at me. "Oh, and we divorced women also make cuter children."

I slumped a little at that. I couldn't tell Joyce about me. She wanted only the best for her son, and I didn't blame her. She wouldn't want Trevor to continue dating me if she knew the truth.

"I'll prove it to you," Joyce continued. "Do you want to see pictures of when Trevor and Jessie were little?"

"Yes!"

"Come with me into the den. The fondue can wait."

Trevor looked up from the television as we walked past the living room heading for the den. "Where are you two going?"

"I just wanted to show Chrissy something really quick."

Joyce pulled out a couple of photo albums from the shelves in their den and I sat down on a soft sofa to look through them. She was right. Trevor had been an adorable baby and little boy. You could tell how much Joyce had enjoyed every moment of her boys' childhoods. She'd snapped pictures of everything: birthday parties, playing in the bathtub, riding tricycles in the driveway, attending Cub Scout and Boy Scout outings, going on family campouts and vacations. Trevor's little dimples were right there in every picture. It seemed he had spent his whole childhood smiling, laughing, playing, being

300

followed everywhere by picture-snapping parents. In some of the photos, he reminded me of my little brother Ronnie. And my heart hurt just a little that Ronnie's childhood had been so different from that of Trevor and Jessie. All of my brothers and sisters had deserved a better childhood than the one they got. Every child deserved to be as well cared for and as happy as the little boys in that photo album, I thought to myself, but unfortunately not all children are as lucky.

I turned page after page, smiling at the pictures but also feeling a sadness I couldn't control. It was so strange to think that the Townsends had been here the whole time, breezing through life and celebrating non-holidays, while my family suffered so greatly on the other side of town. It wasn't their fault. It's not as if they could have known what we were going through. Besides, these people and places, these events captured in photographic images, were the things that had made Trevor into the person that he was today. I couldn't begrudge him his good upbringing and family life. I could only hope that there were also photo albums somewhere out there in other family dens that had pictures of my smiling, happy, well-cared-for siblings.

I turned another page that showed Trevor in his early teen years, complete with acne on his face and braces on his teeth. "Of course, he had his awkward phases as well," Joyce explained.

"Okay, I heard that!" Trevor entered the den just then to check on why we were in there for so long. "Chrissy, I'll have you know, Mom has doctored some of those pictures to make me look worse than I actually did," he explained.

"Now why in the world would I go and do something like that?" Joyce asked him indignantly.

"To keep me humble."

"Well, it didn't work very well, did it?"

"So you admit that you did doctor them."

"I did no such thing!"

"Children! Children! Behave yourselves now," I said. "The pictures really aren't that bad. I've seen worse."

"That's the nicest compliment you've ever paid me," Trevor said, leaning his head in to steal a kiss.

"Oh hush!" I said, laughing and pushing his head away from me.

I turned the page and a picture caught me by surprise. A youthful Trevor stood in a tuxedo with his pretty young date in a formal yellow gown. She had a corsage pinned to her chest. They stood there smiling into the camera. "You went to the prom!" I said, a little too wistfully. I touched the picture and studied it for a moment.

"You didn't?" Trevor and his mom asked in unison.

I just shook my head. "I never did anything back then," I said.

They both waited silently for me to say something more, but I didn't. I scanned through the last few pages: Trevor graduating from high school, Trevor working as a lifeguard during the summer, Trevor moving into his dorm room at UNC, Trevor standing in front of various buildings on the university's campus. I closed the photo album and handed it back to Joyce. "I don't know about you, but I'm getting very hungry for chocolate and cheese," I said.

"Well let's go fire up those pots!" Joyce said.

We spent the next hour experimenting with various food and fondue combinations. By 11:30 p.m., we were out in the backyard setting off fireworks. Just before midnight, Joyce pulled out the party hats and noisemakers. We counted down to midnight on the front porch and then ran crazily up and down the streets tooting the noisemakers and shouting "Happy New Year!" to the world. I couldn't stop laughing, and my face was completely frozen by the time we went back inside.

Joyce popped the cork of a bottle of champagne and proposed a toast to 1976. By that time, I had forgotten all about mourning the loss of 1975 and preventing the new year from arriving. At that moment, it seemed we had nothing to dread and not a care in the world. We clicked champagne glasses and believed that 1976 would be the best year yet.

Spring semester started in January. Trevor and I no longer had a class together, but we'd often meet up on campus before or after our classes. I had registered for two classes again. I probably could have increased my course load, but I wanted to spend as much time with Trevor as I could while he was still in Hilldale and attending Pemberton. I told myself that, once he was gone, I could bury myself in mountains of schoolwork and care center duties. That would help me to take my mind off Trevor and hopefully eventually get over him. But for now I had to face the truth and stop denying the fact that I'd fallen in love with him. He claimed to be in love with me too, but I knew that he was in love with only the parts of me that I shared with him. There was so much about me that he didn't know, and if I did tell him, neither Trevor nor his family would love me. I struggled with a constant inner battle, berating myself for not being completely truthful with Trevor. I would vow to tell him everything and then opt out at the last minute. The part of me that was in love with him begged for just a little more time. Just a little while longer with him and then I would tell him everything about me. And then I would lose him forever.

We planned our first trip together. Trevor would be coming with me to New York in March for Nadine and Ty's wedding. Since that was the week we had spring break, we decided to drive up and stay for six days and five nights. That would give us enough time to be part of the wedding festivities and to spend a little time sight-seeing around New York. This would be my first time leaving North Carolina since I'd run away with Marla so long ago. I was so excited to experience New York with Trevor by my side.

On one of the mornings I had off at the beginning of March, I drove to the Townsend home to switch out my Valentine's Day decorations at the care center for St. Patrick's Day decorations. Trevor was in class that morning, but I didn't need him to carry anything for me. I rang the doorbell and waited for someone to answer the door. When no one answered, I reached under the doormat for the spare key and unlocked the door. As I lifted my boxes through the entranceway, I could hear Joyce's voice from upstairs. "Chrissy, is that you?" she called out.

"Yes, it's just me!" I answered. "I let myself in. I didn't think anyone was home. I'm here to switch out decorations."

"Could you come here for a minute?"

"Sure!" I set the boxes down and bounded up the stairs to Joyce's room.

When I walked in, I was taken aback for a moment. There were piles of sheets and blankets and a comforter on the floor. A fitted sheet was halfway on the mattress of Joyce and Hal's bed. Joyce sat at the edge of the mattress, holding herself up with shaky arms. She looked pale, clammy, and dehydrated. She smiled weakly at me. "I had one thing on my to-do list today: to change all the sheets on the beds. I seem to be having some trouble getting it done. It's just one of those bad days, I guess."

I helped her up from the mattress and eased her over to a nearby chair. "Let's get you over here to sit down, okay? You shouldn't be doing stuff like this! I'm going to get you a glass of water, all right? I'll be right back."

I ran downstairs to the kitchen to fill a glass with water and then headed back up to her room. "Sip this very slowly, but I want you to drink the whole thing. You look very dehydrated. Should I take you to the hospital?"

"Oh, no, no, no. This just happens every once in a while. It's nothing." She took a sip of water. "I'll be fine in a minute."

"Can I call your doctor? I'm a little concerned right now."

"Oh, no," she waved off my suggestion. "I have an appointment in a couple of days. Really, I'm just fine."

I turned around and finished putting the clean sheets on the bed along with the blankets and the comforter. I felt that familiar icy fear and dread in the pit of my stomach. I knew the subtle creep of age and disease. When you see someone on a daily basis, you hardly notice it at all. Then something will happen to bring it to your attention, and you realize the downward slide has been happening the whole time, right under your nose. "Why don't you let me or Hal or the boys handle this stuff from now on? You shouldn't have to do everything. They can handle it."

"Pffft," she waved off my suggestion. "They can't do it the right way."

"Well, then they need to learn." I gathered the pile of dirty sheets to put in the laundry. "I'll go change the sheets in the other rooms too. You stay there and sip your water."

When I came back, Joyce had finished her water and was looking a little better. I refilled her glass and made her drink it despite her protests that she was just fine now. Since I had the morning off and didn't feel comfortable leaving Joyce alone, I went around the house and did some light cleaning, dusting, and vacuuming. Their house was never dirty, but I didn't want Joyce to get up and do it herself.

I brought her lunch to her. "Oh, you didn't have to do that," she said.

"It's no bother. I'll feel better once you've had some food. You're looking better, but I think you need to take it easy today."

Just so that she wouldn't have any excuses not to rest that day, I went back to the kitchen and put together a casserole that could be heated for dinner that night. I covered it in tin foil with heating instructions written in a note on top.

I went back up to Joyce's room and took her empty plate away. "Okay, I need to head off to work now, but the sheets are changed. The house is clean. And dinner is waiting in the fridge with heating instructions. Surely the men can handle turning on an oven and a timer. There is no excuse for you to get up and work today, okay? Today's a rest day."

She started to protest, "But I need to run over to ..."

"The Hobby Barn will still be open tomorrow," I interrupted. "Anything you wanted to do today can wait until tomorrow. Your body's telling you it wants to rest, and you need to listen to it. Promise me."

"Okay," she said reluctantly.

"Okay, what?"

"I'll rest."

"Good. I'll see you later. Trevor and Jessie should be home soon." I turned to leave.

"Chrissy," Joyce called out.

"What?"

"Thank you."

"You're welcome."

I drove to work, worrying the whole time. I remembered Miss Candace telling me about her son Danny. She'd been so sure he could fight his disease and win, just as he'd won every battle he'd ever fought. I remembered how she'd started to cry when she told me that three months later they'd lowered her precious war-hero son into the ground. Trevor thought his mother was invincible too. I needed to talk to him. Somehow I needed to prepare him.

30

Trevor and I took turns driving my car on our long drive to New York in mid-March for Nadine and Ty's wedding. I was so excited for him to meet them. It would be interesting to see what Nadine thought of Trevor. She'd hated Stan from the beginning and tried to talk me out of marrying him. If I had listened to her from the start, it would have saved me so much trauma. I was the only non-family member that Nadine had asked to be a bridesmaid. We all had matching yellow satin dresses to wear. I thought I looked pretty good in it. I wondered what Trevor would think when he saw me in it.

The drive up I-95 was long but beautiful. I had good company with Trevor. We listened to music some of the time. He slept a little in the passenger seat during the time that I drove. I loved to watch him when he slept. It was strange how things that I found so annoying in Stan, like occasional snoring or smacking his lips when he slept, were somehow endearing when Trevor did them.

When it was Trevor's turn to drive, I decided to turn down the music and broach the subject of his mom. "Trevor," I said, "have you noticed any recent changes in your mom?"

He shook his head, "No. Why do you ask?"

"Well, when you were in class a few days ago, I had the morning off, so I decided to go over to switch out my decorations for the month. I didn't think anyone was home, but your mom called out to me when I went inside. She was really weak and dehydrated. It scared me a little. I'd never seen her like that. I made her sit down and rest and gave her some liquids. I ended up staying there all morning, in fact."

"She was probably faking it to get you to do something for her," he said. "Believe me, if it's something she wants to do, like shopping, she'll somehow muster the strength for it."

I shook my head, "No, I don't think she was faking this. I actually wanted to call her doctor, but she wouldn't let me."

"Did you do anything for her?" he asked.

"Well, I finished changing the sheets on her bed, and then I did all the beds. Then I did some light cleaning and brought her some lunch. And then I put a casserole in the fridge for dinner that night."

Trevor shook his head and laughed. "Score a home run for Mom! I can't believe you fell for that."

"I wish you would have seen her. You would know she wasn't faking it."

Trevor's face clouded over and he stared straight ahead at the freeway. "Well, what am I supposed to do about it? She never asks for help."

"I think you need to spend more time at home. She can't continue to do everything. You and your brother and dad need to step up to the plate and take care of her."

"I've tried! Whenever I try to do something for her, she tells me that I didn't do it right and to get out of her way."

"Well, she has to learn how to accept help too. You'll both be on a learning curve dealing with each other. At the care center, we have to learn to develop a sense of when to let people handle things for themselves and when to step in. I know it's difficult, but she's going to increasingly need your help as her health goes downhill, and you need to be there for her."

"Oh, I wouldn't write her off just yet." Trevor tried to laugh it off. "If there's anyone who can beat this thing, it's her. Who has time for cancer when 'Blossom Festival' is fast approaching? It's not going to celebrate itself, you know."

I hesitated for a moment. I didn't want to upset him about his mother, but I wanted to be a realist for him, the way Nadine had always been for me. "Trevor, about this time a year ago, one of my very good friends at the care center was dying, and for months I buried my head in the sand and lied to myself about it. Then one day, she was gone. I took it really hard. Even though I'd seen her every day, I felt cheated somehow, like I'd never really had a chance to say good-bye. I just don't want that to happen to you. It will be easier for you to accept it if you're prepared and if you feel like you've made the very most of the time you had left with her."

Trevor continued to stare straight ahead. "So tell me more about Nadine and Tyrone," he said. Trevor was just like me, changing the subject when it wasn't something that he wanted to face.

Once we were in New York, we were consumed with wedding activities. During the rehearsal dinner, we had a chance to visit with Nadine and Ty since we sat at their table. They seemed to like Trevor quite a bit. We joked and laughed all evening. They told stories about me to Trevor, and I countered with stories about them.

Ty asked Trevor how we'd met, and Trevor said that we'd shared a class at Pemberton. "Chrissy was constantly batting her eyes and winking at me from across the room. Then she started passing love notes to me."

"That's a lie," I laughed. "You were the one staring at me constantly like a lovesick puppy dog. I took pity on you."

Trevor turned to Ty. "Actually, Chrissy would rather be dating my mom, but she settled for me instead."

"That is true," I said. "But his mom was taken, so I settled for the son. She decorates her entire house for every holiday," I explained.

"And she makes up her own holidays," Trevor added.

"Ah!" Ty nodded his head. "That'll win Chrissy over every time."

Later, when I had a chance to pull Nadine aside, I asked her what she thought of Trevor. "I really like him," she said. "He's perfect for you. And he seems crazy about you. He brings out the best in you. I think he's a keeper."

"Well, it probably won't work out. He's too good for me. He just hasn't figured it out yet."

"Now why would you go and say a fool thing like that?" Nadine asked in disgust. "You always have to sabotage your own happiness."

"I'm just trying to be a realist about it. I mean, we come from very different backgrounds. We've had very different lives."

"Just because you don't share a past doesn't mean you can't share a future."

"He could have any girl he wanted really."

"It looks like the girl he wants is you." Nadine shrugged her shoulders. "I guess some guys like the scrawny, flat-chested type."

"Ha ha! Somebody's getting a little scrawny herself," I nudged her playfully. "We need to get some of that good old Southern fried food back into you. You're wasting away up here!"

"Mmm! Southern food. That's the one thing I miss about that place." She thought for a moment and then nudged me. "Well, maybe I miss two things about that place."

I smiled sadly. "I miss you too," I said.

I'd almost been hoping that Nadine would tell me that, although Trevor was a nice guy, he just wasn't right for me. It would make it a bit easier for me to let him go. Now that Trevor had Nadine's endorsement, I was more confused about him than ever. Trevor was supposed to be just a temporary pleasant distraction for me. But my feelings kept getting in the way, making things very difficult for the realist in me whose only goal was to protect me from getting hurt in the end.

The wedding was wonderful, and Nadine was the perfect, beautiful bride in white walking down the aisle. When Ty saw her, his face lit up. He was finally marrying the only girl he'd ever loved. I thought about how lucky people are who find their soul-mates without ever having to suffer a broken heart. I remembered how Momma had told me that Daddy was the only man she'd ever loved. Of course, if the time ever comes that you lose that one love, it shatters your heart into a thousand pieces. Momma never did fully recover after Daddy died. No, it's better not to fully give your heart to somebody. That's truly the only way to protect yourself from heartbreak. I stood there in my yellow bridesmaid dress, holding a bouquet of flowers, while they recited their vows. I glanced over at Trevor in the audience and he flashed me a wide, dimpled grin. My heart still skipped a beat when he did that, but I ordered it to calm down. It was just a smile, after all. Anyone can flash a smile. There was nothing particularly special about his, I reminded myself.

But, later on at the reception, I felt myself melting into Trevor's arms as we danced. For just this one time, I would allow myself to imagine we were dancing at our own wedding. I imagined that Trevor could be mine forever, and we'd never have to say good-bye. Tomorrow I'd go back to being a realist. But just for tonight, I'd let the dreamer in me dream away.

Nadine and Ty left for their honeymoon in Hawaii, but Trevor and I had a few days left to take in New York City. We took the train into Manhattan and visited all the places we wanted to see. We walked through Central Park and Times Square. We spent one evening at a Broadway show. We visited Radio City Music Hall and the newly-built twin towers of the World Trade Center. We saw the Empire State Building and the Statue of Liberty. We took a horse-drawn carriage tour of the city. I loved the hustle and bustle of New York. It was so busy and full of people and lights and noise and buildings as tall as mountains. It was everything that I'd always imagined it to be. It was 1976, the year our country turned 200 years old. National pride was in the air, and I loved the feeling of being part of the giant, colorful tapestry that was the United States.

As we drove back home along the Eastern Seaboard, I tried to take in all the sights and commit them to memory. It was a wonderful, beautiful country, all of it. But as the lush green trees of North Carolina came into view, I had an odd sense of comfort and relief. As nice as all those other places were, as busy and wonderful as New York City had been, North Carolina was my home. This was where I belonged.

Even though Trevor avoided any further discussion of his mother's health, I think he took some of what I said to heart. He began spending much more time at home that semester. He and his brother and dad took on increasing shares of the household duties. And Joyce learned to accept and even to ask for help at times. The decorating was still her domain. She wouldn't allow them to take over that part. If something wasn't done to her satisfaction, most of the time she wouldn't redo it. She just learned to let it be as it was. After all, a towel doesn't know whether it's folded correctly or if it's hanging a little askew on the towel rack. Cans in the cupboard don't know if they're facing with the label in front or arranged in the most space-efficient way. If it doesn't bother them, why should it bother Joyce?

Trevor also spent more time just sitting and visiting with his mother. She'd share stories from her past with him. They'd talk and laugh and enjoy each other's company. They'd never been closer. Sometimes I'd join them, and we'd sit out on their rocking chair porch with tall, icy glasses of sweet tea and say whatever was on our minds. At times, we'd get so caught up in our discussions that we'd stay out there until well past our normal bedtimes. Hal would poke his head out the front door and ask if we were ever going to stop our jabbering so he could cuddle in bed with his wife. She'd wave him away. She wasn't about to leave the discussion until she'd finished making her point. Sitting out there late at night while watching the stars reminded me of the warm evenings when Momma and I would sit on the porch swing, talking and laughing. It was as if we were best friends back then, before our relationship was forever fractured. I realized with sadness that I had probably been Momma's only friend ... her last one.

With my birthday fast approaching on May 9, Trevor told me that he would take me out to dinner anywhere I wanted to go that evening. "And it can't be Mike's Diner or the mall food court," he quickly added just as I was starting to say the word "Mike's." I asked around for some suggestions at work and finally settled on an Italian restaurant that sounded pretty good. Trevor had dropped me off at work that day so that he could pick me up and we could go to dinner straight from the care center.

When I climbed into his car after work, he kissed me and wished me a happy birthday. As I was giving him verbal directions to the restaurant, he reached for his back pocket and said, "Dang! I left my wallet at home. We're going to have to stop at home first. Do you mind?"

"I have my purse with me. I can pay for us. It's not a problem."

"On your birthday? No way! It's just a quick stop at home first. It'll take us 10 extra minutes."

Trevor and his mom had the house to themselves that weekend since Hal had taken Jessie and some of his friends on a camping and fishing trip. When we pulled into their driveway, I said, "I'll just wait here in the car for you."

"I think Mom wanted the chance to say happy birthday," Trevor informed me.

"Oh. All right then."

I unbuckled my seatbelt and climbed out of the car. Trevor held open the front door to the house for me and I walked inside. What I saw when I entered took me by complete surprise. "Oh my goodness, look at this!" The entire entryway and living room walls were plastered with images from the ocean: waves, bubbles, rocks, colorful plants, and coral reefs. Cartoonish-looking cardboard cutouts of sea life were attached to strings that hung from the ceiling: all kinds of colorful fish, sea horses, clams, dolphins, an octopus, starfish, and jellyfish. A disco ball with flashing blue lights spun slowly from the middle of the living room ceiling, casting an array of blue speckles on the walls that made it look like a moving sea. A tape recorder played background noise of bubbles moving through water. In the corner of the room stood a card table with a giant punch bowl in the center, surrounded by plastic cups. A banner reading "Night Under the Sea" hung across one wall.

"Chrissy, would you be my date for the prom?" Trevor asked from behind me.

I laughed incredulously and spun around the room slowly, with my hands covering my mouth in astonishment. "Oh my gosh! This is amazing! This is absolutely incredible! I can't believe it. Did you do all of this?" I asked Trevor in amazement.

"Well, I had a little bit of help."

It was just then that I noticed Joyce sitting on the couch, wrapped in a blanket in the dimly lit room. Her face looked shadowed and gaunt, but she smiled as she watched my reaction to the room. "Joyce, I should have known that you were behind all of this!" I exclaimed.

"Well, much of it, yes. No one knows the sea quite like the Hobby Barn. I don't take credit for *that* though," she said, nodding in the direction of a poster from the new motion picture film *Jaws* that was taped to one of the walls. The shark's mouth gaped open, revealing a horrifying display of razor-sharp teeth. It was obviously Trevor's one contribution to the decor.

"Would somebody please explain to me how a man-eating, great-white shark is *not* a creature of the sea?" Trevor asked indignantly.

"It does not go with the rest of the decorations!" Joyce answered him. "It's completely inappropriate here."

"Well, we'll have to agree to disagree on that point."

I was still circling the room in disbelief, taking in all the work that had been done to decorate the room. Near the stairs stood an archway that had been cut out of a refrigerator box, painted with white cross-hatching, and decorated with silk flowers. "I am truly amazed," I said.

"And now for my fairy godmother moment," said Trevor as he opened the coat closet and pulled out a dress hanging there. "You simply cannot attend a prom without appropriate attire."

The dress was a long, powder blue gown with chiffon ruffles from top to bottom. It looked like a giant feather duster. "Where did you get that thing?" I asked with a laugh.

"You'd be surprised what you can find in the formal wear section of Goodwill."

"It's hideous," I remarked.

"You think? I don't know. I look pretty hot in it, but ... not everyone can pull off this shade of blue."

"Give me that!" I yanked the dress from Trevor. "I need to go change."

I started off, then turned back around. "Wait. What are you going to wear?"

"My tuxedo from my high school prom, of course."

"Chrissy," Joyce informed me, "he wouldn't even try it on beforehand to see if it still fits."

"I don't need to. Of course it still fits! I'm the same lean, mean machine that I was back in high school," he said, patting his sucked-in stomach and flexing his muscles.

"That was before you gained your 'freshman 15,'" Joyce reminded him.

Letting out his stomach, Trevor protested, "Mom, you know perfectly well those were sympathy pounds for the girl I was dating at the time. I wanted to make her feel better!"

I left them to their pretend argument, slipping off my shoes, and running to the half-bathroom to change into my dress. This was so much fun! I giggled like a schoolgirl as I slipped the feather duster dress over my head and pulled it down. I did some arm acrobatics to pull up the zipper in back. I checked my appearance in the mirror. The dress was slightly too big for me, and there were a few air pockets in the bust area, but nothing that a few wads of toilet paper couldn't remedy. I stuffed the chest until it looked decent, then rummaged through my purse for a comb and some bobby pins. I did my best version of an "up-do" in the mirror. Then I applied some lipstick and sprayed my open mouth with Binaca. Perfect! I was ready for the prom.

Trevor and his mom were waiting for me when I came out. Trevor's tux was indeed a bit too short and tight for him now. The pants were about an inch above his ankles, and I'm pretty sure he was unable to fasten the top button. He whistled and made cat-calls in my direction, while Joyce exclaimed, "Oh, you just look lovely!" Then Joyce said, "Chrissy, you would not believe this boy. He came down the stairs in the tux with *white socks and tennis shoes!* I made him go back upstairs to change them."

"Thank you, Joyce. I could never have been seen with him like that," I said.

"Wow! Two minutes as a high school girl and she's already turning into a snob," Trevor observed teasingly.

"Okay, you two need to gather under the archway for pictures," Joyce directed us as she got her camera ready.

We made our way over to the cardboard arch. Trevor had a homemade flower corsage that he pinned to my dress while his mother snapped pictures. Then we turned and posed for the camera. After a few pictures we turned silly, making goofy faces and ridiculous poses. Trevor made bunny ears behind my head while I flashed a movie star pose. We turned and gazed dreamily into each other's eyes for a "lovesick puppy dog" photo. In another one, we pretended to dance and Trevor dipped me while pretending to throw out his back.

Joyce was laughing so hard at our antics that she had tears running down her cheeks. Then suddenly she set the camera down. "Wait! I almost forgot something." She ran into the kitchen and came out holding a paper bag with some items inside. "May I have everyone's attention, please!" she called out. "A formal vote was taken, and the senior class has decided that this year's prom queen will be Chrissy Rollings. Her date, Trevor Townsend, was also voted as the prom king."

She pulled from the bag a sash reading "Prom Queen" to drape over me and handed me a little bouquet of flowers. Then she pulled out a little plastic tiara and a crown to secure on our heads. Trevor took a photo while she placed the tiara on my head, and I pretended to bawl my eyes out as I accepted the title. Then I smiled and waved to my invisible adoring fans. "Thank you! Oh, thank you!" I called out to them as I waved.

Joyce placed the crown on Trevor's head while he exclaimed, "This is such a surprise and honor! Well, actually, it's not much of a surprise, since I voted for myself."

"You voted for yourself?" I asked, laughing.

"Yes, I also voted for myself as prom queen."

"Well, then, who voted for me?" I countered.

"Mom did. And Jaws. That's what put you over the top."

Joyce took pictures until she ran out of film. "Okay, I think my work here is done. I can't wait to get these pictures developed. I think we got some good ones." She put the camera away, and then turned to us. "I'll leave you two lovebirds to enjoy your prom night. Don't forget to eat dinner." There was a candle-lit table for two set up in the kitchen with what looked like an Italian meal ready to eat. "Don't play the stereo too loudly. And don't stay up too late. I'm heading to bed."

"Wait!" I called out. I lifted my dress and ran in bare feet across the room to where Joyce stood at the foot of the stairs. I threw my arms around her. "Thank you! This is the best birthday ever. I can't think of when I've ever had more fun!"

Joyce smiled and hugged me back. "I'm glad I could be a part of it. Happy birthday, Chrissy."

I went back to Trevor and Joyce climbed the stairs to go to her room. I noticed that at the top of the stairs she turned around for one last glimpse of us. She loved to see her son happy and wasn't sure how much time she had left with him, two things we shared in common.

Trevor and I sat down for dinner and then went over to the punch bowl for a little drink. "I hope you didn't spike that!" I joked.

Trevor had made a mixed cassette tape of mostly slow love songs, which was just to my liking. I wanted to be in his arms the whole evening. We put the volume down low so as not to wake Joyce and began to sway under the blue disco lights and hanging sea creatures. I felt as if I were melting into in his arms, as I always felt when he touched me. "Would it be all right if I nibbled on the homecoming queen's ear for a few minutes?" he asked.

"I don't know. You'll have to ask her. I'm the prom queen."

He chuckled as he nuzzled my ear. "Prom queen," he corrected himself, talking softly in my ear in a way that always sent a thrill through me.

We swayed for several minutes. I just wanted to take in everything from this night and never see it end.

"Your mom was right," I commented. "That *Jaws* poster is really creepy."

"Now, I think you're both being very unfair to Jaws. If you look around, you'll see that there are plenty of other very dangerous sea creatures in this room. But you don't mind them because they're cute little cartoonish characters. See, there's an octopus right there," he pointed. "You would not want to be next to one in real life. There's a killer whale over there, I think. There's a jellyfish. Have you ever been stung by a jellyfish? And for all we know, this thing could be a piranha," he said, pointing to an innocent-looking fish dangling over our heads. "You just need to give Jaws a chance. He likes *you*!"

"I feel like he's watching me."

"He's just jealous."

"I think he wants to bite my leg off."

"That too," Trevor admitted. "But, let's face it, you're biased toward the cartoon characters. If we changed Jaws into a cartoon character, maybe with a little baseball cap on and a coach whistle around his neck, have him hold a little clipboard with his fin, you'd totally think he fits right in here."

"That would be so adorable!" I exclaimed. "I think we just stumbled upon the theme for your next birthday party: 'Coach Sharky's Birthday Bash.' I need to tell Joyce."

"She'll be at Hobby Barn first thing tomorrow morning to gather her supplies."

We talked, laughed, danced, and kissed until we'd played the mixed tape all the way through at least three times.

318

It was a night I'll never forget — the setting, the music, the company, the feeling of being loved and so completely in love.

And so, for my 24th birthday, I finally attended the prom. I was crowned the prom queen. And I danced, talked, and laughed the night away with the most handsome man in the room.

Later, as I pressed the pictures from that night into my photo album, with our goofy poses in ill-fitting formals and plastic crowns under a cardboard arch, I was reminded of the favorite quote of an old friend: It's never too late to be what you might have been.

31

Spring semester ended, and we were out of school for the summer. I'd managed to add two more A's to my transcript, in spite of the fact that I'd spent less time studying than I would have liked. I agreed to increase my workload at Sunset for the summer, since I wasn't taking classes and the care center was short-staffed again. Trevor spent the extra time at home, taking care of his mother and handling the yard work. He'd often come over to the care center and join me for lunch. We'd sit out on the lawn under a shade tree, talking and eating lunch as I used to do with Nadine and Ty. I remembered how I used to envy the ease of their relationship. How were they able to go days and days without fighting? It was such a mystery to me. Now that I had Trevor, I finally understood how it could be managed. The idea of having a fight with him seemed so foreign. We'd never yelled at each other. There were sometimes slight irritations, which we'd iron out or forget about after a little while. Nothing was ever big enough to go to the effort of arguing.

I was seldom at my apartment except to sleep. I'd drive straight from work over to the Townsends and stay there until late. And I was always over there on my days off. In a way, it felt as if Trevor's parents were my own. Jessie was my brother. And Trevor ... well, he was everything.

One day near the end of June, I received a phone call at work and was surprised to hear Hal's voice instead of Trevor's on the line. He sounded very distressed. He told me that Trevor had come home from a run that morning to find his mother unconscious on the living room floor. He rushed her to the hospital, where she revived. After a battery of tests, the doctors told them that Joyce's cancer had spread to several major organs. There was not much they could do for her at this point except to give her pain medication. Trevor's dad had sent him home after Trevor had caused a scene at the hospital, yelling at the doctors and demanding that they do something to help his mother. He was probably there now, Hal told me. I thanked him for calling me and told him that I would try to leave work early and go immediately to the house.

When I arrived at the Townsend home, I saw Trevor sitting out on the porch steps in front. I could tell he'd been crying. His eyes were red and puffy and his mouth was set in a grim line. He stared straight ahead and didn't acknowledge me as I walked up the driveway. I didn't know what to say that would be of any comfort, so I just stood there, waiting for something brilliant to dawn on me.

But Trevor was the one to speak first. "They told her that it was up to her, what she wants to do. She just said she wants to come home."

"Then she should come home."

"She's giving up, Chrissy. She's coming home to die. To die!" He looked up at me with red-rimmed eyes, as if it had just now occurred to him that his mother could die from this.

I stood there helplessly. You would think, after all the death I dealt with on a regular basis at work, I'd know just what to say to bring comfort to a loved one. But, every time it happened, I was still at a complete loss. I looked around at the front yard and at the bare porch. Joyce hadn't set out her "beach vacation" decorations for June, which had set off an alarm bell for me a few weeks ago. I hadn't mentioned it to Trevor, and he hadn't seemed even to notice that the house was so bare. Other homes on their street had out their American flags. It was almost July 4, the country's Bicentennial celebration. This year, out of all years, was not the year to neglect the recognition of Independence Day. That gave me an idea. Decorating the house for the Fourth of July would give us something to do besides sit here mired in sadness, and I'd always known that keeping busy was the best way to distract myself from an unpleasant situation.

"We should get out all of Joyce's Independence Day decorations and decorate the living room and front porch. We need to get it done before she comes home. She would love that! It would lift her spirits and give us something to do," I suggested.

"I am *not* going to decorate the house and pretend like it's a damn party!" Trevor spat out bitterly. I'd never seen him like this, and it caught me by surprise.

"Trevor, there's going to be plenty of time to feel angry and bitter and sorry for yourself. But right now you need to decide how you want these last memories with your mother to be," I said. "You told me once that you didn't want to live with any regrets. Well then, don't! Be the kind of son that I know you can be. Be the kind of son that your mother deserves to have."

He angrily wiped away a tear, staring straight ahead for a few minutes. Then he stood and spun around and went into the house. I wasn't sure where he was going, so I followed behind. He trudged up the stairs to the attic and started pulling out all the boxes labeled "Independence Day." I set to work helping him with the boxes, and we labored in silence for the next hour decorating the living room and the porch with all of Joyce's things: red, white, and blue lights; American flags; stars and stripes knick-knacks; bald eagles; Uncle Sams; George Washingtons; and "We the People" banners.

By the time we finished, the house looked as festive as it ever had. Trevor caught me in an embrace and we held each other tightly for a long time. "I'm proud of you," I said. I hadn't ever loved him more than at that moment.

The next day, Trevor and I stayed at the house while Hal and Jessie brought Joyce home from the hospital. We stood out in front of the decorated house while they helped her out of Hal's van. "It's beautiful," she said, taking it all in. "I love this."

She went inside the house and gushed over each decoration as if seeing it for the first time. Many of the decorations were things she had made herself, but maybe after not seeing them for a year, they seemed new. "I just love this! Isn't this adorable?" she would say, holding up some knick-knack for me to see.

We tried to put Joyce in her room, but she would have none of that on such a beautiful June day. She wanted to be out on her rocking-chair porch with a tall glass of sweet tea, enjoying her decorations and the summer breezes. We all decided to join her out there. We sat in the porch shade and rocked, sipping our tea and chatting with the neighbors as they went by. I remember watching the American flag blowing in the breeze and feeling happy to be alive at this moment in our nation's history. We all agreed that we were incredibly lucky to have been born in a land of opportunity and freedom.

For the next few days, someone was nearly always at Joyce's side, holding her hand, talking, laughing, reminiscing, saying good-bye. The last time that I sat and talked with Joyce alone, I squeezed her hand and forced a happy smile. "They must be in need of a really good event planner in heaven," I said.

She laughed. "Well, let's Just hope there's a Hobby Barn nearby."

"It's heaven, isn't it? I'm sure there's a Hobby Barn on every corner. And everything is always on clearance."

We both chuckled and sat in silence for a few moments. "Take care of him, Chrissy," she said.

There was really no time to explain my story to her and explain why I couldn't be the one for Trevor. And, at this point, it hardly seemed to matter. So I simply said, "I will." What was the harm in letting her think that Trevor and I could live happily ever after? Was there really any harm in letting her look at my face and believe she saw the mother of her future grand-children? Hopefully, she would understand someday why I'd had to lie.

Joyce died at the beginning of July 1976. And, as the rest of the country celebrated its 200th birthday, we mourned the loss of a woman who'd found something to celebrate in every day of every month of every year. As I watched her casket being lowered into the ground, I thought how lucky I'd been to have her briefly in my life. I hadn't meant to love Joyce, just like I hadn't meant to love her son, but I'd loved them both anyway. As much as we might try, we really have no control over what our hearts choose to do.

I held Trevor in my arms while he cried on the day we buried his mother. "Chrissy," he pleaded, "tell me about when you lost your mother."

I paused for a moment. "I can't."

"Please."

"Trevor, ask me for anything else. Anything else I will give you, but not that."

He was silent. He couldn't think of anything else at the moment that might help ease the pain. He wanted to know that someone understood what he was going through. And I *did* understand. I felt as if I'd spent the majority of my life grieving. But how could I explain it to Trevor? As difficult as it was losing his mother, at least she'd died a natural death surrounded by people she loved. She knew that she was loved. As hard as it was, it was something that he could accept over time. Momma's death was *not* natural, and she'd died feeling completely alone in the world. Giving voice to the way she'd died was in a way like accepting it. And I could never accept it.

I remember that summer as being a quiet and mournful, yet passionate, time of my life. Trevor would be heading back to UNC in the fall for his final year there. We clung to each other that summer, knowing we'd have to say good-bye soon. Trevor seemed to think we'd be able to carry on a long-distance relationship for the year, and I outwardly agreed. But, inwardly, I knew this was the beginning of the end for us. I'd always known this time was coming. But now that I could see it on the horizon, I dreaded it so fiercely.

We'd often drive to the beach and walk along the shore holding hands, lost in our own thoughts. There was something healing about the sight of the ocean stretching into the horizon, the rhythmic sound of waves crashing on the shore. Trevor would tell me stories from his past and reminisce about his mother. On Thursday evenings during the summer, Hilldale would have a farmer's market spanning the main road downtown. We'd often go to dinner at Mike's Diner on those evenings and then stroll through the farmer's market afterwards just to see what there was to see. Sometimes we'd buy some fresh fruit or vegetables. Other times we'd just get a snow cone or an ice cream cone and people-watch. Trevor always had interesting observations about other people. Even when I was feeling down about his upcoming departure, he could always make me laugh.

One of our last Thursday evenings together in late August, the farmer's market was quite crowded with people even though it was a muggy, steamy evening. My ice cream cone had melted faster than I could eat it, and I was wishing I'd worn a tank top that could better conceal the sweat marks beneath my armpits. Suddenly, in the swarm of people we were passing, I recognized a face, and my heart nearly jumped out of my chest. It was Stan. He was fervently explaining something to a girl walking next to him, with his hand iron-gripped onto her shoulder. He didn't glance in our direction.

"Trevor," I hissed. "Walk quickly! Quickly!"

Trevor asked questions as he tried to catch up with me. "Why? What is it? What's going on?"

"Keep walking! Hurry! Hurry!"

After several minutes, we finally slowed down and my heart began to calm down a bit. "I need to sit down," I said, catching my breath.

We sat down on the edge of the curb. "What was that all about?" Trevor asked. "You look so spooked."

"I saw my ex in a crowd of people that we passed."

"Really?" Trevor strained his head to look back where we'd been. "What did he look like?"

"He was the guy with dark hair and cowboy boots. He was with a girl. Oh my gosh, I think I recognized her. She was one of the girls from the youth group at his church!"

"Does that bother you?"

"Yes!"

"So you still have feelings for him?"

"No! Oh gosh, no, Trevor. I just feel sorry for *her*! I mean," I threw up my hands helplessly, "some people should really come with a warning label."

"Do you want to talk about it?"

"No. I have nothing more to say about him. Let's go find the car. I want to get out of here now. I don't want to take the chance that we'll run into them."

We walked quietly back to the car, lost in our own thoughts. I was surprised at how strongly I'd reacted to the sight of Stan. He had no power over me anymore, but even the memory of the two years I'd lived under the thumb of this man was enough to stoke those old fears and insecurities about myself. I just hoped that girl was a submissive little wisp of a woman who had no will of her own. Maybe Stan wouldn't feel the need to stomp her into the ground, if there was nothing left to flatten.

As we climbed into the car, I changed my mind about that. I hoped that girl was just the opposite. In fact, I hoped she was a tiger in disguise who could mightily rage against an attacker when cornered. I hoped she could beat the crap out of him.

The dreaded day when Trevor would be leaving for Chapel Hill arrived at the end of August. I put on a brave, happy face to see him off. He promised that he would call me regularly and try to come home as often as he could. It was about a three-hour drive, less than half a day away from Hilldale, he assured me. I nodded and agreed. I stood and watched, waving, until his car was out of sight. Then I climbed into my car and drove back to my apartment. I made it almost all the way home before bursting into tears.

I climbed the steps to the second floor, where my apartment was. Once inside, I drew closed all the blinds and shades and went straight to bed for the rest of the day to wallow in grief. Tomorrow, I would pick myself back up and begin to adjust to life without Trevor. I'd registered for a full load of classes and would still be working part-time. I'd have plenty of things to keep me busy and distract me from thinking of Trevor. But today was for wallowing. Trevor called me later that evening. He'd moved all of his stuff into the apartment he'd be renting with a roommate. Tomorrow he'd buy his books and go grocery shopping. He asked me what I'd done that day, and I said I'd run several errands. We said our good-byes and he told me he loved me. I hung up the phone and headed back into my dark room to sob into my pillow once again.

When fall semester began at Pemberton, I did start to perk up. My classes looked interesting, and they would keep me busy. I tried not to reminisce about meeting Trevor a year ago, the boy with the dimpled grin staring at me from across the room. I spent nearly all of my free time at the library studying.

Joyce had donated most of her decorations to the care center. I sorted through them and took several boxes to be stored there. The residents loved the decorations and would appreciate them more than Hal and Jessie would back at home. I kept a few of the really nice hand-crafted things at the Townsend home and would periodically go over there to set them out. I figured, even though they didn't have the elaborate decorations of previous years, it would be nice to see little reminders of Joyce around the home.

The Townsend men were learning how to live without Joyce, but I knew from experience that it was a difficult journey. I didn't want to set out so many things that it would be overwhelming to them. Constant reminders can add to the pain, but you don't want to pretend as if your loved one never existed at all either. Typically I would go over there when I knew Hal and Jessie would be at work and school so that I wouldn't disrupt them. I would often do a little bit of cleaning and sometimes make a casserole to leave in their freezer with reheating instructions. They knew how to do all that stuff on their own now, but I liked the idea that they might come home and feel as if Joyce had been there that day. Sometimes it's nice to believe in a fantasy, even when you know it's a fantasy, like how I'd believed in two separate stories of how I'd come into this world, born to Momma in her bed and also discovered underneath a rock by Daddy. Both stories were true in their own ways.

My life was back on an even keel, consumed with my daily tasks of work and school. I was learning how to live without Trevor, or so I thought. I tried not to think about some other girl catching his eye from across the room in class. I tried not to think about the day that was coming soon when he'd tell me that we'd drifted apart over time and distance. He still called frequently and didn't seem to give any indication of finding someone else. But, then again, would he even tell me that he'd fallen in love with someone else? When he finally lowered the ax, he would probably just couch it in terms of our not being compatible or that we were going in different directions.

When he came home for a four-day weekend in October, I clung to him. I hated the feeling of being so weak and weepy around him, needing constant reassurances that he still loved me. But I couldn't help myself. I still needed to hear it. And he claimed that he still did. When he left again, I spent another day sobbing in bed, despising myself for not getting over him by now. Next time, I would be strong, I promised myself. Next time, we would have that much-needed discussion about our lack of a future together.

However, the next time he came home again, which was over the Thanksgiving holiday, I behaved exactly the same way, clinging to him, crying, needing him so much. Those types of weepy, clingy, can't-live-without-her-man girls had always filled me with such disgust. *Have a little pride and self-respect*, I would think to myself, vowing never to act like that over some man. And here I was, acting like the worst of them. But I didn't know how to turn off my feelings for him. The highs were so high when I was around him and the lows were so low when he left. I would eventually pick myself back up again and return to the even keel of life that I preferred. I was never one to enjoy emotional roller coasters. I wasn't sure how I'd gotten on this ride or how to get off it.

I did manage to finish out the semester with all A's again, and I'd enjoyed all of my classes. Sometimes I thought maybe it would have been better if I'd never met Trevor. I'd already had enough drama to last me a lifetime, and now my life would be completely devoid of drama if it weren't for him. Yet I couldn't wish away all the happiness he'd brought into my life either.

Trevor came home for nearly a month during the winter break between semesters, and, like a magnet, I was constantly at his side again. It was wonderful to have him home. I was back at the Townsend home anytime that I wasn't at work. It was almost like old times, except for the glaring absence of Joyce.

We decided to carry on Joyce's tradition of putting together a Christmas box for a family in need and delivering it on Christmas Eve. I somehow inherited the mantle of being in charge of it. Even though I certainly didn't have the creativity or craft-making abilities that Joyce had possessed, I was still pleased with how the box turned out. I'd tried to think of a clever theme for the box but had to settle on just "Christmas." Trevor congratulated me for being able to "think outside the box ... by thinking inside the box." It was wonderful to be with him, even though we all shared a certain melancholy sadness as we reminisced about the way holidays used to be when Joyce was around.

After the holidays, that familiar dread of losing Trevor reappeared in the pit of my stomach as I began the awful countdown toward the day he would go back to Chapel Hill for spring semester. It was quite clear to me now: I was never going to get over Trevor as long as he continued to call me frequently and make periodic visits back to Hilldale. I'd always known I wasn't the right woman for Trevor, so why was it so difficult for me to let him go? Every time he talked about his dreams for the future, wanting a spouse and a family, it felt like a stab in the heart to me. He was talking about a life with someone else, though he didn't know it. But I knew it. And it tore me apart inside.

I did manage to have a little talk with Trevor before he left. It was not the talk it should have been, where I finally opened up and told him the truth about me. But it was at least something that would set us on our separate paths, which would allow us to drift apart over time and distance. "Trevor, since this is your last semester before graduating, I think you really need to concentrate on your classes and your senior project. I don't want to be a distraction for you. So I think you should call me less and maybe ... not try to come home for visits this semester. Okay? That would be better for me too, because I'm really busy with full-time school plus part-time work."

"Is this the brush-off?" he asked.

"No. Of course not! I'd never do that. I just think we both need to set some priorities. And, for the time being at least, we are not each other's highest priorities."

I regretted the way that came out as soon as I saw the hurt look on Trevor's face. It really was for the best, I assured myself. He'd see that over time. He agreed to my request and told me that he loved me before driving away again to Chapel Hill. I, of course, spent the rest of the day sobbing in the darkness of my room. But this was the last time, I promised myself. I had done what I needed to do for the both of us. I was finally getting off this emotional roller coaster. I was finally letting Trevor go.

I started spring semester with the firm resolve to be a strong, single, confident, solitary woman. Trevor's phone calls did dwindle, although they didn't cease completely. I tried not to imagine what was happening in Chapel Hill. Whatever it was, it didn't concern me. Was he dating again? Who cared! It was a free country. It was his life. He could do what he wanted with it.

But I would lie awake at night with tortured thoughts of Trevor falling in love with someone else. What was she like? Was she pretty? Was she smart? Could she make Trevor laugh? Did her knees turn to jelly when he kissed her like mine always did? How I hated her! How I wished the most horrible things on this poor, unsuspecting girl whom I'd never met.

I began to imagine that every single one of the thousands of girls who attended UNC was falling madly in love with Trevor. How could they not? Once they realized how wonderful he was, how could they stop themselves from pursuing him? And how ridiculous it was for me to secretly hope that a simple little Hilldale hillbilly like me could hold onto his heart.

When Trevor didn't come home for spring break, it confirmed the worst for me. Trevor had a girlfriend in Chapel Hill. I imagined that she looked just like that big-boobed bimbo who'd thrown herself on him at the New Year's Eve party that first year. Well, I hoped they had a fantastic life together, running around drinking booze and vomiting in the kitchen sink to their hearts' content! In the meantime, I had a meaningful career to pursue. I spent half of my spring break week congratulating myself on being such a strong-willed, independent, career-focused woman ... and the other half in bed sobbing into my pillow over Trevor.

Trevor did call every once in a while to see how I was doing. I tried to be as brief as possible. I asked him about how things were going for him and then analyzed each sentence that came out of his mouth for clues about his bimbo. So far, he'd given no indication of her, but that didn't mean she didn't exist. He was probably just trying to spare my feelings.

When he called me a few weeks before the end of the semester and said that he wanted to talk with me about something, my heart fell to my knees. This was it: "the talk." This was when he would tell me that he would always care for me but that we'd grown apart. Would I have the courage to ask him if there was someone else? Would he tell me the truth? Would I be able to pick up the pieces after this phone call and somehow find the strength to complete my research papers and take my final exams?

But, "the talk" turned out to be something different. Trevor apologized for not being in touch more in the past few weeks. He'd been very busy finishing his senior project and had applied for several regional planning positions across the state and even in other states. He'd had some phone and in-person interviews and was offered three positions. He wanted my input.

I listened as he described each position and the pros and cons of each one. One was in Tennessee, and he was pretty sure he wouldn't accept it. The other two were in North Carolina. The best offer in terms of salary, benefits, and promotional opportunities was in Raleigh. But he'd also had another fairly decent offer in Hilldale and described that one to me. When he asked what I thought, I said it was a decision he had to make. They all sounded pretty good to me. He'd be making much more than I'd ever make as a high school teacher and certainly much more than I made now as a nurse's aide.

"What do you think of Raleigh? Would you ever be willing to move there? You could transfer to NC State and finish getting your degree there."

All I knew about Raleigh was that it was big. It was the state capital. And some bureaucrats who'd never met me had met in a boardroom there one day and decided that I should be sterilized.

"I'm more of a small town girl," I said. "I like to stick with what I know. And I'm comfortable at Pemberton. But don't let that sway you. You need to pick the position that will be best for your future. What I think hardly matters."

"It matters to me! If you were me, which one would you choose?"

I thought about it for a minute. I knew where I wanted him to be. I wanted him in Hilldale. But I also knew that Trevor wasn't mine to keep. We needed to part ways. And it would be easier if he lived in another city.

"I'd take the Raleigh one. It's the best one … and you deserve to have the best."

I congratulated him and then hung up and just sat there staring at the wall in front of me. There. It was done. End of discussion. It was time for us to move on. His bimbo would be thrilled with his relocation to Raleigh. It was a mere half-hour drive from Chapel Hill. They could carry on whatever they were doing together.

But then, a week before his graduation and the end of the semester for both of us, Trevor called me again and told me he'd accepted the position in Hilldale. I was overjoyed but tried not to betray my emotions over the phone. "What made you decide to take that one?"

"Well, I like Hilldale. It's a good place to live. Even though the salary for this position isn't as much, the cost of living is also lower in Hilldale than it is in Raleigh, so I don't think I'm really giving up that much. And it would be good for me to be close to my dad. I worry about him without my mom around anymore. Jessie's graduating and will be leaving home to go off to college. This way, my dad doesn't have to be alone. Plus, I hear rumors that the prettiest girl in North Carolina lives in Hilldale, so I wanted go there and see for myself," he joked.

I rolled my eyes, but I was secretly thrilled. He'd picked Hilldale! He'd picked me! Trevor was coming home.

It wasn't until after I'd hung up the phone that the pessimism and guilt started to cloud my good mood. I should never have let it get this far, I told myself. I should have told him the truth a long time ago. Now I was affecting his life, his decisions for the future. He was making them based on incomplete information about me. And there was no way to handle this delicately anymore. However he found out the truth, it would look bad for me. The fact that I'd withheld critical information from him for so long, even when he was making decisions about his future, was a deal killer. He'd be so angry with me. He wouldn't beat me the way Stan had, he would just tell me that he wished he'd never met me and then turn around and walk away.

32

I finished out the semester at Pemberton and then took a trip with Jessie and Hal to Chapel Hill to attend Trevor's graduation. Trevor looked so handsome in his cap and gown as he walked up to receive his degree. I thought my heart would burst as I watched him from the audience. I loved him so much. He was so close, yet so far away. He was the man of my dreams, but I wasn't the woman of his dreams. Now he was coming home to Hilldale, and my day of reckoning was coming. I could feel it.

We took Trevor out to dinner that night to celebrate and I feigned happiness over the occasion. The next day, Trevor wanted to show me around the UNC campus. It was a beautiful campus. Trevor had been lucky to attend school there. I didn't see any big-boobed bimbos on the campus, but that didn't mean they weren't there. He also drove me around different areas of Chapel Hill that he wanted me to see. It was a wonderful city. It was strange to imagine Trevor's life here without me. In my mind, I'd exalted this place called "Chapel Hill" to almost mythical proportions. I could hardly believe that it was actually a real city, beautiful but ordinary.

Trevor moved back home with his dad and brother for the time being and started work at his new job in Hilldale the week after his graduation. I'd once again increased my hours at Sunset for the summer, but I'd grown so listless and tired of working there. I was tired of watching people die, tired of feigning enthusiasm and energy on the outside when I didn't feel it on the inside, tired of being tired. My dread for the day of reckoning with Trevor was growing, but I kept putting it off. It's better to let him get used to his new job before springing this on him, I told myself. Once he feels comfortable there, I'll tell him.

Trevor liked his new job and was thrilled to be out of school, making real money, and feeling like more of an adult now. He would excitedly describe the different projects that he was working on and the new people that he was meeting daily. I listened with a fake smile on my face, and all the while my heart was sinking. So this is how I would lose Trevor, I thought. He would meet some beautiful, brainy civil engineer and fall in love with her. This was even worse than the big-boobed bimbo in Chapel Hill! At least with the bimbo, I could console myself with the thought that their relationship was purely superficial. It was nothing compared to what we had together. A woman like that could never hold Trevor's attention for long.

But the beautiful, brainy civil engineer was a deep threat to me. What if he found that he had much more in common with her than he did with me? She was probably an atheist who liked baseball too! They'd eat lunch together, talking about the advantages of a life guided by science, logic, and reason. They'd have deep philosophical conversations and then comment on some of the latest baseball stats. She would think that things like road placement and suspended bridges were actually interesting topics of conversation. They'd work on projects together until late in the night. Then she'd whip off her glasses and pull the pin out of her bun, spilling waves of soft, shiny hair down her back. Trevor would be mesmerized. I couldn't bear the thought of it, yet I tortured myself with such thoughts constantly.

I'd be so tired during the day, but once my head hit the pillow I could not fall asleep or stay asleep for very long. It was so frustrating. The more I panicked over not getting enough sleep, the longer I stayed awake in the dark, wondering how I'd ever managed to fall asleep so easily in the past. I started taking different brands of sleeping pills at night to see if any of them worked for me. They did sometimes help, but then I'd feel groggy and listless the next day. The sleep I did manage to get was restless and full of the tortured thoughts that I carried around during my waking hours.

One night, I awoke with a terrible thought that was even worse than my usual painful renditions of Trevor falling in love with another woman. What if Trevor had fallen out of love with me a long time ago and was just with me now out of a sense of obligation since I'd helped him through the loss of his mother? Hadn't Joyce told me that she worried about Trevor with women because he was too nice and they might take advantage of that? He never wanted to hurt anyone's feelings. On her deathbed maybe Joyce had even encouraged him to stay with me. He wouldn't leave me if his mom's dying wish was to have us be together. Even if he didn't love me anymore, he would stay with me to honor her memory. I wasn't sure which was worse: to have Trevor leave me for another woman or stay with me when he felt no real emotion for me anymore. After lying awake for more than an hour, I got up and took another sleeping pill. Tomorrow would be another rough day of trying to work through a groggy, pill-induced fog, but it was better than lying awake nursing my anxieties.

Trevor had noticed the change in me since returning to Hilldale. He often asked me if I was all right. Was I worried or upset about something? I just told him that I'd been having trouble sleeping and felt tired all the time. He encouraged me to visit a doctor to make sure everything was normal. There was no way I was going to see a doctor to try to explain what was happening to me. I knew that I was caught in the same downward spiral of depression that had plagued Momma in the years prior to her death. I'd eventually claw my way back out of it as I'd always done in the past. Bringing up all these issues with a doctor would only make it worse.

Jessie's graduation from Central High School was held one month after Trevor's graduation. I sat in the audience with Trevor and Hal with the same mask of a happy face that I'd worn at Trevor's graduation. Trevor held my hand, but it didn't make me feel any better. My heart felt so heavy and down. Here I was, attending another graduation. I'd never even attended my own high school graduation. The thought occurred to me that maybe all these graduations were the trigger for my most recent bout with depression. All those ghosts from my past refused to stay there. They banged and shrieked at my door, demanding that I face them. Graduation day. And the anniversary of Momma's death was tomorrow, another thing I had to face.

Trevor squeezed my hand. "Are you all right?" he asked with a smile.

"Yes." I turned the corners of my mouth upward, in what I hoped would pass for a smile.

The graduates walked past us down the aisle to take their places near the front. I watched Jessie walk by, wearing his cap and gown and an honors sash. An honors sash! Suddenly an image popped into my mind of Momma standing in my bedroom doorway, holding a letter in her hand the night before my high school graduation. She'd told me she was proud of me for graduating with honors. And then a terrible thought hit me that took my breath away: *Momma was planning to attend my graduation ceremony!* She'd said she couldn't wait to see me get my diploma. All it would have taken was one word of encouragement from me. One word. Or even a nod. And she wouldn't have died that night. I couldn't even give her that much. Momma had stood at the edge of a cliff and instead of offering her a hand to help her back to safety, I'd reached out and given her a final push over that edge. I'd told her that I was leaving Hilldale and never coming back. It was unforgivable.

Pounding migraine pain started closing in on me and I felt claustrophobic in my seat. I needed to get out of there. I pulled my hand from Trevor's and rubbed my temples. Trevor turned to me again. "Are you sure you're okay?"

"Yes. I just have a little headache," I answered.

The ceremony seemed to drag on and on. First the endless list of speakers, and then the reading of names, followed by the clapping. More names followed by more clapping. And still more names followed by evermore clapping. By now, it was quite clear to me that the entire town of Hilldale was comprised of graduating seniors at Central High School!

When the ceremony finally ended and we reunited with Jessie, Trevor told me that his dad was taking us out to dinner to celebrate. "I think I'm going to head on home," I said. "My headache hasn't gone away."

"Are you sure?"

"Yes." I turned to Jessie and gave him a hug. "Congratulations, Jessie. I'm really proud of you. It's a great accomplishment."

Trevor walked me to my car in the parking lot. "I'm a little worried about you. You don't look very well."

"I'm fine. I'll be all right."

"Should I come over afterward?"

"No. I'll be asleep I'm sure."

"I'll at least call to check on you."

"No, Trevor. It's Jessie's night tonight. You should go celebrate with him. Maybe you can meet me at the care center for lunch tomorrow."

"Okay." He kissed me and opened the door for me.

I climbed into my car and sped off to my apartment. I could hardly get inside fast enough. I locked the door, closed all blinds and shades, changed into old boxer shorts and a tank top, took two pain pills, and headed for bed where I drifted off to sleep at last. When I awoke, it was 10 p.m. I should get something to eat, I thought. But I just stayed there in bed and stared at my guitar leaning against the wall.

Why do I even bother to hope, I asked myself. There's no point. There is no hope. No matter how hard I try, I will never be able to escape from my past. It will always be able to find me. There was no future with Trevor. My day of reckoning with him was coming. It was just a question of when. And then I'd be all alone again. Being alone was fine before I'd met Trevor. Now that I knew what life was like with him in it, I didn't want to go back to life without him. There was really no way out.

The thought occurred to me that I would rather be dead than watch Trevor turn his back on me and walk away. When the time came for him to marry and start a family with another woman, it would just be better if I didn't exist at all. If I didn't exist, it couldn't hurt me. I could finally be free from my past, free from pain. I could just go to sleep and never wake up. The idea of feeling nothing ever again seemed so appealing at that moment.

I walked to the medicine cabinet and opened it. Did I have enough? There were several packages of different brands of sleeping pills and two bottles of pain pills. I took the packages and bottles of pills back to my bedroom, sat on my bed and spread the various pills across the bedspread. It was probably enough to do the job. I left the room and came back with a tall glass of water. I sat on my bedspread with my glass in hand, contemplating what I was about to do.

Then I started thinking about the aftermath. Who would eventually find me here, dead in my bed? It would probably be Trevor, who had lost his mother just a year ago. I remembered that horrible morning so long ago when Trisha stood over my bed telling me that Momma wouldn't wake up, the realization of what she had done, the horrifying chorus of screams and cries, and the approaching ambulance as I held Momma's head in my lap, begging her to come back.

I couldn't do that to Trevor. I gathered the pills across my bedspread in two fistfuls and walked over to my bathroom where I dumped them into the toilet and flushed. Then I went back to my room and climbed into bed, drifting in and out of a fitful, restless sleep. I was beginning to wish I'd saved at least one of those sleeping pills, because now I could really use one.

When my alarm clock buzzed the next morning, I switched it off and walked over to my phone across the room. I called Sunset and said that I was ill and wouldn't be able to make it into work that day. Then I climbed back into bed and tried to get some sleep. It was the anniversary of Momma's death today. I went through my annual tradition of calculating how old all my siblings would be now and wondering what they were doing. Little memories of each one would trigger a fresh bout of crying. Get it all out today, Chrissy, I told myself. Tomorrow I would try to pull myself together and get on with life.

In the early afternoon, my phone started to ring. It was probably Trevor. I'd forgotten that I'd told him yesterday we could meet for lunch at the care center. I watched the phone as it rang and rang until it went silent. After a few minutes, the phone started ringing again, and I watched it until it went silent. *Take a hint, Trevor*, I thought. *I am not getting up to answer the phone*. After a third round of ringing, the phone finally stayed silent. Well good, I thought. I'm in no mood to be a "chatty Kathy" today.

After about an hour, I heard a knock on my front door followed by the doorbell. Trevor certainly was persistent, I'd give him that. But I wasn't about to open that door and let him see me like this. He could just think I wasn't home. I'd think up an excuse to give him tomorrow as to why I was unreachable today. I heard footsteps going down the outside stairs and waited to hear the sound of his car leaving the parking lot.

But instead, I heard his voice calling out from below my bedroom window. "Chrissy! Chrissy are you in there?" I threw the blankets over my head, mortified at what the neighbors must be thinking. Did he have to be so loud? "Chrissy, it's me, Trevor." No, duh! "Um, they said at work that you were home sick. Your car's here in the parking lot. I'm starting to get a little bit worried. I'm thinking of trying to break the door down. I'm not quite sure how that's done. So ... if you hear the sound of bones breaking, would you mind calling an ambulance? Thanks!"

I sighed and threw off the covers to climb out of bed and stop the poor man before he threw himself like a rag doll against my front door. A quick glance in the hallway mirror confirmed the worst: I looked horrifying, with a puffy red face and swollen eyes, no make-up, stringy, unkempt hair, and the same dingy tank top and boxer shorts that I'd worn since last night that probably smelled of body odor. Well, fine then. Maybe it was time Trevor had a glimpse of the *real* me.

I swung open the front door just as he was reaching the top of the steps, carrying a small crockpot in his hands. He seemed a bit taken aback by my appearance. "Oh! There you are. So you *are* home."

"Yes. I ... must not have heard you before."

"I brought you some chicken soup."

I took the crockpot out of his hands and placed it on top of the small table in my kitchen. Then I turned back around to face him.

"So," he said, "you're sick. Do you think it's a virus or something?"

"No," I ran my hand through my greasy hair. "It's nothing contagious. It's more like ... just stuff going on in my head. I get depressed sometimes, especially at this time of the year. I'll get through it."

"Do you want to talk about it?"

"No. It's just ... stuff from my past. You don't want to know about it."

"Well," he persisted, "does it, possibly, have anything to do with me?"

"No. Well, yes, maybe a little. But mostly no," I answered.

"Well, if it has something to do with me, I'd like to know about it."

"It's not really any of your business."

"Chrissy, you just can't tell me it has something to do with me and that it's also none of my ..."

"Do you have a girlfriend in Chapel Hill?" I blurted out the question.

Startled, he said, "Do I have a girlfriend in Chapel Hill? No, not to my knowledge."

"Oh, okay. I was just wondering about that."

"So you've been thinking I was seeing someone in Chapel Hill this whole time?"

"Well, it's just that ... you didn't call me much last semester. And then you didn't come home for spring break. I just figured ..."

"You told me not to come!"

"I know, I know!" I put my hands over my face in anguish. "But then, when you didn't come home, it just … made me really sad."

"So, is that what's been bothering you for the past month? You thought I was seeing someone else?"

"Well, it's just part of a larger narrative I have going on in my head all the time. I have this constant fear that I'm losing you. I don't know how to get past it." My voice felt caught in my throat.

"Why would you think you're losing me?"

"I don't know. Maybe it's because I've lost everyone I've ever loved. Why should it be any different with you? I guess that's sort of my strange reasoning about it."

"Chrissy, I tell you that I love you all the time. I took a lower-paying job just so that I could move to Hilldale and be with you!"

"I know. And you shouldn't have done that!"

"I mean," he threw his hands up in the air in exasperation, "what more do I have to do to let you know that I'm not going anywhere?"

"I don't know, Trevor. Truly, I don't." I rubbed my hands over my eyes in exhaustion.

"Would this help?" Trevor asked. He held a small box and opened the lid, revealing a beautiful diamond ring.

My breath caught in my throat, and for a moment my heart began to soar. Then the old Chrissy Killjoy inside of me reached up and yanked it back down to the ground. He wouldn't be asking me if he knew the truth about me.

"Trevor," I hesitated, "you shouldn't be asking me. What were you thinking?"

His face fell. "You don't want to marry me?"

"It's not that," I said. "I do! I want to marry you more than anything in the world. But if there's one thing I've learned from a horrible marriage, it's that you don't marry somebody that you don't really know."

"What more do you want to know about me?"

"It's not that. You don't really know about me."

"I know enough," he said. "I know that I love you."

I shook my head. "But it isn't enough. You don't know about my past. And it's a deal killer."

"Then tell me about this terrible past so that I can convince you that it's not so bad! Please! I mean," his voice raised slightly in exasperation, "are you a secret Russian spy or something? Were you abducted by aliens and forced to do terrible things?"

I shook my head sadly "I wish it were that simple," I said.

"Then tell me what it is!"

It was time. I was going to lose him anyway. We might as well finally end things on a note of truth.

"Do you remember that I told you once how I was born under a rock?" I asked.

"Dear God!" he exclaimed. "You're one of the Mole People!"

"Would you quit joking for a minute? This is serious!"

"I'm sorry," he said. "You were born under a rock."

"Yes. And I still have that rock."

I went back into my room and reached up in my closet for my Chrissy rock. The day of reckoning was here. There was no going back. He needed to know.

I walked back to the living room where he stood. Tears were already coming down my face as I turned the rock around so he could read the childish lettering scrawled on it:

"Christine Rollings, Born May 9, 1952. Died August 13, 1966."

Trevor read the words on the rock and then looked back up at me in confusion. "I don't understand what this means."

"It means there's no future with me, Trevor. I should have told you this a long time ago, but I was too afraid. Part of me is dead inside. This was the day I was sterilized as a young girl by order of the state. They didn't want poor, trashy girls like me running around having babies."

Trevor reached for the rock with one hand and then reached for my hand with the other and led me over to the couch. We sat down and I began to explain. The dam had cracked and my story spilled out of me. I couldn't stop it. I told him everything. I told him about the family I'd come from, all the siblings I'd had, and how we lived in a small house very near the place where we'd delivered the Christmas box when Joyce was still alive. I told him about Daddy's death, being plunged into poverty and becoming a welfare family. I told him about running away with Marla and ending up prostituting ourselves for survival. I told him about the visits from Blue Lids, the threats to take away our welfare check unless I was sterilized. I told him of Momma's betrayal by consenting.

Sometimes I would cry, and Trevor would hand me a tissue and rub my back to comfort me. But he encouraged me to continue. When I got to the part about how I'd pleaded with the doctor not to sterilize me and just say that he had, Trevor grew visibly angry. "How can something like that even happen here? This is the United States, not Nazi Germany! We have rights! Constitutional protections!"

I shrugged my shoulders. "Those rules didn't apply to me for some reason."

I told him about my strained relationship with Momma after that, her spiraling depression and our final, painful exchange on the night she took her life. I told him about how all my siblings had been taken away and placed in foster care or adopted. I told him about moving out of the house and living in my car, how Mike had saved me and found me a place to live with the Stakers. I told him about my marriage to Stan and the physical abuse, the help from Nadine and Ty and the inheritance from Miss Candace, which had enabled me to go back to school.

We talked until well into the night, taking a break once to eat the soup he'd brought. Sometimes Trevor would ask questions, but mainly he just listened. The only part I left out was how I'd seen the little girl in the hallway the night of Stan's last attack. For some reason, I didn't want to share that part with Trevor. He would have dismissed it as a delusion caused by trauma to the brain. Perhaps that's what it indeed was, but I couldn't stand to have her so easily dismissed. She was real to me. She'd given me the strength to leave a toxic marriage.

When I finished, Trevor was silent for a while, reflecting on everything I'd just shared. It was a lot to digest in a short amount of time. Then he spoke.

"Chrissy, the things that have happened to you were heartbreaking and tragic. I can understand why it would be so hard for you to relive some of those events. But I don't understand how you think this changes anything between us."

"Stan said he never would have married me if he'd known."

"Well, in case you hadn't noticed, I'm not Stan. I'm nothing like him. Sorry, but intact fallopian tubes doesn't even make the list of what I want in a woman. Maybe I haven't made myself very clear when I've talked about wanting a family in the future. I consider the couple, the partnership between two people, to be the core of the family. Everything else is just sort of an add-on to that. Kids are great and cute and all, but they're just temporary little boarders. They're not for keeps. Eventually they grow up and leave to form families of their own. And then it's back to just the core. And there are other ways of having children! We could adopt or take in foster children. Or we could decide not to have children. That's not set in stone! We could decide to move to Alaska and get a team of sled dogs. Or we could, I don't know, decide to raise raccoons or something." I couldn't help laughing at the image of that. "My point," he said, "is that when I talk about wanting a future family with you, what I'm really saying is that I just want *you* in my future." His eyes shone in the dim lamplight of the living room and he flashed his dimples at me. "Well, maybe you and my girlfriend in Chapel Hill."

I laughed through the tears running down my face. How silly I'd been to paint all those ridiculous scenarios when the truth was so simple and right in front of my eyes the whole time. How could I have imagined that Trevor might turn his back on me and walk away? Suddenly, I felt so free as the crushing weight of my past lifted from shoulders. I could breathe and I could see with clarity. Perhaps for the first time, I could see things as they really were. I saw Trevor in front of me. I knew that he loved me. For years I'd believed that I was completely on my own and that, in my darkest hours of need, no one would ever come crashing through the door to try to save me. But I'd been wrong. Trevor would. Trevor, carrying a crockpot of soup, was willing to crash right through my front door to come and get me.

And I knew just as surely as he loved me that I loved him right back, now and forever. I loved his smile, his dimples. I loved the feel of his reassuring hand on my back. I loved his stupid jokes. I loved how he knew exactly what to say to clear the fog that clouded my vision and distorted my perception.

I smiled, wiping the tears away. "So, are you a damn genius or something?"

He chuckled softly. "You hadn't heard? I was just awarded the Medal of Honor for being the 'damn genius of North Carolina.'"

"I always wanted to marry the 'damn genius of North Carolina,'" I said.

He pulled out the ring again, and this time I held out my hand and let it slide onto my ring finger. Even in the dim lamplight of the room, it sparkled and glistened as brilliant as my future with Trevor.

"You're still crying," Trevor said.

"Well, I was crying before because I thought I was losing you. Now I'm crying because I'm keeping you."

"It's that bad, huh?"

"No. It's that good."

And so, on a beautiful, colorful autumn day in North Carolina, we gathered together with our closest friends and family members at the Town Hall, and I married the man of my dreams. He was a man who didn't believe in fairy tales, yet made me believe that a fairy tale kind of love could exist. A picture of our smiling, happy group — with Hal and Jessie, Mike and his wife, Tyrone and a pregnant Nadine, and a few of the Townsend extended family members surrounding Trevor and me — rests on the nightstand next to my bed to this day, right next to my Chrissy rock:

"Christine Rollings, Born May 9, 1952.

Died August 19, 1966.

Reborn Chrissy Townsend, October 24, 1977."

33

I quit my job at Sunset Care Center right before fall semester began that year. It was a difficult decision, but I felt it was time to concentrate on finishing school. Trevor made enough money to pay the bills, and we liked to keep our weekends as free as possible. We used some of the money I'd inherited from Miss Candace for a down payment on a small brick starter home in the same neighborhood where I'd lived with Nadine and Ty. I loved our little home! It had three small bedrooms, two bathrooms, and a decent-sized, fenced-in backyard where I could grow a vegetable garden.

Married life with Trevor was so different from married life with Stan. It was so easy in comparison. I didn't find myself suddenly stuck with all the cooking and housework. We didn't have a chore chart like Nadine and Ty, or divide the duties exactly in half. We both had the attitude that if one of us saw something that needed to be done, we just did it without regard for whose turn it was or which job belonged to which gender. During the times that I was home more, I took on a greater portion of the domestic work. Trevor did the same during the times he was home more, when I had class. If one person cooked dinner that night, then typically the other one would clear the table and handle the dishes. More often than not, we'd both do them together because it went by faster and we enjoyed the company.

On weekends we'd often work on home or yard projects. When the weather was nice, we'd find hiking trails to explore or go on bike rides together. Sometimes we'd still visit the care center to read to the residents or play board games. We also loved to go on "weekend jaunts" to nearby areas just to find out what there was to see and do in that area. We'd drive out on a Friday night or Saturday morning and come back on Sunday. They were quick trips, but we always enjoyed them so much. One of the many great things about North Carolina is that you are never very far from the mountains or the ocean. A couple hours of driving in one direction will take you to the ocean and a couple hours of driving in the other direction will take you into the mountains.

Often, we would leave for one of our "jaunts" without a particular destination in mind. We'd just pack enough to handle anything and then decide once we were on the road. Trevor would typically be the one driving, and he would ask, "Right or left?" and I would just pick right then what sounded best to me at the moment. I could never decide which one I loved the best, the mountains or the beach. When I was at the beach, listening to the roar of the waves, feeling the sun on my back and the warm, soft sand between my toes, I knew that I loved the beach the very best. But then, when I was breathing in the cool mountain air, the scent of the earth and the trees, listening to the birds singing and looking down at the miles and miles of undisturbed nature below me, I knew that I actually loved the mountains the best. We spent weekends in Asheville, Boone, Wilmington, and the Outer Banks. We went furniture shopping in Highpoint. We visited bigger cities like Charlotte and Winston-Salem and smaller towns that we just found on a map without knowing anything about them. We also traveled into Virginia, Tennessee, and South Carolina, staying for weekends in Myrtle Beach, Virginia Beach, Richmond, and Chesapeake. Often, someone from school or Trevor's work would tell us about an interesting place to visit, and Trevor and I would add it to our list of places to explore next.

The spring that I turned 27, I graduated with my bachelor's degree from Pemberton State College. I was a bit older than most of my graduating peers, but my degree was just as valuable as theirs. It was a proud day. I interviewed for a job teaching English at Central High School and I was hired! I couldn't wait to start teaching that fall. I spent the summer working on my lesson plans, growing vegetables in my garden, and going on weekend jaunts with Trevor. I'd never been happier. All the things that I'd previously thought were impossible were becoming reality after all. Maybe Miss Candace had been right about believing in my dreams and in my own capabilities.

I loved being a teacher from the moment I first walked into my own classroom. Here was where the playing field was as level as it would ever be in an imperfect world. Here was where the "melting" of the great melting pot happened. Children, regardless of their race, ethnicity, class, gender, color or creed, could enter this classroom and be given a chance to dream, a chance to succeed. I'd often think about the people from other countries who came here and spent their lifetime working low-wage, demeaning jobs, never feeling truly integrated into American society and culture. People wonder why they do it, but I think it's because they know things will be different for their children who make their way through the public education system. These children will be able to fully integrate with American society and culture. They'll have a better life because of the sacrifices their parents made.

Not only did I love being part of the public education system, I loved my subject: English. Books had been my escape for years and years. But little did I know back then that books would also build the stairway to my success in school. I'd done well in every subject because I was a good reader. I was a good reader because I'd read as many books as I could get my hands on. I could write well because I'd read books written by people who could write well. I had consciously tried to write and speak the way people wrote and spoke in the books I read throughout my youth.

And, finally, I loved my job because I loved my students, all of them: the quiet and shy ones who sat in the back and never talked and the ones who talked so much that you wondered whether they ever took a breath. The teen years are such a precarious time of life, when you are caught in a sort of limbo between being a child and being an adult. You feel every emotion so intensely during those years. Hurtful remarks cut so deeply and affirmations are so very scarce. You want so badly to fit in at the same time that you desire to stand out and be seen as a unique individual. Remembering how I'd felt about my teachers in high school, I tried to be somebody they might feel comfortable turning to in a time of need. I always made myself available after hours if someone wanted to talk to me. I tried to reach out to the kids who probably wouldn't try to reach out to me. I hoped to find some way to get through to them. There were times when I discovered that a student was being abused physically or sexually at home. I worked with the school counseling system and social services to get help for students in problem situations, sometimes even removing them from abusive environments if necessary.

Some of the other teachers saw me as being too idealistic. They thought I tried too hard to save everyone. Some students were unreachable, they explained to me. There's no hope for them. Comments like that upset me. No one is ever past all hope. At one time, I'd been labeled a bad seed who shouldn't be allowed to reproduce. And quite often in life I'd believed in that label and the idea that there was no hope for me. Then people like Mike, Nadine, Miss Candace, and Trevor had reached out to me and lifted me up each time I hit bottom. So when I came across a troubled student who seemed to be unreachable, I still thought it was worth a try to reach out.

One thing I remembered from my years of growing up was how much I loved music. I'd spent so many hours alone or with Marla playing my guitar and learning new songs. The lyrics, to me, were like poetry. In one song, you could convey volumes just by the simple act of putting the right few words together and setting them to a tune. I noticed that most of my students were also into music. Many of them wore T-shirts with logos of their favorite bands, and they talked about various concerts and new albums that were coming out. One of their favorite assignments was to write an essay about a set of song lyrics that spoke to them. They could either write about what they thought those lyrics meant or how those lyrics applied to the world around them or to themselves personally.

I was amazed with the content of the essays. These students were much deeper than most people realized. I would read passages aloud to Trevor from their papers, and he would agree that these kids showed a lot of insight. Although I wasn't as knowledgeable about the popular music of the day as I'd been in earlier years, I could still keep up. I'd learn how to play several of the songs that my students had chosen, and then I'd bring my guitar in on the days that we shared the essays in class. The students were usually too embarrassed to sing along, but they liked it when I quietly played the tune in the background while they read their essay to the class. It helped to take some of the "spotlight" off the shy students, and it was just fun to bring an added element to the classroom.

I would lie awake at night either worrying about certain students with problems or coming up with new ways to make my English classes more interesting to the students. Trevor had grown accustomed to the nights when I'd abruptly sit up in bed. "I need to write this down so I don't forget." Then I'd be in our office for the next hour working it out on paper. Trevor would tell me that I should get some sleep and that I could work on it tomorrow, but whenever an idea popped into my head, I felt as if I had to get started on it immediately.

"Sometimes it seems like you won't rest until English is the favorite subject of every single student at Central High," Trevor said to me one day.

"Well, one of the subjects has to be their favorite. Why shouldn't it be English?"

"Some kids just aren't into all that reading and writing."

"Nonsense. They just need to find the right things to read and write about."

"I never liked English much."

"If I were your teacher, it would be your favorite subject."

"Well, that might be true, but only because I'd be hot for the teacher," he joked.

352

Truthfully, Trevor and I both enjoyed our chosen careers very much. We often commented on how quickly the days, weeks, and months flew by when you enjoyed your work.

In the spring of 1980, Trevor and I took a day off to drive to a state adoption agency in Winston-Salem, where we were scheduled for an interview. I'd already filled out several forms that I was bringing with us. I wore the tan suit that I'd worn during my job interview the previous year. It had brought me luck before. Hopefully it would do the same again. I had on my matching tan shoes and carried my matching purse. It was only last year that I'd discovered that purses and shoes should match. I'd read it in a fashion magazine. Trevor wore his nicest suit as well. We certainly looked like happy, responsible, mature adults who were ready to take on parenthood.

When I'd filled out the forms, I couldn't help but get my hopes up about the whole thing. We were the perfect prospective parents on paper: not too old, not too young. We'd been married a few years and had a stable, solid relationship. We both had college degrees and steady employment. We owned a home and had the financial resources to care for a child. I'd been thrilled to discover that the neighbor diagonally across the street from us had a licensed daycare home. When I visited her and talked to her about our desire to adopt an infant soon, she said she'd be willing to provide daycare for the baby. In fact, she really liked to provide daycare for teachers because she enjoyed having a lighter daycare load during the summer. How convenient to have her right across the street! And the home had been clean and well kept. She had all the children on a good little daily routine. Her license allowed her to care for up to six children, including up to two infants. She said she'd hold open one of the infant slots for our baby.

We used one of our spare bedrooms as an office, but the third bedroom was completely empty except for some storage boxes. It would make a perfect baby's room. Everything seemed to be falling into place. It was time. And the more I thought about it, the more excited I became.

As Trevor drove, I happily listed all of our qualifications to him again. "You don't have to convince me," he said.

"I know. I'm just wondering how anyone could *not* choose us! Who could be more qualified than us? Ideally we'd get the baby at the very end of this school year. That way I'll have all summer to bond with the baby. Then, near the end of summer, when I'm preparing for classes, I'll bring the baby over to Miss Julie's house for a few hours at a time so the baby can adjust to the new environment. I'll feel better going back to work if the baby is a few months old by then."

"Chrissy, remember, sometimes these things take a little time. I hope you don't have it set in your mind that we'll have a baby within just a couple of months. It's possible, for sure. But I don't want to get too fixated on the timing of this whole thing. We need to be flexible. Even couples who can get pregnant naturally don't have a lot of control over the exact timing of it all."

"I know. I just like to be prepared," I said, as I attempted to flatten a cowlick on the back of his head. "Trevor, I really wish you'd had your hair cut last weekend. We don't want to go to the adoption agency looking like a couple of country bumpkins!"

"So I guess I shouldn't black out a tooth, chew on a straw of hayseed, and do my 'Hee-Haw' impressions at this thing?"

"Not if you want to live to see the light of day tomorrow."

"This is it, I think," he said, pulling into the parking lot.

I checked my make-up in the car mirror and stepped out of the car, smoothing out my suit and adjusting my purse. Then I straightened Trevor's tie. "Are we really doing this?" I took a deep breath. "Let's go."

We entered the building and waited in the front lobby for one of the agency representatives to call us into her office. She seemed like a nice woman, probably in her 40's. She told us to call her Sandra. She smiled at us and said it looked like most of our paperwork was in order. They'd do their best to get us a baby as soon as possible. She asked several questions that I had already answered on the forms, so I gave her my well-rehearsed answers. I had to remind myself to let Trevor do some of the talking so that I didn't look like an overbearing wife. But it was hard to stay silent when I was just so excited about this whole thing.

"Now, we also typically like to put a little background here as to reasons for choosing to adopt," Sandra stated. "Could you tell us a little bit about your attempts to have children naturally? Have you been to a doctor? Have you been told that one of you has a fertility or sterility issue?"

My mouth dropped open. I was stunned by the question. There was no question like this on the forms that I'd completed. How should I answer? I could be vague. I could just say that I had a fertility issue. It was a state agency though. What if they had access to my records? Lying or giving incomplete information about my sterilization would make me look worse. It would make me look like I had something to hide. And I *did* have something to hide.

Seeing the frozen, deer-in-the-headlights expression on my face, Trevor decided to step in. He cleared his throat. "Uh, actually we haven't been to a doctor for fertility treatments. My wife already knows she is infertile. She was sterilized against her will as a young girl under the state's eugenic sterilization program."

"It wasn't my fault," I offered weakly. "They threatened me. They were going to take away my momma's welfare benefits unless I complied. My brothers and sisters would starve. I had no choice."

There were a few moments of painful silence. Sandra nodded her head and gave me a look of pity. "I'm familiar with the program," she said quietly. "It's a regrettable period of North Carolina's history. The program ran for about four decades and ended only about six years ago. Many states had eugenic sterilization programs, but most of them ended after World War II when the horrors of the Holocaust were uncovered. Eugenics was just too closely tied into these ideas of creating a master race and getting rid of the weak and the unfit. But for some reason, maybe because of the way North Carolina's program operated, it just continued for years and years. It was also one of the few states that authorized sterilizations outside of state-run institutions. Almost anyone in a position of authority in the general population could petition the Board to sterilize anyone else. The Board would typically rubber-stamp approval on almost all of them. In the last two decades, especially, the program became more of a way to control the welfare rolls than anything else. The Board just operated quietly and efficiently all those years, never really answering to anyone. And because they targeted the weak and defenseless, no one ever spoke out about what was happening."

Who would have listened to me back then? All the people who had authority over me knew I didn't want the procedure: Momma, Blue Lids, and the doctor. It didn't matter that I didn't want it. They had all the power. I had nothing.

Sandra continued, "You're actually not the first person I've met who was sterilized under the program and I'm sure you won't be the last. What's especially upsetting to me is the number of children in state-run juvenile detention centers and training schools who were sterilized as a matter of routine. Sometimes it was a condition for their release. They didn't even know what was happening to them. They were just told they had to have an operation before they could leave. Then, as adults, they were left to figure out on their own what happened to them."

My heart stopped for a moment as her words sunk in. Brad! He'd spent so much time in juvie. Had he been sterilized too during one of his stays? I wasn't aware that he'd had any kind of surgery. But, then again, he'd never known anything about mine either. It's not the kind of thing that you brag about.

As if reading my mind, Sandra continued, "They'd often target entire families for sterilization. If one was a bad seed, they probably all were. That was the thinking of the time. Eugenics philosophy was sort of a mixture of junk science, race, and class prejudice, and giant leaps of logic about people and what traits they passed on to the next generation. It's incredible that we allowed it to shape a policy that was put into practice for decades, leaving thousands of North Carolinians sterilized in its wake." She shook her head sadly. "And now here we are in the 80's scrambling around trying to find babies for all the young people we sterilized in the 60's. It makes no sense. I am truly sorry for what happened to you."

From the look in her eyes, I could tell that she meant it. I was still too shaken to speak because of having this old wound ripped open without warning. Luckily, Trevor stepped in and finished out the interview with Sandra. I wasn't paying attention anymore to what was said. I felt that I'd been stripped bare of my classy tan suit with matching purse and shoes. Those things weren't fooling anyone! I sat in that chair naked with the word "Unfit" scrawled across my forehead. I had to fight the urge to openly plead with her to leave that part out of our application. No one need know! Did it really truly matter how we came to the point of wanting to adopt? Wasn't it enough just to know that we wanted to adopt?

But I sat there quietly until the interview was finished. Then I stood on wobbly legs, grabbing my purse. I managed to thank Sandra and shake her hand as we left. Trevor's hand was on my back as we walked to the car. I held it all in until the car started, and then I burst into tears. I cried all the way home, while Trevor assured me that someone would still pick us as a couple to adopt her child. In fact, he said, they were even *more* likely to pick us, because they'd feel badly about what I'd been through and want to give me a chance.

No they wouldn't, I thought. Trevor just assumed that everyone saw me as he did. But who in their right mind would pick a person as an adoptive parent who was once thought to be so unfit for parenting that she needed to be sterilized? No one would. In a pile of applicants, mine would be the first one weeded out. I knew that *I* wouldn't pick me. If I were in the difficult situation of giving up a child for adoption, I would scrutinize every application for possible red flags. And the fact that I'd been a troubled teenager who had been eugenically sterilized was a giant red flag. I would pick only the very best possible parent. Sure, I might appear on paper to be rehabilitated. I did have the other qualifications. But, when making such an important decision, who is really going to take that kind of risk?

Trevor and I went for a long walk that evening and talked things through. I felt a little better. But I knew our chances were very slim now and that I shouldn't count on having a baby by the beginning of the summer, or maybe ever. I was happy. I had a good life. Trevor was my family, and he was all I ever really wanted. I had a job I loved. I had my students. They were my children in a way too. I had everything I needed to be content. I needed to let go of the idea of being able to adopt a baby.

But then a few weeks later, as Trevor and I were driving around town running our weekend errands, I spotted something. "Trevor," I said, "pull over! Stop the car! I need to look at something."

"What? What is it?" He pulled the car to the curbside, and I immediately hopped out and headed back to the giant yard sale that we had just passed. They were selling a beautiful set of oak baby furniture. There was a crib with a mattress, a cradle, a chest of drawers, a nightstand, a diaper-changing table, and a rocking chair. I ran my hands over the solid oak. This was the nicest baby furniture I'd ever seen.

When Trevor caught up with me, I exclaimed, "Just look at all of this, Trevor! It's a complete matching set!" I pulled him to the side and lowered my voice. "Trevor, this is name-brand furniture. It looks practically new. And it's at a fraction of the price we would pay to buy all this brand new. Do you think we should get it?" I asked hopefully. "We're not going to find another deal like this."

Trevor hesitated a moment. Then he said, "Chrissy, don't you think this is jumping the gun a little bit? I mean, we don't have a baby yet and it might be some time before we actually get one. We don't even have all the furniture for the house yet. Maybe we shouldn't worry about stuff like this for now. I'm just afraid having all of this around might make you more depressed than anything else."

Trevor was right. It was completely impractical for all the reasons he listed. And, though he wouldn't say it out loud, there was always the chance that we might not get a baby at all. Having this beautiful set of baby furniture around all the time would just be a continual reminder for me of what we didn't have. It was a good thing I had Trevor around to talk some sense into me.

We walked back to the car and drove home. Along the way, I stared out the passenger window and suddenly had a flashback to the time so many years ago when Momma's bus had passed by a yard sale and she had spotted a guitar for sale. She'd gotten off at the next stop and ran back to the sale. At first, she'd decided it was too expensive, and she walked away. Then she turned around, went back and bought it anyway. She'd decided I just had to have it, and that's all there was to it! I smiled at the memory. Then the thought occurred to me that this was the first time I'd been able to relive a memory with Momma and just smile about it. It was a small step forward but still progress.

We pulled into the driveway and parked. I opened the passenger door and started to climb out.

"Wait!" Trevor called out. "Get back in the car."

"What? Why?"

"Well, now I can't stand the thought of someone else getting that furniture."

I happily hopped back into the car and kissed him on the cheek while he backed out of the driveway. He knew me so well! We went back to the yard sale and bought all the baby furniture. Hal borrowed a friend's truck so that we could haul it over to our house and move it all in. I directed exactly where I wanted everything to be placed in that room.

For the next few weekends, I busied myself with decorating the baby's room. I painted the walls and put in a wall border. I figured I couldn't go wrong with shades of green and yellow. Those were pretty gender-neutral baby colors. I bought matching bedding for the cradle and crib and cushions for the rocking chair. I found a mobile with baby animals on it to go over the crib and a couple of lamps with the same baby animals on them for soft lighting in the room. I filled a little bookcase with baby books and stuffed animals. I thought how much Joyce would have loved to help me decorate this room. I'd see a little baby stuffed animal at the store and I could almost hear Joyce exclaiming, "Chrissy, isn't this adorable? I have to buy it for the baby's room!" Before I knew it, that animal had made it to the checkout counter. Surely we could find a place for one more stuffed animal in that room. I even had little bottles of baby lotion, baby powder, baby soap, and baby oil placed in a row along the changing table. They let off just enough of a scent to make it smell like a baby's room.

When the room was finished, it became my favorite room in our little house. It was like my little sanctuary from the world. I would bring in piles of papers and tests to grade and sit in the rocking chair. Somehow the work was more pleasant when I could do it in that room. Other times, I would just go in there with a book to read or to play my guitar. I'd sit in the rocking chair and play every lullaby that I knew. Sometimes I'd wind up the little mobile over the crib and watch it spin around and around to the soft tinkle of a lullaby. It would start out fast and then slow down until the last few notes of the song were slow, distinct plinks before it stopped. The room was just big enough to fit all the furniture without looking crammed. The window let in just enough sunlight to make the room bright without being overpowering. It was a perfect room for a baby. Any baby could be happy here, I would think as I rocked in the chair. It was just missing one thing, I thought, and my eyes would drift to the empty baby crib.

The end of the school year drew near. People were back outdoors again to enjoy the nice weather before the heat and humidity of the South drove them back indoors again. Everywhere I went these days, it seemed I would encounter women with babies balanced on their hips or being pushed in strollers. Pregnant women were out walking everywhere too. Sometimes I'd see pregnant women who were also pushing strollers with older children walking next to them. One day, I counted five pregnant women out walking just on my drive home from work. At the grocery store, at the mall, everywhere I went it seemed I was bumping into baby strollers or overhearing pregnant women talking about trimesters and cravings or complaining about swollen ankles. It seemed the "Baby Boom" of the 1950's hadn't reached Hilldale until the early 80's. We always were a bit behind the times when it came to national trends. It not only affected the people living in Hilldale, it also affected anyone who'd ever lived in Hilldale. Nadine had just given birth to her second baby.

Trevor thought I was imagining things. He said that the pregnant women and babies had always been there and that I was just noticing them more now because it was on my mind.

"No. I am not imagining things, Trevor. There really are more pregnant women and babies than at any time in Hilldale history. I was just at the mall the other day and I overheard some women talking about how everyone who can have a baby is having one right now. They said there must be something in the water!"

Trevor contemplated this for a moment. "Well, it's never a bad idea to stay hydrated."

"I'm glad you find this so amusing, Trevor. I could walk around all day with an IV drip of Hilldale water in my arm, and I *still* would never get pregnant! How do you think it makes me feel that, for everybody but me, getting pregnant is as easy as breathing the air?" My voice briefly caught in my throat by the lump forming there.

Trevor's face softened. "I'm sorry for joking. I know this is a sensitive area for you. Are you dissatisfied with your life, Chrissy? Tell me what to do and I'll do it. I'd do anything to make you happy."

"No," I shook my head and reached for him, burying my head in his chest. "I love my life with you. I wouldn't trade it for anything. I think I just need to find some projects to work on this summer while I'm not teaching so that I don't sit around feeling sorry for myself."

That summer, I kept myself very busy. I signed up for several teacher development seminars and workshops in various nearby cities. I spent countless hours working in my vegetable garden in the backyard. I attended morning aerobics classes or swam laps at the local public pool. Trevor and I continued our weekend jaunts to the mountains or the beach. I researched different places that might be interesting for us to visit. I read all the books that I'd put on my list for when I had more time to read. By mid-summer, we had more tomatoes, carrots, bell peppers, cucumbers, and strawberries than we could eat. I gave some of it away to Hal and to our neighbors. I found and tried out new recipes for utilizing our home-grown produce. I canned several jars of homemade salsa that Trevor loved to put on everything. It was an enjoyable summer.

On one of the last summer days, I awoke to one of those rare August mornings when the humidity is low and the air feels downright cool compared to the stifling heat of most August days. I decided to go for a walk around the neighborhood instead of my usual aerobics or lap swim. I passed by Miss Julie's daycare, where children were playing in her fenced-in yard. They wanted to enjoy the nice weather while it lasted as well. I smiled at two little girls who were drawing with chalk on the concrete driveway.

They squinted up at me in the morning sunlight. "We're going to play hopscotch!"

"That sounds like a lot of fun," I said.

Miss Julie waved over at me from across the yard. I noticed she was carrying an infant on her shoulder. Another baby was placed in a little shaded baby-seat nearby. Miss Julie gave me an apologetic look. "I'm sorry," she said. "I couldn't hold that spot open any longer. I needed the money, and there's such a demand right now for infant caregivers."

"It's all right," I said. "I understand."

I continued walking. The sound of laughing, playing children slowly faded into the distance behind me.

34

When the new school year began, I was able to immerse myself in teaching again. It was amazing how quickly the days, weeks, and months flew by. I'd been married to Trevor now longer than I'd been married to Stan. Even though my marriage to Stan felt like a miserable eternity at the time I was enduring it, from my perspective now it just seemed like a little blip in my past. It hardly seemed to matter now. Maybe someday, I'd feel about it the way Joyce had felt about her first marriage, something that I barely remembered. The physical damage from him had long since healed, but the emotional damage would take more time. I still battled those old feelings of inadequacy and self-doubt that Stan had reinforced. Those emotional scars were still there. Perhaps they never would completely heal.

Even though I knew that Trevor and my students thought highly of me, sometimes I wondered how I'd managed to fool them for so long. Would they wake up one day and realize that I was an imposter and a fraud? I had a sort of ongoing personal narrative, fueled by self-doubt, that I had somehow managed to "cheat the system" and didn't really deserve anything that I had: My degree was a fake. I didn't really know anything. I wasn't sure how I'd fooled all those professors into giving me A's while I was in college. I didn't deserve my job. I'd portrayed myself in the interviews to be someone that I really wasn't. I'd given them the answers that I thought they wanted to hear rather than what I truly thought about things. I didn't deserve my husband. He could have been much happier with a better woman, someone with a better background who could give him children. Of course, I kept all these thoughts to myself and only nursed them during those insecure moments. Most of the time, I was too busy with my life to reflect on all the things that I hadn't really earned and didn't really deserve.

As the school year drew to an end, life had another major change for us. Trevor was offered another regional planning position in Raleigh. This one was an even better position with better pay than the one he'd been offered there when he first graduated from college. We weighed the pros and cons of taking this offer. I was, frankly, terrified of the idea of leaving Hilldale and moving to Raleigh. I didn't want to leave my house, my job, my memories, and the life we'd created here. But it was time to think about what was best for Trevor's future. He'd chosen Hilldale once for my sake. This time, I was the one who insisted that he accept the offer in Raleigh. We put our house up for sale, with the hopes of moving that summer. And I applied for a high school teaching position with Wake County Schools in Raleigh.

Jessie also graduated from college that spring and had accepted a job offer in New Jersey. We offered to help him move to New Jersey as soon as I was off work for the summer. That way we could take the opportunity to visit Nadine and Ty in New York. They'd bought a home and had two little girls now. I hadn't seen them since their wedding, although we talked on the phone periodically. Now, with Jessie up in New Jersey, we'd have an additional reason to make periodic visits to the Northeast.

After we helped Jessie move into his new apartment, we spent a few days with Nadine and Ty. Their little girls were so cute. They looked like little miniature versions of Nadine. The youngest one, Mandy, had just turned a year old and was beginning to toddle around the house. She was adorable, but I found myself drawn to their older daughter, Charlotte. At only 3 ½ years old, she seemed so grown up for her age. We had several little chats and I was amazed at how much knowledge she'd managed to accrue in her few short years of life.

After dinner on our first night there, Nadine and I went into their living room to talk while Ty and Trevor went down to their basement to play foosball. I'd noticed that Charlotte had cleared her own plate from the dinner table and put it in the kitchen sink. "Have the girls been added to the chore chart yet?" I jokingly asked Nadine.

"Charlotte, yes. But Mandy's still too young." She was serious! At Charlotte's young age, she was already making her own bed, picking up toys, scrubbing the bathroom sinks, and dusting the living room. Nadine didn't kid around with teaching her children how to work. "Charlotte, honey, will you take your little sister to the playroom while the grown-ups talk?" she asked her daughter.

I smiled and watched as Charlotte dutifully took her little sister's hand and led her to the playroom. She reminded me of myself in a way. At her age, I already had a little brother and a baby sister on the way. I guess that's how we big sisters are, I thought to myself. We grow up quickly, and we take care of everybody.

"You have a great little family," I told Nadine. "It's interesting to see how having children has changed the dynamic around here. You and Ty are wonderful parents."

"It has its good moments," she said. "What about you and Trevor? Have you thought about having kids?"

I paused for a moment, then nodded my head. "Yes. We're actually on a waiting list to adopt an infant. It turns out that I can't have kids. I'm infertile."

"Oh," Nadine just accepted what I'd told her at face value. "How long have you been on the waiting list?"

"A little over a year. Sometimes these things take time."

She nodded. "Did you list any preferences?"

"We have no preferences for gender or race. We were hoping to get an infant though rather than an older child. It's just," I shrugged, "we have a lot of baby furniture. I'd like to be able to use it one of these days."

"Well, I'll keep my fingers crossed for you."

"Thank you."

I don't know why I couldn't share the story of my sterilization with anyone but Trevor. It just seemed too private and personal. It required too much of an explanation and reopened too many old wounds. People like Nadine, Joyce, and Miss Candace would have understood, but it required too much emotional work for me to share it with them. The woman at the adoption agency had said that the sterilization program had continued for decades because people wouldn't speak out about what had happened to them. I understood why. I couldn't even share my story with the people I trusted most in the world, not to mention people that I didn't know who might jump to conclusions about me, perhaps assuming that I'd deserved what I got.

After our trip to the Northeast, we came back to Hilldale and accepted an offer on our house. I spent the next month packing while Trevor was at work. I tried not to betray my emotions about moving to Trevor. He was excited about our move to Raleigh and his new job there. But Trevor was the type of person who looked forward eagerly, while I lagged behind, glumly looking back. He was especially looking forward to showing me a neighborhood in North Raleigh that was close to his work and filled with big, beautiful homes in a fancy new development. He couldn't wait to buy me a home that I "deserved." How could I explain to him that I struggled with the idea that I "deserved" the tiny little place that I loved to call home right now? I didn't want to move to a big city and live in a big, fancy home and work at a high school filled with snobby rich kids.

But I kept all these thoughts to myself and packed up our life in Hilldale. As we pulled away in our big rented moving truck, I watched our first home in the rear-view mirror fade into the distance and sadly said good-bye to our lovely little brick house with its vegetable garden in the backyard and the baby's room that never saw a baby.

We lived in an extended-stay hotel room in Raleigh and kept most of our stuff in storage until we could find a home to buy. Trevor excitedly drove me to where his new office was in North Raleigh. It was a beautiful glass building with an atrium in the middle. I agreed that it looked like a very nice place to go to work every day. We timed the drive to the neighborhood that he wanted me to see. It took 10 minutes. It would be nice for him to have a quick commute. I stared out the window at the large, spacious homes with well-manicured, nicely landscaped lawns and fancy cars parked in the driveway. They were about as big and as nice as the Townsend home, but for some reason, the Townsend home had seemed friendlier and more welcoming. Maybe it was just because it had been located in Hilldale and I'd known the people who lived in it.

I agreed with Trevor that it was a very nice neighborhood. I did mention that I felt that "I didn't belong" in a neighborhood like this. But Trevor dismissed that as nonsense. I belonged here as much as anyone belonged anywhere, he said. In fact, I think my comment made him more determined than ever to buy a home in that neighborhood, to prove to me that I was as deserving as anyone else to live in a nice home and a neighborhood like this. We looked at several homes and made an offer on the one that seemed to appeal the most to Trevor.

A month later, we hired movers to get our stuff from storage and move it into the new home. Even with all the furniture moved in from our old home, there were still several bare, empty rooms. Trevor said we would fill them over time. We were in no hurry to fill every square inch of our new home with stuff. Trevor was at work while I directed the movers.

When they placed all the baby furniture in one of the rooms, a mover turned to me and said, "I have a baby too, a little girl, about six months old. How old is your baby?"

"Oh, uh... We actually don't have our baby yet. It hasn't arrived." That reminded me I needed to call the adoption agency to change our contact information on file.

"Oh, congratulations!" he exclaimed. "When are you due?" he asked, looking at my belly.

It was too complicated to explain to him, so I just said, "In about six months." I walked away patting my belly and vowing to start exercising again.

I was hired for a teaching position at a Raleigh high school about 15 minutes away from our neighborhood and started teaching in the fall. The students in North Raleigh were indeed different from my Hilldale students. Many of them were from well-to-do families. But I did grow to love them as much as my students in Hilldale. After all, they had no control over what kind of homes they lived in or what their parents did for a living. They had their own sets of problems, and life could be just as lonely and traumatic for a teen in North Raleigh as it could be in Hilldale.

I slowly began to carve out my own little niche at my new job, my new neighborhood, and my new life. Eventually, I felt less like a guest as I drove through the neighborhood. The houses didn't seem quite as enormous and uninviting as they had initially. I can't say that I ever fully fit into my new neighborhood. I still had my few areas of resistance: I continued to shop for clothes and shoes at discount stores. I owned one purse at a time that I used for everything and only replaced it when the straps broke. The nicest piece of jewelry that I ever owned was my wedding ring. When my Toyota Corolla finally died, I bought another Toyota Corolla. We always did our own yard work and house cleaning instead of hiring help for that kind of stuff. I grew another vegetable garden in the backyard. The neighbors didn't see us as "Hilldale hillbillies." They just knew that we liked doing things our own way.

We enjoyed all the interesting and fun things to do now that we lived in "The Triangle." Not only were there tons of restaurants, museums, and interesting places to visit in Raleigh, there were also nearby cities with even more ways to pass the time and stay entertained. We explored Raleigh, Durham, Chapel Hill, and other nearby cities and towns. Whenever one of us would hear about an interesting museum, restaurant, park, or place to explore, we would note it and suggest it as an activity for that weekend. I did miss our "weekend jaunts" to the mountains and beach. We promised ourselves we would visit them soon, but there were just so many options locally that we put off the longer trips for the time being.

Trevor excelled at his new job. He enjoyed it for the most part. He often had to work longer hours now and sometimes he brought work home with him. My biggest complaint was that people at work often called him at home. He spent enough time at the office during the workweek, and I seldom bothered him while he was there. But I was possessive of his time away from work and didn't want the interruptions during evenings and weekends. I was glad I didn't get calls from the high school during my time at home. I mean, I could understand the need for calls at home for someone who worked in the medical field or had some sort of emergency-response profession, but "city planning" emergencies? Come on.

"With our move to Raleigh, I thought I would have more time to spend with my girlfriend in Chapel Hill," Trevor observed one day. "But I've just been too busy!"

"Ha ha, such a funny guy. You missed your calling in life as a comedian," I replied. One thing I'd learned about Trevor was that he never forgot a thing. If something tickled his funny bone, he would file it away and bring it up years later when I'd long since forgotten it. Then he would laugh as if it were the funniest thing in the world. He laughed at his own jokes much more than anyone else did. We never paid a visit to Chapel Hill without some reference to his "girlfriend" there. Then he would laugh away, while I rolled my eyes. It was a good thing I'd never told him about the brainy, beautiful civil engineer who was about to steal him away from me in my tortured imagination. He would have gotten such a hoot out of that, and then never let me forget it.

My 30th birthday approached in early May. We decided it was time for one of our weekend jaunts to the mountains or the beach. I could decide which one it would be. I hadn't yet figured out which one I needed to visit more. I'd probably just pack for both and then decide once we hit the road and Trevor asked, "Right or left?" We'd arranged to have that Friday off of work so that we could make a three-day weekend of it. I was so excited when we woke up early that Friday morning and began packing for our trip. It looked like the weather would be gorgeous all weekend, and I felt more than ready for a vacation.

We scurried through the house gathering our things for the trip. I had already filled the gas tank the day before so that we would be ready to go. As I went into the kitchen to load the cooler with ice, drinks, and snacks, the phone rang.

"We're not answering that!" I called out. "We've already left the house!"

Trevor walked past the phone and hesitated. "It could be someone from work."

"Don't answer! Whatever it is, it can wait until Monday! Don't they know you're on vacation this weekend?"

Trevor picked up the phone anyway. I sighed as he leaned his head down, listening intently. Good old responsible Trevor couldn't bear the thought of letting some detail about a project wait until Monday. I went out to the car and loaded the trunk. All I needed was a good book, my beach chair, umbrella, and a nice view. That was the perfect way to spend my birthday.

When I went back into the house, Trevor was still bent over the kitchen countertop, writing something down on a piece of paper. He balanced the receiver between his shoulder and ear as he wrote.

"Trevor! We really do need to go now!" I called out loudly, so that the person on the other end would be able to hear.

He held up a finger in my direction, "One moment."

I sighed and went back to loading our stuff, making plenty of noise to convey my impatience. This was so annoying! They *would* be calling right as we were about to leave for my birthday weekend! We should have left earlier, I thought to myself.

After a few more minutes, Trevor hung up.

"Finally! Let's go! Did you have just the one bag with your stuff?"

"Actually, Chrissy," Trevor said, "slight change of plans. What do you say we go to Hanksville instead for the weekend?"

I stood there dumbfounded. "Hanksville? Hanksville! Do you mean Hanksville, North Carolina, as in no-beach, no-mountains, no-nothing Hanksville?"

"I believe that's the one."

"Trevor, no!" I whined, stomping one foot. "If this is one of your ideas to do something different, please let me talk you out of it! I do not want to go to Hanksville for any reason. I drove through Hanksville once a couple of years ago, and, let me assure you, there is nothing of interest in Hanksville!"

"Oh, I think you're wrong there."

"I'm not wrong. Trevor, please! Shouldn't I get to decide since it's my birthday weekend? Frankly, if that's my only choice, then I'd just rather stay here. There's more to do in the Triangle. Really, Trevor, I..."

"Our baby's in Hanksville," Trevor interrupted me. His voice broke with emotion.

I stood there, frozen, registering what he had just said. His face was red and flushed and his hand holding the sheet of paper shook. He wasn't joking.

"I'll get my bag," I said.

35

As we drove in the direction of Hanksville, I grilled Trevor for every detail of his phone conversation with the adoption agency representative. A 16-year-old girl in Hanksville had found out she was pregnant after breaking up with her boyfriend. She'd been leaning toward the idea of keeping the baby and raising it on her own, but she'd visited the adoption agency as her back-up plan. She'd chosen us as potential adoptive parents for the baby. Only us! We hadn't been contacted because they didn't know whether or not she'd end up keeping the baby. Apparently, the girl didn't have much of a support system at home. After a little more than a week handling the newborn on her own, she'd decided the baby would be better off with us.

"Tell me every detail you know about the baby," I said to Trevor. "I want to know exactly what they said. Don't leave out a single word."

"All I know is that it's a girl, she's white, and she's 10 days old. That's all the representative told me about her."

"What does she look like? Did they describe her at all?"

"No. Don't all newborns kind of look alike anyway?"

"Trevor, I'm going to pretend that you did not just say that."

"Well, we'll see her in person tomorrow morning. A social worker will meet us with the baby at 10 a.m. at a little café on the outskirts of town. We'll sign some more paperwork and then take her home. Can you believe it?" He laughed incredulously.

"No, I really can't. In fact, I don't think I'll really believe it until I see her. I wish I could just picture her now. Are you sure they didn't give you more information? Oh, this is really, really important: what is her length and how much does she weigh?"

"Why is that incredibly important?"

"Well, I'm not exactly sure. But it's always the information that people give when they have a baby. They give the gender and then the weight and length. So I assume it has to be important."

"Do you even know what is considered to be optimal length and weight ranges?"

"No," I admitted quietly. "Dang it! We should have brought our book, 'More Than You Ever Want to Know About Babies.' I could have answered that question in 10 seconds if I had that book with me! I feel like we're trying to cram for a major exam and we don't have the appropriate study materials! I should be reading that book aloud for this entire drive. It has everything in it."

"More than everything, it sounds like."

"Oh, you know what else we need? A baby book. Why didn't we get one before? I should be recording everything about this day in her baby book: how we got the news, what the drive was like, our first impression of her. We need to stop and buy one right now."

"That's probably something that can wait."

"Oh, what color are her eyes?" I asked.

"They didn't say."

"But she has eyes?"

"I didn't think to ask. I assume she comes with all the standard features: eyes, ears, mouth, nose, etc."

"Oh, my gosh, I'm going crazy without a thorough description of each feature!"

"You'll see her soon enough."

"If this thing actually happens. I won't believe it until I actually see her. Is this possible, Trevor? Are we actually driving to Hanksville as a family of two and coming back as a family of three? Oh, you know what? We have to stop at the store right now to get a safety seat! I can't believe I didn't think of it before. We cannot go anywhere with the baby without a safety seat!"

We pulled off the highway to a nearby town and found a K-mart. I loaded a cart with newborn diapers, bottles, baby formula, a few onesies with matching caps and socks, blankets, and a baby book. I looked for a copy of the "More Than You Ever Want to Know About Babies" book, but K-mart didn't have it. I worried and fretted because I remembered it had a big section about what to look for in a quality baby safety seat. Without this knowledge, we just decided that our safest bet was to buy the most expensive seat on the shelf. After we bought everything, we stopped at a deli for sandwiches and Slurpees. I nervously sucked down my Slurpee while poring over the baby book. "Now I know why the weight and length are so important. It's so that you can note it in the baby book along with her head circumference. And look! There's a little spot right here where we can put her handprint and footprint! And there's a space here for a little lock of her hair. Does she have hair?"

"Once again, I have no information on that."

"Trevor, I really wish you would have gotten more details about her."

"Well, it was a little difficult to carry on a detailed conversation with all the background noise going on at the time." I chose to ignore that remark.

We loaded everything into the car and then continued our drive to Hanksville. I read the directions aloud for how to mix the formula from the back of the label. When I got to the directions for sterilizing and using the bottles, Trevor held up a hand. "Chrissy, must you?" I finished reading all the labels in silence and then set the baby stuff back down.

"Go exactly five miles over the speed limit, Trevor. I want to get there as soon as possible without risking a speeding ticket."

I leaned my head over to the driver's side to check the speedometer. Trevor cleared his throat, "I'd be better able to go exactly five miles over the speed limit if I could actually see the speedometer." I pulled my head back over to the passenger side. "Remember," Trevor said, "we can't get her until tomorrow morning. There's no rush to get there early today."

"I know, but I'll feel better once we're in the town limits. I want to make sure this place actually exists."

"I thought you'd already seen it. Weren't you the one telling me just a few hours ago what a horrible little town it was?"

"Trevor, I never said that! And don't you dare ever tell our child that I said her place of birth was a horrible little town! Hanksville is a charming, quaint little town! It represents everything that is good and decent about small-town America. Oh, that's good! I'm going to write that down in her baby book."

I reached for the baby book and began writing. Trevor sighed. "And the revisionist history begins," he remarked.

We made it to Hanksville by late afternoon and checked into a nearby decent-looking motel. Then we drove around Hanksville, while I exclaimed over the beauty, warmth and charm of this little-known town. We drove past the café where we would get our baby in the morning. I could hardly breathe when I saw it. It was indeed a real place. I took a picture of it for the baby book.

We had dinner at a little restaurant near our motel and then went back to our room. Trevor turned on the TV. I sat on the bed and stared at the screen, but I didn't pay attention to any of the shows. I just wished that I had that "More Than You Ever Want to Know About Babies" book with me so that I could spend the evening reading it and preparing for the next day.

I would need to call the high school and arrange for a substitute to finish out the school year for me. There was about a month left before the summer break. I would be back in the fall, but the baby would be about four months old then, and hopefully I would find a good daycare arrangement for her by then. They wouldn't be pleased about my springing this news so suddenly, but I'd really had no idea that something like this could actually happen. I'd hoped, yes, but I'd never actually believed.

Trevor would need to add the baby right away to our health insurance plan. And we needed to find a pediatrician for her and bring her in for her immunizations. Oh! There were just so many things that would need to be handled right away. Why had I ever thought that just having some baby furniture arranged nicely in a room somehow made us well-equipped and qualified to be parents?

After watching the local news, we got ready for bed, climbed into the sheets, kissed each other good night and flipped off the bedside lamp. I lay there in the dark wide awake, worrying and fretting over all the details. A human life would be depending on me for her every need, starting tomorrow, and I was so ill-equipped and ill-prepared to take on that important responsibility! I tossed and turned and fretted more for the next few hours. The old self-doubts and insecurities came bubbling up until I was in a state of sheer panic. My heart pounded in my chest, and I felt that I could hardly breathe. At 2:15 a.m., I sat up in bed.

"Oh no. This is not good. This is not good at all," I said out loud.

Trevor stirred beside me. "What is it? What's the matter?" he asked groggily.

"I just realized something. I only know how to change cloth diapers on a baby. All we have are disposables!"

"Don't most people use disposables now because they are much easier than cloth?"

"The point is that my experience is with cloth diapers. That's what I know!"

"Didn't they sometimes use disposable diapers for some of the residents at the care center?"

"Yes, but that's very, very different. You can't compare the needs of babies with the needs of seniors. It's just different!"

"Well, we're a couple of college-educated, intelligent people. I'm sure between the two of us, we can figure it out. But I'll tell you what, if somehow that baby ends up with a disposable diaper wrapped around her head like a football helmet, I will personally go out and buy us a package of cloth diapers to use."

I slowly eased my way back down to my pillow, but my eyes were still wide open. The curtains were cracked open, letting a small stream of moonlight into the room. That, and the sound of Trevor's breathing next to me should have been enough of a comfort, but it wasn't. After a few more minutes of tossing and turning, I sat up again.

"This is very, very bad," I said.

"What is it now?" There was a hint of exasperation in Trevor's voice.

"I really do wish we'd brought that book with us, Trevor. I haven't taken care of a newborn since I was 10 years old! There's a lot that I've forgotten. I mean, I can't even remember how much to feed a newborn! Momma nursed Trisha in the beginning. I sometimes fed her a bottle, but was it two ounces? Was it four? Beats me! And how often do you feed a newborn? Is it every two hours? Is it every three hours? Don't ask me! I haven't a clue! And then there's the whole burping thing. They must be burped after every feeding! I can't remember how much force to use!"

I grabbed my pillow and flung it over my shoulder. "I mean, I know you need to use a fair amount of force to get those bubbles up, especially when a baby is bottle-fed. But is it more of a ..." I patted gently on the pillow, "or is more like a ..." I thwacked the pillow with the palm of my hand a few times. "You definitely don't want to use too much force on a newborn. They're very fragile. Oh my gosh! What if I fracture one of her ribs without knowing it? What if it punctures one of her little lungs and collapses it?"

"Chrissy," Trevor propped his head up on one arm, "what's going on? I've never seen you like this! I thought this was what you wanted."

"It *is* what I want!"

"Then why all of this anxiety about it?"

"I'm just ... afraid! I'm so afraid that I'll fail!"

"Chrissy, you've never failed at anything in your life!"

378

"I failed Momma. I failed to keep my siblings together after her death. I failed my first marriage. Now that I think about, I've failed at a lot of things," I said quietly.

"Those things were out of your control! Okay? You can't hold yourself responsible for every bad thing that ever happens! Bad things do happen, and you have to just pick up the pieces and somehow move on. You blame yourself for all the bad stuff, but then you never take credit for any of the good things that happen."

"Trevor, good things have happened *in spite* of me, not *because* of me. I don't deserve them."

"That's exactly what I'm talking about."

I shrugged and slowly pulled the pillow down from my shoulder and held it in my arms in front of me. "It's just how I see things. I don't know why. All those years ago, when they sterilized me, they labeled me as feeble-minded, a person so unfit to be a parent that she needed to be surgically altered to prevent her from ever having that kind of responsibility. And even though I know they were wrong, I know I was targeted for reasons that were out of my control. I know I'm a smart, capable person. But somewhere deep down inside of me, there's still a little hopeless welfare girl … who still believes they may have been … right."

Even in the pale moonlight of the room, I could see Trevor's eyes on me. "Now, listen to me," he said. "You're always telling me that I have no faith. But you're wrong. I *do* have faith in things that are real and things that are true. What we have is real. And true. I have faith that you are going to be a terrific mom. I don't just believe it. I know it! We're going to be terrific parents and have a great family. That little girl is going to have a great life, with every opportunity available to her. And part of that will be because we came into her life. I know that somewhere out there tonight, not far from here, there is a little baby peacefully sleeping. She doesn't even know that her life is about to take a major turn tomorrow, a turn for the better. She's going to join our family! And none of us will ever have doubts that it was the right move for us. Listen to me." His eyes glistened in the moonlight. "We are *not* going to fail her."

"What if you're wrong?"

"I'm not wrong."

"How do you know?"

"I just know."

"But how?"

"How?" Trevor contemplated this for a moment. "Because I'm the damn genius of North Carolina. That's how!"

I hit him with the pillow while he laughed. Then he pulled my face in and kissed me softly on the lips. "Now get some sleep," he said, "because you're driving me crazy."

I settled down into the crook of his arm and let go of my worries and fears for the moment. I still didn't believe in myself much. But Trevor believed in me. And I believed in Trevor, so in a roundabout way, I could believe in myself a little too. My heart rate and breathing slowed in unison with Trevor's. And after a little while, I finally drifted into a deep and peaceful sleep.

The next morning, I awoke with the sun shining through the crack in the motel room curtains. I checked the clock. It was already 8:30! I couldn't believe we'd slept so late. We jumped out of bed and scurried around the room getting ready and gathering our things. We were both excited and nervous about the day and hardly spoke as we got ready. I showered, fixed my hair, and did my make-up. I knew the baby wouldn't remember this day, but I still wanted to make a good first impression. We packed our bags and set them by the door.

Trevor went out to install the safety seat in the backseat of our car, and I followed him out to the parking lot to offer helpful advice. "Would you like me to read the instructions aloud?" I asked.

"No."

"Really? Because it would be no bother."

"Trust me. It would."

"Make sure you get it in there really tightly. I saw a news report on this. Most people do not install these things correctly."

"That is what I am attempting to do here," Trevor grunted as he struggled with the seat and the safety straps. "It's easier said than done."

"We don't want her head bouncing all around back there. It could rattle her brain and cause brain damage," I added.

"Chrissy, why don't you go back into the room to make sure we've gathered all of our stuff together," Trevor suggested.

"I will. But first I wanted to talk to you about SIDS."

"Is that a name you were considering for her?"

"No! It's a condition that strikes infants for no known reason. I've been worrying about it all morning. I really wish I had that book so that I could read up on it. Have you heard of it?"

"No. And I do not *wish* to hear of it at the moment."

"It stands for 'Sudden Infant Death Syndrome.'"

"Of course it does."

"Babies can just stop breathing and die in their sleep. Just like that. They're alive one minute, dead the next. It's baffling. I'd never really pondered the phenomenon before, but it just popped into my head this morning. It's very strange."

"Indeed."

"Do you think it means anything?"

"Yes. It means that you are over-thinking it."

"Put all your weight on it, then fasten the strap as tightly as possible."

Trevor sat up abruptly, red-faced. "There are too many instructors here right now!"

Since I was the only person standing there, I could only assume that he was referring to me. I went back to the motel room to make sure we'd gathered all of our stuff. I never stored anything in motel room cabinets and drawers, but I always opened them all before we checked out just to be sure.

Finally, the car was all packed and we were on our way to the café by 9:45. We drove in nervous silence. Trevor tried not to show his annoyance when I repeatedly reached to the back seat to try to jiggle the safety seat. It didn't budge in any direction.

When we arrived at the café, I was relieved to see there were very few cars parked. I was worried that it might be busy and chaotic on a Saturday morning, as it had often been at Mike's Diner. This place seemed more peaceful and private. But, as we parked the car, I started to panic again. It was *too* peaceful, *too* quiet. We clasped hands as we walked toward the building and Trevor gave my hand a reassuring squeeze. But all I could think was *she isn't here*. Why hadn't I known from the beginning that this was too good to be true? Why had I allowed myself to believe it? The birth mother had probably changed her mind last night. She'd decided not to go forward with the adoption. She'd decided to keep the baby. Or, even worse, what if they'd had an accident on the way here? What if the baby hadn't been strapped into a properly installed safety seat? Or maybe she had died of SIDS last night in her sleep. Of course! That's why it had popped into my head this morning. I braced myself for the worst as we walked through the entrance.

And then I saw her.

A tiny little bundle wrapped in blankets. A woman stood holding her next to a table where a small diaper bag was placed. She turned as we walked through the entrance. "Townsends?" she asked hopefully.

"Yes." Trevor stepped forward. "Hi, I'm Trevor Townsend. This is my wife, Chrissy."

I stood behind, frozen in place, unable to move.

The woman turned to me and smiled, holding up the bundle of blankets a little more so that I could see. "There's somebody I'd like you to meet," she said.

I slowly stepped forward on shaky legs and peered down at the little bundle in her arms. She was the most beautiful baby I'd ever seen. Her bright, silver-blue eyes blinked up at the bright lights overhead. Miss Candace's eyes! She had a tuft of dark hair on top of her head. A tiny fist had escaped the blankets, and I marveled at the smallness of that little hand. I stroked over her little fist with one finger and then gasped as she closed her fist around my finger. "I think she likes me!" I said.

Trevor laughed softly and wiped at a tear. "I think she does," he agreed.

"May I?" I asked the social worker.

"Please." She transferred the little bundle into my arms, and I just stood there, mesmerized by this little person.

"She's precious," I said. We all nodded our heads in agreement. "Does she have a name?" I asked.

"Well, she was given a family name by her birth mother, but of course when we send in her paperwork, we can go with any name that you like."

"What is it?" I asked.

"Mildred."

"Mildred!" I objected. "That sounds like something growing on the shower curtain!"

Trevor interrupted, "She said we could change it to any name that we want."

I looked down at her little face for a moment. She still had that one fist clamped around my finger. "How about Hope?" I suggested.

"I think that's a lovely name." Trevor's eyes glistened with tears.

Her official name was Candace Hope Townsend. But we always called her Hope.

There were a few more papers that needed to be signed. Trevor busied himself with the formalities of the adoption, while I tended to Hope. I realized that I needn't have worried so much about knowing how to care for an infant. The 10-year-old Chrissy inside me sprang to life again. And she knew exactly what to do.

I found a bottle of formula in the little diaper bag that her birth mother had carefully packed for her and sat down at the table to feed her. Trevor brought me the forms that I needed to sign and I hastily signed them so I could get back to focusing on the baby.

When the social worker had everything she needed, she congratulated us and wished us well before leaving the café. I burped the baby and then took her to the restroom to change her diaper, where I managed on my own to figure out how it was done. Her old diaper had been soiled and was pretty full. Now she was fed, changed, clean, and ready for her long car ride to our home in Raleigh.

As we walked out with our new baby to the car, the panic started to set in again. Why did we have to live so far away? And how did people ever feel comfortable strapping these fragile, precious little infants into giant moving vehicles of death and then tearing through the streets with them? At that moment, I would have just preferred to buy a house in Hanksville to spend the remainder of our days there.

Trevor opened the door to the backseat so I could place Hope in her safety seat. "I'm going to sit in the backseat with her on this trip home in case she needs me," I stated.

"Chrissy, come on. Really?" Trevor protested. "I don't want to feel like I'm the chauffeur."

"Trevor, she is literally clinging to my finger! This is a very difficult day for her, and I am not about to wrench my finger from her grasp and leave her alone in the backseat to fend for herself!"

"You're ascribing some pretty deep emotions to a one-week-old," he observed. I gave him a look, and he sighed. "Fine. Sit in the backseat."

Once we were all securely fastened, Trevor started the engine and began to back out of the parking space. I could already feel beads of sweat forming on my forehead and the back of my neck. Hope was still grasping my pinky finger, but her eyes were slowly closing. "Everything's going to be just fine.

Don't worry. Mommy's here." I glanced around nervously watching for oncoming cars. "Trevor, do not take any chances. Take extra time. Let people go around you. There's no need to go tearing through town."

He turned on the blinker to turn left. "Look out for that car," I cautioned him.

"The one car that's about 10 miles away?"

"Just let him pass. I can tell he's speeding."

We finally made it to the outskirts of town and onto the highway. I was even more nervous as we encountered more traffic at higher speeds. "Trevor, please stay at least five miles below the speed limit. Remember, there's a reason why it's called a speed *limit*. That's the maximum speed you can go. It doesn't mean you have to go that speed. It's better to stay below it."

"I thought one could safely go five miles *above* the speed limit."

"Trevor, just … indulge me, would you please? Can't you see that I'm a nervous wreck back here?"

Trevor dutifully went five miles below the speed limit, and a small train of cars lined up behind us on the two-lane highway. One particularly impatient man behind us was visibly enraged, throwing his hands up above the steering wheel and shouting obscenities that we couldn't hear. I rolled down the window and waved my hand at him to pass us. "Well, just go around, you moron, if you're in such a big hurry!" He zoomed past us while I called out, "Can't you see there's a baby on board!"

I sighed and fell back into my seat. Hope remained quietly and peacefully asleep, still holding my finger. She was completely unaware of all the peril, danger, and anxiety surrounding her.

After what was arguably the longest, sweatiest car ride of my life, we all made it home miraculously unharmed. Hope had slept through almost the entire trip. Was it just yesterday morning that I was packing for a trip to the beach or the mountains? It seemed like a lifetime ago. Hope had opened her eyes, and I quickly fed and changed her again so that I could carry her around the house to show her where she lived now. "And this is your backyard. Isn't it pretty? Don't worry, we'll get a swing set and some riding toys. You're going to have a great time back here in a couple of years."

I knew she wouldn't remember any of this tour, but I still wanted to show everything to her. Trevor and I sat down at the table, armed with our "More Than You Ever Want to Know About Babies" book and came up with a list of things we still needed to get, a list of people that we would need to call, and arrangements we would need to make during the next week.

Trevor went to the store to buy some of the more critical items, while I grabbed the phone, still cradling Hope in one arm to call our friends and family with our news. People were surprised and thrilled for us. Hal promised to come out for a visit the next weekend to meet his new grandchild.

It wasn't until Trevor came home with Chinese take-out that I realized how hungry I was. I hadn't eaten anything all day. We placed Hope in a baby carrier near the kitchen table while we ate. That was the first time we'd heard her cry all day, which was good because I'd started to worry that she couldn't cry and that we would have no way of knowing when she needed something.

By the time it grew dark that night, we were feeling a little more confident as new parents, having kept a newborn alive and well for several hours now. I warmed another bottle and brought Hope into her new room and turned on the little table lamps. I sat and rocked in the rocking chair while I fed her and stroked her soft little head and sang every lullaby that I knew. It was as blissful, tranquil, and peaceful as I'd always imagined it would be. Hope's silver-blue eyes were open and she sucked greedily on her bottle while staring absently overhead.

I remembered Momma, sitting so peacefully in her rocking chair with baby Trisha in the days before we lost Daddy.

The sound of her voice singing softly was so comforting to me back then. Even though none of us can consciously remember what it was like to be a baby, I think there must be a little part of the subconscious mind that does remember the feeling of being so peaceful and safe in the arms of our parents as they rock us to sleep.

And suddenly in that room, I could feel the presence of Momma so powerfully. I knew she was watching me rocking my own baby to sleep for the first time. "You sent her to me, didn't you, Momma?" I asked aloud softly. "I know you did. Thank you." Hope sighed softly in my arms. Her sucking slowed and her eyes closed. "We're even now." The presence faded from the room. Momma could go now. She could finally rest in peace.

I set the bottle on the table next to me and continued rocking. After a few minutes, I felt another presence watching me and looked up to see Trevor standing in the doorway. "I've come to take my shift," he said softly.

"Give me just a few more minutes with her. Okay?"

"Okay." He added, "I was just in our bedroom reading from that book."

"What did you learn?"

"More than I ever wanted to know about babies."

"Go read one more chapter and then come back."

"Okay," he said. He started off down the hallway toward our room.

"Trevor?" I called out softly.

He turned back around. "What?"

"I love this."

"I know you do. I'll be back in a little while."

He left me there, quietly rocking back and forth in the baby's room that finally had an occupant.

36

Never was there a more loved baby than our little Hope. We marveled over every tiny feature. Surely a more beautiful and perfect baby had never existed before Hope was born. She was a peaceful, contented baby who seldom cried and was easily comforted when she did cry. I enjoyed every single day of my four months off work with her that summer. I took her for daily walks through the neighborhood in her baby carriage. After a few weeks, I was even comfortable enough to start driving around town with her in her safety seat. I became a pro at quickly strapping her in and out of various baby carriers and seats. She was my little companion, running errands around town with me. She'd watch me from her carrier while I cleaned or worked in the garden or chopped vegetables in the kitchen.

We fell more in love with Hope by the day, especially as she began to recognize us and interact with us. She'd break into a huge smile whenever one of us would walk into the room, and we'd immediately go straight over to her to baby talk and coo with her, completely forgetting our original reason for going to that room. She gained weight quickly and very soon lost her "newborn" look. I loved how she'd kick out her chubby, dimpled baby thighs while I changed her diaper and gave her a bath. I loved how she always tried to eat her clenched fist. We didn't travel that summer, but every day seemed to be a new adventure with our new little family member. We snapped pictures of her and filled her baby book with every detail of her life.

I dreaded the idea of going back to work in the fall, but I didn't want to give up the job I loved. I found a good daycare center near the high school. The first day back to work was the worst. Hope did just fine at the daycare center. I was the one who had a hard time handing her to one of the workers. I cried all the way to school, feeling like I had just abandoned my child. Fortunately, the first few days were shorter, teacher-prep days, and I didn't have to face the students just yet. By the time the full days started, we were in a pretty good routine and I felt comfortable that she was happy and well cared for at the daycare center. I still loved my job as a high school English teacher and didn't love my students any less. But, whereas before I saw myself as a teacher first and foremost, now I saw myself as a mom first and a teacher second. I no longer stayed awake at night worrying and fretting over my students. I tried to leave my work at work, though that wasn't always easy to do.

The year passed by so quickly. Every holiday was a big event since it was Hope's first. We dressed her up in a little dragon costume for Halloween and took her to several community Halloween events and then carried her around the neighborhood for trick-or-treating, mainly so that we could hear the neighbors tell us how cute she was in her costume.

Hal made frequent trips to visit Raleigh from Hilldale. He loved being a grandfather and didn't want to miss out on anything. He and Jessie and the girl Jessie was dating in New Jersey came out to spend Christmas with us. Hope was, of course, the highlight of the occasion. We dressed her up as an elf and took pictures of her sitting on Santa's lap at the local mall. She did just fine until she looked up and saw who was holding her. Then she began to cry and reach for us. Trevor wanted me to leave her in Santa's lap so we could get some good, classic "crying with Santa" pictures, but I couldn't stand the sight of her crying and reaching for us. Trevor ended up purchasing and framing the photo that shows me swooping in to snatch a crying Hope from Santa's lap.

It was wonderful to see Hal in the role he loved, grandfather. There was sometimes a twinge of sadness to his laughter though, and he would often comment on how much Joyce would have loved to have been part of this. It was true. No one would have been a better grandmother than Joyce, and I felt sad that both Joyce and Hope had been cheated out of that relationship. There were always those moments when people from my past would pop into my mind, and for a few minutes I would miss them so intensely that it would hurt. But then the pain would ease and I could continue on as before. I found that recognizing the pain of loss and just feeling it for a few moments, rather than always pushing it away, was the best way to keep me from becoming consumed with depression as I'd done in past years.

Since we knew that Hope would most likely be our only child, we wanted to enjoy every moment. We didn't want to miss a single "first," first smile, first rollover, first of each holiday, first sitting up, first crawling, first words. I carefully recorded all the "firsts" in her baby book, so that we would always remember them. The days, weeks, and months of Hope's first year flew by, marked by her steady progression from an infant to a toddler. Right around her first birthday, she took her first steps. Fortunately, Hal was there for the week to celebrate her first birthday. We all got such a kick out of watching her, mainly because of the look on Hope's face when she realized she was walking without support. She knew she was doing something pretty spectacular! With all the cameras flashing in her face, you would have thought she was a famous actress stepping out on the red carpet.

After that, Hope suddenly found that she detested being carried or being pushed in a stroller. If she was going somewhere, she wanted to be walking. In the beginning, it was adorable, until I realized that everything now took us 10 times as long. Sometimes, to speed things up, we had to pick her up and carry her and she'd yell out "Me gok!" which meant "Let me walk!"

The next summer was even more enjoyable than the previous summer with Hope as a newborn. Now she was a toddler and so much fun to play with. I registered us for a "parent-toddler" water play class at the local pool, and we had a great time splashing in the water and playing with floating toys. We joined playgroups at the park and reading time at the library. Hope had no idea what the stories were about and would have preferred to just wander around the library pulling out all the books from the shelves, but I did my best to keep her in the story-time area, listening to the stories. We did our daily walks, but now that Hope had to walk by herself, our walks usually consisted of going down to the end of the street and back. The things like gardening, cleaning, and cooking were a bit more difficult now that she was so mobile. Sometimes it was just easier to save those things for when she was down for a nap.

We loved her little gummy smile and dreaded the time when her teeth would come in. However, once those first tiny teeth came, we realized that they made her cuter than ever. She had a little gap between her two front teeth. My first thought, when I noticed it, was that she had inherited that from her father. But, of course, she wouldn't have gotten that from Trevor because she wasn't his biological daughter. That's the thing about adopted children though. You forget that they aren't related to you by blood because they are yours in every other way. In fact, in some ways, I felt as if the bonds were even tighter with an adopted child because we'd waited and wanted a child for so long before finally getting her. You hear of plenty of "accidents" when it comes to biological children, but there are no "accidental" children for adoptive parents. These children are very much wanted and very much loved.

We'd always assumed that Hope would be our only child. But we were wrong. Near the end of the summer, which had passed far too quickly, the phone rang. I answered it, and a woman introduced herself and said she was calling from the state adoption agency. For a moment, I panicked. Had Hope's birth mother changed her mind and decided she wanted her back? She couldn't take her! The adoption was already final. But that wasn't what this was about.

"Mrs. Townsend, we wanted to let you and your husband know that the birth mother of your adoptive daughter recently gave birth to another child. This one's a little boy and he's about two months old. It's gotten to be too much for her, and she wants to give up this one too. She was hoping you might take him so that he could be with his sister. We wanted to give you the first opportunity to adopt him, but we completely understand if that's too much for you take on right now. I should also tell you that this baby has a different father. He's black. So the child is of mixed race."

All this news was coming at me so fast that I could hardly comprehend it. Hope had a brother? He was two months old?

"So, if he's two months old, that means that he and our daughter are only 14 months apart?"

"Yes, that's right," she answered with a tone of disgust. "She didn't learn her lesson the first time. Some people should just be *sterilized*!"

That stung. This woman obviously hadn't read through my file or she wouldn't have made such an insensitive remark.

The woman continued, "I'm sure that you and your husband want a chance to talk this over and think about it, so we'll give you some time. There are a lot of drawbacks, I know, since you work full-time and you just adopted a baby last year. There's also the matter of him being a mixed-race kid and all..."

I suddenly felt myself boiling with rage at this ignorant woman. How dare she talk about my son with such disrespect! *My son.*

I interrupted her abruptly. "We don't need to think about it. He's the brother of our daughter, which means he's part of our family, and he belongs with us." We discussed the details of going to get him in Hanksville that weekend.

Later I worried that maybe I'd gone too far by making such a big decision for our family without even discussing it with Trevor first. But when I relayed the conversation to him that evening, he agreed with me that of course the baby belonged with us. The timing wasn't as ideal as before with the new school year beginning, but we'd figure something out.

And that was how Scotty came into our family. Scott was the name his birth mother had given him. Since we didn't have any objections to the name and couldn't think of a better one, we just decided to go with what she'd named him. This time around, we felt much more confident in our parenting skills, having made it through the first year with Hope. I'd practically memorized "More Than You Ever Want to Know About Babies" from cover to cover. We knew quite a bit about raising babies.

I did worry in the beginning, however, that I would never be able to love a baby as much as I loved Hope. Even when I saw other babies in TV commercials or in our playgroups and swim classes, I always secretly acknowledged that Hope was about 10 times cuter and more lovable than any of them. But perhaps all parents feel that way about their children.

I shouldn't have worried about that though. Scotty won us over from the day we got him. He was such an agreeable baby, even more so than Hope. He was just as happy and content at daycare as he was at home. And he loved to be held. He would cling to me like a little koala bear and peek out at the world with his dark brown eyes and long lashes. Unlike Hope, who always insisted on walking, Scotty preferred to be held and carried everywhere. It was really no bother, especially when he was lighter, because he would clamp on to me with both his arms and his legs so that I barely had to hold onto him. I found that I could still do plenty of household chores while carrying Scotty because he pretty much supported himself on my hip. Hope had never been a very good baby to carry around because she made me do all the work. Her legs would fall straight down, and she'd be on a constant slow slide down my body until I hoisted her back up on my hip again.

Hope was immediately fascinated by this little person and wanted to be involved in all aspects of baby care. She loved to rub the brown curls on the top of his head. After a while, it became sort of an unconscious habit of hers to rub the top of his head whenever he was within her reaching distance. Trevor and I joked that Scotty was her own personal security blanket. We had our family portrait taken when Scotty was nine months old and Hope was almost two, and the photographer had to keep asking Hope to take her hand off her brother's head because it ruined the pose. She would remove it briefly. But then pretty soon it would find its way back to his head. We ended up choosing the picture with Hope's hand on top of her baby brother's head as our official family portrait, framed and mounted on the hallway wall. We felt it was more of an accurate representation of our family. I still smile when I see that picture.

Scotty, in turn, developed a real liking for holding onto long female hair. Both Hope and I became his victims. I would never put up with it when he would yank at my hair. I would grab his hand as soon as he started pulling, removing his grip on my hair and firmly saying, "No, Scotty! We don't pull on Mommy's hair. That hurts!"

But Hope was always so patient with her little brother. She never wanted to scold him or hurt his feelings. Perhaps the nerve endings on her scalp weren't as sensitive as mine, because she endured an awful lot of yanking and pulling. She would sometimes hold onto the roots with her own hand so that it wouldn't hurt so much, while she gingerly tried to untangle the hair from his grasp, but she never yelled at him or tried to hurt him. One time, Trevor and I peeked through the doorway to their playroom as Hope sat at her coloring table working on her coloring book. Scotty was next to her with a toy in one hand and a fistful of her hair in the other. We wondered how long she would last. She did whisper, "Ow, ow!" a few times and asked him to stop. When he wouldn't, she just sighed and continued her coloring.

"I know I was never that patient with my brother when we were little," I whispered to Trevor. My smile faded as I thought of Brad. I wondered where he was and what he was doing. I wondered if anything might have been different if he'd had a big sister like Hope, who treated him with love and patience, instead of me.

I distinctly remember a time when Hope came home from pre-school and was giving me her usual rundown of her entire day while I prepared dinner. Her head was tilted at an odd angle while Scotty yanked and pulled from one side. All the while, her head bobbed and she never missed a beat. That was my first clue to Hope's ability to focus on one thing, to the exclusion of any and all distractions. That ability would eventually serve her well in school, as she was always at the top of her class through her entire school career. Scotty did well in school too, but he needed a little more parental intervention and prodding to finish his homework and turn in assignments on time.

My favorite time of year was always the summers that I had off and could be home with the kids. I'd take them to local parks and to swimming lessons. We'd work on craft projects or go for nature hikes. We'd read books and go to the matinee. Sometimes we'd drive to the beach and spend the day there. I remember watching the kids playing with their sand toys on the beach against the backdrop of the waves and wishing that I could capture and bottle that moment to replay whenever I felt like it later in life. I knew that my kids wouldn't stay small forever, and it was always so hard for me to let go of each year. I faced each of their birthdays with both happiness and a bit of dread. I just tried to remind myself that I was lucky to be their mom and to be able to enjoy their childhood for the time that I did have.

Scotty liked to be held and rocked to sleep while I told him stories or sang lullabies until well into his toddler and pre-school years. Since I wanted to keep him little, I indulged him for as long as he would let me. I remember watching my precious boy as he slept in my arms, his lips slightly parted while he breathed noisily. Is this what my old elementary school teacher had been referring to when she talked about the terrible, terrible things that would happen if the races were allowed to mix? We are fed so many lies, but every once in a while we have those moments of clarity and truth that have the power to cut through all the lies.

One thing we noticed about Scotty from the time he was very young was that he had a great amount of love and compassion for animals. In any situation that involved animals, he would make a beeline straight for them and stay there trying to make friends the whole time. One time, when he was two years old, we took a vacation to a horse ranch in the mountains. When we woke up one morning, Scotty was missing. After a frantic search, we found him in the horse corral, hanging out with all the horses. Fortunately, they seemed not to mind his presence. He could have been kicked and badly injured, but the horses let him be.

When he grew older, he began asking for a pet. At first, I flatly refused. We'd never had pets growing up since we couldn't afford their care, and I'd always just viewed them as another thing I'd have to feed and clean up after. Whenever we'd see a television show or movie in which an animal might have been hurt, Scotty would immediately want us to reassure him that no animals were actually hurt during the filming. He didn't seem to worry that much about people who were hurt in these shows. I guess he just assumed they could fend for themselves. For a time, I noticed that food was going missing from our house, and I discovered that Scotty was going around the neighborhood to feed all the cats and dogs that looked as if they might be "starving." I tried to assure him that all the pets in our neighborhood were well cared for, and that their owners didn't necessarily want him going around feeding them food that was meant for human consumption.

Eventually, we gave in. For Christmas one year, we got him a little terrier mix that we named "Bubbles." Scotty and Bubbles became fast friends and were inseparable until Scotty went off to college. To Bubbles, Scotty was the entire world. The rest of our family came in a distant second place, but she would put up with us if she had no other choice. That dog ended up living for 18 years, and begrudgingly started following me around when Scotty wasn't home. I'll be damned if I wasn't the one who cried the most when we finally had to put her to sleep due to age and disease.

Jessie eventually married the woman he'd been dating in New Jersey and they had three children together. They would frequently come down to visit us, or we'd head to the Northeast to see them along with Nadine and Ty's family. Hal was overjoyed to be a grandfather of five. He could rarely go more than a month without a visit to someone's home to see his grandkids. He still kept himself busy in Hilldale with work, playing golf, and going fishing. He periodically dated other women but never did remarry. Let's face it: Joyce's shoes were too big for someone to ever truly fill.

Trevor and I had always planned to be open and honest with our children about how they'd come to join our family. We wanted to wait until they were old and mature enough to have that discussion. But, as it turned out, Hope beat us to the punch. One summer day, when Hope was seven and Scotty had just turned six, we watched in the stands as Scotty played one of his first Junior League T-ball games. Hope watched Scotty for a while and then turned to me. "Scotty doesn't look like us. Was he adopted?" She squinted up at me in the morning sun.

I was caught by surprise with that question, but I tried to answer it honestly and calmly. "Actually, um, you were both adopted, honey. But you and Scotty are really related by blood. You have the same birth mommy and different birth daddies. That's why you don't look that much alike."

"Oh. Okay." She turned back to the game, and I thought that was the end of it. I'd tell Trevor about it that evening and we'd sit down with the kids to have that discussion that we'd always planned.

Scotty's team won the game, and we rushed over at the end to congratulate him. "Scotty! Scotty!" Hope yelled as she ran to him with her arms outstretched. "Good job! I'm so proud of you!" She hugged him and then immediately pulled away, holding him by the shoulders. "Unfortunately, Scotty, I have some very bad news. We were both adopted!"

There was an abrupt silence and several heads turned in our direction. I cleared my throat and clapped my hands together. "Hey kids! Why don't we take this conversation home, shall we?" I gathered them together and scurried us out of there as fast as I could before Hope had a chance to explain to Scotty that they looked different because they had different daddies.

When Trevor came home that evening, we sat down with the kids and told them the whole story about how excited we were when we found out they'd been born and that their birth mommy chose us as their parents, and how happy we were that we could all be a family now. They asked a few more questions and seemed satisfied with the answers. After they went to bed, Trevor and I chuckled about how the news had come out that day. "You should have seen how quickly Hope ran to him after the game. She couldn't get there fast enough to break the bad news."

"Well, let's face it, who *doesn't* love to be the bearer of such juicy gossip?" he asked.

But then, later, as I walked past Hope's bedroom, I could hear a little muffled whimper coming from inside. I knocked softly on the door and then opened it. "Hope? Is that you? Are you all right?"

Her head was propped up on pillows and the nightlight gave off enough light that I could see her tear-streaked face in the darkness. "I'm sad that I was adopted," she said. "Somebody didn't want me! Why wouldn't they want me?"

I walked over and switched on the lamp beside her bed and pulled the desk chair over to sit next to her. "Oh, Hope, you couldn't be further from the truth! Lots of people wanted you, including your birth mommy. In fact, she tried really hard to keep you and raise you. But she was very, very young, and she was all alone. She didn't have anyone who could help her. Finally, she decided that your life would be better if Daddy and I could adopt you. It wasn't what she wanted. But sometimes, when you really love someone, you do the things that are best for that person, even if they aren't the things that you really want for yourself. That shows real love that your birth mommy would do that. Don't you think?"

She nodded her head and wiped the tears from her eyes.

"I'll tell you something else too. It's kind of a secret, so I don't want you tell anybody else about this. But, when I was a young girl, there were some bad, mean people who didn't like me. And they told me that I would be a very bad mommy and so I shouldn't be allowed to have any children. Then they did stuff to me to make it so that I could never be a mommy."

Hope gave a look of shock and indignation. "Well, that was very rude of them!"

"It was extremely rude! And it made me really sad for a very long time, because I thought that I would never have a chance to be a mommy. But do you know what? Your birth mommy didn't pay any attention to what those bad people had to say about me. She thought I deserved a chance to be a mommy, and that Daddy deserved a chance to be a daddy. So she picked us to be the parents for you and Scotty. Do you think she made a good choice?"

Hope nodded her head emphatically. "She made a really good choice!"

"I'm glad you think so. And so now, when I think of your birth mommy, I just feel really grateful to her and so happy that somebody gave me a chance to raise two of the best, most wonderful children on the planet. Isn't that amazing, how one person's decision could end up making four people's lives so happy and complete? So, if you could think of some words to describe your birth mommy, what would they be?"

"Um, smart. And brave."

"I think she is smart and brave too. Who knows? Maybe someday you'll get a chance to meet her and you can tell her those things. I think she would really love to know that that's what you think of her."

Hope thought for a moment. "Do you think I could make a thank you card for her? Scotty could sign it too. He can sign his name now."

"Well, I'm not exactly sure where we would send it. But maybe we could send it to the adoption agency and they could find a way to get it to her. I think that's a brilliant idea. Remind me about it tomorrow and I'll pull out some supplies for you to work on it."

"I will."

I gave her a kiss on the cheek. "You know you're the most loved girl on the planet, right?"

"And you're the most loved mommy on the planet."

"I guess we're pretty lucky girls, huh?"

"Yes."

I switched off the lamp and left her room, sending vibes of love and gratitude to a young woman somewhere in Hanksville.

37

Despite my very best efforts to bottle and preserve my children at every age, they continued to grow, mature, and develop. Don't get me wrong, I loved having older children who were more capable of handling the everyday tasks of their own self-care, but I'd look at the old pictures and miss that little pre-schooler Hope, telling me about her day with her head tilted sideways while her brother pulled her hair. I missed that baby Scotty, clamped to my body, peeking out at the world while I did household chores. Where had those little children gone? I could only visit them now in pictures and in my memory.

Trevor actually preferred the children at an older age. He was thrilled that Hope showed a special interest in science and that Scotty liked baseball as much as he did. Our home life more closely resembled Trevor's upbringing than mine. That was for the best. It wasn't as if I thought I'd had a stellar upbringing, but I did worry sometimes that my children would take for granted all the things that came so easily for us now. I still remembered what it was like to live in poverty, and I didn't want to forget that viewpoint.

It turns out that all the things that I'd thought were the realm of the super-rich were actually just a regular part of middle-class life: birthday parties, Cub Scouts and Girl Scouts, piano and swimming lessons, dentist and orthodontist visits, doctor check-ups, trips to national parks and Disney World, restaurant meals, brand-new store-bought clothes and toys for birthdays and holidays. Did my kids even realize what a luxury these things were? Did they know that some kids their age go to school with no breakfast or lie awake at night listening to their growling stomachs? Did they know that some parents struggle just to pay the most basic monthly household bills and sometimes don't have enough, even for the necessities?

My children not only had everything they could possibly need, they also had most of the things they truly wanted, within reason. It wasn't as if I wanted my children ever to experience the lack of real necessities. I didn't want them to know what it felt like to skip meals because there wasn't enough food, or show up to school in the same outdated, ill-fitting clothing day after day, announcing to their peers that they couldn't afford to dress like everyone else. I didn't want them to experience the hurt that comes when people think they can demean and dehumanize them just because they fall into a lower social class than their peers. But at the same time, I wanted them to be able to imagine how those things *might* feel. I wanted them to empathize. Somewhere within me, there was still that little welfare girl who wanted them to understand her. She wanted them to know that she might have dressed differently and lived in a home that wasn't as nice as theirs, but that, where it counted, on the inside, she was just like them. She was just as worthy of respect as anybody else.

But how do you get people to understand a situation that they haven't experienced themselves? I decided that all I could do was try my best to explain what it was like. I always talked in general terms. It was still too difficult for me to go into specific details about my life, but I would point out situations and ask my children questions and then explain my viewpoint on it. We encouraged them to immerse themselves in the community and learn about the world around them. We volunteered regularly as a family at homeless shelters and soup kitchens. We continued the Townsend tradition of putting together a Christmas box for a family in need. I tried to make the box the major focus of our efforts during the Christmas season, rather than coming up with lists of things we wanted for ourselves. I remembered how Joyce told me once that it made her happy to know that her sons would have good lives, and she hoped they might carry on some of the traditions they'd shared as a family. I often thought of her and wondered if she would approve of the family that Trevor and I had formed. I hoped that she would.

As with my high school students, I encouraged my own children to read, read, read and grab knowledge wherever they could find it. When you think about it, reading the words of somebody else is probably as close as you will ever get to being able to step outside of your own lens for a moment and experience the world through someone else's eyes. I always told my students and children that if you want to understand somebody else, you read their words. And when you want to be understood, you write. Maybe that's the reason why I sit here now and I write. The words tumble out faster than I can type them. Maybe they make no sense at all. But I hope that somewhere in this jumble of words, someone out there will see the world through my eyes for a moment — and finally be able to understand.

I'm not sure that all of our efforts to help our children grow into unselfish and socially conscious people were enormously successful, but I think some of it did sink in because of the choices they made later on in life with how they would spend their time and resources. Scotty, especially, seemed to be sensitive to the problems and needs of others. He would come home sometimes so troubled by something he'd learned at school or in the news, as when he heard of people suffering from a natural disaster or from the ravages of war, disease, and lack of resources. We would sit down and talk about the situation and the things that had caused it. We'd talk about possible things that could be done to help alleviate the human suffering or prevent that type of problem from happening again.

"Scotty, you've always been a doer, not a bystander," I would say to him. "When you see or hear about something that tugs at your heart, that's your conscience telling you that you need to do something about it. People like you change the world. They make it a better place." He was always the first one to sign up to volunteer for fund-raisers in the name of some cause. He'd go around the neighborhood collecting pledges, and he'd sign up for races and get sponsors to raise money for his causes. When he'd tell us about his latest endeavor, we always supported him in any way we could. The only thing we asked is that he not let his schoolwork suffer in the process. Sometimes Scotty was too busy saving the world to bother with trivial things like homework assignments.

I loved to watch my children become older and more independent. At the same time, my protective nature and tendency to worry about them too much threatened to hold them back. Trevor was a good balance for me as a parent. I remember one time when Hope came home from elementary school in tears. She was heartbroken that a group of kids had taken to calling her "Hopeless." She told me that she was always picked last for sport teams in P.E. class because she wasn't very good at sports and no one wanted her on their team. The idea of Hope being so sad and alone at school while other kids tormented her and called her names was more than I could bear. I decided we needed to have an "intervention" with all the offending children and their parents to talk about treating one another with kindness and respect.

When Trevor caught wind of my plans, he decided to have a little "intervention" of his own. "Chrissy, you can't step in and fix things every time there's a problem. You'll end up making things worse for them. Our kids are going to be hurt sometimes. They'll be called names. They'll feel alone. We have to let them fight their own battles. I know it's hard, but they'll come out stronger in the end if they have to handle their problems themselves."

I knew he was right, but it was still so hard to stand back when my children were hurting. Goodness knows, I knew what it felt like to feel so alone at school. I knew what it felt like when everyone seemed to have friends except for me. For years, I sat by myself at lunchtime reading my books while my peers talked, joked, and laughed all around me. But, for some reason, I couldn't bear the thought of my children having to deal with the same loneliness and sadness that I'd endured.

Just like Hope, Scotty had his moments of heartbreak. The worst time was when he came home from school as a

404

young teenager feeling so dejected. He'd finally worked up the courage to ask the girl he'd liked for some time to go to a school dance. She turned him down, telling him callously that she didn't go out with "dark-skinned boys." When Scotty admitted what she'd said, I felt as though I'd been punched in the gut myself. Who could treat my kind-hearted son in such a dismissive, disrespectful way? Then I felt immediate anger.

"Well, Scotty, I wouldn't want you to take her anyway! She can just stay home and pick her nose all evening, for all we care! I want you to ask another girl to the dance right away, someone who is good enough for you!"

Scotty just shook his head. "It doesn't matter," he said. "I really didn't want to go anyway."

He spent the rest of the afternoon and evening sitting out by himself on the back lawn, with Bubbles at his side trying to offer some comfort. I stood looking through the kitchen window worrying and fretting about him the whole time. Would this scar him emotionally for life? Would his self-esteem be forever damaged?

"I have a mind to march right up to that school and slap that little bigot all the way home to her parents," I fumed to Trevor. "Then I'll give the parents a piece of my mind for raising such a dreadful, heartless girl!"

Trevor put a hand on my back and peered through the kitchen window at our son. "He's handling it just fine without interference from you. He'll be okay. It's not our job to shield our kids from all the blows that life will deal them. Our job is to provide a loving and supportive place for them at home. As long as they have that, I think they'll have the confidence and sense of self-worth they'll need to withstand the blows that life will deal them."

But then, the next day, Trevor surprised Scotty with tickets to see the Yankees play during our upcoming trip to the Northeast. We couldn't help it that we indulged our children sometimes. We just loved them so much and wanted nothing more than their happiness. I used to think that was something people just said about their kids. Why would people care about their kids' happiness more than their own? But it's true. Nothing hurts parents more than witnessing the pain of their children. And nothing brings them more joy than witnessing the joy of their children.

I remember one time in Hope's early teens when I asked her to write down the three worst things about her life. Maybe it was because I remembered so clearly the worst things about my life at her age, and I wanted to make sure Hope's list wasn't as awful. When she handed me her list, I read it with almost a sigh of relief: "1) My hair. 2) Having to share a bathroom with my brother (and his aim is very bad). 3) Having a locker right beneath the lockers of Lidia Claycomb and Nina Cox, the two nastiest, meanest girls in school."

We sat down and discussed ways that she could choose to deal with those problems. I did get her to admit that, compared to the problems of 99.9% of the world's population, hers were really very minor.

People complain about the problems of raising teenagers. But, really, as with my high school students, I quite enjoyed my children during their teen years. We had our moments of frustration, and there were certainly things that we didn't quite understand about them. Hope went through an entire year during which she dyed her hair black and wore all black all the time and listened to grunge music. To Trevor and me, all those songs sounded exactly the same, and we didn't quite get the appeal of her color choices (or lack thereof). But her grades never slipped and she continued regular and open communication with us. We decided it was a relatively harmless way to express herself at that stage in her life.

In the tradition of Joyce, we'd often sit out on the screened porch with tall glasses of sweet tea and talk about the news of the day. By this time, all four of us were an opinionated bunch, and our discussions would often become quite animated and carry on until the wee hours of the morning, especially if we didn't have to get up early the next day. Trevor and I often used these discussions to probe a little bit into our children's lives and figure out how they viewed the world.

"I hate being smart," Hope stated one day. "Boys don't like smart girls."

"That's not true," Trevor said. "One of the things that first attracted me to your mom was how smart she was. She read a paper aloud in class and I was blown away. I was not attracted at all to girls I didn't think were very smart."

"That's right, Hope," I said. "Maybe there are some boys out there who only care about what's on the outside, or feel threatened by intelligent girls, but you just need to stay away from boys like that. Find someone like your dad."

"Gross! He's my dad!"

We talked about messages from the media and society in general that might make a girl feel that she should "dumb herself down" to make a boy like her, and why a boy might not feel that same pressure but feel pressured in other ways. Trevor and I liked to ask them questions that would help them clarify and refine their own viewpoints. We didn't expect our children to be able to solve the world's problems, but we wanted them to be able to think critically about a wide variety of issues and to articulate their viewpoints in a thoughtful manner.

During the high school years, our household was a constant whirlwind of busyness. We often had more than just two teenagers running up and down the stairs and inhaling all the food from our cupboards and refrigerator. Our house was a favorite hang-out spot for our kids and their friends. I taught at a different high school from the one our kids attended, which was probably for the best since I didn't want them to be known as "Ms. Townsend's kids."

They made a name for themselves in their own high school, which was quite different from my high school experience. While I'd had no friends, never spoke, and basically just blended into the background scenery watching everyone else participate in high school life, my children had lots of friends and a fair amount of confidence in themselves. They threw themselves into many different before- and after-school clubs and activities. Scotty played on the baseball team and ran track. Hope was in the science and drama clubs. They were both on the debate team and in the National Honor Society. Scotty played the guitar and Hope played the piano. Not only did they participate in various school clubs and events, they also signed up regularly as volunteers in community events and fund-raisers.

A giant calendar hung on the wall with color-coded items for each person in our family. Every month it was a mad mess of colorful scribbles. At times it was truly chaotic, leaving me longing for the summer when things would quiet down somewhat. Hope and Scotty both worked as lifeguards and swim instructors at the local community pool during the summer. When Hope turned 16, we bought a used car that both kids were supposed to share. However, once Scotty turned 16, there were enough arguments over car use and scheduling conflicts that we ended up buying another used car for him. We figured he'd need one anyway when Hope went off to college and took her car.

Hope's life was forever changed when she went with a group of high school kids on a visit to Duke Children's Hospital and spent the afternoon with children battling cancer. When she came home, she went straight to her bedroom and spent most of the evening crying into her pillow. Later, when Trevor and I talked with her, she told us that she'd figured out what she wanted to do with her life. She wanted to attend Duke University for her undergraduate degree and then medical school there so that she could become a pediatric oncologist.

"I looked into their eyes, and I felt so strongly that they needed me. I knew I had to do something to help them."

It reminded me of that day that I'd interviewed at Sunset Care Center many years ago and felt so strongly that I was needed there. And I *was* needed there. Little had I known then that I would also need the people that I met there just as much.

Hope worked harder than ever at school so that she'd be able to get into Duke. And in the spring of her senior year of high school, she received not only a letter of acceptance there but also a partial tuition scholarship. Even with the scholarship, though, it was a long and expensive road ahead if we wanted to put her through college and medical school at Duke. And we had another child's college education to think about as well. We'd have to make some sacrifices and dip into retirement funds, but we decided that we would cover the expenses that Hope couldn't cover herself. We didn't want her to graduate with a load of debt on her shoulders. And we were thrilled with her choice of vocation. After having witnessed Joyce's courageous multi-year battle with cancer, we were overjoyed that she had chosen to make a career of battling this dreaded disease. We opened a separate savings account for Hope's college expenses and called it "The Joyce Townsend Scholarship for Hope" fund. Joyce never knew her grandchildren, but I think she would have been very proud of them.

In a way, I lived vicariously through my children during their teenage years. I didn't want to be one of those parents who pushed activities onto their children, but I was more than supportive of everything they wanted to do. Maybe it was because I'd felt so alone and deprived during my teens. But it gave me such happiness to see them running up and down the stairs, off to yet another activity or event. They went to football games and cheered for their school. They had their senior portraits taken and went on class trips and excursions. They attended homecoming and the prom.

The night that Hope went to her senior prom, I scurried around helping her with her hair, her dress, her jewelry and make-up. We took dozens of pictures of her with her date. When the limo showed up to take them off, Trevor and I watched them from the front porch. I turned to Trevor and said with a smile, "I hope she has a wonderful time, but her prom couldn't possibly top mine."

"I was just thinking the same thing," Trevor said. "She looked pretty darn good, but she is really no match to the hottie that graced the dance floor so many years ago in my parents' living room." Then he added, "Oh, and *you* looked pretty good that night too, by the way."

I laughed and swatted at him. He was still the same Trevor, all these years later.

A few weeks later, we sat in a stadium for Hope's graduation and swelled with pride as that year's class valedictorian was introduced. "Candace Hope Townsend" walked confidently up to the podium to receive her diploma and shake the principal's hand. Then she turned and spoke eloquently into the microphone before an audience of thousands of people.

Trevor handed me tissue after tissue, as my memories and emotions overflowed. I thought of her namesake, Miss Candace, and how she'd told me so many years ago that there was hope in my future. She'd been right, in more ways than one. I wished that she could be here now, witnessing this moment. Who knows? Maybe she was.

As Hope's voice rang confidently over the sound system, I thought of all those years when I'd remained silent at the back of the classroom, fear and shame had such power over me back then. But the voice of my fearless, brilliant daughter echoed through the stadium and filled me with such pride and joy.

I thought of Momma and felt that familiar stab of sadness that I'd denied her a moment like this. I'd denied her the opportunity to watch her daughter walk across that stage, draped with an honors sash, to receive her diploma. She'd told me that she couldn't wait to see me receive that diploma and that she wanted to try to help me go to college. I'd scoffed at the idea and belittled her suggestion. Back then, I was so full of anger, bitterness, and sadness. I thought everything was about me. What I didn't realize is that parents share in their children's accomplishments. We feel pride and joy when they feel pride and joy. We share in their heartbreak and sadness too. We hurt when they hurt and we cry when they cry. We gladly make sacrifices so that our children can achieve their dreams. It's what we parents do. I understand that now.

The subtle quivering of Trevor's lower lip told me that he was having a hard time containing his emotions as well. I'm sure he was thinking back, just as I was, to that night so long ago when he promised me that we wouldn't fail this little girl, that she would have a bright future with every opportunity available to her, and that part of that would be because we came into her life. Maybe that was true. Hope had done the work to get where she was standing today, but we'd been there to clear the path and light the way for her.

I thought of the moment I first laid eyes on her at that café in Hanksville. I could hardly believe she was real. I remembered how she held onto my pinkie and slept peacefully in the car all the way to Raleigh while I nearly had a heart attack over every car that sped around us. I thought of her as a pre-schooler working so diligently at her coloring table or making sandcastles on lazy summer days at the beach. I thought of how patiently she handled her brother's constant hair pulling, how her head would be tilted to one side as she described every detail of the events at pre-school that day. Her kindness and patience would serve her well in her profession, working with little children enduring very traumatic situations. I thought of all the hours reading to her and watching her grow into a thoughtful and mature young woman.

And, oddly, during Hope's speech, I thought so much about her birth mother. I wondered what life was like for her now. I wished that she could have been sitting here next to us in the stadium, watching her beautiful, brilliant daughter deliver the valedictorian address. Surely, she would feel the same pride and joy that I felt, knowing that this young woman carried her blood and genes. Maybe she would see some feature of Hope's that reminded her of a family member or herself. I wished she could have heard this speech 18 years ago as she packed that tiny diaper bag for her newborn baby, hoping that she was doing the right thing.

A year after Hope's graduation, we sat in the same stadium to watch Scotty, or Scott, as he had by now asked to be called, receive his diploma. He had also graduated with honors and followed in the footsteps of his father by choosing the University of North Carolina at Chapel Hill for his bachelor's degree. He majored in International Law and took some time out of his college career to serve in the Peace Corps. We were so proud of both of our children and their dedication to bettering themselves and the world around them.

They both had chosen to live in dorms on campus at first and then in apartments near campus. Both schools were a short distance from Raleigh, and they could have lived at home and commuted, but we felt it was part of the college experience to live on their own. They still came home frequently with piles of dirty laundry and empty sacks with which to "grocery shop" in our kitchen and pantry, but it was still hard for me to let go of them. Now I wouldn't be able to see them every day.

Trevor had once said that children were temporary little boarders. They weren't for keeps, and that was partially true. Of course, they would always be part of our family, and there was always a place for them in our home, but we did sense the change that came over our house when they went off to college.

Overnight, it seemed, we had gone from being a busy, bustling house full of teenagers running up and down the stairs and heading off to this activity or that event to being a quiet, reserved house with just a middle-aged couple and their dog.

"Just think of all the hobbies you can pursue now," Trevor said to me. "Think of all the projects you've put on the back burner that you can tackle now. I think you're really going to love this new phase of life. We could go back to doing our 'weekend jaunts' to different places again. We'll have time now. You could get started on that book you've always wanted to write …"

I nodded silently, staring at the empty kitchen table. I could almost see little Scotty sitting there for lunch singing, "I'm a snowman! I'm a snowman!" with a baby carrot dangling from each nostril and raisins held in front of his eyes. The nearly blank, white calendar hung sadly on the wall next to the table. There was one appointment, written in pencil, for me to get my cholesterol checked on the 25th.

Unable to bear the forlorn look on my face, Trevor reached over and placed his hand on my back. "I miss them too," he said. "So does she." He nodded to the living room window, where Bubbles sat perched in her usual spot, watching and patiently waiting for her loved ones to come home.

38

In early 2003, one of my high school students came to me with a disturbing article she'd found in the *Winston-Salem Journal*. It was a part of a five-part series titled "Against Their Will." The series, she said, documented a shocking program in which thousands of North Carolinians were sterilized against their will. My heart froze as she described the series to me, but I tried to maintain the look of mild interest and nodded my head. I said it sounded like an interesting series and I would look into it when I had a chance.

As soon as school was out that day, I went straight to the City Library and found the series. I hastily made copies of the entire series, checking around me to see if anyone was watching. I had to remind myself that I wasn't doing anything suspicious. I was an English teacher, for heaven's sake, and we *do* read things. Yet I still hoped that no one would notice my shaking hands and the sweat beading on my face as I made copy after copy. Maybe they'd wonder whether I might be one of the "feeble-minded" people described in the series who was forcibly sterilized.

I took the copies home and then pored over each article as I sat on the living room floor. Bubbles was at my side, very concerned by my periodic sobs and frequent dabbing at my eyes with tissues. So there were more people like me, so many more. Our shared pain, silence, and shame connected us together.

A few brave souls spoke out and shared their stories with the investigative reporters from the *Winton-Salem Journal*. I admired them for their courage, but I knew I could never do something like that. The only person I'd ever told was my husband, and even then it wasn't a subject either one of us cared to revisit. I'd always meant to talk to my children about my past, including my sterilization. They knew I'd had a troubled past, had lived in poverty and lost my family, but they knew very few actual details. Something always got in the way of having that conversation. Maybe this series would be a good way to broach the subject with them someday. I put the articles away, feeling emotionally and physically exhausted from absorbing all of that information.

Scott was out of the country on a study-abroad program, but the next time that Hope was home from school for a visit, I set out the copies of the "Against Their Will" series on the kitchen table. Hope was rummaging through the refrigerator, looking for a snack.

"Hope, honey, sometime when you have a chance, there's something I'd like you to read on the kitchen table. It'll take some time, so it doesn't have to be right now, just when you have a chance."

"Oh?" Her head popped out of the refrigerator. She was gnawing on a carrot as she walked over to the kitchen table and glanced at the articles. "What's it about?"

"Just read it when you have time."

Hope stopped chewing for a moment and sat down at the table, setting aside the carrot. For the next two hours, she pored over the series, closely studying every chart and diagram, reading all of the pull-out quotations, and examining the pictures, her brow furrowed the way it does when she is completely focused on something.

I puttered around the house doing chores while she read. Bubbles, my little shadow, followed me from room to room. With Scott gone, she was my new best friend. When I went back into the kitchen to empty the dishwasher, Hope was still reading. The carrot still sat, half-eaten, on the table next to the articles.

I went to the refrigerator to pull out a pitcher of sweet tea and began to fill two glasses. Suddenly I felt two arms wrapping around me from behind. "You were one of them, weren't you, Mom? You were one of the people sterilized under North Carolina's eugenics program." I just nodded and swallowed down the lump rising in my throat.

"I remember you told me something a long time ago," she continued, "about how mean people did things to you so that you couldn't have babies. But I really didn't understand back then." She squeezed me for a few moments. "Would you tell me about it?"

We brought the glasses to the kitchen table and sat down. I told her everything that I'd finally told to Trevor so many years ago on the night he'd proposed. This time, though, I was less emotional, more stoic. The pain from these memories was less raw, less intense. Hope shed more tears than I did as she listened.

When I finished, she sat there for a little while staring into her drink. Then she shook her head. "As a future doctor, I just can't even fathom the idea of forcing an unnecessary, invasive procedure on somebody who clearly doesn't want it. What about medical ethics? You make that oath to act in the best interest of your patient..."

"Well, he was sure he was doing the world a big favor," I said. "It seems there is no limit to what people are willing to do to each other when they are so sure that they are in the right. Most of the people that they interviewed who were involved in the program's operation remain unapologetic about the whole thing. They said it may not be the politically correct thing to say today, but it was the right thing to do back then. Some of the anonymous people who have commented on the series have wondered why the program isn't still in operation today."

"You shouldn't read those comments, Mom. There will always be A-holes like that who have to add their worthless two cents to every topic out there. All they manage to convey is their own ignorance on the matter."

"The governor recently issued a formal apology from the state for the eugenics program," I told her.

"Hmm, just in time for when this story broke, what a coincidence!" she noted sarcastically. "'Oh yeah. That. We're sorry about that.' Hopefully it doesn't turn into one of those 'we said we're sorry, now get over it' things."

"Well, there's a representative in the state House who has sort of taken up this issue and is trying to get some justice for the survivors. He's proposed a bill to take the eugenics law off the books."

"It's still on the books? Good grief."

"And there's talk about trying to include information about the program as part of North Carolina's history program in schools and doing some type of outreach program for survivors, perhaps providing counseling and health benefits, maybe even some type of monetary compensation."

"Do you think that will ever happen?" Hope asked.

"Well, I don't know. They'll probably study it to death for years and years in various committees and commissions. By the time they finally come to an agreement on what, if anything, should be done and how to do it, we'll all be dead. Who knows? Maybe that was the plan all along."

I reached down and patted Bubbles' head. "I don't even care about the money or benefits," I added. "I doubt I would even come forward to claim them. I just want it for the other survivors out there who might desperately need it. Some of their stories are much worse than mine. If there's something that could be done to make their lives better, it should be done."

"Come here, Bubbles," Hope said. "I need some love too."

"She only goes to me now."

"You brat," she scolded Bubbles. "Why can't I ever be your favorite?"

"I wouldn't even begin to know what amount should be proposed for compensation. How would I quantify what's been taken from me? How would I even explain the impact these events have had on me? It would take an entire book to articulate how my sterilization has affected my life."

Hope reached across the table and grabbed my hand. "Well, then maybe you should write it," she said.

"Maybe someday ... when I'm ready."

We sipped our tea for a few moments in silence, lost in our own thoughts.

"Mom," Hope said, "do you think you and Dad would have had Scott and me if you hadn't been sterilized?"

"Oh, I think we were meant to be together as a family. Somehow we still would have found our way to each other. Who knows? Maybe there would have just been more of us. It's hard to say for sure. Everything has such a ripple effect."

Hope nodded and took another sip.

"You know," I added, "something very strange happened that very last time that Stan beat me. I could have easily been beaten to death that night. He threw me into the hallway mirror and I fell to floor. Then he kicked me in the head until I went unconscious ..."

Hope put her hand over her mouth and her eyes welled with tears.

"But, when I came to, I could have sworn there was someone standing there in the hallway. It was a little girl about three or four years old. She reached out to me and called me 'Mommy.' Then she disappeared. At the time, I thought she was the ghost of a child I would never have. But then later on, I wondered if it might have been you instead. She looked kind of like you did back then, with long brown hair and a sweet little face. I don't know. Maybe it was nothing. I've never even told your father about that. You know how he feels about supernatural things."

"Tell me about it. I had to listen to an hour-long diatribe yesterday when I made the mistake of telling him I had visited a psychic with a friend. It was just for fun. I don't really believe they have any special powers."

"You have a science-oriented mind like your dad. There's always a rational explanation for everything. He's probably right. It was probably just a hallucination brought on by trauma to the brain."

Hope considered this for a few moments, running her finger along the rim of her glass. Then she reached out again and put her hand over mine. "No, I think you're right, Mom. I think it was me. Because I know that, at that moment in time, nothing could have kept me from being by your side. Nothing at all."

I smiled through tears and squeezed her hand back. So someone *had* come to save me on that terrible, dark night so long ago. It was a little girl named Hope.

39

The sterilization law was taken off the books, thanks in large part to a lone House representative who refused to forget about the people that the law had hurt. It was a relief to have that hateful law finally removed from the books forever. The years passed and little else came of the promises to reach out to program survivors and try to help them. The *Winston-Salem Journal* would occasionally publish an article revisiting the issue and decrying the lack of action taken to benefit the victims. Hope's gloomy prediction of the "We said we're sorry, now get over it" sentiment seemed to prevail. I'd had so many apologies like that during my marriage to Stan that I was pretty much immune to them by now.

I read in the paper that a traveling museum exhibit describing the program was created. The information for the exhibit was mainly pulled from the "Against Their Will" series. When it came to Raleigh, I briefly considered visiting it, but then decided against it. I already knew everything from the series. Rehashing all of that information wouldn't make me feel any better. Scott went to it and said it was a nice exhibit but that I probably wouldn't learn anything new from it. So I stayed away.

Then, in 2009, a historical roadside marker recognizing the program's victims was unveiled near the corner of Jones and McDowell Streets in downtown Raleigh. I considered attending the unveiling ceremony. I'd heard that some of the program survivors might be in attendance and would maybe even speak at the ceremony. But, then I decided against it. What if someone recognized me and wondered what I was doing there? Maybe they'd sense that invisible word "Unfit" stamped across my forehead. So I didn't go to the ceremony. I told myself I would visit the roadside marker someday, alone and on my own terms.

And now, nearly a decade after the "Against Their Will" series was first published, a governor's task force has recommended that each survivor of North Carolina's eugenics program receive a one-time cash sum of $50,000 in reparation for his or her compulsory sterilization. It still needs to be approved by the legislature, but if it passes, North Carolina will be the first state ever to accomplish some sort of restitution for a past wrong in time for a few of the people affected to attain a measure of justice before they die. We shall see. It's taken a while, but it's progress at least. It's something.

Dr. Martin Luther King Jr. once said, "The arc of the moral universe is long, but it bends toward justice." Maybe that's true, but it doesn't just bend on its own. It bends because there are people out there struggling, straining, and tugging to make it bend. Maybe someday I will have the courage to join them.

The $50,000 would certainly come in handy. We're still paying off bills for medical school for Hope and then law school for Scott. I doubt I will ever come forward to claim it though. In fact, very few of the nearly 8,000 people who were sterilized under North Carolina's eugenics program have been identified to date. The majority of them are already dead. There are others who never knew they were sterilized. It turns out there were some doctors who took great liberties with the eugenics program and, after delivering a baby or performing some other medical procedure, tied the woman's tubes on the way out without her knowledge. The Board was willing to backdate approval for such procedures as long as the victim met the specifications for eugenic sterilization. And this didn't just happen in North Carolina. In fact, sterilization procedures were performed so commonly in the South, especially on poor, black women, with or without their knowledge or consent, that they were given the nickname "Mississippi Appendectomies."

Another reason some victims have not come forward is that many of them were disabled people or children at the time they were sterilized and were not informed of what the procedure was or why they needed it. When you are a child or a disabled person, you tend to trust that the people caring for you have your best interest at heart even when they do not. Surely, the children at the training and detention centers who were told they needed to have "a little operation" before they could leave did not know what else they could do but comply.

Then there are people like me who knew exactly what was happening to us and what it meant for our future. We simply don't want to come forward. We don't want to rip open those old wounds again. We will take our stories with us to the grave, or share them with the precious few people who will understand. We cannot bear to put ourselves and our lives before the harsh court of public opinion.

I figure I've already received my leg up from the people who have truly loved and cared about me. So, as far as I'm concerned, they can keep their $50,000.

I did see that there was a number I could call to verify that my name was on record as one of the program participants, and that I could request that a copy of my file from the Eugenics Board be sent to me. I called the number and requested the records.

When the envelope arrived from the North Carolina state archives several days later, I stood frozen at the mailbox for a few moments. My first impulse was to quickly stuff it in the trash and pretend I'd never seen it. But then I slowly walked back into the house, deposited the other mail on the kitchen counter, and sat with the envelope at the kitchen table. I stared at it for several minutes, wondering if I really wanted to open this door to a past I'd rather forget.

I am brave. I am strong. I slowly opened it.

There, before my eyes, was the petition filled out and signed by T. Pickard, aka "Blue Lids." The petition was reviewed and approved by the Eugenics Board of North Carolina on May 15, 1966, just days after my 14th birthday. Happy birthday to me. Momma's signature of parental consent was dated June 10 of the same year.

"Christine Rollings, 14 years old, is the oldest of six children in a single-parent, welfare-dependent household. Her mother works nights in a bar, leaving the children completely unsupervised to run around and do as they please at all hours of the day and night. A year ago, Christine ran away from home with a friend and was missing for three weeks before turning herself in at a local police station in Little Rock, Arkansas. She is believed to have been working as a teenage prostitute at the time. I suspect she still may be prostituting herself from time to time for the extra cash. Christine is a rude, obstinate, and reckless young girl with no respect for authority. Unless immediate action is taken, I fear she will become pregnant within a year and continue the cycle of poverty, reckless breeding, and government dependence instilled in her by her mother. This feeble-minded, promiscuous young girl cannot care for herself and will never be able to function in any way as a parent. I recommend eugenic sterilization for her own safety and protection, as well as the safety and protection of the community at large."

The record noted that the procedure was completed by M. Blake, M.D., at Community Hospital in Hilldale on August 13, 1966. Case closed. Problem solved.

I read the words a second and a third time. Who was the girl being described on this page? I hardly recognized her. Was this an accurate depiction of the girl I once was? There were elements of truth here, yes, but the facts were stretched, twisted, and distorted to serve a specific purpose. I conjured an image of the young girl that I used to be, trying to reconcile her with the person described on this page. I stared at the words until they blurred and swam before my eyes.

That evening, when Trevor was home, I placed the petition in front of him without saying a word. He picked it up and read it, his mouth set in a grim line the way it does whenever something upsets him. Then he set it down abruptly. He told me that I should tear it up and throw it away. Burn it.

But I've decided to keep it. It's part of my past, and I'm tired of running away from my past. I'm tired of burying my head in the sand and pretending like bad things didn't happen.

They *did* happen, and burying them will never make them go away.

Part of the healing process is being able to face your past and acknowledge the things that have hurt you and the things that have made you stronger. And so I will face my past: All of the beautiful, the terrible, the tragic, the splendid, the mundane, the triumphant, the lonely, the tender, and the joyful moments weave the rich tapestry of my life. What I will *not* do is allow my past to cloud my present or impede my future.

I've learned that healing is a difficult, sometimes lifelong, process. But it can be done. I continue to heal.

As of this book's writing, I've taken the first steps toward reconnecting with my long-lost siblings by hiring a private investigator to try to locate them. And, just this morning, I received an e-mail from him with two very promising leads: There is a 56-year-old woman named Jenny Winters who was put into foster care at age 14 out of Hilldale, North Carolina. She was later adopted by a foster family, and she currently works as a professional photographer in Wilmington. This small tidbit of news fills me with such indescribable joy, to think that Jenny might have had a good life with a family that loved her and supported her dreams! How wonderful!

But it was the second piece of news that made me actually sob out loud right there at my computer. There's a Brad Rollings, a 58-year-old father, proud grandfather, and police officer, of Durham, North Carolina. That's a mere 30-minute drive from my house! Hope drives there every day to treat her young patients at Duke Children's Hospital. Is it possible that Brad and I have lived so close to each other all these years? Perhaps we've passed each other on the freeway. Or maybe we've sat in the same movie theater, his head blocking my view as it did in the back of Daddy's pick-up at the drive-in movie theater so long ago.

I don't know whether my siblings will be happy to hear from me. Maybe they are still working through issues of their own from the past. And I don't know whether they will want to have any kind of relationship with me in the future. But I think it's worth a try. Maybe there's still a chance for us to be a family again. Maybe there's still a chance for me to be the kind of sister that they always deserved to have. After all, it's never too late to be what you might have been …

*****

On a beautiful, sunny Saturday morning in North Carolina last spring, Trevor and I awoke bright and early and decided to take a scenic drive. We stopped at a café first to pick up some breakfast bagels and orange juice and then hit the road.

"Right or left?" Trevor asked.

I paused for a moment. "To Jones and McDowell Street." I keyed the location into our car's GPS system.

We found a parking space near the end of the street and slowly walked to the place where the historical roadside marker stood. Funny. I'd imagined it to be 50-feet tall, looming hauntingly and casting a dark shadow over the entire street. But it was just a simple roadside marker, like any other marker you might pass daily and never notice. The sign sparkled pleasantly in the morning sunlight:

EUGENICS BOARD
State action led to the
sterilization by choice or
coercion of over 7,600
people, 1933-1973. Met
after 1939 one block E.

I stood there before the roadside marker with my arms dangling helplessly by my sides, feeling strangely intimidated and defeated by those few words embossed on a road sign. And, for a few moments, I was transformed back into that lost and lonely 14-year-old girl I once was, standing vulnerably before the harsh judgment of the Board. They had all the power. I had nothing.

But the touch of Trevor's hand on my back brought me back to the present day, and, after a few moments, I found my voice. "One block east. That's where five people who didn't know me met one day and read a sheet of paper written about me by someone else who didn't know me. And they proceeded to make a decision that would alter my life forever. Then they probably went home that day, had a nice meal with their own families, and never thought of me again."

Trevor nodded his head silently and squinted at the words on the sign in the bright morning sunlight. He raised a hand to shade his eyes as he reflected on the words and his own thoughts on the matter. Then he spoke. "They didn't win, you know."

"How do you figure?" I asked.

"Well, think about it, Chrissy. Every assertion they made to make their case against you, every single ignorant assumption, you went out and proved to be wrong 10 times over. They said you were feeble-minded. And you went on to become an honor student and a college graduate. You became a high school English teacher, instilling a love for reading and writing in the thousands of students who have passed through your classroom the past few decades. They said you were promiscuous, and you've been faithfully married to the same man for about 35 years now. They said you couldn't care for yourself or anyone else. And you've spent a lifetime caring for other people: first your own siblings, your customers at the diner, the residents at the care center, my mother before she died, your high school students, your own family. They said you could never be an effective parent. And I know of two happy, confident, capable adult children who would beg to differ on that point. So, they may have won a battle, that's true. But you won the war, Chrissy."

I looked up at Trevor's profile as he spoke. His temples were graying and his hairline slightly receding. There were a few more wrinkles around his eyes and mouth. But he still had the same eyes, the same smile, the same dimples. He was still the

426

same Trevor who won my heart so many years ago. I felt his hand on my back. For decades, his reassuring voice and touch had comforted me and provided clarity in times of insecurity and need. His other hand still shaded his eyes from the morning sun as he spoke.

His hands were a bit more calloused and weathered with age now but still capable and strong. They were hands I trusted, hands I loved. I reached up impulsively and planted a solid kiss on his cheek.

"What was that for?" he asked.

"For being the damn genius of North Carolina," I answered.

"Don't forget it."

"As if you'd let me."

We clasped hands and slowly made our way back to the parked car at the end of the street.

Afterword

     This story is a work of fiction. But many of the people and events described are inspired by or based on real people and real events. North Carolina's eugenics program operated quietly and efficiently from 1929 until 1974, with the Eugenics Board formally organized in 1933. The program's purpose was to weed out the "unfit" from society by stopping them from breeding.

     Tens of thousands of people across the United States were victims of eugenic sterilizations, and many states had active eugenics programs in the early 20th century. But North Carolina was something of an anomaly. When the horrors of the Holocaust were uncovered after World War II, most of the states that had eugenics programs quietly and shamefully dismantled them. The "science" behind eugenics — which held that things like poverty, disease, and alcoholism were inherited genetically and could therefore be bred out of society by controlling the reproductive lives of the population — had already by that time been disproven. North Carolina, however, ramped up its eugenics program in the post-war years. Early on, the program focused on those who were in state-run mental hospitals and institutions, which admitted those who were believed to have developmental disabilities or psychiatric disorders. But then it began to extend its reach beyond state-run institutions into the general population. North Carolina was the only state in which social workers were empowered to start the sterilization petitioning process. By the 1950's and 60's, the program increasingly targeted women who were poor, women who were black, and, most especially, women who were both poor *and* black.

     By the program's end in 1974, North Carolina ranked third among the states for number of eugenic sterilizations performed, with at least 7,600 over 45 years. The Eugenics Board, comprised of five bureaucrats who met monthly in Raleigh, approved 90 percent of the sterilization petitions, often deciding cases within 15 minutes and without interviewing the individual to be sterilized. They were not elected to their positions and had virtually no accountability to the public. More than 70 percent of the victims were sterilized for "feeble-mindedness," a vague term open to the board's interpretation, from supposedly possessing a low IQ to being "promiscuous," "rebellious," or even "untidy."

The records of the Eugenics Board were closed to the public, and, since few sterilization survivors ever spoke out about what had happened to them, most people in the state had no clue that such a program had ever existed. The story might never have been told were it not for the work of a professor of women's history at the University of Iowa and graduate of UNC-Chapel Hill. In the late 1990's, Dr. Johanna Schoen was researching the history of birth control, sterilization, and abortion and had repeatedly requested access to the sealed records of the North Carolina Eugenics Board. Finally one day, perhaps by accident, she was handed a roll of microfilm and was quite shocked to discover it contained all the Eugenics Board's records kept during the program's tenure. Recognizing that the stories of thousands of victims desperately needed to be told, she shared her research with a team of reporters at the *Winston-Salem Journal*, who then combined Schoen's research with their own investigative reporting to publish the series, "Against Their Will."

The articles revealed terrible abuses within the program. For example, the Board sometimes backdated approval for procedures that had already been performed. Families who feared the stigma of a pregnant teenage daughter sometimes petitioned the Board to have that daughter sterilized. In one case, a father suspected of sexually molesting his daughter petitioned the Board for her sterilization. The petition was approved and the sterilization performed. More than 2,000 of the victims were younger than 18. Hundreds of children who passed through the doors of state training schools and detention centers ended up sterilized. Caswell Training Center had the most, with nearly 600 sterilizations. The State Home and Industrial School for Girls was second, with 300 sterilizations. It was assumed that these North Carolina children would grow up to be unfit parents, so they were sterilized before they ever had the chance.

Eighty-four percent of the sterilization victims overall were women. And by the 1960's, nearly all of the sterilization victims were female. Eugenic sterilizations for women and girls were secured and performed at a remarkably rapid pace at a time when women in the general population had an extremely difficult time accessing birth control, sterilization, and abortion. Most hospitals followed the "120 formula" back then. In order to be considered for elective sterilization, you multiplied the woman's age by the number of children she had, and the number had to reach or exceed 120. So if a woman was 30 years old and had four children, for instance, she *might* be allowed to have a tubal ligation. Even then, she would often need the endorsement of two doctors, plus a psychiatrist, to obtain the procedure.

I researched North Carolina's eugenic sterilization program during my graduate studies at North Carolina State University in Raleigh. I had a chance to interview several survivors of the program, resulting in a cover story for the March 24, 2010 issue of *The Independent Weekly*, "The Ultimate Betrayal: N.C. Eugenics Survivors Seek Justice."

Details from these real survivors are woven into Chrissy's story. One interviewee was raped and impregnated at age 13 and sterilized immediately after the birth of her only son at age 14. She was not aware of her sterilization until she was married and trying to have children years later. A doctor, after examining her, told her she'd been "butchered." This woman suffered through years of physical abuse, which she blames, in part, on her inability to bear children. She told me that she avoided people from her past and was "always hiding, hurting, and crying." She felt that she had the word "sterilized" stamped across her forehead and that people judged her harshly for it.

Another survivor was the oldest child in a welfare family who was threatened and bullied into her sterilization by a social worker who told her that they would take away her mother's welfare check unless she complied. The social worker said that her siblings would starve and it would be all her fault. She tearfully pleaded with her doctor before the surgery not to go through with it and just say that he had, but he showed no mercy.

"Agnes" is the pseudo-name I used in the article for a woman in her early 80's who shared her story with me but asked to remain anonymous. No one but her husband knew of her sterilization, which happened during her brief stay in a psychiatric hospital when she was suffering from severe postpartum depression in her early 20's. When she was told she needed to have an operation, she remembers asking the doctor why. She said he answered, "We don't want you to have any more children." I had found her because her name was listed in the legislative library as someone who had contacted the state archives office about eugenics records. I was struck by the shyness and shame she exhibited so many years after her forced sterilization. Later, after the article was published, she told me that her grandson, who taught high school, had read the article and recognized his grandmother even though her real name was not used. She admitted to him that she was the person described in the article. She was not upset that the truth came out that way. She told me that she was happy to have a way to talk to her family about what had happened. She said that her grandson has used the article in his classroom to teach North Carolina students about this chapter of state history.

Another survivor whose spirit I've tried to include in Chrissy's narrative was sterilized as a young boy during his stay at Caswell Training School. He remembers being told that he needed an operation before he could leave. But, he said he wasn't told what it was or why he needed it. Later on in life, he figured out on his own what had happened to him. He learned from his records that the Eugenics Board had tried but failed to sterilize his mother as well. This boy was from a desperately poor, single-parent household on welfare, but he fondly recalled how his mother had once scraped together enough money to buy him a guitar, and he taught himself how to play it. We sat in my car on a rainy North Carolina day outside a café while he played song after song for me from memory. I remember thinking how strange it was that someone so musically gifted could be labeled as "feeble-minded."

The stories and voices of those that I interviewed echoed through my mind as I wrote this book.

The fingers of the American eugenics movement reached out to affect a broad array of people, but no one was affected more than women who were both poor and black. By portraying Chrissy as a white girl, I do not mean to diminish the issue of race, especially as eugenics was played out in the South. I felt that I did not know enough about what it was like growing up as a black female in the Jim Crow South to provide a genuine voice for her. Having been raised in a white, working-class family that struggled to pay the bills, I felt that I could imagine what it would be like to be thrown into poverty by the death of a breadwinner. Indeed, many women today still learn the hard way that they are just one full-time working male away from poverty, and the vast majority of welfare recipients are single women with children who are struggling to hold down one or more low-income jobs. I wish I could say that they and their children are no longer demonized or labeled as lazy, degenerate, and a burden on society. But current politics and discourse surrounding welfare recipients, such as mandatory drug testing for welfare eligibility, indicate to me that little has changed in the harsh court of public opinion.

While this book deals with some very heavy topics and a dark chapter of North Carolina's history, I hope that the reader will sense my love for this state and ultimately view this as a book about the strength of family bonds, the resilience of the human spirit, and the transforming power of love.

Acknowledgements

I would like to extend my thanks to Meredith Maslich and Susan Garlock of Possibilities Publishing for taking a chance on an unpublished author and for being such wonderful advocates for this book. Their insight and expertise have proven invaluable in shaping and guiding an unpolished manuscript into the book it was meant to be. I owe a debt of gratitude to my talented father-in-law, Dr. Joseph K. Torgesen, for the cover art that so beautifully captures the spirit of this novel.

Fiction is often drawn from real-life people and events, and this book is no different. Researching North Carolina's eugenics program had a deep impact on me, and the stories of those whom I interviewed stayed with me. The eugenics program is often studied in terms of facts and statistics, but I felt that the lived experience of being sterilized was mainly ignored or glossed over in the news stories that covered the program. Such an experience would echo and reverberate throughout one's lifetime. As Chrissy stated, it would take a book to capture the lifelong effects of mandatory sterilization. When I thought of all the ripple effects it might have on a person's life, the character of Chrissy began to take shape in my mind. I couldn't stop thinking about her.

Many events in Chrissy's life were also drawn from real-life experiences of my own family members. I cannot name them all, but I would like to acknowledge three people in particular. The story of Chrissy's running away was inspired by my dear aunt, Teresa Eames, who ran away from home with a friend at age 13 and was missing for three weeks, crossing two state lines before turning herself in at a local police station. The dysfunctional home-life situation of Miss Candace and her son Danny largely mirrors the environment that my father, Donald Cleveland, experienced growing up in a home characterized by alcoholism, fear, and violence. The marriage of Chrissy and Stan was inspired by a past relationship of one of my sisters. Her quiet suffering during that time still breaks my heart. I borrowed cautiously and carefully from their lives, recognizing that many of these events and situations are deeply personal and traumatic. I wanted Chrissy's story to be realistic, and I did not know how to do that other than drawing from real life. After reading the parts dealing with domestic violence, my dad called to tell me that he felt as if I had been there, standing in his childhood home, witnessing everything. That comment means much more to me than any sort of critique from someone who's never experienced domestic violence or abuse. Dad, I love you dearly, and I'm so grateful that you chose to end the cycle of violence with your own family.

Very special gratitude goes to my family for their support and encouragement throughout this entire process: my husband Ben and my three children, Chloe, Paige, and Tyler. They are my biggest fans, along with my parents, Don and Julie Cleveland, and my sisters, Tami Wagner, Natasha Cleveland, and Dadra Call. This book would never have been written if Tasha hadn't first suggested the idea and then convinced me I could write it.

A big thank you also to my early draft readers for their edits, comments, and insights: Brigid Gorry-Hines; Elizabeth Gibbons, M.D.; James Barrington; Jian Bao, Ph.D.; Joanne Means; Julia Lerche; Karen Torgesen; Kirsty Blowers, M.D.; Laura Warner-Torgesen; and Rachel Lukowski. For me, at least, writing a book takes a village. These family members and friends are my village.

About the Author

Lara Cleveland Torgesen lives in Cary, NC, with her husband and children. This is her first novel.

CPSIA information can be obtained
at www.ICGtesting.com
Printed in the USA
BVOW06s1143061216
469936BV00011B/47/P